Edward L. Nichols

A Laboratory Manual of Physics and Applied Electricity

Volume 1

Edward L. Nichols

A Laboratory Manual of Physics and Applied Electricity
Volume 1

ISBN/EAN: 9783337405830

Printed in Europe, USA, Canada, Australia, Japan

Cover: Foto ©Andreas Hilbeck / pixelio.de

More available books at **www.hansebooks.com**

A LABORATORY MANUAL

OF

PHYSICS AND APPLIED ELECTRICITY

A LABORATORY MANUAL

OF

PHYSICS AND APPLIED ELECTRICITY

ARRANGED AND EDITED

BY

EDWARD L. NICHOLS

PROFESSOR OF PHYSICS IN CORNELL UNIVERSITY

IN TWO VOLUMES

VOL. I

JUNIOR COURSE IN GENERAL PHYSICS

BY

ERNEST MERRITT AND FREDERICK J. ROGERS

New York

MACMILLAN AND CO.

AND LONDON

1894

Norwood Press:
J. S. Cushing & Co. — Berwick & Smith.
Boston, Mass., U.S.A.

PREFACE.

THIS work has been written to supply in some measure the needs of a modern laboratory, in which the existing manuals of physics have been found inadequate. In its present form the book is the work, chiefly, of Assistant Professors George S. Moler, Ernest Merritt, and Frederick Bedell, of Instructors Frederick J. Rogers, Homer J. Hotchkiss, Charles P. Matthews, and of the editor. Certain parts, however, have been taken from written directions to students which had been prepared by instructors who are no longer members of the department from which the book emanates, and who have taken no immediate hand in its final preparation.

No attempt has been made to provide a complete and sufficient source of information for laboratory students. On the contrary, it has been thought wise to encourage continual reference to other works and to original sources. It is assumed that in all laboratories in which a work of this kind will be found useful, there is accessible to the student a small collection of reference volumes, including the Laboratory Manuals of Kohlrausch, Glazebrook and Shaw, Stewart and Gee, Witz, and of Wiedemann and Ebert; also that the larger treatises on experimental physics of Jamin, Winkelmann, Violle, Wiedemann, Preston, etc., together with the best known of the lesser works in English, are available.

The Manual has been divided into two volumes; and it is designed for three classes of students, differing from each other in experience, maturity, and purpose. The method of treatment has been varied in accordance with the principle, that with increasing experience the student should be divorced more and more from the use of the Manual and also from the close supervision of the instructor, and that he should be thrown gradually upon his own resources, and be led to make a wider and wider use of the literature of the science.

It will be found that the first volume, which is intended for beginners, affords explicit directions, together with demonstrations and occasional elementary statements of principles. This volume is the outgrowth of a system of junior instruction which has been gradually developed during a quarter of a century. No attempt has been made to include the whole of physics. On the other hand, the principle has been followed here, as indeed throughout the book, of incorporating only such experiments as have been in actual use.

It is assumed that the student possesses some knowledge of analytical geometry and of the calculus; also that he has completed a text-book and lecture course in the principles of physics. It is not expected that the experiments will be taken consecutively, nor that a student, in the time usually given to the work, will complete more than a third of them. The experiments have been divided into groups, an arrangement of the work for which there were two reasons. On the one hand, it serves to guide the practicant and the instructor in the selection of experiments; on the other hand, it furthers the development of the system by making it easy to add or to exclude material. It is expected, indeed, that the book will be used thus by those into whose hands it may come, each one adding such experiments to the various groups as he may desire to include in his course, and dropping out those which he may deem useless.

In the second volume more is left to the individual effort and to the maturer intelligence of the practicant. This volume differs from the first also in another respect. In the junior course no attempt is made to leave the beaten track. The very nature of the subjects with which we have to deal in Volume II, however, has compelled the introduction of new materials. The writers trust that where the ripeness and maturity of treatment which comes from long-continued experience in the teaching of a subject is missing, some recompense may be found in the freshness and novelty of the themes.

A large proportion of the students, for whom primarily this Manual is intended, are preparing to become engineers, and especial attention has been devoted to the needs of that class of readers. In Parts I, II, and III of Volume II, especially, a considerable amount of work in applied electricity, in photometry, and in heat has been introduced, with particular reference to the training of students of engineering. It is believed, nevertheless, that selections from these parts may be made which will be of value to students of pure physics also.

The final chapters (Part IV), which are intended for those who have already had two years or more of laboratory instruction, consist simply of certain hints for advanced work. These are accompanied by typical results, the object of which is to show in brief form what has already been accomplished by the methods proposed, and to lead the student to a suitable starting-point for further investigation. Through-out this portion of the book theory and experimental detail alike have been omitted. The outlines which have been given are designed to afford suggestions only, and by virtue of their very meagreness to compel the student to read original memoirs in preparation for his work.

EDWARD L. NICHOLS.

CORNELL UNIVERSITY, ITHACA, NEW YORK,
    May, 1894.

TABLE OF CONTENTS.

VOLUME I.

VOLUME II.

PART I.

EXPERIMENTS WITH DIRECT CURRENT APPARATUS.

PART II.

EXPERIMENTS IN ALTERNATING CURRENTS.

A LABORATORY MANUAL OF PHYSICS AND APPLIED ELECTRICITY.

VOLUME I.

JUNIOR COURSE IN GENERAL PHYSICS.

By ERNEST MERRITT AND FREDERICK J. ROGERS.

INTRODUCTION.

THE object of all of the experiments described in the following pages is twofold : (1) to illustrate, and therefore impress more thoroughly on the mind, the principles and laws which have previously been taught by text-books or lectures ; (2) to familiarize the student with proper methods of observation and physical experimentation. These two aims should be kept in view throughout the work which follows.

GENERAL DIRECTIONS.

Before beginning any experimental work, the student is advised to read carefully the directions for the experiment that is to be performed, making sure that the object of the experiment and the means to be employed in accomplishing this object are fully understood. If the experiment involves principles which are unfamiliar, the matter should be looked up in some reference book before the observations are begun. If this is done, the significance of each step in the experimental work will be appreciated, and the experiment will therefore be more instructive.   The likelihood of essential observations being omitted is also less when the bearing of each observation upon the result is fully understood.

Record of Observations.—All original observations should be recorded in a note-book *at the time when they are taken*, and should be preserved. It is a saving in the end to devote enough time to the original records to make them neat and clear, and so complete as to enable any person who is familiar with the experiment to understand the meaning of each figure recorded.

In all cases, it is the *original* observations that are to be recorded. A derived result should in no case be recorded as an observation, no matter how simple may be the process of derivation.

For example, it may be required to find the duration of a certain phenomenon ; let us say that it begins at half-past three o'clock and lasts until twenty-two minutes of four ; the time is eight minutes, but this is a derived result obtained by subtracting 3.30 from 3.38. The actual time of beginning and end should be recorded, and the subtraction performed afterward.

The uniform observance of this rule will save annoyance from simple mistakes due to carelessness or haste, which are frequently made even by the best observers, and which, without the original observations, it would be impossible to correct.

The time at which each observation is taken should always be recorded, including the day, hour, and minute.

An example of the possible usefulness of this rule might occur in the case of observations taken with a sensitive galvanometer. Let us suppose that it is found on working up the data that the results of certain observations disagree with those of the remainder. The very annoying question then arises whether this disagreement represents an actual change in the phenomena observed, or whether it is due to the effect on the galvanometer of some outside disturbance. Knowing the time at which the observations were taken, it will be possible to investigate the matter, and if it is found that there was a change in the magnetic conditions (due to varying currents, moving iron, or other causes) at the time when the irregularities were observed, then these observations may be legitimately discarded.

Observations. — It is to be remembered that the object of scientific observations is not to confirm preconceived theories, or to obtain a series of results which shall arouse admiration on account of their uniformity, but to discover the truth in regard to the phenomenon investigated, no matter what the truth may be. It is of the greatest importance, therefore, that the observer should be entirely unprejudiced, either by a knowledge of the results of other experimenters, or by any preconceived notion as to what the results should be. It is not meant by this that the observer must be ignorant of the probable results : but that his observations should be taken with as much care as though he were ignorant ; and that great precautions must be taken to avoid the almost unconscious tendency, to which all observers are more or less subject, of making the observations correspond with what is thought to be the truth.

In many cases artificial devices can be used to insure unprejudiced observations. For example, the scale of a micrometer screw may be covered, so that it is kept out of sight until the setting is made. Or, in an experiment like that on the Coefficient of Friction (No. C_1), one experimenter may adjust the weights while the other observes whether the motion obtained is uniform. Since the latter does not see the weights, his judgment is uninfluenced by any assumption as to the law by which they vary.

In the measurement of almost all physical quantities the results will be better if the observation is repeated several times. The individual observations will doubtless differ from one another on account of slight unavoidable errors ; but the mean of the results will in all probability be nearer the truth than any single observation. To gain the advantages of taking an average, however, it is necessary that each observation should be independent of all the rest. Knowing that all the measurements should be alike except for accidental errors, there is an unconscious tendency to make them agree. This tendency must be carefully guarded against, as in the cases cited above. Each observation should be taken as carefully as though the final result depended upon it alone.

Estimation of Tenths. — In measurements in which a graduated scale of any kind is used it often happens that the result sought cannot be expressed by any exact number of scale divisions. For example, in using a thermometer graduated to single degrees, the top of the mercury column will probably come between two divisions on the scale. In such cases always estimate the fractional part of a division by the eye, expressing the fraction in tenths. Even if the estimation is poor, it gives results nearer to the truth than if the fraction were disregarded; while after a little practice it will be found possible to estimate tenths with great accuracy.

Choice of Conditions. — It often happens that the accuracy of the results of an experiment can be improved by a proper choice of the conditions under which the observations are made. An example of this fact occurs in the experiment where the internal resistance of a cell is determined by measurements of the current sent by the cell through two different external resistances. If I_1, R_1, and I_2, R_2, represent the corresponding values of current and resistance, the internal resistance of the cell is

$$x = \frac{I_1 R_1 - I_2 R_2}{I_2 - I_1}.$$

It is evident that if I_1 and I_2 are nearly alike, a slight error in the measurement of either may cause a very large error in x. To make the results reliable it is therefore necessary to choose R_1 and R_2 so that the two values of the current shall differ widely. There are many cases similar to this, where an inspection of the formula by which the results are to be computed will suggest what conditions will make the influence of accidental errors as small as possible.*

Computations.—In computing results every precaution should be used to avoid simple numerical mistakes. Mistakes due to careless adding or subtracting, to incorrect copying from one sheet to another, to the misplacing of a decimal point, etc., are a source of great annoyance, and unless care is used to avoid them they will appear with a frequency that is startling to one unaccustomed to computing. The best safeguard against mistakes is neatness and an orderly arrangement of the work. In many cases four or five place logarithms are a help, not so much on account of any saving of time, as because of the diminished liability of mistakes. Tables of squares, reciprocals, etc., can often be used to advantage, and the slide rule, when one is accustomed to its use, affords a considerable saving in time and worry. When a number of similar computations are to be made, the work should be done systematically and the results arranged in tabular form.

In working up the results of an experiment time is often wasted by carrying the results to a degree of refinement that is not warranted by the observations upon which the computations are based. Very few of the experiments that are described here will give results that are accurate to within less than one-tenth of one per cent. In most cases, therefore, it is useless to express the result by more than three, or at most four, significant figures. If it is decided from an inspection of the observations that the result should be carried to three places, then the computations should be made with four places in order to insure the accuracy of the last significant figure of the result.

---

* In this connection see the paragraph dealing with the "Influence of errors of observation upon derived results," p. 18.

In the progress of the work numbers may be obtained in which five or six significant figures appear; in such cases all beyond the fourth may be discarded.

In many cases approximate methods may be used which will effect a considerable saving in time without diminishing the accuracy of the results. For example, it often happens that a factor of the form $\dfrac{1}{1+k}$ appears as a multiplier, k being a very small quantity. In most cases it is sufficiently accurate to say that

$$\frac{1}{1+k} = 1 - k;$$

and in general

$$(1 + k)^n = 1 + nk \text{ when } k \text{ is small. *}$$

Units. — In almost all physical measurements, the units employed are based upon the centimeter-gram-second system. Since this system differs in several important particulars from that generally used in engineering work, it is essential that these differences should be clearly understood.

In physics, all derived units are defined in terms of the fundamental units of length, *mass*, and time. In the foot-pound-second system, commonly employed in engineering work, the fundamental units are length, *weight*, and time. Now the terms "weight" and "mass," although technically quite different in meaning, are frequently confused in ordinary conversation, and it is probably from this cause that the relation between the two systems is so often misunderstood.

It must be remembered that the weight of a body is defined as the force with which the body is pulled downward by gravity. By the word *pound* is meant, not the block of metal which weighs a pound, but the force by which that block is drawn toward the center of the earth. Since a force is numerically equal to the product of the mass moved into the acceleration, we have

---

* Other examples of the use of approximations will be found in Kohlrausch, Glazebrook and Shaw, and in Stewart and Gee, Appendix to vol. 1.

$W = Mg$, and in order to find the mass of a body whose weight in pounds is known, we must divide the weight by g; *i.e.*

$$M = \frac{W}{g}.$$

The mass of a pound weight is therefore $\frac{1}{32.2}$, and the unit of mass in the foot-pound-second system is the mass of a body which weighs 32.2 lbs.

In the *C. G. S.* system the gram is the unit of *mass*. By the word *gram*, therefore, is meant the amount of matter contained in a certain standard piece of metal. The weight of this piece of metal is found by multiplying its mass by the acceleration of gravity, and for the latitude of Ithaca (about 40°) is a little more than 980 dynes.

The process of weighing a body by means of a balance consists of choosing the weights so that both scale pans are pulled downward by gravity with the same force. When the adjustment is correct, the weight is therefore the same on each pan. But since, so long as g remains unaltered, the mass of a body is proportional to its weight, the two masses must also be equal. The balance may therefore be used either for comparing weights, or for comparing masses. In physical experiments the weight is seldom required, so that the balance is used almost entirely for the measurement of mass. The standards used, being grams, or multiples of a gram, are standards of mass, and the term "weights," which is so commonly applied to them, is really a misnomer.

If it is found, therefore, in making a weighing by the balance that 100 grams are required to produce equilibrium, the mass of the body weighed is shown to be 100 grams. The *weight* of the body is $100 \times g = 98{,}000$ dynes.

If care is used in distinguishing between the terms "weight" and "mass," no difficulty should be experienced in passing from one system of units to the other. The two systems are perfectly consistent with each other when properly used, and each has special advantages for the kind of work in which it is commonly employed.

Graphical Representation of Results. — When a series of observations has been taken to show the manner in which one quantity depends upon another, it is often of advantage to present a summary of the results to the eye by means of a curve. Points upon such a curve are located on cross-section paper by using the values of one quantity as abscissas, and the corresponding values of the other quantity as ordinates, the scales used in measuring the various co-ordinates being any that are convenient. It is customary to use the values of the independent variable as abscissas.

As an example of the use of the graphical method, we may consider the experiment on the coefficient of Friction (C_1). In this experi-

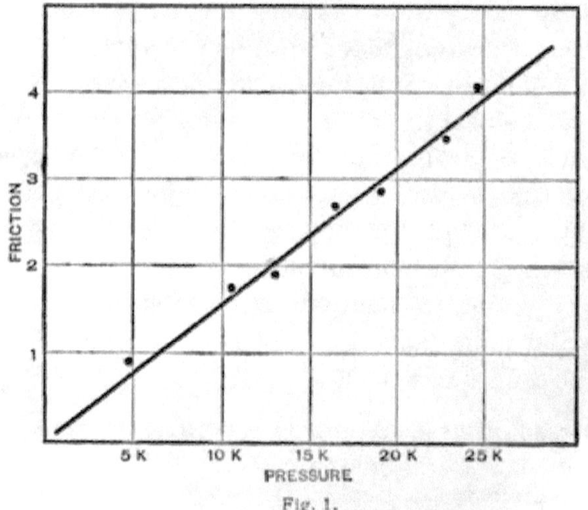

Fig. 1.

ment the force necessary to overcome the friction between iron and wood is measured for a number of different values of the pressure between the two. It is natural to suppose that the amount of friction depends in some way upon the pressure. To determine the law of this dependence, a curve is platted, in which pressures are used as abscissas, and the corresponding values of the friction as ordinates. If the observations have been carefully taken, the points located in this way will be found to lie very nearly upon a straight line passing through the origin. If the divergence from a straight line is not great, it is proper to assume that such divergence in the case of individual points is due to the accidental errors of observation, and that a straight line, passing as nearly as possible through all the points, really represents the relation sought. Now the equation of a straight line passing through the origin is $y = mx$, in which m is a constant. But the x's of our line represent pressures, while the y's represent the corresponding values of the friction. The law established by the experiment is therefore that $F = mP$; *i.e.* friction is proportional to pressure.

It is to be observed that when a curve is platted in order to show the relation between two variables, it is by no means necessary that the horizontal and the vertical scale should be the same. Either scale may be assumed at pleasure, and without reference to the other.

In the case just cited, for example, the horizontal scale may be taken as 5 kilograms to the inch, while the vertical scale may be 1 kilogram, $\frac{1}{10}$ kilogram, or any other quantity that proves convenient. In taking readings from the curve, however, regard must be paid to the scale employed. If, for example, the horizontal scale adopted is 5 kilograms to the inch, 5 inches would be read 25 kilograms. If the vertical scale at the same time is $\frac{2}{10}$ kilogram to the inch, 5 inches on the vertical scale would be read 1 kilogram.

The example referred to above, where the curve obtained is a straight line passing through the origin, illustrates the simplest case that could arise. In other cases where the graphical method is used the curve obtained may prove to be a straight line which does not pass through the origin; or it may be any form of curved line, such as a parabola or a hyperbola. In any case the law sought is determined as before, and can be expressed, either in words or by a formula, as soon as the curve is recognized.

Since the straight line is the curve which is most readily tested, it is often convenient to transform the results of an experiment in such a way that they will give a straight line when platted.

Suppose, for example, that the volume of a gas has been measured when subjected to à number of different pressures. We know from Boyle's Law that $PV =$ a constant $= k$. If the results were platted, therefore, with pressures and corresponding volumes for co-ordinates, the resulting curve would be a hyperbola whose equation is $xy = k$. If, however, we plat instead of volumes the products PV, the curve will be a straight line with the equation $y = k$. By observing whether this line is accurately straight, the law can be tested more readily than if the first curve had been used, while if the line is not straight it affords a simple means of exhibiting the deviation from Boyle's Law to the eye.

If the method described in Exp. H_1 for verifying Boyle's Law is employed, the data may be platted in still a different way to advantage. In this method the total volume V is not measured, but merely a portion v, while a part v_0 of the volume remains unknown, but constant.

Then
$$V = (v + v_0), \qquad (1)$$

$$PV = P(v + v_0) = k. \qquad (2)$$

If now P and V are taken as co-ordinates, a hyperbola should be obtained. But if v and $\frac{1}{p}$ are used, the resulting line should be straight, its equation being

$$ky = x + v_0. \qquad (3)$$

If the data are platted in this way, a means is therefore afforded of determining both v_0 and k. Since the line obtained is straight, we know that the form of its equation must be

$$y = ax + b, \qquad (4)$$

and the numerical values of a and b can be at once computed. From Boyle's Law, however,

$$ky = x + v_0,$$

or
$$y = \frac{1}{k}x + \frac{v_0}{k}. \qquad (5)$$

Since these two equations represent the same line, we must have

$$\frac{1}{k} = a, \text{ and } \frac{v_0}{k} = b. \qquad (6)$$

Graphical methods are of such great value in all branches of physical investigation that their use is recommended in a large number of the experiments which follow. The student is strongly advised to make himself familiar with graphical methods and their interpretation, as early as possible.

Reports. — As soon as the observations required in an experiment have been completed, and the results computed, a report is to be written, describing in detail the work that has been done. This report should be sufficiently clear and complete to enable it to be understood by any person having a good general knowledge of physics, even though the particular experiment described is entirely unfamiliar to him. Each report should therefore contain the following :

(1) A statement of the object of the experiment and an explanation of the means employed to accomplish this object.

(2) A description of the apparatus used.*

(3) All formulas used, which express relations between physical quantities, should be proven.† The object of putting such demonstrations in the report is to make it clear to the instructor that the principles involved are fully understood. The student will find, also, that there is no better way of making a subject perfectly clear to himself than by presenting it in such a form as to be readily intelligible to some one else. Those steps or details of a demonstration which are merely referred to in the text-books should therefore be very clearly explained. Originality in the methods of proof is desirable, but of course cannot be expected in every case.

(4) The report should contain *all the original data*, and an indication of the numerical work by which the results are obtained. It is not necessary to include all the computations in

---

* In case the same apparatus has been employed in previous experiments, however, it is not necessary to describe it a second time.

† The proof of purely mathematical formulas, such as the trigonometrical relations used in solving triangles, is not required.

the report, although where this can be done systematically and neatly, it is an advantage.   In case the results are obtained by substitution in a formula, the numerical work should be given in detail in at least one case.

(5) When possible the results obtained should be compared with the results of previous experiments as found in various reference books.

When graphical methods have been used in connection with an experiment, the curves obtained are to be included in the report.   In such cases the scale by which the co-ordinates have been measured should be clearly indicated on the drawing itself.

In writing reports, it is always to be borne in mind that one important benefit which practice in this work may accomplish is the acquirement of clearness and facility of expression in the description of scientific investigations.   The arrangement and wording of each report should therefore be carefully considered with this object in view.

ERRORS OF OBSERVATION AND METHOD OF LEAST SQUARES.

Sources of Error in Physical Measurements. — All physical measurements are subject to error from a variety of sources. Although the choice of proper methods, the employment of carefully constructed instruments, and great care in the observations themselves may enable results to be reached which are quite close to the truth, yet absolute accuracy can in no case be expected. The effort of the experimenter should always be to reduce these errors to a minimum; yet he may feel perfectly sure that to completely eliminate them is quite impossible.

As an example of the different ways in which inaccuracies can occur, we may consider a case which represents probably the simplest measurement imaginable; namely, the measurement of a length by means of a graduated scale. The chief sources of error in this measurement may be summarized as follows:

1. The scale may be incorrect either in total length or in graduation.

2. Even if it were possible that the scale were constructed with perfect accuracy, it can only be correct at one definite temperature. The coefficient of expansion of the scale must therefore be known, while its temperature must be determined at the instant of making the measurement. Two sources of error are here introduced.

3. The end of the length to be measured will in all probability lie between two divisions of the scale. The fractional part of a scale division must therefore be estimated, and on account of a variable illumination of the scale, an improper location of the observer's eye, or lack of experience on the part of the experimenter, this estimation is always subject to error.

4. Lastly, the observer may make a mistake; *i.e.* may read 10 for 20, $\frac{7}{10}$ for $\frac{3}{10}$, etc.

A little consideration will show that all possible errors may be made to fall under four classes:

1. Errors of method.
2. Inaccuracies in instruments.
3. Accidental errors of observation.
4. Mistakes.

The avoidance of errors due to the employment of faulty methods is largely a matter of judgment and experience on the part of the experimenter. No general rule can be given. Probably the best means of testing for the presence of errors in the method of measurement employed is to repeat the determination by several radically different methods. If the results agree, it is to be presumed that the methods contain no fundamental errors.

The presence of inaccuracies in the instruments used may similarly be tested by making the same measurement with several different instruments. Special methods may also in most cases be devised by which the errors of any given instrument may be determined. These methods are different for each particular case, so that it is useless to give illustrations here.

After the errors of method and of apparatus are as far as possible eliminated, there still remain the "accidental errors of observation." Two measurements of the same quantity made by the same observer, with the same instrument, and to all appearances under the same conditions, will, in the great majority of cases, differ from each other by an appreciable amount. Such discrepancies are entirely accidental, and a cause for the disagreement in the two results can in no case be assigned. The discussion of these errors can therefore only be undertaken with the aid of the theory of probabilities, and numerous treatises have in fact been written which deal with the "theory of errors" and the "method of least squares."* The principal results of such discussion, in so far as they have an application to physical measurements, will be briefly stated here.

---

* Merriman, Method of Least Squares; Violle, Cours de Physique (see Introduction to vol. 1); Weinstein, Handbuch der Physikalischen Maassbestimmungen, vol. 1; Holman's Precision of Physical Measurements; also, for brief discussions, Kohlrausch, Physical Measurements, and the Appendix to Stewart and Gee, vol. 1.

Probable Error, etc. — If a large number of *independent*[*] measurements of the same quantity are made, it is evident that one result is as likely to be correct as any other. As a matter of fact, all of the results are doubtless in error. It is also evident that the *most probable* value of the result sought will be found by taking the average of all the values found. This average will probably be more correct than any one of the single determinations. For this reason it is always advisable to repeat a determination a number of times when the conditions are such as to make this possible.

If a series of independent observations has been taken under favorable conditions and by a skillful observer, so that the individual results do not differ greatly from one another, it is obvious that the average has greater probable accuracy than if the conditions had been unfavorable so that the individual results showed a wide divergence among themselves. From an inspection of a series of determinations we may therefore form an estimate of the probable accuracy of the average. In order to express this estimate numerically the **term "Probable Error"** has been introduced, which is defined as follows :

The *probable error* of a result is a quantity e such that the probability that the actual error is *greater* than e is the same as the probability that the actual error is *less* than e. [†]

A result whose probable error is small is thus in all probability more accurate than one whose probable error is large.

The probable reliability of a result is often indicated by writing the probable error with the sign $\pm$ after the result itself: *e.g.* $l = 27.36 \pm 0.21$.

---

[*] Too much stress cannot be laid on the condition that the observations must be *independent*; *i.e.* the observer must be entirely uninfluenced by results previously obtained, or by his own opinion as to what the result "ought" to be. The avoidance of this bias in making a series of readings of the same quantity is one of the most difficult things which an observer has to learn.

[†] The name "probable error" is an unfortunate one and is apt to lead to confusion. That the probable error of a result is e does *not* mean that the result is probably in error by this amount.

If another series of measurements of the same quantity gave the result $l = 27.51 \pm 0.38$, it is clear that the first result is more reliable.

If a series of observations $a_1, a_2, \ldots, a_n$ has been taken, the average being a, then the probable error of the average may be shown to be *

$$e = \pm 0.67449 \sqrt{\frac{(a - a_1)^2 + (a - a_2)^2 + \cdots (a - a_n)^2}{n(n-1)}}. \qquad (7)$$

It may happen that it is desired to determine the probable accuracy of the result obtained from a single reading. The *probable error of a single observation* is given by the formula

$$e' = \pm 0.67449 \sqrt{\frac{(a - a_1)^2 + (a - a_2)^2 + \cdots (a - a_n)^2}{n-1}}. \qquad (8)$$

That is to say, if a single observation of the quantity in question is made, the error is as likely to be greater than e' as it is to be less.

As an example of the computation of the probable error we may consider the following case where ten independent settings are made with a spherometer on the same surface.   (See Exp. A$_1$.)

Readings of micrometer.	Deviation (d) from the mean.	d^2.
3.445 mm.	− 0.001	0.000001
3.448	+ 0.002	0.000004
3.442	− 0.004	0.000016
3.450	+ 0.004	0.000016
3.451	+ 0.005	0.000025
3.444	− 0.002	0.000004
3.446	± 0.000	0.000000
3.442	− 0.004	0.000016
3.445	− 0.001	0.000001
3.447	+ 0.001	0.000001
Mean 3.446		$\Sigma d^2 = 0.000094$

Probable error of the mean $e = .0007$

Probable error of single observation $e' = .0022$

* For the derivation of this formula, see any text-book of least squares.

It is to be observed that the computation of the probable error has no significance unless n is large.   Unless at least *ten* observations have been taken, it is useless to compute e.

On account of the annoyance in computing the probable error, the "average deviation" is often used instead; *i.e.* the average (disregarding signs) of the deviations of the individual observations from the mean.

It is to be observed that the probable error affords no means of estimating the so-called "constant errors" that are caused by improper methods of measurement or by imperfections in the instruments used. These may be very large even when the "probable error" is quite small. The use of the "probable error" may be looked upon as merely an arbitrary means of showing at a glance how closely the individual observations have agreed among themselves, and it indicates, therefore, to what extent the accidental errors of observation have been eliminated.

Assignment of Weights in taking an Average. — When the same quantity has been measured by several different methods, the results will in general differ, and it is often desirable to combine all the results by taking an average. In such cases "weights" should be assigned to the different determinations in accordance with their probable accuracy. The theory of probabilities shows that in taking an average, each quantity should be given a weight equal to the reciprocal of the square of its probable error; *i.e.* if the various values determined by the different methods are A_1, A_2, A_3, etc., the probable errors being, respectively, e_1, e_2, e_3, etc., the most probable value of the quantity in question, as determined from *all* of the observations, is

$$A = \frac{\frac{1}{e_1^2}A_1 + \frac{1}{e_2^2}A_2 + \cdots}{\frac{1}{e_1^2} + \frac{1}{e_2^2} + \cdots} \tag{9}$$

In Exp. A_1, for example, the length l of one side of the triangle formed by the three legs of the spherometer may be determined in several different ways. Let the result obtained by one method be $l = 6.12^{cm} \pm 0.03$, while that determined by another and less accurate method is $l = 6.20^{\text{cm}} \pm 0.11$. It is certainly not right to use the average $\dfrac{6.12 + 6.20}{2} (= 6.16)$, for much more reliance can be placed on the first result than on the second. According to the rule above stated the most probable value of l is

$$l = \frac{\dfrac{1}{(0.03)^2}6.12 + \dfrac{1}{(0.11)^2}6.20}{\dfrac{1}{(0.03)^2} + \dfrac{1}{(0.11)^2}} = 6.126. \tag{10}$$

Influence of the Errors of Observation upon Derived Results. — It often happens that the final result sought must be computed from the observations themselves by substitution in some formula. In such cases it is of importance to know how the final result will be influenced by possible errors in the individual observations. If an error in one of the quantities involved will produce a large error in the result, then this quantity must be observed with especial care. On the other hand, if an error in another of the observed quantities has only a slight influence on the result, it is needless to occupy one's time in measuring this quantity with a high degree of refinement. By considering this question before the actual measurements are begun, it is thus possible not only to obtain better final results, but also to save time in the observations themselves.

The general case may be discussed as follows: Let the result R, which is sought, be some function ϕ of the quantities to be observed;

i.e. $$R = \phi(x, y, z, \cdots).$$

Now if x, y, z, etc., are measured with absolute accuracy, R will be correct. But if one of the quantities x is in error by the amount e, then an error E_x will be introduced into the result, and

$$E_x = \phi(x + e_1, y, z, \cdots) - \phi(x, y, z, \cdots). \tag{11}$$

Since e will in general be quite small in comparison with x, no great inaccuracy will be introduced by treating it as an infinitesimal; *i.e.* neglecting powers higher than the first:

Then
$$E_x = e_1 \frac{d}{dx} \phi(x, y, z, \cdots).$$

Similarly,
$$E_y = e_2 \frac{d}{dy} \phi(x, y, z, \cdots), \tag{12}$$

$$E_z = e_3 \frac{d}{dz} \phi(x, y, z, \cdots),$$

etc.

If the probable errors e_1, e_2, etc., are known, the corresponding errors E_x, E_y, etc., in the result may thus be readily computed. The probable error in the result due to the combined effect of the errors in all of the observed quantities may then be shown to be *

$$E = \sqrt{E_x^2 + E_y^2 + \cdots}. \tag{13}$$

Take, for example, the case which occurs in Exp. A_1. The radius of curvature is given by the formula

$$r = \frac{l^2}{6a} + \frac{a}{2}. \tag{14}$$

Let us suppose that $l = 7.14 \pm 0.05$, and $a = 0.423 \pm 0.004$. Substituting in the formula $l = 7.14$ and $a = 0.423$, we obtain

$$r = 20.09.$$

To compute E_a and E_l, we have:

$$E_a = e_a \frac{d}{da} \phi(a, l) = e_a \frac{d}{da} \left[\frac{l^2}{6a} + \frac{a}{2} \right] \tag{15}$$

$$= e_a \left[-\frac{l^2}{6a^2} + \frac{1}{2} \right] = 0.004 \left[-\frac{\overline{7.14}^2}{6 \times \overline{0.423}^2} + \frac{1}{2} \right] = -0.188.$$

---

* See Merriman's Method of Least Squares, etc.

$$E_1 = e_1 \frac{d}{dl}\phi(al) = e_1 \frac{d}{dl}\left(\frac{l^2}{6a} + \frac{a}{2}\right) \tag{16}$$

$$= e_1 \frac{l}{3a} = 0.05 \times \frac{7.14}{3 \times 0.423} = 0.28.$$

$$E = \sqrt{0.188^2 + 0.28^2} = 0.34. \tag{17}$$

$$\therefore r = 20.09 \pm 0.34.$$

When the formula is known by means of which the result of an experiment is to be computed, it is often possible to determine the most favorable conditions before beginning the observations. The method of procedure in such cases can best be explained by means of the following example : *

A tangent galvanometer is to be used in measuring a current. What are the most favorable conditions for making the measurement?

The formula for computing the result is :

$$I = I_0 \tan \theta. \tag{18}$$

The only observed quantity is θ; and if this angle is read from a circular scale, it is liable to the same error, e, no matter from what part of the scale it may be read. Let the resulting error in I be E.

Then
$$E = e \frac{d}{d\theta} \cdot I_0 \tan \theta = \frac{eI_0}{\cos^2 \theta}. \tag{19}$$

The *relative error* is

$$E' = \frac{E}{I} = \frac{eI_0}{\cos^2 \theta} \div I_0 \tan \theta = e \frac{1}{\sin \theta \cos \theta} = \frac{2e}{\sin 2\theta}. \tag{20}$$

It is, however, evident that E' reaches its smallest value when $\sin 2\theta$ reaches its greatest value, namely unity. In other words, the relative error in the result will be least when the deflection of the galvanometer is 45°. If the galvanometer used has several coils, these should therefore always be so connected as to make the deflection as near 45° as possible.

---

* Numerous instructive examples will be found discussed in detail in Holman's Discussions of the Precision of Physical Measurements.

Determination of Constants by the Method of Least Squares. — It often happens that a series of observations is made, not of the same quantity, but of quantities which are known to be related to one another. If the form of the equation expressing this relation is known (as is usually the case), the question then arises as to what values should be given to the constants of the equation in order that it should represent the results of experiment as accurately as possible.

A case of this kind is illustrated by Exp. C_2, where a series of observations is made to determine the relation between "power" and "load" in the case of a wheel and axle. If the results are platted, the points corresponding to the different observations will probably be found to lie nearly in a straight line, as shown in Fig. 2. Although it is impos-

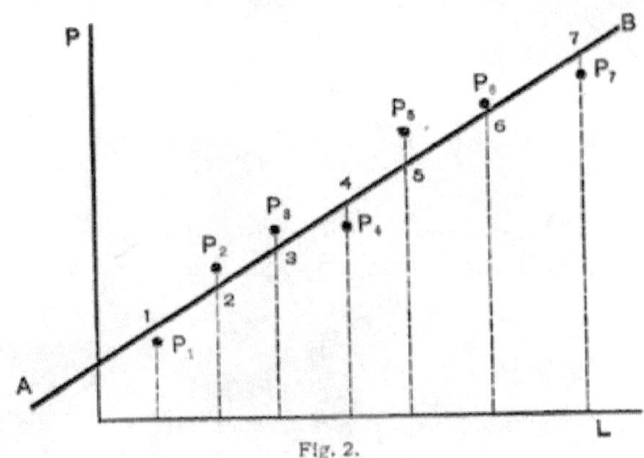

Fig. 2.

sible to draw a straight line which shall pass through all the observed points, yet it seems probable that these points would have formed a straight line, had it not been for accidental errors of observation. The problem, therefore, is to draw a straight line which shall pass as nearly as possible through all the points. This can often be done by the eye ; but when the highest degree of accuracy is required, the Method of Least Squares should be used as explained below.

The method of procedure in all such cases rests upon the principle * that the results will best be represented by the

---

* For the proof of this principle see any text-book of Least Squares.

equation in question when the constants are so chosen that the sum of the squares of the deviations of the individual observations from the values computed from the equation is a minimum.

In the example just cited the formula which expresses the relation between "power" (y) and "load" (x) is evidently

$$y = ax + b; \tag{21}$$

for the observations when platted have been found to give roughly a straight line, and the general equation of a straight line is of the form stated. As the result of experiment a number of values y_1, y_2, y_3, etc., of the power have been observed, corresponding respectively to loads of x_1, x_2, x_3, etc., kilos. Now, if the constants a and b were known, it would be possible to compute y from x : *e.g.*

$$y_1' = ax_1 + b,$$
$$y_2' = ax_2 + b, \tag{22}$$
$$\text{etc.}$$

[The y's have been primed in order to distinguish them from the observed values y_1, y_2, etc.]

The principle of least squares, which has been stated above, now says that a and b must have such values that the sum

$$(y_1 - y_1')^2 + (y_2 - y_2')^2 + \cdots$$

shall be a minimum.

Interpreted graphically, this means that the line must be so drawn that the sum of the squares of the distances $1\,P_1$, $2\,P_2$, etc., shall be as small as possible. (See Fig. 2.)

To determine a and b it is therefore merely necessary to apply the ordinary methods for maxima and minima :

$$(y_1 - y_1')^2 + (y_2 - y_2')^2 + \cdots = \Sigma (y - y')^2 = \text{a minimum.}$$

But
$$y' = ax + b.$$

$$\therefore\ (y_1 - ax_1 - b)^2 + (y_2 - ax_2 - b)^2 + \cdots = \Sigma (y - ax - b)^2$$
$$= \text{a minimum.}$$

It is to be observed that x_1y_1, x_2y_2, etc., are not variables, but constants, being the quantities determined by observation.

It is a and b that must be varied *until* such values are found that the above expression is a minimum.*

The conditions are therefore that

$$\frac{d}{da} \Sigma (y - ax - b)^2 = 0 \quad \text{and} \quad \frac{d}{db} \cdot \Sigma (y - ax - b)^2 = 0. \qquad (23)$$

On performing the differentiation the following equations result :

$$\begin{aligned}
- 2 (y_1 - ax_1 - b) x_1 - 2 (y_2 - ax_2 - b) x_2 - \cdots \\
= -2 \Sigma (y - ax - b) x = 0, \\
- 2 (y_1 - ax_1 - b) - 2 (y_2 - ax_2 - b) - \cdots \\
= - 2 \Sigma (y - ax - b) = 0.
\end{aligned} \qquad (24)$$

These equations may be more readily utilized if written in the following form :†

$$\begin{aligned}
\Sigma xy - a\Sigma x^2 - b\Sigma x = 0, \\
\Sigma y - a\Sigma x - bn = 0.
\end{aligned} \qquad (25)$$

In the last equation n represents the number of observations.

Since the quantities Σxy, Σx^2, etc., are readily computed from the observations, these two equations make possible the determination of both a and b. In fact,

$$a = \frac{\Sigma x \Sigma y - n\Sigma xy}{(\Sigma x)^2 - n\Sigma x^2},$$

and

$$b = \frac{\Sigma x \Sigma xy - \Sigma y \Sigma x^2}{(\Sigma x)^2 - n\Sigma x^2}. \qquad (26)$$

---

* Note that this variation of a and b in the algebraic work corresponds to shifting the line AB in the graphical consideration of the problem. In the one case a and b are varied until certain mathematical considerations indicate that $\Sigma (y-y')^2$ has reached a minimum; in the other case the line is shifted until it looks to the eye as though a good intermediate position had been reached.

† The student is cautioned in regard to the use of the sign of summation. Σxy means $x_1 y_1 + x_2 y_2 + \cdots$, while $\Sigma y = y_1 + y_2 + y_3 + \cdots$. Σxy is therefore *not* equal to $\Sigma x \Sigma y$.

In the general case, where the relation between x and y is expressed by an equation of any form, the method of procedure is the same as that illustrated by the example above.

Let
$$y = \phi(x, a, b, c, \cdots),$$

where a, b, c, etc., are the constants to be determined.

The observed values of y are then y_1, y_2, y_3, etc., while the computed values are y_1', y_2', etc. The principle of least squares requires that the sum

$$(y_1 - y_1')^2 + (y_2 - y_2')^2 + \cdots \text{ shall be a minimum};$$

i.e.
$$[y_1 - \phi(x_1, a, b, c, \cdots)]^2 + [y_2 - \phi(x_2, a, b, c, \cdots)]^2 + \cdots$$
$$= \Sigma[y - \phi(x, a, b, c, \cdots)]^2 = \text{ a minimum.}$$

$$\therefore \frac{d}{da}\Sigma[y - \phi(\ )]^2 = 0,$$

$$\frac{d}{db}\Sigma[y - \phi(\ )]^2 = 0, \tag{27}$$

$$\frac{d}{dc}\Sigma[y - \phi(\ )]^2 = 0,$$

$$\text{etc.}$$

The number of equations obtained in this way is always equal to the number of constants sought, so that the problem is in all cases determinate.

In applying the method of least squares, the numerical work is always somewhat tedious, especially when the number of observations is large. For this reason the computations should be made with especial care; for if a mistake occurs, considerable difficulty will be met with in discovering it. The following example illustrates a systematic way of arranging the computations, which will be found of advantage:

Equation is known to be of the form $y = ax + b$.

$$\therefore a = \frac{\Sigma x \Sigma y - n \Sigma xy}{(\Sigma x)^2 - n \Sigma x^2},$$

$$b = \frac{\Sigma x \Sigma xy - \Sigma y \Sigma x^2}{(\Sigma x)^2 - n \Sigma x^2}. \tag{28}$$

x.	y.	xy.	x^2.
5	0.20	1.00	25
10	0.34	3.40	100
15	0.48	7.20	225
20	0.64	12.80	400
25	0.80	20.00	625
30	0.93	27.90	900
35	1.10	38.50	1225
40	1.24	49.60	1600
45	1.38	62.10	2025
50	1.54	77.00	2500
275	8.65	299.5	9625

$$\therefore \Sigma x = 275$$
$$\Sigma y = 8.65$$
$$\Sigma xy = 299.5$$
$$\Sigma x^2 = 9625$$

$$a = \frac{275 \times 8.65 - 10 \times 299.5}{275^2 - 10 \times 9625} = 0.299,$$

$$b = \frac{275 \times 299.5 - 8.65 \times 9625}{275^2 - 10 \times 9625} = 0.433.$$

The equation which most accurately represents the relation between the quantities measured is therefore

$$y = 0.299\,x + 0.433.$$

A simple means of detecting large mistakes in computation is always afforded by platting the curve represented by the equation found by least squares upon the same diagram as the original data. This curve should then pass close to all of the observed points, although it may not actually pass through any one of them.

CHAPTER I.

GROUP A: LENGTH, TIME, AND MASS.

(A_1) *Curvature of a lens;* (A_2) *The cathetometer;* (A_3) *Calibration of a thermometer tube;* (A_4) *Volumes and densities by measurement;* (A_5) *Time of periodic motion.*

EXPERIMENT A_1. **Measurement of the curvature of a lens by means of the spherometer.**

The spherometer, as indicated by its name, is intended primarily for the determination of the radius of a spherical surface. It can also be employed, however, for other measurements:

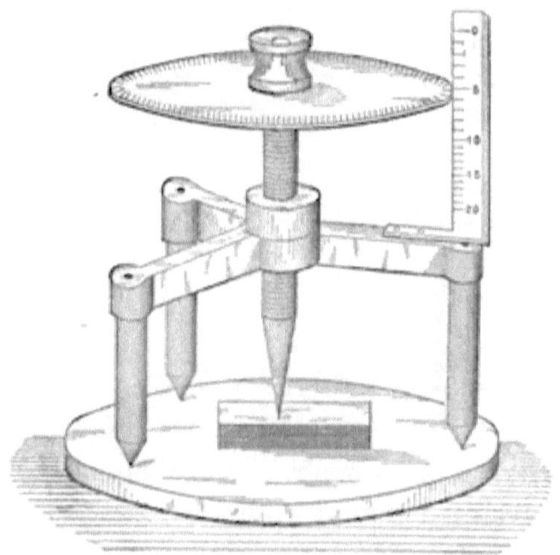

Fig. 3.—The Spherometer.

for example, the thickness of plates of glass or other materials can be determined by means of the spherometer, although unless the plates are almost perfectly plane, the results will not possess a high degree of accuracy.

As will be seen by reference to Fig. 3, which represents a simple type of spherometer, the instrument consists essentially of four metallic rods connected in the manner shown, each rod being sharply pointed at the lower end. Three of these rods are fixed in position, and constitute a tripod upon which the instrument rests. The three supporting points are made to form an equilateral triangle. The fourth rod may be moved in a direction at right angles to the plane of this triangle by means of a micrometer screw.

In using the spherometer to determine the curvature of a surface (see Fig. 4) which is known to be spherical, such for example as that of a lens, the reading of the micrometer is

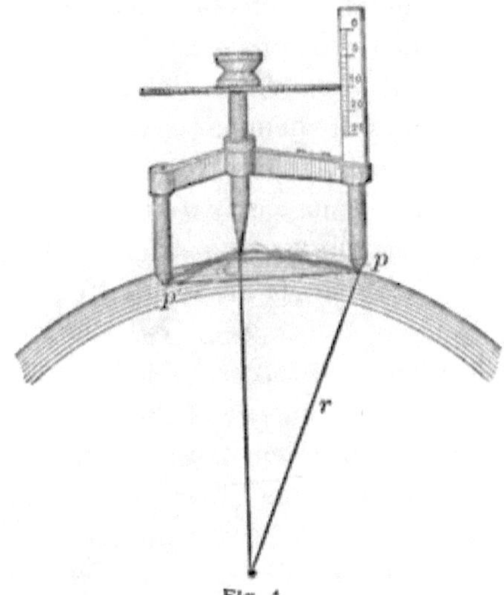

Fig. 4.

taken, first when the instrument rests upon a plane surface, and then when it is placed upon the lens in question. All four points must in each case be in contact with the surface. The difference between the two micrometer readings then gives the height of the fourth point above the plane of the other three. If this height be represented by a, and the length of one side of the triangle formed by the three fixed points by l ($l=\overline{pp'}$; Fig. 4), then the radius of curvature is readily shown to be *

$$r=\frac{l^2}{6a}+\frac{a}{2}.\tag{29}$$

In determining l, two methods may be employed; viz. (1) the three sides of the triangle may be measured directly by a millimeter scale; (2) the instrument may be placed upon a piece of paper, and the distances between the impressions left by the feet may be measured. After making a number of measurements by both methods, estimate the degree of accuracy attainable by each, and obtain the mean, giving to each measurement its proper weight.†

Since a, which enters as numerator in the formula for r, is in general a very small quantity, its value must be determined with especial care. It is therefore advisable to make a number of independent settings of the micrometer, and to use the mean of the readings obtained. Make at least ten readings for the plane surface, and the same number for the spherical surface. Compute in each case the "probable error of the mean" and the "probable error of a single observation."

After the value of r has been computed, determine the influence upon the result of the probable error in measuring the vertical height; also the influence of the error which is liable to occur in measuring the distance between the legs; and finally the probable error in the result, arising from both these causes.

In making a series of readings with the spherometer upon the same surface, it is best not to look at the scale until the setting has been made. Otherwise it is difficult to avoid being influenced by a knowledge of previous readings. Each reading

---

* For a more detailed description of the spherometer and derivation of this formula, see Stewart and Gee, vol. I.

† See Introduction, p. 17.

should be the result of an independent attempt to obtain an exact setting.

EXPERIMENT A₂. **Adjustment of a cathetometer, and determination of the sensitiveness of the level.**

A general description of the cathetometer will be found in any text-book of physics. The various adjustments should be made in the following order.

I.

To make the level parallel to the axis of the telescope. — Adjust the vertical column and bring the bubble to the middle of the level tube ; then reverse the telescope in its Y's. If the bubble settles away from the middle, it must be brought back, partly by the screws that attach the level to the telescope, and partly by changing the direction of the telescope itself. Repeat until the bubble remains in the middle of the tube when the telescope is reversed.

II.

To adjust the telescope to a right angle with the column, and to make the column vertical. — Unclamp the column and turn it till the telescope is parallel to the line joining two of the leveling screws at the base ; bring the bubble to the middle of the tube, and then turn the column through 180°. If the bubble moves from the center, it must be brought back, partly by the screw that adjusts the angle between telescope and column, and partly by the leveling screws at the base, using only the two to which the telescope is parallel. Turn now through 90°, and adjust the third leveling screw. Turn back to the first position, and repeat the adjustments till the bubble will remain in the middle of the tube for the entire revolution.

III.

To adjust the line of collimation. — Bring the point of crossing of the spider lines exactly upon some well-defined point and turn the telescope upon its axis. If the spider lines move away from the point, they must be brought back, partly by the small screws in the ring near the eye-piece, and partly by moving the telescope. Repeat until the point of intersection of the spider lines remains fixed while the telescope is rotated.

IV.

To determine the angular value of one division of the level.— Incline the telescope as far as possible, at the same time making sure that the position of both ends of the bubble can be read on the scale; raise or lower the telescope till the intersection of the spider lines coincides with some well-defined point, and take the reading on the vertical scale; then incline the telescope in the other direction, and raise or lower it till the spider lines again coincide with the fixed point; read the vertical scale, and measure the distance from it to the point. This may be taken as the radius of a circle, of which the difference in readings upon the vertical column may be considered as an arc. The angle subtended by it may then be computed. This, divided by the number of divisions through which the bubble has moved, is the angle sought.

EXPERIMENT A_3. Calibration of a thermometer tube.

The object of this experiment is to determine how completely the variations in the bore of a thermometer tube have been corrected by the graduation of its scale. The experiment is also of value in affording practice in the use of the dividing engine.

As usually employed in the Physical Laboratory, the dividing engine is merely an instrument for the accurate measurement of lengths. The more or less complicated modifications which make it possible to use the dividing engine in constructing scales and in ruling diffraction gratings need not be here considered.

The essential parts of one of the common forms of dividing

engine are shown in Fig. 5. The most important part of the instrument is the carefully constructed screw, which extends the whole length of the "engine." The figure shows only a portion of the screw and bed. The reading microscope *m* is attached to a carriage which rests upon a nut fitting this screw. By the rotation of the latter, the carriage can be moved through any distance within the range of the instrument. If the pitch of the screw is known, the distance through which the micro-scope has been moved can be computed from the number of rotations of the screw. A large divided circle at one end enables fractional parts of a complete revolution to be measured.

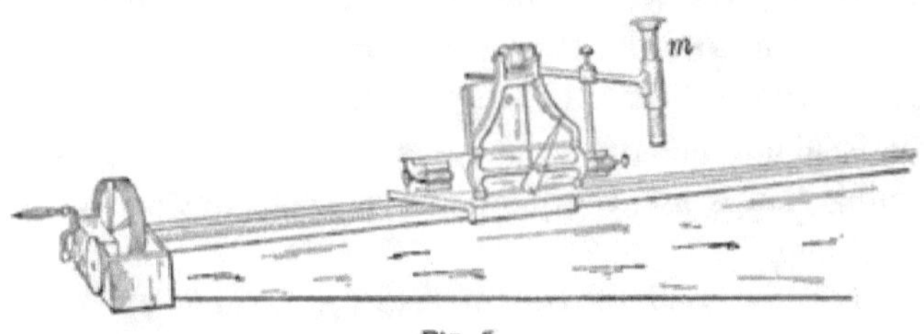

Fig. 5.

In using the engine, the object whose length is to be measured is placed upon the massive support underneath the reading microscope, and in such a position that the line to be measured is parallel with the screw. The microscope is then moved until the intersection of the cross-hairs is directly above one end of this line. After the reading of the divided circle has been recorded, the microscope is again moved until the other end of the line to be measured lies directly below the cross-hairs. From the number of turns of the screw necessary to accomplish this the length is computed. The chief source of inaccuracy in the use of the dividing engine is the "lost motion" between nut and screw. To avoid errors arising from this source, the screw should be turned during each measure-ment *always in the same direction.* If the microscope has by accident been carried too far, do not attempt to correct this by moving the carriage backwards, but begin the measurement again.

No matter how carefully the screw of a dividing engine has been cut, it is impossible to obtain one that is perfect. For the most accurate determinations the screw must therefore be *calibrated; i.e.* the pitch must be determined at different points along the screw by comparison with a standard scale. In most of the experiments which follow, the results will, however, be sufficiently accurate if the errors of the screw are neglected.*

The method of the experiment is as follows :

(1) Invert the thermometer, and allow a portion of the mercury to run into the bulb at the upper end of the tube.

(2) Separate from the rest a thread of mercury whose length is about one-tenth as great as that of the whole tube. Assuming that a 40° thermometer is used, this thread will be about 4° long.

(3) Let the end of this thread be at the 40° mark, and measure its length on the dividing engine; then by gently jarring the thermometer while in a slanting position, move the thread until the end that was at 40° arrives at 36°. Having measured its length in this position, move the thread through another 4°, and continue in this way until it has reached the bottom of the tube.

A curve is to be platted from the results of these measurements in which the positions of the middle point of the thread are used as abscissas, and the reciprocals of its length as ordinates. The reciprocal of the length of the thread is obviously proportional to the average cross-section of the tube at the place where the thread is measured. This curve, therefore, shows the relative values of the cross-section at different points along the tube. Fig. 6 (I) shows such a curve.

---

* For more detailed description of the dividing engine, see Anthony and Brackett; also Stewart and Gee, vol. 1.

(4) Measure the length of each four-degree space on the dividing engine. The product of the length of a four-degree space by the reciprocal of the length of the thread of mercury in this space will be a quantity proportional to the volume of the space. If the thermometer is accurately graduated, this product should be a constant in all parts of the tube. Fig. 6 (II) shows the actual result attained in the graduation of a fine thermometer.

From the above measurements, the error in graduation at any point may be determined in the following manner: Suppose

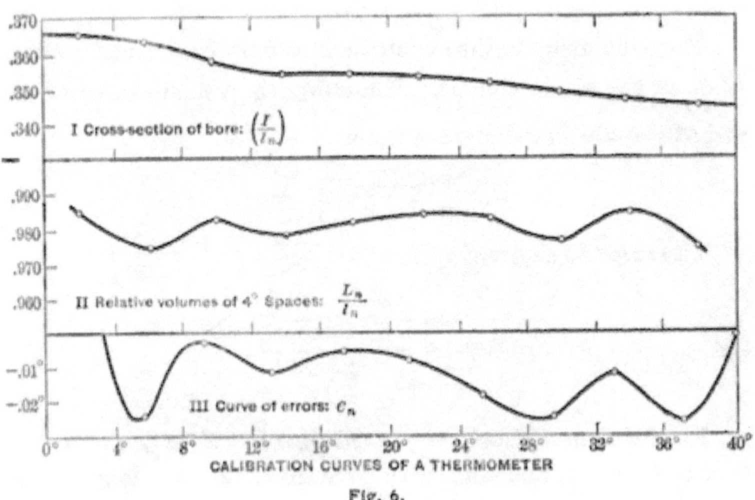

Fig. 6.

that the range of the thermometer is from 0° to 40°. Let v be the volume of a thread of mercury which is very nearly equal in length to a four-degree space. Let $l_1, l_2, \cdots, l_{10}$ be the measured length of this thread when its mid-point is at the two-degree mark, six-degree mark, and so on. Let $L_1, L_2, \cdots, L_{10}$ be the measured length of 1st, 2d, $\cdots$, 10th four-degree space. Then we shall have for the mean cross-section of the nth four-degree space

$$S_n = \frac{v}{l},$$ (30)

and for the volume of the nth four-degree space

$$V_n = \frac{vL_n}{l_n}. \tag{31}$$

Now the error of any graduation is a cumulative one; *i.e.* it depends on all the errors preceding it. The volume up to the end of the nth four-degree space is

$$\sum_1^n V_n = v \sum_1^n \frac{L_n}{l_n}, \tag{32}$$

and the total volume is

$$v \sum_1^{10} \frac{L_n}{l_n}.$$

The volume up to the end of the nth four-degree space *should be* $\frac{n}{10}$ of the whole volume. Therefore the volume error at the end of the nth four-degree space is

$$E_n = \frac{nv}{10} \sum_1^{10} \frac{L_n}{l_n} - v \sum_1^n \frac{L_n}{l_n}. \tag{33}$$

The error in degrees will be

$$e_n = 4\,n\ \frac{\sum_1^n \frac{L}{l_n} - \frac{n}{10} \sum_1^{10} \frac{L}{l_n}}{\sum_1^n \frac{L_n}{l_n}}.$$

Finally a curve should be platted (See Fig. 6, III), with values of e_n as ordinates, and with corresponding values of n as abscissas.

EXPERIMENT A_4. Determinations of volumes and densities of solids by measurement of their dimensions.

I.

Determination of the volume of a regular solid by measurement of its dimensions.

If the solid is a parallelopiped, measure each of its twelve edges on the dividing engine. If it is a cylinder, measure its altitude in four places, and measure the diameter of each base in four different places. In each case great care should be taken that the microscope moves parallel to the line measured. From the data obtained compute the volume. If the solid proves to be pyramidal or conical, treat it as a frustum. As a check upon the result, weigh the solid in air and in water. The difference of these weights, in grams, is numerically equal to the mass of the displaced water, and this quantity divided by the density of water at the observed temperature will give the volume of the solid. In weighing in water, free the solid from air bubbles, and correct for the weight of the suspending wire. More accurate results may be obtained by correcting for the buoyancy of the air. (See Exp. G_3.)

II.

Determination of the volume and density of a wire, from measurements of length, diameter, etc.

If the wire is insulated, it should first be carefully stripped in such a way as not to scratch the surface or change the shape of the cross-section. Then measure the diameter, at ten or twelve different points throughout the length, with a micrometer wire gauge. Before using the micrometer, its zero point should be tested; if it is found to be incorrect, a suitable correction must be made to each reading. Measure the length of the wire as accurately as possible, and compute its volume, treating it as a cylinder whose diameter is the mean of the diameters measured.

(If, however, the diameter is found to decrease progressively from one end to the other, the wire should be treated as the frustum of a cone.)

Finally, weigh the wire and compute its density. Check the last result by determining the specific gravity by weighing in water. (See Exp. G_1.)

III.

Measurement of the diameter of a wire by the microscope, and determination of density from diameter, length, and mass.

First determine the value in millimeters of one division of the micrometer eye-piece. To do this, focus the microscope on an accurate scale, and observe how many divisions of the scale are covered by any convenient number of micrometer divisions.

Measure the diameter of the wire at ten or twelve different points, by means of the micrometer eye-piece, and then compute the volume and density of the wire as in II, above.

Check the result by finding the specific gravity as directed in Exp. G_1.

EXPERIMENT A_5. **Determination of the time of a periodic motion by the method of middle elongations.**

The method illustrated by this experiment affords a means of determining the vibration period of any vibrating body with great accuracy. It is used, for example, in determining the time of vibration of the suspended magnet of a magnetometer, in determining the period of a pendulum, etc. With the object of affording practice in the use of the method, the apparatus is arranged as described below :

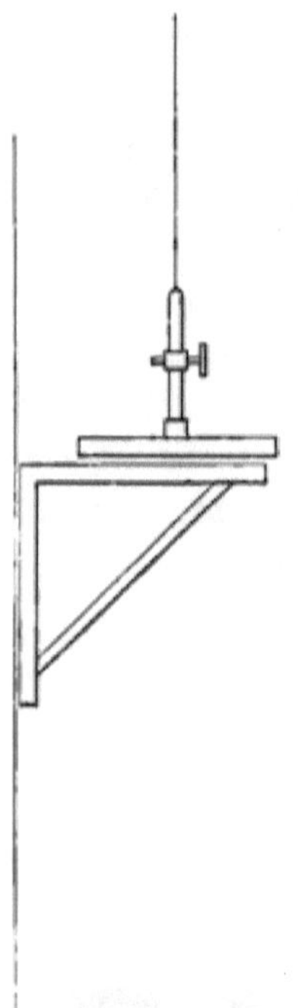

Fig. 7.—Disk for Torsional Vibrations.

A heavy disk (Fig. 7), having a black spot or a pencil line on the edge, is suspended by a long wire, and is kept in vibration, when once started, by the torsion of the wire. Place a telescope in some convenient position near a clock, and adjust it so that the vertical cross-hair is in the prolongation of the wire. The black spot will then move back and forth in the field, passing the cross-hair twice in each vibration. Note the time of day (hour, minute, second, and *tenth of a second*) of each passage of the spot across the hair, for ten successive transits. To obtain the time accurately, observe the second hand of the clock and count seconds as indicated by it. Continue the count while observing the transit, looking occasionally at the clock to see that no mistake is made. In most cases the time of transit will not correspond exactly to the beginning of a second. Observe the position of the spot at the second just before, and again at the second just after the transit : from the relative distances of these two positions from the cross-hair the tenths of a second can be estimated. This will doubtless at first be somewhat difficult, but after a little practice the estimation can be made with considerable accuracy. An experienced observer should be able to estimate twentieths of a second with certainty. Repeat the ten readings mentioned above at intervals of about fifteen minutes until three sets have been taken of ten observations each.

To utilize these data in computing the period in question, add together the fifth and sixth time of transit in each set and divide by two. The result will be the time of the " Middle Elongation," or the time at which the spot was at its greatest distance from the cross-hair between the fifth and sixth transits. If all the observations were correct, the same time of middle elongation would be found by adding together the fourth and seventh, the third and eighth, etc., and in each case dividing by two. In general, however, the five values obtained for the time of middle elongation will differ slightly on account of errors in the observations, and their average should be used. Subtracting the time of one middle elongation from that of the next, and dividing by the number of vibrations in the interval, gives the time of vibration with great accuracy. It is not necessary to count the vibrations ; the number may be deduced from the observations themselves. Between the first and ninth, or second and tenth observations of each set, there were four vibrations. Dividing the interval between the first and ninth observations by four, gives an approximation to the periodic time. If the interval between two middle elongations is divided by this quantity, the quotient would, if the observations were all exact, be a whole number ; * *i.e.* the number of vibrations in the interval.

---

* It is to be observed that this quotient might also be a whole number plus *a half.* This will be the case if the disk moved in opposite directions at the beginning of the two sets of observations.

It should, with reasonably accurate observations, be near enough to a whole number to leave no doubt as to the true number of vibrations. Dividing the interval by this number gives the periodic time desired. As a check, the time of vibration should also be computed from the interval between the second and third middle elongations.

It is to be observed that the interval which it is safe to allow between two sets of observations depends upon the accuracy of the observations, and upon the length of the period to be determined. If the period is short, the interval between two sets of observations must also be short. Determine, from a comparison of your observations, how long an interval would have been safe.

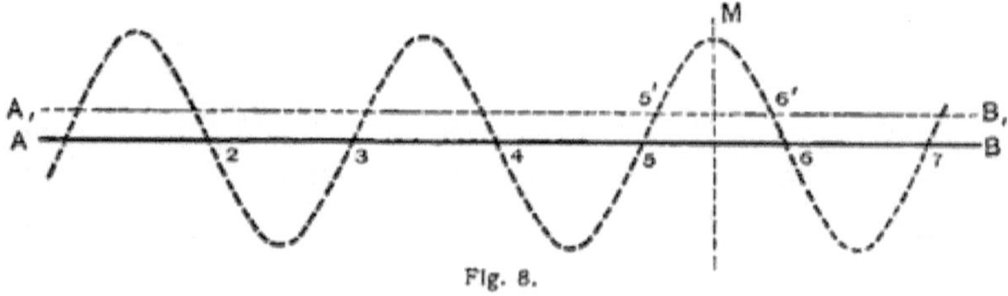

Fig. 8.

Repeat the experiment with the cross-hair to one side of the center, and show that the method pursued eliminates any such want of symmetry.

The principle of this method may perhaps be more clearly understood if the motion of the disk is represented graphically, as in Fig. 8. Horizontal distances here represent times, while vertical distances correspond to the displacement of the disk from its middle position.

The sinuous line in Fig. 8 thus represents graphically the displacement of the disk as a function of the time. The passage of the spot across the cross-hairs of the telescope corresponds in the figure with the intersection of the curve with the line $A'B'$. When the cross-hairs are placed in the prolongation of the suspending wire, this line coincides with the middle line AB. In general it is displaced as shown. The time of middle elongation corresponds to the point M on the curve, and lies midway between the times 5 and 6, 4 and 7, etc. It is evident also that M lies midway between $5'$ and $6'$, $4'$ and $7'$, etc. In other words, the method is independent of the position of the cross-hairs. Since M corresponds to the time at which the vibrating body was at rest, it is clear that the time of middle elongation is independent of the position of the telescope. A movement of the latter between two sets of observations is therefore without effect on the result.

When the time of vibration is less than four or five seconds, the observations become difficult, and in such cases an electrical contact is provided by means of which the successive transits are automatically recorded upon a chronograph. The principle of the method remains, however, unaltered.

As an example of the employment of the method, the following set of observations is appended :

DATE: JAN. 4, 1894.

First Set.		Second Set.	
No. h. m. sec.		No. h. m. sec.	
1....3 : 14 : 10.2		1....3 : 35 : 9.3	
2....3 : 14 : 23.7	Middle Elongations.	2....3 : 35 : 22.8	Middle Elongations.
3 ...3 : 14 : 35.9	5–6....3 : 15 : 8.25	3....3 : 35 : 35.0	5–6....3 : 36 : 7.45
4....3 : 14 : 49.3	4–7....3 : 15 : 8.25	4... 3 : 35 : 48.4	4–7....3 : 36 : 7.4
5....3 : 15 : 1.5	3–8....3 : 15 : 8.30	5....3 : 36 : 0.7	3–8....3 : 36 : 7.4
6....3 : 15 : 15.0	2–9....3 : 15 : 8.35	6....3 : 36 : 14.2	2–9 ....3 : 36 : 7.45
7....3 : 15 : 27.2	1–10....3 : 15 : 8.30	7....3 : 36 : 26.4	1–10....3 : 36 : 7.45
8....3 : 15 : 40.7	Average, 3 : 15 : 8.29	8....3 : 36 : 39.8	Average, 3 : 36 : 7.43
9....3 : 15 : 53.0		9....3 : 36 : 52.1	
10....3 : 16 : 6.4		10....3 : 37 : 5.6	

Interval between first and second middle elongations $=$ 20 m. 59.14 second $=$ 1259.14 second.

Approximate time of one vibration computed from interval between 1st and 9th observation of first set $=$ 25.7 second.

$$\frac{1259.14}{25.7} = 48.9 + \; ; \textit{nearest whole number} = 49.$$

$$\therefore \text{Period} = \frac{1259.14}{49} = 25.697.$$

It is propable that the result is correct to within a unit in the third place of decimals.

GROUP B: STATICS.

(B$_1$) *Parallelogram of forces;* (B$_2$) *Parallel forces;* (B$_3$) *Principle of moments.*

EXPERIMENT B$_1$. **The parallelogram of forces.**

To illustrate the principle of the "parallelogram of forces," the simple apparatus shown in Fig. 9 may be employed. It consists of a circular board about a meter in diameter, which is held in a vertical plane by any suitable support. Cords, joined

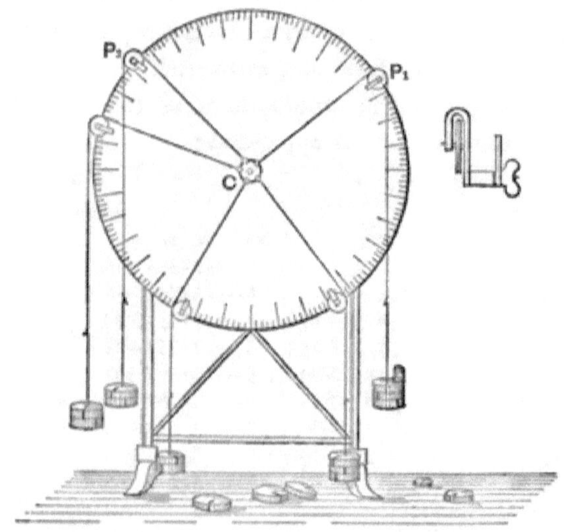

Fig. 9. — Circular Blackboard for the Study of the Parallelogram of Forces.

together at the center of the board, may be made to take any desired directions by passing over adjustable pulleys P_1, P_2, etc. By properly adjusting the position of these pulleys, and by hanging suitable weights on the cords, it is possible to obtain any desired system of forces acting at the point C. If the system of forces is in equilibrium, the point of intersection of the cords will not move, even when free to do so. The apparatus thus affords a means of testing roughly the solutions to problems which involve the equilibrium of forces acting in one plane and applied at a single point.

The student should test in this way the solutions to three problems such as those given below : *

1. Two forces being given, together with the angle between them, their resultant is to be computed both in magnitude and direction.

2. Three forces being given, compute the angles that they must make with each other in order to be in equilibrium.

3. Four forces are given in magnitude and direction. Compute their resultant.

In the last problem, the simplest method of solution is to resolve each force into two components along arbitrary rectangular axes. †

In testing the results, it will be found most convenient to fasten the point of intersection at the center of the board until the weights have all been applied. If, when the cords are now left free to move, their point of intersection still remains at the center, it is clear that the various forces are in equilibrium, and that the solution of the problem is reached. In the first problem, for example, the two given forces should be in equilibrium with the equal and opposite of their resultant. To show that the equilibrium is not due to friction, the junction of the cords may be displaced from the center ; it should then vibrate back and forth about its position of equilibrium, and finally come to rest not far from the center.

In the report on this experiment the dependence of the computations upon the principle of the parallelogram of forces should be clearly explained in each of the three cases. Diagrams should also be drawn showing the exact position in which the weights were placed when testing the results.

---

* Numerical data will be furnished by the instructor.

† See Church's Mechanics.

EXPERIMENT B₂.   **Parallel forces.**

The apparatus used in this experiment consists of a horizontal graduated bar, whose weight may be counterbalanced. At any point along the bar weights may be suspended by means of stirrups ; while forces may be made to act upwards on the bar by means of short levers, which can be attached at any point desired.   Three or more problems involving the equilibrium of parallel forces are to be given to the student, and the experiment consists in verifying the results that are obtained by computation.   In the first problem two forces and their points of application are given, to determine their resultant in position and magnitude.   In the second problem three or more forces acting in the same direction are given, together with their points of application, to determine the resultant.   In the third problem three or more forces acting in different directions are given, and the resultant is required as before.

In the report on this experiment the method of working the problems should be fully explained.   Diagrams should also be given showing the position and magnitude of the weights actually used in testing the results.

EXPERIMENT B₃.   **Principle of moments.**

The apparatus used in this experiment consists of a light frame which is free to revolve about an axis placed at the center

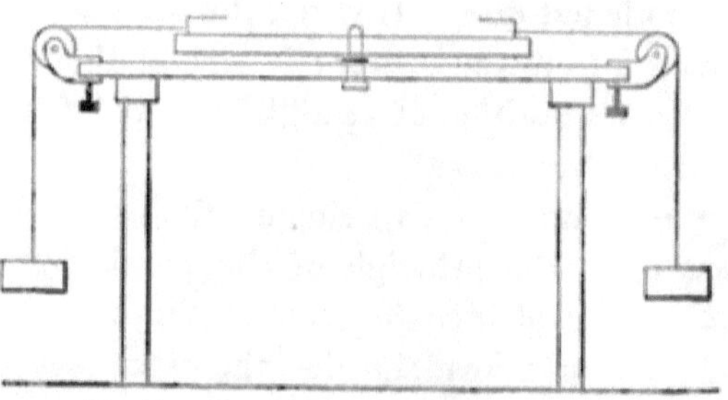

Fig 10. — Apparatus for the Study of Moments.

of a rectangular table (Fig. 10).   Cords passing over pulleys on the edge of the table may be attached to the frame at various points by means of hooks or pins (see Fig. 11). By hanging suitable weights at the ends of these cords and properly adjusting the position of the pulleys, it is therefore possible to obtain forces acting on the frame, whose magnitude and direction are under control.

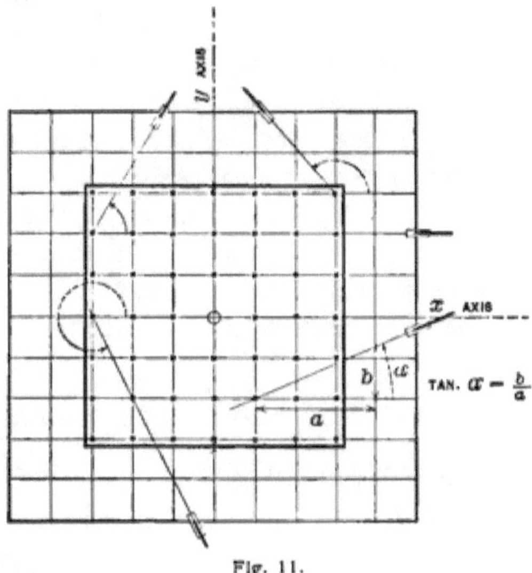

Fig. 11.

The object of the experiment is to verify by means of this apparatus the solutions of problems involving the principle of moments.

1. Four forces are given in direction, magnitude, and point of application. It is required to find the magnitude of a fifth force which will produce equilibrium when applied at a given point and acting in a given direction.

2. Four forces are given as above, together with the magnitude and point of application of a fifth force. It is required to find the direction in which this last force must act in order to produce equilibrium.

To verify the results obtained by calculation, fasten the frame by means of a pin in one other point besides the axis, so that it is no longer free to revolve. Then attach the cords to the frame, and adjust the position of the pulleys, so that the forces to which the frame is subjected are as given in the problem. Adjust in like manner the direction and intensity of the force which is to produce equilibrium. Now remove the pin, so that the frame is again free to rotate. If the computations are correct, the position of the frame should remain unaltered. To prove that the frame is not held in position by friction, it may be displaced through a small angle by the hand. The action of the various forces will then cause it to return, after a few vibrations, to its original position.

In the report on this experiment the method of working the problems should be clearly explained. Diagrams of the apparatus should also be given, in which are shown the directions and magnitudes of the forces actually used in each test.

GROUP C: FRICTION AND SIMPLE MACHINES.

(C_1) *Coefficient of friction;* (C_2) *Law of wheel and axle;* (C_3) *Law of systems of pulleys.*

EXPERIMENT C_1. **To determine the coefficient of friction between two surfaces.**

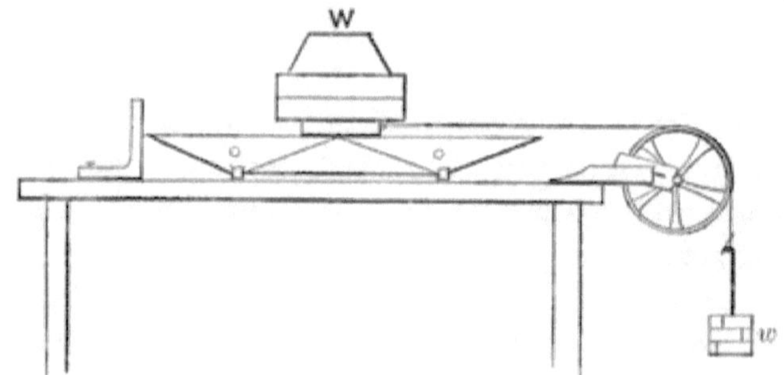

Fig. 12.—Coefficient of Friction.

The apparatus, which is shown in Fig. 12, consists (1) of a smooth plate made of one of the materials to be tested and capable of being adjusted so that its upper surface is accurately horizontal ; (2) a small block of the second material in question which can be made to slide across the plate by means of a cord passing over a pulley and loaded with suitable weights.

Observations should be taken as follows :

First adjust the plate so that its surface is horizontal. Place the block upon it, and add enough weights to make the total pressure five kilograms. Then hang weights on the cord until the force is just sufficient to keep the block moving uniformly when once started. Repeat the observations with pressures of 10, 15, 20, etc., kilos on the block until a pressure of 50 kilos is reached.

It is to be observed that the weights upon the cord do not represent exactly the force required to overcome the friction between plate and block. A correction must be applied in each case on account of the friction of the pulley itself. To determine this correction, a cord may be passed over the pulley, carrying equal weights at its two ends. A definite pressure is thus exerted on the bearings of the pulley, and to overcome the resulting friction, a slight additional weight, whose amount is determined by experiment, must be placed on one side. In this way the relation between the friction of the pulley and the pressure on its bearings can be determined, after which the corrections to be applied to the former observations can be readily computed.*

The results may now be best shown by platting a curve on cross-section paper, using pressures, W (Fig. 12) as abscissas and forces necessary to overcome friction, w (Fig. 12) as ordinates. If friction is proportional to pressure, this curve should be a straight line passing through the origin. Find its equation by the method of least squares, and so deduce the coefficient. A typical curve of the kind described is shown in Fig. 13.

Each of the observations at different pressures should be

---

* It is to be observed that the friction of the pulley is determined by the *pressure on its bearings*, and is independent of the direction of this pressure. The weight of the pulley itself is usually so small that it can be neglected.

independent, and uninfluenced by any assumption as to the probable result.   Friction, under the best of conditions, is irregular, so that it need not be at all surprising if the observations are somewhat discordant.   The best final results will be obtained by making a number of entirely independent observa-

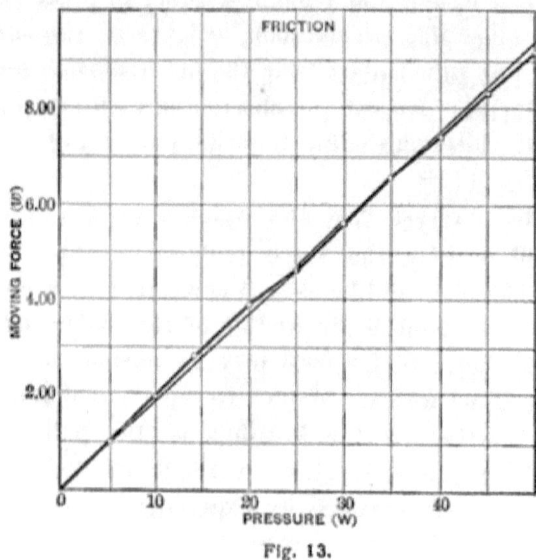

Fig. 13.

tions, each one being as carefully made as though it alone were to determine the coefficient.

The same apparatus may be employed to determine the influence of the area of contact upon the coefficient of friction, and also to study the "friction of rest," or "starting friction."

EXPERIMENT C_2. Law of the wheel and axle and determination of efficiency.

In this experiment a small weight suspended by a cord from a large wheel is made to lift a larger weight which hangs from the axle of the wheel.* The object of the observations is to

---

* The experiment will perhaps be more instructive if a compound wheel and axle is used, or a compound system consisting of an endless screw and gear wheel.   In these cases the influence of friction on the results will be much more marked.

determine experimentally the relation between the two weights when the smaller is just sufficient to keep the system moving. It is to be observed that the conditions differ from those considered in the simple theory of the wheel and axle, in the fact that the friction of the various parts is not negligible. The system forms, in fact, a simple type of machine, whose object we may consider to be the raising of weights. The effect of friction in reducing the efficiency of this simple machine is exactly the same in *kind* as it is in larger and more complicated machines, and the experiment thus affords an opportunity of studying the influence of friction in a simple case where the various disturbing factors may be readily isolated.

Observations are to be taken as follows :

Find by experiment the weights necessary to raise loads of 5, 10, 15, up to 50 kilos, the small weight being adjusted in

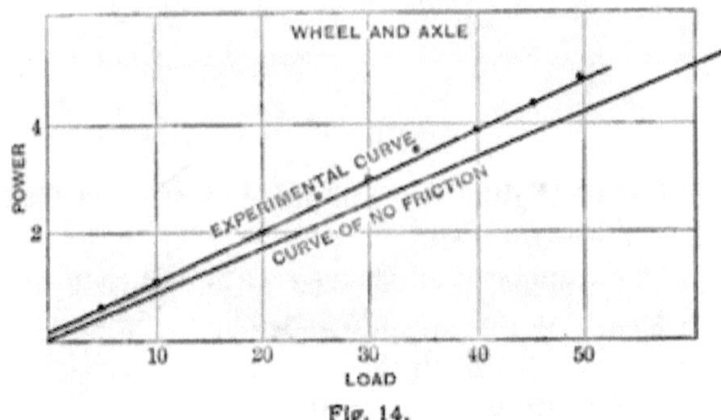

Fig. 14.

each case until it is just sufficient to keep the system moving with a slow, uniform motion, when started by the hand. Make several trials with each load and use the mean of the results. It is essential that each observation should be entirely independent of all the rest, and uninfluenced by any assumption as to what the relation should be between " power " and " load."

From the data thus obtained, plat curves showing the relation between the power and the load in each case. Fig. 14 shows such a curve. To locate points on these curves (which should be accurately drawn on cross-section paper), the loads are to be used as abscissas and the corresponding powers as ordinates.* From the appearance of the curves decide upon the form of their equations, and find the constants by the method of least squares. The lines represented by the equations that are obtained by least squares should be drawn on the

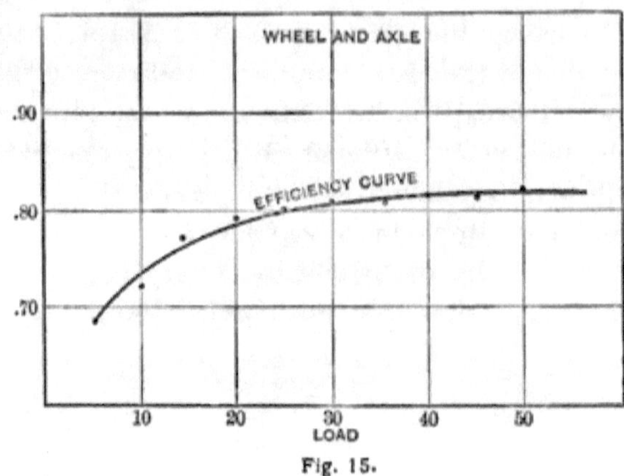

Fig. 15.

same sheet as the original ones, in order to see how closely they represent the observations.

Having determined the velocity ratio in each case, show what the behavior of the apparatus would be if there were no friction, and compute the efficiency of the apparatus, considered as a machine for lifting weights, for loads of 5, 10, 25, and 50 kilos. A curve showing the relation between efficiency and load may then be drawn (see Fig. 15).

The velocity ratio may be roughly computed from the diameters of the wheel and axle; but on account of the appreciable thickness of the rope used, it is better to obtain the velocity ratio by actually measuring the distance passed over by the load when the wheel is turned a known number of times.

---

* Note that the horizontal and vertical scales need not be the same. See Introduction.

Addenda to the report :

(1) Interpret the curves obtained in detail. For example, the friction of the machine consists of two parts: (1) a constant frictional resistance, which is independent of the load; (2) a variable resistance becoming greater as the load increases. Each of these is readily determined from the curve.

(2) Indicate the greatest possible efficiency that can be attained by the machine, and the load to which this corresponds.

EXPERIMENT C_3. **To determine the efficiency of a system of pulleys.**

In this experiment a system of pulleys is used by which a small weight moving through a considerable distance is enabled to lift a much larger weight through a comparatively small distance. The objects of the experiment are: (1) To determine experimentally the relation between "power" and "load" for uniform motion; (2) to determine the efficiency of the system considered as a machine for raising weights. The procedure is as follows:

(1) Find by experiment the weights necessary to raise loads of 0.5, 1.0, 1.5, up to 6 kilos, the small weight being adjusted in each case until it is just sufficient to maintain uniform motion when the system is started by the hand. Make several trials with each load, and use the mean of the results.

(2) With the data obtained, plat curves showing the relation between power and load for both cases, and from the appearance of the curves decide upon the form of their equations. The constants are to be determined by the method of least squares. The lines represented by the equations obtained by least squares should be drawn on the same sheet as the original curves.

(3) Having determined the ratio of the distances passed over by the two weights, show what powers would be necessary to raise the same loads if there were no friction, and compute the

efficiencies of the two systems for loads of 0.5, 1, 3, and 6 kilos.

The results are to be discussed in the manner explained in the previous experiment.

GROUP D: UNIFORMLY ACCELERATED MOTION.

(D_1) *Atwood's machine.* (D_2) *Determination of gravity from the motion of a freely falling body.*

EXPERIMENT D_1. Atwood's machine.

In Atwood's machine a vertical standard, from two to three meters high, carries at the top a light pulley, P (Fig. 16), which is mounted in such a way as to make the friction of its bearings as small as possible. To the standard is attached a scale graduated in centimeters or inches for convenience in measurement. Over the pulley hangs a light silken cord, to which weights, w_1, w_2, may be hung. If equal weights are hung on the two sides of the pulley, it is evident that the system will remain at rest. But if a small additional weight be placed on one side, the condition of equilibrium will be destroyed, and the heavier side will begin to fall with a uniformly accelerated motion. The force of gravity acting on the small added mass, or "rider," r (Fig. 17), is thus utilized to set in motion a much larger mass, and the acceleration is, in consequence, smaller than if the rider alone were moved. By suitably choosing the various weights, the motion may be made so slow that the velocity can be readily measured. The apparatus thus affords a means of illustrating the laws of uni-

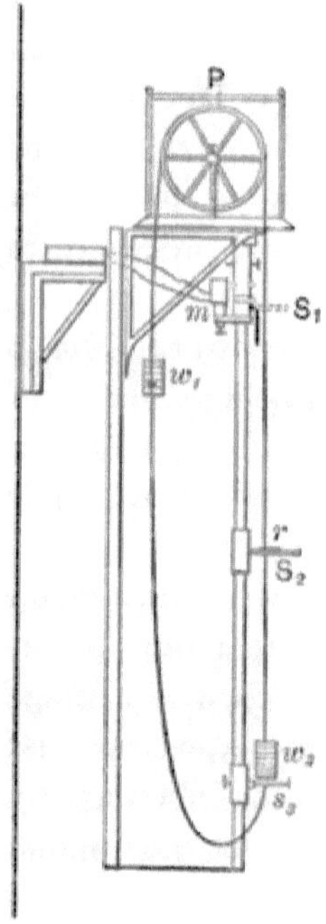

Fig. 16.

formly accelerated motion, and can also be used, as explained below, to determine the acceleration of gravity, g.

For convenience in measuring time, most forms of Atwood's machine are provided with an electric bell or sounder, which can be connected with a seconds pendulum. By means of an electromagnet, m (Fig. 16), placed at the top of the vertical standard, and connected with the same circuit as the sounder, the weights may be released exactly at the beginning of a second, so that the necessity of estimating fractions of a second is avoided. A bracket, s_3 (Fig. 16), movable along the upright standard, may be adjusted so as to stop the fall at any point desired, while a ring, s_2, also adjustable in position, serves to remove the rider at any desired time without disturbing the motion of the weights themselves.

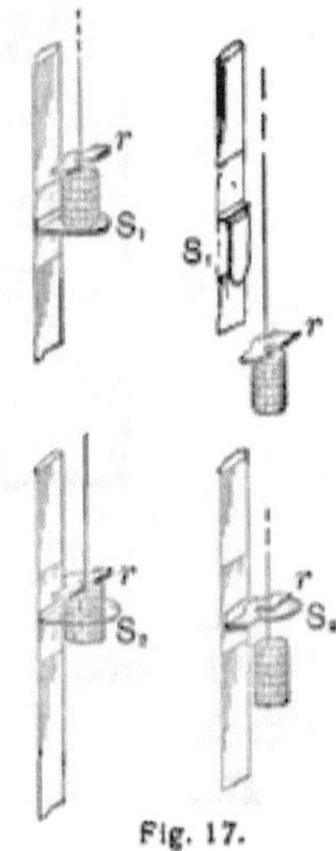

Fig. 17.

I.

To test the laws of uniformly accelerated motion.

Hang equal weights on the two sides of the pulley, and then put enough additional weight on the side which is to fall during the experiment to overcome the friction of the apparatus. This can be done by adding small pieces of paper or tin-foil until the weight will continue to move uniformly downward when once started. When this adjustment is completed, place the rider in position, and adjust the ring by trial to such a position on the vertical bar that it will remove the added weight after a fall of exactly two seconds. Measure the distance traversed by the rider and record it, together with the time of fall. To determine the velocity acquired, adjust the bracket to such a position that the space between it and the ring shall be traversed in some exact number of seconds. This distance between ring and table being measured, the velocity can be computed. To insure accuracy, each of these observations should be repeated several times and the average of the results used. Now shift the position of the ring until the time of fall is three seconds; then four

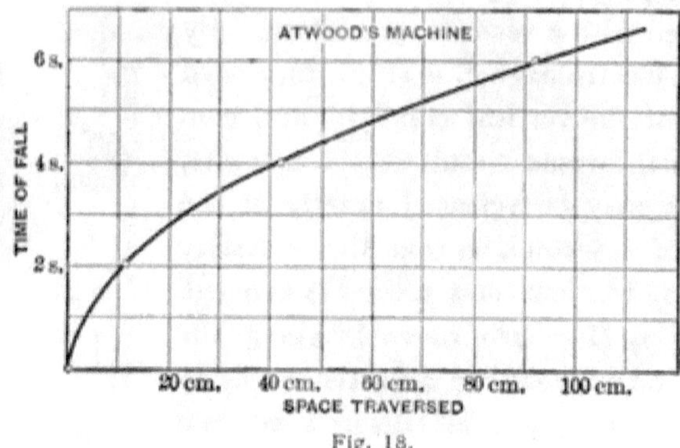

Fig. 18.

seconds; and so on, repeating the observations described above in each case.

The results can be best shown by platting two curves, one

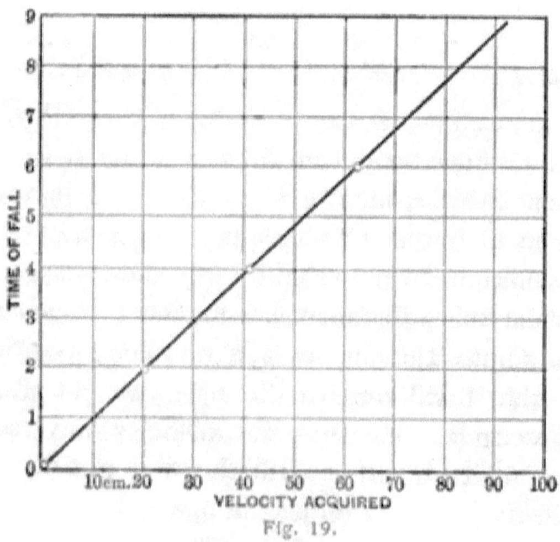

Fig. 19.

showing the relation between time of fall and the space traversed (Fig. 18), the other showing the relation between time of

fall and the velocity acquired (Fig. 19). Discuss the results and show whether or not they are in agreement with the laws of uniformly accelerated motion.

II.

To use Atwood's machine for the determination of g.

If the mass of the rider is m, the resultant force acting on the system is mg. This force is equal to the product of the total mass moved into the acceleration imparted. If, therefore, the total mass except the rider be denoted by M, and the measured acceleration by a, we have

$$mg = (m + M)a ; \qquad (34)$$

g can therefore be computed as soon as m, M, and a are known. The mass m can be at once determined by weighing, while a can be computed from the observations. But the value of M cannot be so simply obtained, since the pulley itself forms a part of the mass set in motion. The "equivalent mass" of the pulley must therefore be first determined. To accomplish this, proceed as follows :

(1) Remove one of the small weights from each side of the cord ; adjust again with tin-foil to overcome friction, and determine by experiment the spaces corresponding to falls of two, three, four, etc., seconds, respectively.

(2) Determine also the mass upon the cord.

(3) Repeat the observations after removing another weight from each side, and continue until only one weight remains.

From these observations, compute the acceleration imparted by the rider in each case. Since the equivalent mass of the pulley is known to be a constant, it may now be readily computed, either algebraically or graphically. The graphical method which follows is, however, recommended.

Plat a curve (see Fig. 20) upon cross-section paper in which the masses hung upon the pulley are used as abscissas, and the reciprocals of the corresponding accelerations as ordinates. This curve should, if the observations are good, be nearly a straight line. The equation of the line is, in fact,

$$mg \cdot \frac{1}{a} = m + M_0 + M, \qquad (35)$$

where M_0 denotes the constant equivalent mass of the pulley, and $m + M$ the sum of the masses hung from the cord. The co-ordinates of the curve are therefore $x = m + M$ and $y = \frac{1}{a}$; i.e.

$$mg \cdot y = x + M_0. \qquad (36)$$

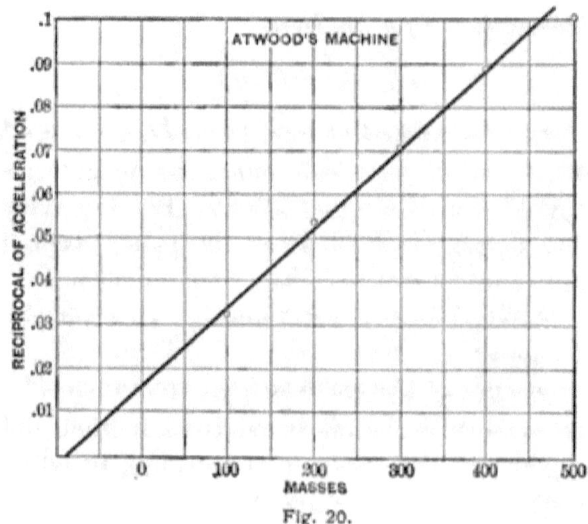

Fig. 20.

This is an equation of the first degree, and therefore represents a straight line.

Owing to errors of observation, the curve obtained will not be exactly straight. A straight line should, however, be drawn which passes as nearly as possible through all the points platted. A little consideration will show that the intercept of this line on the axis of abscissas is equal to the equivalent mass of the pulley.

The computation of g can now be easily performed.

It may be readily proved that what has been called the equivalent mass of the pulley is really its moment of inertia divided by the square of the distance from its center to the cord. The work done by gravity when the rider has moved a distance, l, is mgl, but this work must be equal to the kinetic energy gained.

$$\therefore \; mlg = \tfrac{1}{2}(m+M)v^2 + \tfrac{1}{2}K\omega^2, \tag{37}$$

in which v is the final velocity of the suspended masses, ω the final angular velocity of the pulley, and K its moment of inertia. Remembering that $v^2 = 2\,al$ and $v = r\omega$, this equation reduces to

$$mg = \left(m + M + \frac{K}{r^2}\right)a, \tag{38}$$

in which r is the radius of the pulley.

EXPERIMENT D_2. **Determination of g from the motion of a freely falling body.**

The apparatus for this experiment, Fig. 21, is so arranged that a piece of smoked glass may be allowed to fall freely in

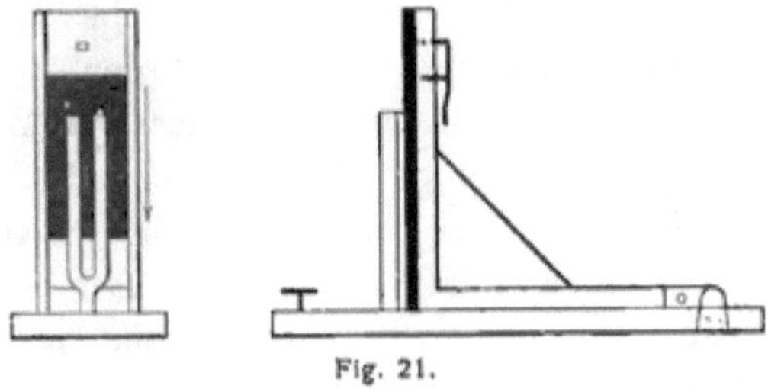

Fig. 21.

front of a vibrating tuning-fork of known pitch. A stylus attached to one prong of the fork is adjusted to trace a sinuous line on the glass as it falls. By measuring the length of the successive waves of this curve, it is possible to compute the acceleration of gravity. As a means of measuring g, the method is not at all accurate, since any friction in the apparatus will introduce a considerable error. The experiment is valuable, however, in illustrating the laws of falling bodies, and in familiarizing the student with the use of the dividing engine as an instrument for measuring length.

Having covered the glass with a *thin* layer of smoke (preferably from burning camphor), adjust the stylus until it traces a smooth and distinct curve when the glass is allowed to fall. Several trials may be necessary before this adjustment is satisfactory. When a good curve has been obtained, stop the vibration of the fork, and allow the glass to fall a second time without changing the position of the glass.

The stylus will then be made to trace a straight line nearly through the center of the sinuous curve. (See Fig. 22.)

Now adjust the glass under the microscope of the dividing engine, assume some sharply defined intersection of the straight line and curve as a starting-point, and measure the distance from this to the third, fifth, seventh, etc., intersection. These distances evidently represent the spaces passed over during one, two, three, etc., complete vibrations of the fork. It is best not to start with the beginning of the curve, since the line may be more or less blurred and irregular in this region.

From these measurements, the acceleration of gravity can be determined in the following manner: Let v_0 be the velocity with which the falling body passed the point of the sinuous curve taken as origin. Let L be the distance from this point to an intersection passed t vibrations later. Then we shall have

$$L = v_0 t + \tfrac{1}{2} g t^2, \tag{39}$$

Fig. 22. in which g represents the acceleration of gravity. If the series of observations taken be platted, with values of L as ordinates and values of t as abscissas, the resulting curve will be a parabola. The constants v_0 and g may be determined from this curve by the method of least squares. As this is a quadratic equation, the numerical computations will be very laborious.

It will therefore be desirable to use a linear equation if possible. This may be done as follows: Let l be the distance traversed *during* the tth vibration of the fork, counting from the assumed origin; then we shall have

$$l = v_0 + \tfrac{1}{2}g + gt. \tag{40}$$

If a series of corresponding values of l and t be platted, this will give a straight line, from which the constants v_0 and g may be determined either directly by measurement or indirectly by the method of least squares.

The constants may also be derived from two independent equations like the above. If this is done, the two values of l taken should differ considerably, one being about twice the other.

In the above discussion, the unit of time is the period of the fork. Therefore the values of v_0 and g obtained will be referred to the period of the fork as the unit of time. Since v_0 varies inversely as the time, it is necessary, in order to express that constant in centimeters per second, that the values obtained be divided by the period of the fork. For a similar reason, the value of g obtained must be divided by the *square* of the fork's period if the acceleration of gravity is to be expressed in centimeters per second per second.

GROUP E: MOMENT OF INERTIA AND SIMPLE HARMONIC MOTION.

(E) *General statements;* (E₁) *The physical pendulum;* (E₂) *Kater's pendulum;* (E₃) *Relation between the time of vibration and the position of the knife-edges in a uniform cylindrical pendulum;* (E₄) *Determination of the moment of inertia of a body.*

(E). General statements concerning the moment of inertia and simple harmonic motion.

The moment of inertia of a body, with respect to a right line taken as an axis, is the sum of the products of each element of mass by the square of its distance from the axis. If K_a is the moment of inertia of any body with respect to the axis a, dM any element of mass, and r its perpendicular distance from the axis a, we have

$$K_a = \int r^2 dM, \tag{41}$$

in which the integral is extended to every element of mass of the body.

Moment of inertia bears the same relation to motion of rotation that mass bears to motion of translation. The following dynamical relations may readily be derived from definitions and Newton's second law of motion.

1. $\begin{cases} \text{Momentum} = \text{mass} \times \text{velocity.} \\ \text{Moment of momentum} = \text{moment of inertia} \times \text{ang. vel.} \end{cases}$

2. $\begin{cases} \text{Resultant force} = \text{mass} \times \text{acceleration.} \\ \text{Resultant moment} = \text{moment of inertia} \times \text{ang. acc.} \end{cases}$

3. $\begin{cases} \text{Kinetic energy} = \frac{1}{2}\ \text{mass} \times (\text{velocity})^2. \\ \text{Kinetic energy} = \frac{1}{2}\ \text{moment of inertia} \times (\text{ang. vel.})^2. \end{cases}$

The moment of inertia of a body with respect to any axis is equal to the moment of inertia of the same body with respect to a parallel axis through the center of gravity, plus the mass of the body multiplied by the square of the distance between the two axes.

Let dM be an element of mass whose co-ordinates with respect to an axis through the center of gravity are x, y. Let c be an axis parallel to the axis through the center of gravity (Fig. 23) at distance a from it. Let K_0 and K_c be the moments of inertia with respect to the two axes. Then we shall have

$$K_c = \int [(a+x)^2 + y^2]\, dM = a^2 \int dM + \int (x^2 + y^2) dM + 2\, a \int x dM \quad \text{or}$$

$$K_c = Ma^2 + K_0. \tag{42}$$

The term $\int x dM$ is zero, for the origin is at the center of gravity of the body; this means that the sum of the positive products xdM is just equal to the sum of the negative products $- xdM$.

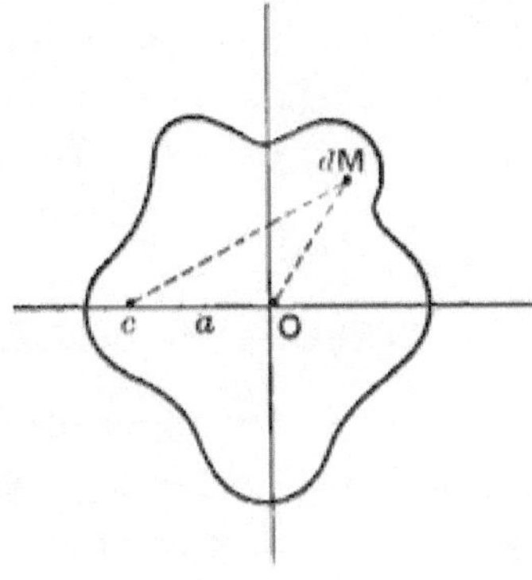

Fig. 23.

Moment of inertia of an infinitely thin rod about an axis perpendicular to its length.

Let L be the length of the rod, S its cross-section, δ its density. If dx is the length of the element of mass, we shall have $dM = \delta S dx$. If x (Fig. 24) is the distance of the element

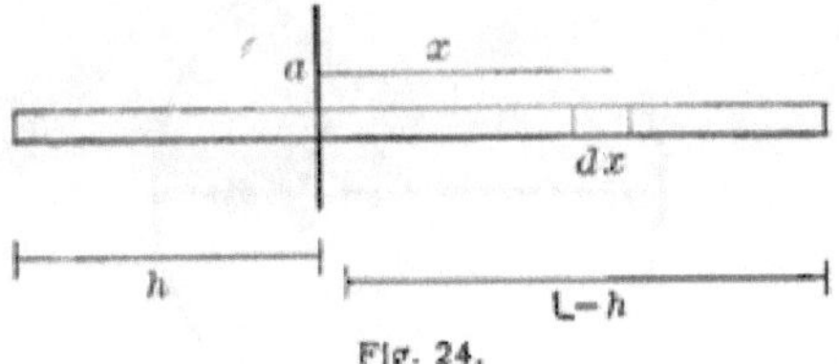

Fig. 24.

of mass from the axis a, and h is the distance of the axis from either end of the rod, we shall have

$$K_a = \delta S \int_{-h}^{L-h} x^2 dx. \tag{43}$$

If M is the mass of the whole rod, this reduces to

$$K_a = M\left[\frac{L^2}{3} - hL + h^2\right]. \tag{44}$$

Two particular cases are of especial interest; namely, when $h = 0$ and when $h = \frac{L}{2}$.

Moment of inertia of a cylinder about its axis of figure.

Let L be the length, a the radius, and δ the density of the cylinder. Take as element of mass an indefinitely thin, hollow cylinder, concentric with the axis, of radius r and thickness dr.

We shall then have $dM = 2\pi r L \delta dr$. Therefore we have

$$K_0 = 2\pi\delta L \int_0^a r^3 dr = M\frac{a^2}{2}, \qquad (45)$$

in which M is the mass of the whole cylinder.

Moment of inertia of a circular lamina about any diameter.

Let a be the radius of the lamina, ϵ its thickness, and δ its density. Taking the element of mass in polar co-ordinates, we have

$$dM = \epsilon\delta r d\theta dr.$$

As the distance of the element of mass from the diameter is $r\sin\theta$ (Fig. 25), we have

$$K_0 = 2\epsilon\delta \int_0^\pi [\sin^2\theta d\theta \int_0^a r^3 dr] = M\frac{a^2}{4}. \qquad (46)$$

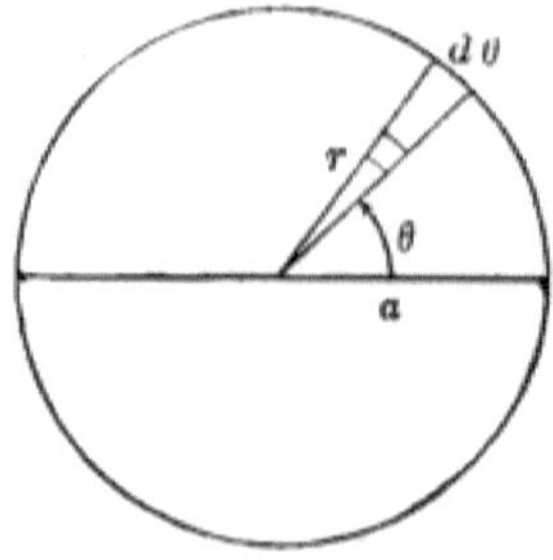

Fig. 25.

Moment of inertia of a cylinder about any axis perpendicular to its geometrical axis.

Let L be the length of the cylinder, a the radius, δ the density, and h (Fig. 26) the distance of the axis from one end of the cylinder. Taking as element of mass a lamina of thickness dx, we have

$$dM = \pi a^2 \delta dx.$$

From equations 42 and 46 we have for the moment of inertia of this lamina, with respect to the axis a,

$$dK_a = x^2 dM + \frac{a^2}{4} dM. \tag{47}$$

$$K_a = \pi a^2 \delta \int_{-h}^{L-h} x^2 dx + \frac{\pi a^4 \delta}{4} \int_{-h}^{L-h} dx,$$

and

$$K_a = M \left[\frac{L^2}{3} - hL + h^2 + \frac{a^2}{4} \right]. \tag{48}$$

Two particular cases are of especial importance; namely, when $h=0$ and when $h=\frac{1}{2}L$.

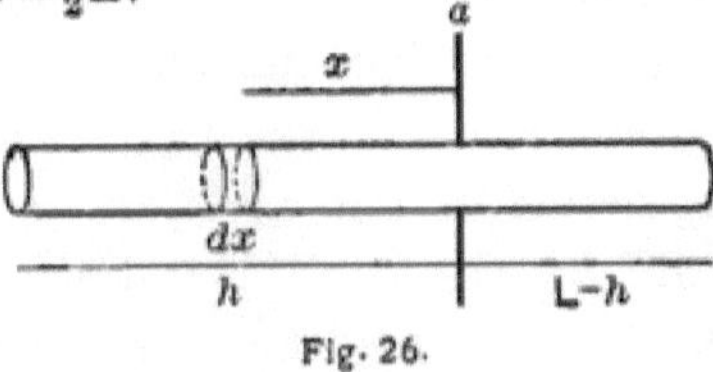

Fig. 26.

Simple harmonic motion.

An oscillating body is said to have simple harmonic motion when its distance, either linear or angular, from a fixed position is a simple harmonic function of the time of either of the forms,

$$x = A \cos [p(t+t_0)],$$
$$x = A \sin [p(t+t_0)], \tag{49}$$

in which A, p, and t_0 are constants.

The distance of the body, either linear or angular, from the fixed position is called its *displacement*. The maximum displacement occurs when the cosine becomes unity. This maximum displacement is called the *amplitude* of the simple harmonic motion. In the above equation t_0 is a constant interval of time. This constant is obviously zero if time be reckoned from the instant when the displacement is a maximum in the positive direction, using the first of equations 49. When the time t has increased to the value $\frac{2\pi}{p}$, the displacement x is exactly equal to what it was at the instant, $t=0$. Moreover, at any time, t_2, the displacement has the same value that it had at the time t_1 if $t_2-t_1=\dfrac{2\,\pi n}{p}$. The constant interval of time $\dfrac{2\,\pi}{p}$ during which the displacement takes all possible values, and the motion begins to repeat itself, is called the *period* of the simple harmonic motion. It is usually represented by τ or T.

Simple harmonic motion of translation.

The rectangular projection of uniform circular motion upon any diameter is simple harmonic motion; *i.e.* if the point N (Fig. 27) revolves about a circle with a uniform velocity, the point P will move along the diameter BC with simple harmonic motion.

Let A be the radius of the circle, let p be the constant angular velocity of the radius ON, and suppose time to be reckoned from the instant that the point P leaves the right-hand end of the diameter BC; then at any time, t, we shall have *

$$x=A\cos\beta=A\cos pt. \qquad (50)$$

The distance, x, is the displacement, and A the amplitude, of the simple harmonic motion.

If the point P moves through the distance dx in the time dt, we have, from the definition of velocity,

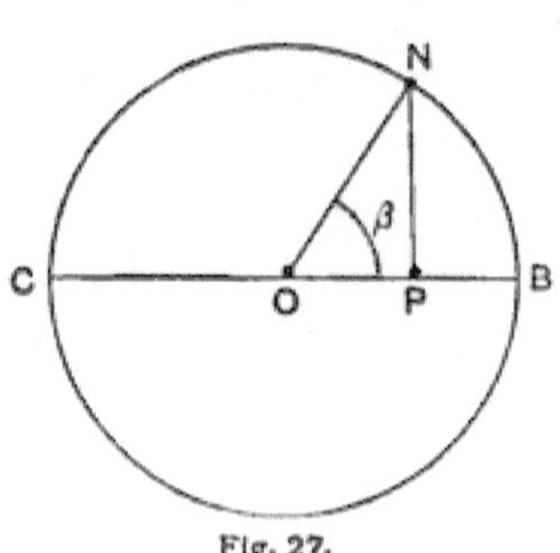

Fig. 27.

$$v=\frac{dx}{dt}=-pA\sin pt. \qquad (51)$$

If the velocity of the point P changes by the amount dv in the time dt, we have, from the definition of acceleration,

$$a=\frac{dv}{dt}=-p^2A\cos pt. \qquad (52)$$

---

* It is to be understood that these equations hold for any simple harmonic motion, that the circle is an auxiliary circle, and that the motion of N is only to aid in understanding the real motion, which is along BC.

Substituting for $A \cos pt$ its value from equation 50, we have

$$a = -p^2 x. \tag{53}$$

Equation 53 shows that the acceleration of a point whose motion is simple harmonic is at any instant proportional to its displacement from the mid-point. The negative sign shows that the acceleration is always directed oppositely to the displacement; *i.e.* when the point is at the right of the mid-point, its acceleration is directed towards the left, while the reverse is true when the point is on the left.

Multiplying both sides of equation 53 by the mass of the moving point, and remembering the dynamical equation $F = Ma$, we have

$$F = Ma = -Mp^2 x. \tag{54}$$

This is a dynamical equation, and shows that the force which produces the acceleration of the mass M in simple harmonic motion is directed towards the mid-point and is proportional to the displacement.

Conversely, it may be proved that whenever the resultant force acting on a body is proportional to its displacement from a fixed position, the motion of the body will be simple harmonic.

From the equations 50, 51, and 52, it follows that the displacements, velocities, and accelerations of the point P begin to repeat themselves when t has increased from o to $\frac{2\pi}{p}$. This constant value of the time $\frac{2\pi}{p}$ is the period of the simple harmonic motion; and is obviously the same as the time required for the point N to revolve about the auxiliary circle.

Substituting T for $\frac{2\pi}{p}$, equations 50, 51, and 52 now become

$$x = A \cos \frac{2\pi}{T} t, \tag{55}$$

$$v = -\frac{2\pi}{T} A \sin \frac{2\pi}{T} t, \tag{56}$$

$$a = -\frac{4\pi^2}{T^2} A \cos \frac{2\pi}{T} t. \tag{57}$$

It is often especially desirable to know the velocity with which the moving body passes the mid-point. It will first pass the mid-point after one quarter of a period has elapsed, and it will pass the same point for every odd number of quarter periods. Substituting for t in the equation for velocity any of the values $\frac{1}{4} T, \frac{3}{4} T, \frac{5}{4} T, \cdots$, we have

$$v_0 = \mp \frac{2\pi}{T} A = \mp pA. \tag{58}$$

Simple harmonic motion of rotation.

Let M be a body oscillating about an axis O (Fig. 28) perpendicular to the plane of the paper. The line OA, fixed in

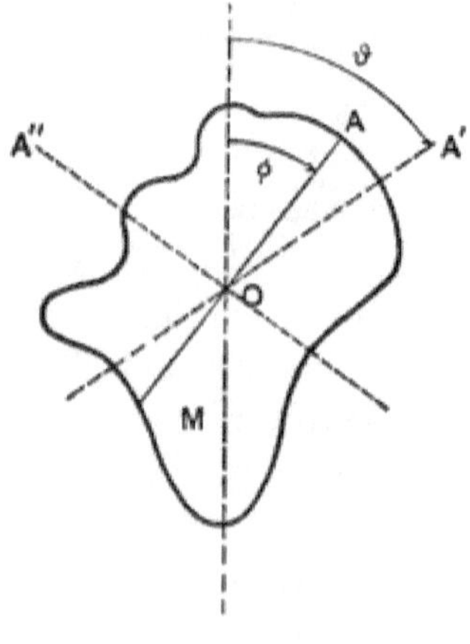

Fig. 28.

the body, oscillates between the extreme positions OA' and OA''. The motion of the body will be simple harmonic motion, according to the definition above given, if we have at any time t,

$$\phi = \delta \cos pt, \tag{59}$$

δ and p being constants.

If $d\phi$ be the angle turned through during the time dt, we shall have, from the definition of angular velocity,

$$\omega = \frac{d\phi}{dt} = -p\delta \sin pt. \tag{60}$$

If $d\omega$ is the change of angular velocity in the time dt, we shall have, from the definition of angular acceleration,

$$a = \frac{d\omega}{dt} = -p^2\delta \cos pt. \tag{61}$$

Substituting the value of $\delta \cos pt$ from 59, we have

$$a = -p^2\phi, \tag{62}$$

from which it follows that in simple harmonic motion of rotation the angular acceleration at any instant is proportional to the angular displacement.

Multiplying both sides of equation 62 by the moment of inertia of the rotating body with respect to the axis of rotation, we have

$$G = Ka = -Kp^2\phi. \tag{63}$$

Since, however, Ka is equal to the resultant moment, with respect to the axis of rotation, of the forces acting on the body, it follows that the moment of the force producing the angular acceleration in simple harmonic motion is directly proportional to the angular displacement.

Conversely, it may be proved that if the resultant moment of the forces acting on a body with respect to the axis of rotation is proportional to the angular displacement from a fixed position, the resulting motion of the body will be a simple harmonic motion.

Here, as in simple harmonic motion of translation, the motion begins to repeat itself in all respects after a time $\frac{2\pi}{p}$ has elapsed. This constant time is the period of the simple harmonic motion, and, calling it T, equations 59, 60, and 61 become

$$\phi = \delta \cos \frac{2\pi}{T} t, \tag{64}$$

$$\omega = -\frac{2\pi}{T}\delta \sin \frac{2\pi}{T} t, \tag{65}$$

$$a = -\frac{4\pi^2}{T^2}\delta \cos \frac{2\pi}{T} t. \tag{66}$$

If ω_0 be the angular velocity with which the body passes its mid-position, we have, in a manner similar to equation 58,

$$\omega_0 = \mp \frac{2\pi}{T} \delta. \tag{67}$$

Examples of simple harmonic motion of translation:

(1) If a mass be suspended by a spiral spring, it will oscillate along a vertical line with simple harmonic motion, if it is first displaced upwards or downwards from its position of equilibrium, and then set free.

(2) Any molecule in a sounding body or a sound-wave, when the sound is absolutely simple, *i.e.* without harmonics or overtones.

(3) The bob of a simple pendulum, or any point in a compound pendulum, when the arc of vibration is very small.

(4) Any point in a magnet vibrating in a uniform magnetic field when the arc of vibration is very small.

Examples of simple harmonic motion of rotation:

(1) A mass suspended by a wire or cord, and rotating about a vertical axis, the only force acting being the force of torsion.

(2) A compound pendulum when the arc of vibration is very small.

(3) A magnet vibrating in a uniform magnetic field when the arc of vibration is very small.

In these examples, as well as in all other cases, there are certain retarding forces, as friction, imperfect elasticity, or induced currents of electricity, which prevent the motion from being absolutely simple harmonic. This "damping," as it is called, has an extremely small effect upon the *period* of the simple harmonic motion, and may be safely neglected when the period is the quantity desired. When the amplitude of the simple harmonic motion is the quantity to be used, a correction for "damping" must generally be introduced.*

---

* See Nichols, The Galvanometer, Lecture 3; also Stewart and Gee, Vol. 2, p. 364 *et seq.*

EXPERIMENT E_1. **Determination of g by the physical pendulum.**

If a physical pendulum be displaced from its position of equilibrium through an angle so small that the angle may be substituted for its sine without appreciable error, the moment of the force acting on the pendulum will be proportional to the angular displacement. The pendulum must therefore have simple harmonic motion.

From the principle of the conservation of energy, in any transformation, the two forms of energy must be equal to each other. As the energy dissipated in a single swing of the pendulum is small enough to be negligible, we are justified in equating the kinetic energy of the pendulum when at its lowest point to the gain in potential energy when it reaches its highest point.

The kinetic energy of a rotating body is $\frac{1}{2} K_a \omega^2$. Since the pendulum has simple harmonic motion, the angular velocity at the mid-position will be $\frac{2\pi\delta}{T}$. (See equation 67.)

$$\therefore\ E_K = \frac{2\pi^2\delta^2}{T^2} K_a.$$

The potential energy at the highest point is equal to the work required to turn the pendulum through the angle δ from the lowest point. This work is equal to the average moment multiplied by the angular distance moved, or,

$$E_P = \frac{MgR\delta}{2}\delta$$

Since $E_K = E_P$, we have

$$\frac{2\pi^2}{T^2} K_a = \frac{MgR}{2}, \tag{68}$$

in which T is the period of a complete oscillation, K_a the moment of inertia of the pendulum with respect to the axis of suspension, M its mass, R the distance of the center of gravity from the axis of suspension, and g the acceleration of gravity.

If T and R be observed, and K_a computed, the acceleration of gravity may be determined.

In this experiment a uniform bar of metal, provided with an adjustable pair of knife-edges (Fig. 29), is to be used as a pendulum.   The method of procedure is as follows :

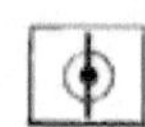

(1) Fasten the knife-edges firmly at some point not at the end of the bar, and set the pendulum to vibrating through a *small* arc.

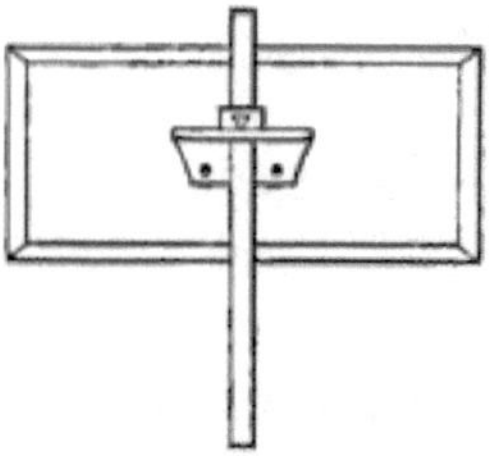

(2) Determine the time required for the pendulum to make some large number of oscillations.

(3) From the result compute the period of the pendulum.   An ordinary watch or clock may be used for determining this time, although a stop-watch is better.   In any case, several determinations of the period should be made, in each of which the time is at least five or six minutes.

Fig. 29.

(4) After the period has been determined, measure the dimensions of the bar and the distance of the knife-edges from one end.   From these data, the moment of inertia can be computed.

As the bar is homogeneous, the center of gravity will be at the center of the figure, and thus R is known. M will be found to cancel out ; consequently g may be computed.

The knife-edges and clamp slightly affect the moment of inertia and the center of gravity of the pendulum, thus slightly changing the period.   If greater accuracy is desired, the effect of the knife-edges and clamp on the period may be made zero by fastening to the knife-edges an auxiliary mass, a portion of which extends above the axis of suspension, and varying the center of gravity of this mass until the period of vibration of the knife-edges without the bar is approximately the same as the period of the bar pendulum.

The observations and results of the experiment are to be tabulated in the manner indicated below :

GRAVITY BY THE PHYSICAL PENDULUM.

No. of Transit to Right.	Time.			Duration of 100 Oscillations.	Dimensions of Pendulum and Results.
	hr.	min.	sec.		Distance of axis from upper
1	1	27	00		end of bar, 3.5 cm.
101	1	30	24	204 s.	Length of bar, $L = 159.6$ cm.
201	1	33	49	205	Diameter of bar, $2r = 1.6$ cm.
301	1	37	13	204	Distance of axis from center
401	1	40	$38\frac{1}{2}$	$205\frac{1}{2}$	of gravity of bar, $R = 76.3$ cm.
					Moment of inertia, $K_a = 7945$ M.
	hr.	min.	sec.		Periodic time, $T = 2.047$
1	1	42	50		Computed value of gravity,
101	1	46	14	204	$g = 981 +$ cm. per sec. per sec.
201	1	49	40	206	Most careful determination
301	1	53	3	203	for Cornell laboratory, 980.28
401	1	56	29	206	

Addenda to the report :

(1) Explain how the mass of the pendulum cancels so that it does not need to be known. Compute the acceleration of gravity in centimeters per second per second and in feet per second per second.

(2) Explain what is meant by the statement, The force of gravity is g dynes.

(3) Explain why a small error in the period will make an error relatively twice as great in g.

EXPERIMENT E₂. **Determination of g by Kater's pendulum.**

The equation for the physical pendulum may be put into the form

$$\frac{4\pi^2}{T_1^2}(K_0 + MR_1^2) = MgR_1, \tag{69}$$

in which K_0 is the moment of inertia of the pendulum with respect to an axis through the center of gravity parallel to the axis of suspension. (See equations 42 and 68.) If the pendulum be inverted, and the time of vibration determined for an axis on the opposite side of the center of gravity, a new equation will be obtained similar to the above, except that there will be new values of R and T. Between these two equations K_0 may be eliminated and g determined. To this end we substitute l for $R_1 + R_2$ in the equation derived by the elimination of K_0 from two equations like the above. It will then reduce to the equation for the simple pendulum, provided that the two times of oscillation are the same, and the two values of R are *not* the same. Kater's pendulum is an apparatus which makes use of this fact.

The use of Kater's pendulum depends upon the principle that the center of oscillation and the center of suspension of any pendulum are interchangeable; *i.e.* if a pendulum is reversed, so that the point which was the center of oscillation is made the center of suspension, the time of vibration will remain unchanged. The distance between these two points being equal to the length of the corresponding simple pendulum, the measurement of this length, together with the observation of the time of vibration, is sufficient to determine the force of gravity. The experiment consists, therefore, in adjusting the positions of the two knife-edges by trial until the time of vibration about one pair as an axis is the same as that about the other.

The pendulum used consists of a hollow cylindrical bar, one end of which is loaded by a filling of lead (Fig. 30).* There are two pairs of knife-edges, one being placed near each end of the bar; both are capable of adjustment along the bar, so that the distance between them can be altered.

---

* The pendulum here referred to is a very simple one, but with careful observations is capable of giving quite accurate results. A homogeneous cylindrical bar is sometimes used, but with such a pendulum one pair of knife-edges will be at such a point that considerable variation of its position will produce but little change in the time of vibration. (See Exp. E_3, and Fig. 31.)

The method of the experiment is as follows:

(1) Fasten one pair of knife-edges to the bar at some point near the end which is not weighted.

(2) Determine the rate of vibration roughly by observing with a watch or clock the time occupied by some large number of oscillations (20–50).

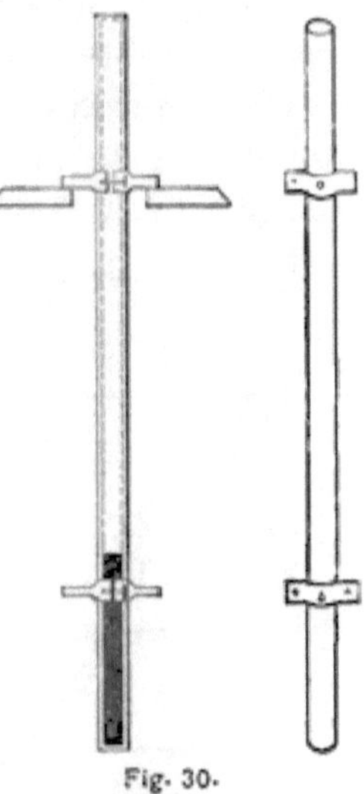

Fig. 30.

(3) Locate approximately the position of the center of oscillation by hanging a simple pendulum (a small weight suspended by a cord) near by, and adjusting its length until it vibrates nearly in unison with the bar. The length of this simple pendulum is then a rough approximation to the distance from the center of suspension of the bar to its center of oscillation. To obtain this distance more accurately, set the second pair of knife-edges at a distance from the first equal to the length just determined; then *reverse* the bar, and determine its time of vibration as before. The period should now be nearly the same as at first. If the two periods differ, one or both of the knife-edges should be shifted until the time of vibration is very closely the same with either suspension.

(4) The final determination of the time of vibration must be made very carefully, and should be repeated several times.

(5) Finally, the distance between the knife-edges is to be measured as accurately as possible. From this distance and the two times of vibration, the value of g is to be computed.

Determine the value of g in the C. G. S. system, and also in the foot-pound-second system.

EXPERIMENT E_3.   **Relation between the time of vibration and the position of the knife-edges in a uniform cylindrical pendulum.**

In the equation for the physical pendulum given in the preceding experiment, everything is determined for any given pendulum except R and T.   The object of this experiment is to show the relation which exists between these two variables.

To this end, fasten the knife-edges at one end of the bar, and determine the period of vibration by observing the time occupied by a large number of oscillations.   Then shift the

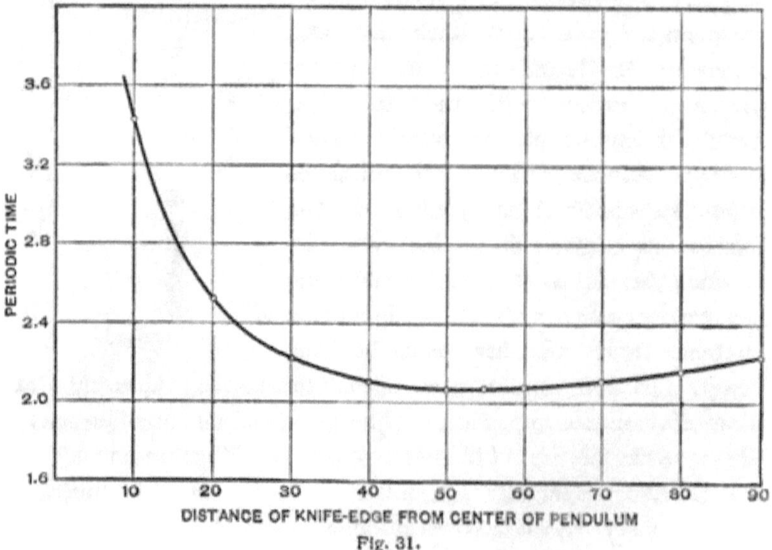

Fig. 31.

knife-edges down the bar three or four centimeters, and determine the new period.   Continue shifting the point of suspension and observing the period until the center of the bar is reached. From eight to ten different positions of the knife-edges should be used, and the distance of the knife-edges from one end of the bar should be carefully measured in each case.   In determining the time of vibration, a stop-watch will be found of considerable assistance.   From the data obtained, plat a curve, similar to that given in Fig. 31, using for abscissas the distances of the point of suspension from the center of the bar, and for ordinates the corresponding times of vibration. Discuss and explain the shape of this curve, and determine the form of its equation from a knowledge of the law of the physical pendulum.

The following is a tabulated statement of a set of observations taken as indicated above. The results are shown graphically in Fig. 31.

RELATION OF PERIODIC TIME TO POSITION OF KNIFE-EDGES.

Distance from Center of Gravity.	No. of Transit to Right.	Time.			Duration of 100 Oscillations.	Periodic Time.	Other Data and Results.
		hr.	min.	sec.			
	1	2	16	50			Length of bar = 183 cm.
90	101		20	30	220	2.21	Diam. " " = 2.5 "
	201		24	12	222		Equation of curve from
	1		29	00			theory of pendulum:
80	101		32	34	214	2.15	
	201		36	10	216		$T^2 R = \dfrac{4\pi^2}{g} R^2 + \dfrac{4\pi^2 k^2}{g}.$
	1		42	00			
70	101		45	30	210	2.10	
	201		49	00	210		From pairs of points on
	1	3	22	00			curve having equal ordi-
60	101		25	27	207	2.07	nates.
	201		28	54	207		
	1		35	00			$T = 2.20, \quad g = 970;$
55	101		38	25	205	2.05	$T = 2.16, \quad g = 989;$
	201		41	50	205		$T = 2.12, \quad g = 977.$
	1		51	40			
50	101		55	6	206	2.06	
	201		58	32	206		
	1	4	6	30			
40	101		10	1	211	2.10	
	201		13	30	209		
	1		17	10			
30	101		20	$52\frac{1}{2}$	$222\frac{1}{2}$	2.225	
	201		24	35	$222\frac{1}{2}$		
	1		28	40			
20	101		32	54	254	2.535	
	201		37	7	253		
	1		42	40			
10	101		48	24	344	3.435	
	201		54	7	343		

Addenda to the report:

(1) The equation of this curve expressed in its simplest form will contain two constants. Show what relation these constants bear to the pendulum and to the acceleration of gravity.

(2) From any pair of points on the curve compute the values of these constants, and hence determine the acceleration of gravity.

(3) Prove that the abscissa corresponding to the minimum ordinate is equal to the radius of gyration of the pendulum with respect to its center of gravity.

EXPERIMENT E_4. **Determination of the moment of inertia of a body.**

The pendulum furnishes a means of determining the moment of inertia with respect to an axis through the center of gravity of any body to which a pair of knife-edges may be attached, and whose center of gravity may be determined.

In the equation for the physical pendulum given in experiment E_2, K_0 may be computed if T, M, and R be determined, g being known.

Take any body whose mass is great with respect to the knife-edges to be used; fasten the knife-edges to it at some distance from the center of gravity. Determine the period of oscillation as in any of the preceding experiments; weigh the body, and measure the distance of the knife-edges from the center of gravity. From the data thus obtained compute the moment of inertia, K_0. Repeat the same observations and computations for two or three other bodies.

If any of the bodies are regular solids, check the values thus obtained by direct integration, as described at the beginning of this chapter. Express the results obtained both in the C. G. S. system and in the foot-pound-second system.

GROUP F: ELASTICITY.

(F_1) *Young's modulus;* (F_2) *Moment of torsion;* (F_3) *Moment of inertia by torsion.*

EXPERIMENT F_1. **Young's modulus by stretching.**

Elasticity of tension is defined as the ratio of force applied to extension produced. If the elastic limit has not been reached, the extension of a weighted rod or wire is proportional (1) to the force applied, (2) to the length, (3) inversely proportional to the cross-section, or

$$l = E\frac{LF}{\pi r^2},\qquad(70)$$

in which E is the coefficient of elasticity.   From this equation it is seen that E is the increase in length produced by unit force applied to a rod of unit length and unit cross-section.

Young's modulus is defined as the reciprocal of the coefficient of elasticity.   Calling this modulus M, we have

$$M = \frac{LF}{\pi r^2 l}.\qquad(71)$$

Young's modulus may be computed if the quantities on the right of this equation are determined in the proper units.

Fasten a wire two or three meters in length to some firm support.   A small vice rigidly attached to the brick or stone wall of the room makes a support which is satisfactory in most cases.*   Suspend from the end of the wire a weight which is just sufficient to take out the kinks; for a wire whose diameter is 1 mm. a weight of from two to four kilos will be required.

A horizontal microscope containing an eye-piece micrometer is now to be adjusted so that a slight scratch on the wire is sharply focused in the lower part of the field.   As the tension of the wire is increased by the addition of weights, this mark will move across the field, and by means of the micrometer the elongation corresponding to each increment in weight can be measured.   Measure in this way the elongations produced by successive increments in weight until the mark has passed out of the field.   Each increment in weight should be sufficient to cause an elongation of three or four scale divisions.

---

* If there is any reason to suspect that the support is not rigid, two microscopes must be used, one at the upper and the other at the lower end of the wire.

After the wire has been fully loaded the weight is to be gradually reduced and the measurements repeated until the original load is reached.   Note whether equal increments of tension produce equal increments of length, and whether the elastic limit has been passed.

The results can be best shown by a curve in which abscissas represent force applied, and ordinates the increments in length produced.

Determine the value of one division of the micrometer as described in Exp. A_4 (III), and measure the length and diameter of the wire.

Since the square of the radius enters in the above equation, a small error in determining it will be relatively doubled in the computed value of the modulus.   For this reason the diameter of the wire must be measured with unusual care. The cross-section may be most accurately determined by computation from the density and the mass of a given length. Since the density of various specimens is liable to differ, the density should be carefully determined by weighing in water.

EXPERIMENT F_2.   **Determination of the moment of torsion of a wire.**

When a wire of elastic material, such as steel, bronze, or hard drawn copper, is twisted by a moderate amount, the moment of the couple by which it tends to regain its original condition is proportional to the angle of torsion; *i.e.* if θ is the angle, and G the moment of the elastic return force, $G = G_0\theta$. The constant G_0 is called the moment of torsion, and depends upon the length, diameter, and material of the wire.

To determine the value of G_0, a heavy weight, of such shape that its moment of inertia can be readily computed, is hung upon the end of the wire, and set to vibrating through an angle of twenty or thirty degrees.   Since the moment of the return force is proportional to the angular displacement, the weight will have simple harmonic motion, and the vibration will be isochronous.   From equation 63 we will have

$$G_0\theta = -K\frac{d^2\theta}{dt^2},\qquad(72)$$

in which $G_0\theta$ is the resultant moment due to torsional displacement through an angle θ, and $\frac{d^2\theta}{dt^2}$ is the angular acceleration of the suspended weight.   An integration of this equation gives

$$T = 2\pi\sqrt{\frac{K}{G_0}},\qquad(73)$$

in which T is the period of the harmonic motion.

The same equation may be derived more easily from the energy relations.   If δ is the maximum angular displacement, the kinetic energy of the rotating weight as it passes the mid-position will be

$$E = \tfrac{1}{2}K\omega_0^2 = K\frac{2\pi^2\delta^2}{T^2}.\qquad(74)$$

The potential energy of the twisted wire, when the suspended weight is at its greatest displacement, is equal to the work that must be done on the wire to twist the lower end through the angle δ.   The moment of the force at any instant to be overcome is $G_0\theta$; as this varies between o and $G_0\delta$, the average moment is $\tfrac{1}{2}G_0\delta$, and hence the work done and the potential energy gained is

$$E_P = \tfrac{1}{2}G_0\delta\cdot\delta.\qquad(75)$$

As the dissipation of energy during a single vibration may be neglected, the potential energy at the extreme, when the weight has no motion, must be equal to the kinetic energy when the weight is at its mid-position and there is no twist in the wire. Hence we have

$$T = 2\pi\sqrt{\frac{K}{G_0}}.\qquad(76)$$

To determine the period of vibration, the method of Exp. A_5 should be used.   It is to be observed that since it is the square of T that appears in the formula, an error in the determination of the period will introduce a considerable error in the result. The moment of inertia is to be computed from the mass and linear dimensions of the vibrating weight.

From the result obtained for G_0 compute the force, both in dynes and in pounds, which would twist the wire through a complete revolution when acting at a distance of one centimeter from the center.

EXPERIMENT F_3.   **To determine the moment of inertia of an irregular body by torsion.**

The preceding experiment offers one of the best means of determining the moment of inertia of an irregular body. G_0 is a constant for any given wire, independent of the mass suspended by it and of the period of oscillation. Therefore, if it is already known, the moment of inertia of the suspended weight may be computed after the period has been determined. If G_0 is not known, it may be eliminated between two equations of the form (76), in one of which the moment of inertia of the suspended weight is known.

To perform the experiment, suspend the body by a wire of phosphor bronze or some other elastic material, the upper end of the wire being rigidly fastened. The axis about which the moment of inertia is required should lie in the prolongation of the wire. Set the system to vibrating, and determine the period as in the previous experiment. Then hang upon the wire a body whose moment of inertia is known, and determine the vibration period as before. If the two periods are T_1, T_2, then

$$K_2 = K_1 \frac{T_2^2}{T_1^2}. \tag{77}$$

CHAPTER II.

GROUP G: DENSITY.

(G) *General statements;* (G$_1$) *Rough determination of specific gravity by weighing in water;* (G$_2$) *Specific gravity of solids and liquids by the specific gravity bottle;* (G$_3$) *Determination of density with corrections for air displacement and temperature;* (G$_4$) *Specific gravity by the Jolly balance;* (G$_5$) *Nicholson's hydrometer;* (G$_6$) *Fahrenheit's hydrometer;* (G$_7$) *Graduation of a hydrometer of variable immersion;* (G$_8$) *Specific gravity of a solid by means of a variable immersion hydrometer;* (G$_9$) *Density of a liquid by Hare's method.*

(G.) **General statements concerning specific gravity and density.**

The specific gravity of a substance is the ratio of the weight of a given volume of the substance to the weight of an equal volume of water at its maximum density.

Specific gravities being ratios of like quantities are abstract numbers, and hence the same for all systems of units. The unit used in comparing the weights may indeed be entirely arbitrary, such as the unit extension of a spring made use of in the Jolly balance.

The density of a substance is the ratio of the mass of a given volume of the substance to the volume which it occupies; or in symbols

$$D = \frac{M}{V}. \qquad (78)$$

Since density is not an abstract number, its numerical value in any particular case must depend upon the units used. For example, the density of water in the foot-pound-second system is $62\frac{1}{2}$. The density of water in the C. G. S. system is unity, for the reason that the unit of mass is equal to the mass of a cubic centimeter of water. Hence it follows that the densities of all substances in the C. G. S system are numerically equal to their specific gravities. This is not *absolutely* true, however, for the mass of a cubic centimeter of water at its maximum density is not exactly a gram.

The term "relative density" is sometimes used. It has the same meaning as "specific gravity."

EXPERIMENT G_1. **Rough determination of specific gravity by weighing in water.**

I.

Specific gravity of a body more dense than water. — Weigh the body in air; then suspend it from a hook under one of the scale-pans of a balance, immerse it in water, and weigh again. The specific gravity is to be computed from these two weights, no correction being made for the temperature of the water or the buoyancy of the air. The wire used for suspending the body must be quite fine. It should be immersed in water to the same extent that it will be when the body is attached, and balanced with shot or sand, before the second weighing above is made.

II.

Specific gravity of a body lighter than water. — First weigh the body in air. Then suspend a heavy sinker from one scale-pan, and find its weight when immersed in water. Finally attach the body to the sinker, and find the weight of the two when entirely submerged. From these three weights compute the specific gravity.

The results should be tested by placing the vessel of water on the scale-pan and suspending the substance in the water from some outside support. The gain in weight of the vessel should be the same as the loss of the substance.

Errors in this method of determining specific gravity are apt to arise from small bubbles of air adhering to the substance when immersed; such bubbles must, therefore, be carefully shaken off before the weighings are made.

EXPERIMENT G_2. **Specific gravity of solids and liquids by the specific gravity bottle.**

The specific gravity bottle is simply a small bottle which is provided with an accurately fitting ground-glass stopper. A very small hole through the center of this stopper leads to the interior of the bottle, its object being to allow the bottle to be *completely* filled with any liquid.

To use the specific gravity bottle, proceed as follows:

I.

Specific gravity of a liquid. — First weigh the bottle alone, when perfectly clean and dry. Next fill with distilled water and weigh again. Finally fill the bottle with the liquid whose density is required, and weigh a third time. These three weights are sufficient for the computation of the specific gravity.

II.

Specific gravity of a solid.[1] — Place the substance in the specific gravity bottle and determine the combined weight. Then add sufficient distilled water to entirely fill the bottle, insert the glass stopper, and after wiping off any drops which may adhere to the outside, weigh again. Finally determine the weight of the bottle when filled with water alone. These three weights, together with the weight of the bottle, are sufficient to determine the specific gravity of the substance. This method is of course only available when the substance is insoluble in water. In the case of soluble substances some liquid of known density must be used in which the substance does not dissolve.

---

[1] The specific gravity bottle is especially useful when the solid is in the form of small fragments or powder.

It sometimes happens that difficulty is met with in shaking off the small bubbles of air which tend to adhere to the substance, and which will introduce a considerable error. In such cases the bottle containing the substance, and about half full of water, should be placed under the receiver of an air-pump, and the air exhausted until bubbles are no longer formed.

If greater accuracy is required, corrections for temperature and air displacement must be made, similar to those described in Exp. G_3.

EXPERIMENT G_3. **Determination of density, with corrections for air displacement and temperature.**

The balance is nearly always used for comparing masses, but it should be remembered that it is merely a lever with equal arms, by which two *forces* may be proved to be equal. Each of the two equal forces is the resultant of the *weight* of the body on the scale-pan acting *downwards*, and the buoyant effect of the weight of the fluid displaced by the body acting *upwards*. This gives

$$W_1 - w_1 = W_2 - w_2.$$

Since weights are directly proportional to masses, we have

$$M_1 - m_1 = M_2 - m_2, \tag{79}$$

in which M_1 and M_2 are the masses of the bodies on the two scale-pans, and m_1 and m_2 are the masses of the displaced fluid in the two cases. Nearly always in using the balance, m_1 and m_2 are supposed to be equal, or at least it is assumed that their difference is negligible.

If M_s is the mass of the substance of density δ_s, then from the definition of density the volume of the displaced fluid will be $\dfrac{M_s}{\delta_s}$. If δ_a is the density of the displaced air, then its mass is $M_s \dfrac{\delta_a}{\delta_s}$. If M is the mass of the counterpoise, and δ_c its density, equation 79 becomes

$$M_s - M_s \frac{\delta_a}{\delta_s} = M - M \frac{\delta_a}{\delta_c}. \tag{80}$$

In order to determine M_s from the known mass of the counterpoise, δ_a, δ_s, and δ_c must be known. Approximate values for these quantities will serve quite as well as more accurate values, because the term in which they appear is always a very small quantity.

The object of this experiment is to determine the density of the substance s with all possible accuracy. If the substance is suspended from the scale-beam, so as to be immersed in water of density ρ, and is then counterpoised with the mass M', equation 79 becomes

$$M_s - M_s \frac{\rho}{\delta_s} = M' - M' \frac{\delta_a}{\delta_c}. \tag{81}$$

If equation 80 be divided by 81, and the resulting equation solved for δ_s, we shall have

$$\delta_s = \frac{M}{M - M'} (\rho - \delta_a). \tag{82}$$

In deriving equation 82 it has been assumed

(1) That the density of the counterpoise M is the same as that of M'

(2) That the density of the air has not changed between the two weighings.

(3) That the density of the substance or of the weights has not been changed during the experiment on account of expansion. The value of ρ depends on the temperature of the water. The value of δ_a depends on the temperature, pressure, and humidity of the atmosphere at the time of performing the experiment. The effect of humidity in altering the density of the air may be neglected except when the substance weighed is a gas or a vapor.

Use the most accurate balances that are available, counterpoise the substance whose specific gravity is required, first in air, and then when suspended by a fine wire, in distilled water. Observe also the temperature of the water and the temperature and barometric pressure of the atmosphere. The distilled water used should first be thoroughly boiled in order to expel the dissolved air.

The values of ρ for different temperatures can be found in most reference books, while δ_a can be computed from the temperature and pressure of the air.*

In this experiment all observations must be taken with great care. A suitable correction should be made for the weight of the wire used in suspending the substance in water, and all air bubbles that may adhere to the wire or specimen must be carefully removed.

When the value of δ_t is finally obtained, it must be remembered that this is the density of the substance at the temperature of the water in which it was weighed. For comparison, this must be reduced to 0° by using the coefficient of cubic expansion.

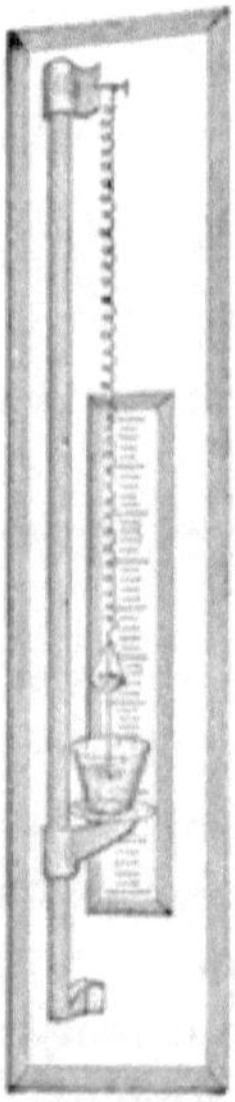

EXPERIMENT G_4. **Specific gravity by the Jolly balance.**

The Jolly balance consists of a spiral spring hanging in front of a vertical graduated scale, and carrying at its lower end two small scale-pans. The lower of these should always be kept immersed in water, as shown in Fig. 32, and in order to render this possible, the bracket which supports the vessel of water is made adjustable in position.

The instrument may be used in determining specific gravity in two different ways:

I.

Place the body whose specific gravity is required upon the upper scale-pan and observe the elongation of the spring. The weight of the body is now determined by finding what known weight is required to produce the same

Fig. 32.

---

* Tabulated values of ρ and δ_a will be found in Landoldt and Börnstein, in Stewart and Gee, Vol. 1, etc.

elongation. Then place the body on the lower scale-pan (under water), and observe what weight must be placed on the upper pan to make the elongation the same as before. These two observations are evidently sufficient to determine the specific gravity.

II.

The specific gravity may also be determined without the use of weights, upon the assumption that the elongation of the spring is proportional to the force tending to stretch it.

The specific gravity of some solid should be determined by each of the above methods, and the assumption made in method II (*i.e.* that the elongation is proportional to the weight) should be tested by observing the elongations produced by five or six different weights. Compute the value in grams of an elongation of one scale division. Find also the number of *dynes* required to produce an elongation of one division.

EXPERIMENT G_6. **Specific gravity by Nicholson's hydrometer.**

This hydrometer (Fig. 33) consists of a hollow cylinder which is made to float with its axis vertical by means of a heavy weight at the bottom. At the top a wire projects two or three inches above the end of the cylinder and supports a small scale-pan. At the bottom another pan is provided, upon which can be placed the object whose density is required.

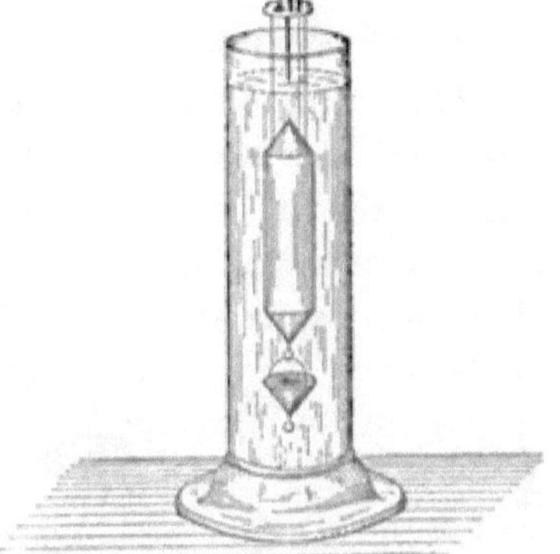

Fig. 33.

To determine the specific gravity of a solid, place the hydrometer in water, and find by trial the weight which must be placed on the scale-pan in order to bring some well-defined mark to the surface of the water. In the instrument shown in Fig. 33, which is a slight modification of the hydrometer of Nicholson, this mark consists of the point of a wire which projects downward from the center of the scale-pan. Then place upon the scale-pan the body whose density is required, and add weights until the instrument has sunk again to the same level. Finally place the body upon the lower pan or basket, and again determine the weight necessary to sink the hydrometer. From these three weights the specific gravity can be computed. In case the specimen is lighter than water it must be fastened in some way to the bottom of the instrument to prevent it from floating away. The instrument may also be used in determining the specific gravity of a liquid.

This form of hydrometer is not very sensitive, and therefore cannot be expected to give results of great accuracy. In this experiment, however, as in all specific gravity determinations, the most common source of error is the presence of air bubbles, which will adhere both to the specimen and to the instrument unless carefully shaken off.

The report should contain a full explanation of the principles involved, including Archimedes' Law.

Experiment G_6. Fahrenheit's hydrometer.

This hydrometer consists of an elongated glass bulb (Fig. 34), weighted at the bottom, and carrying at the top a small scale-pan supported by a wire sealed into the bulb.

To determine the density of a liquid, first float the instrument in distilled water and place weights on the scale-pan until some well-defined mark on the stem is brought to the surface of the water. It will be found preferable to use bits of tin-foil for weights. The tin-foil corresponding to each separate observation should then be wrapped in a piece of paper, labeled, and afterwards weighed on a pair of balances. Then place the hydrometer in the liquid whose specific gravity is required and determine the weight necessary to sink it to the same point.

From these two weights, together with the weight of the hydrometer, the specific gravity of the liquid can be computed. A correction should be made for the temperature of the water.

I.

Use the instrument in the manner just described, to determine the variation in the density of a salt solution as its degree of concentration is altered. To accomplish this, first dissolve in water sufficient salt to make a nearly saturated solution, weighing both the salt and the water. Having determined the density of this solution, dilute it by the addition of a known weight of water, and again determine its density. Continue in this way until the solution is so dilute as to have nearly the same specific gravity as water. At least eight or ten different observations

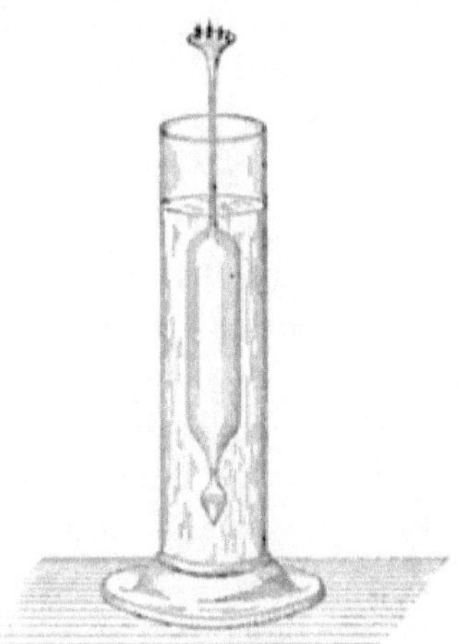

Fig. 34.

should be taken. With the results obtained, plat a curve in which the strengths of the solution are used as abscissas and the corresponding densities as ordinates.

II.

Fahrenheit's hydrometer may be used for determining the density of water at different temperatures. In this experiment it will not be allowable to assume that the volume of the submerged portion of the hydrometer is constant, for as the temperature is changed, the hydrometer expands or contracts. The volume of the hydrometer at temperature t may always be expressed in the form $V_0(1 + kt)$, in which V_0 is its volume at $0°$, and k is the coefficient for cubical expansion of glass.

If M is the mass of the hydrometer, m the additional mass necessary to sink the hydrometer to the point of reference, and δ_t the density of the water at the temperature t, we shall have

$$M + m = V_0 (1 + kt)\delta_t. \tag{83}$$

If another observation be now taken in which t, and consequently m, are different, we shall have another equation similar to the above. Between these two equations V_0 may be eliminated, and the ratio of δ_t to δ_r determined. If one of these values is already known, the other may be computed in absolute measure.

For this experiment fill a vessel nearly full of distilled water, and cool it by means of ice and salt down to 2° or 3° C. Make eight or ten determinations of corresponding values of m and t. The values of t should differ by approximately equal increments, with two or three additional observations at temperatures as near as possible to 4°.

From the observations near 4°, determine by interpolation the value of m that would correspond to a temperature of 4°. Assume the density at 4° to be unity, and compute the densities at the other observed temperatures. From the results thus obtained, plat a curve with temperatures as abscissas and densities as ordinates. The ordinates should be on a greatly enlarged scale, the axis of abscissas not being shown at all. Upon the same paper, plat the results of some standard determination.

EXPERIMENT G_7. **Graduation of a hydrometer of variable immersion.**

The density of liquids is very frequently determined by means of variable immersion hydrometers. These hydrometers consist of an elongated glass bulb weighted at the bottom with mercury, and supporting a graduated stem of uniform cross-section. The graduations on the stem are not equidistant, however, for equal increments of submersion in different liquids do not correspond to equal decrements in density.

If M is the mass of the hydrometer, V_0 the volume of that part below the lowest division of the scale, a the cross-section of the stem, and l the added length of stem submerged in a liquid of density δ, we have, from Archimedes' principle and the definition of density,

$$M = (V_0 + la)\delta = (V_0 + l'a)\delta' = (V_0 + l''a)\delta'' = \cdots. \tag{84}$$

The product of density by volume submerged is a constant. Therefore the volumes submerged in different liquids vary inversely as their densities. It also follows that as the densities increase in arithmetical progression, the volumes submerged must decrease in a *corresponding* harmonic progression. For example, if the series of densities is 1, 1.1, 1.2, 1.3, $\cdots$, the series of volumes must be numerically $\dfrac{M}{1}$, $\dfrac{M}{1.1}$, $\dfrac{M}{1.2}$, $\dfrac{M}{1.3}$ $\cdots$. If M, V_0, and a were known, the values of l could be computed corresponding to any particular arithmetical series of densities. However, if the values of two points on the scale be experimentally determined as described below, it will be possible to determine the values of other points by the harmonic law

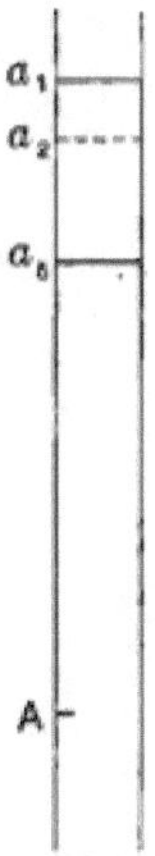

Suppose a_1 and a_5, Fig. 35, to be the two experimentally determined points of the scale corresponding to densities of 1 and 1.4, respectively. Let it be required to find a point a_2 which shall correspond to a density of 1.1. Let A be a point such that distances measured from A to a_1, a_2, $\cdots$, will be proportional to the volume of the hydrometer up to these points. Then we shall have

$$1.(Aa_5 + a_5a_1) = 1.4\,(Aa_5) = 1.1\,(Aa_5 + a_5a_2). \tag{85}$$

If Aa_5 be eliminated between these equations, the position of a_2 may be determined, that of a_1, a_5 being already known. Other points may be determined in the same way.

The graduation may be performed much more easily and quite as accurately by the following graphic method. Let it be remembered that the end will be attained if the scale is divided harmonically so that the fixed points a_1 and a_5 shall correspond to densities 1 and 1.4, respectively. Take any line PP_1 (Fig. 36), and divide it so that PP_1, PP_2, $\cdots$, PP_5 are in the harmonic progression $1, \dfrac{1}{1.1}, \dfrac{1}{1.2}, \dfrac{1}{1.3}, \dfrac{1}{1.4}$. From any point, O, at a convenient distance from PP_1, draw lines through the points P_1, P_2, $\cdots$. Any line drawn across this series of diverging lines

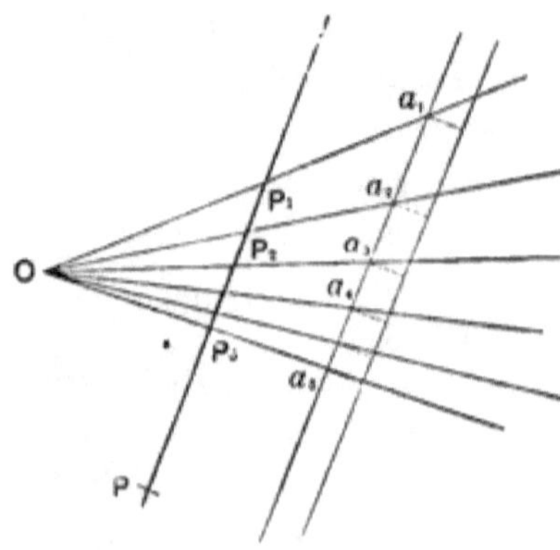

Fig. 36.

parallel to PP_1 will be divided by them in the same harmonic progression as PP_1. Now take the paper scale and lay it across these lines (keeping it parallel to PP_1) so that a_1 will fall on the line drawn through P_1, and a_5 will fall on the line drawn through P_5. If the distances between the graduations so determined are not great, these distances may be subdivided into equal parts without introducing an appreciable error.

To determine experimentally the two fixed points, proceed as follows :

Place the instrument in distilled water, and adjust the paper scale in the tube until its zero is at the level of the water. Next determine (by one of the methods of Exp. G_2 or G_9) the density of some liquid considerably heavier than water (*e.g.* a strong salt solution). Place the hydrometer in this liquid and observe the reading. Having now two points on the scale, the intermediate divisions can be determined by either of the methods described above.

Finally test the accuracy of the calibration by using the hydrometer to measure the specific gravities of one or two liquids of intermediate density.

EXPERIMENT G_8. **Density of a solid by means of a variable immersion hydrometer.***

If a hydrometer of variable immersion is provided with two pans, one above and the other below the surface of the liquid, it may be used for the determination of the density of a solid.

Let a be the cross-section of the stem, l the added length of the stem submerged when a substance of mass m is placed on the upper scale-pan. From Archimedes' principle, the increased mass of liquid displaced must equal the mass of the substance. Therefore, we have, from the definition of density,

$$m = al\delta, \tag{86}$$

in which δ is the density of the liquid in which the hydrometer is placed. If the substance is placed in the lower pan, the same volume of liquid will be displaced as before, but since the substance itself is below the surface, a shorter length of the stem will be submerged. And we have

$$m = al'\delta + \frac{m}{\delta_s}\delta, \tag{86 a}$$

$\frac{m}{\delta_s}$ being the volume of the mass m. From (86) and (86 a) we have

$$\frac{\delta_s}{\delta} = \frac{l}{l - l'}. \tag{87}$$

From this equation it follows that either δ_s or δ may be determined if the other is known.

---

*This form of hydrometer is due to G. H. Failyer of the Kansas Agricultural College.

To perform the experiment, first observe the division of the scale which coincides with the surface of the liquid when no substance is placed on the hydrometer. Next observe the scale reading when the substance is placed successively on the upper and lower scale-pans.

From these observations the density of the subtance may be computed if the density of the liquid is known.

Determine in this way the densities of several solids. The determination will be most accurate when the sample tested is as large as possible.

To verify the statement that the volume of liquid displaced by a floating body is proportional to its mass, proceed as follows: Place a known mass on the upper pan, and observe the corresponding scale reading. Repeat these observations with a series of masses, varying from zero to the maximum that can be used. Plat a curve with masses as abscissas and scale readings as ordinates. Show that this curve verifies the above statement. From its constants determine the cross-section of the stem, assuming the density of the liquid to be unity.

Experiment G_9. Density of a liquid by Hare's method.

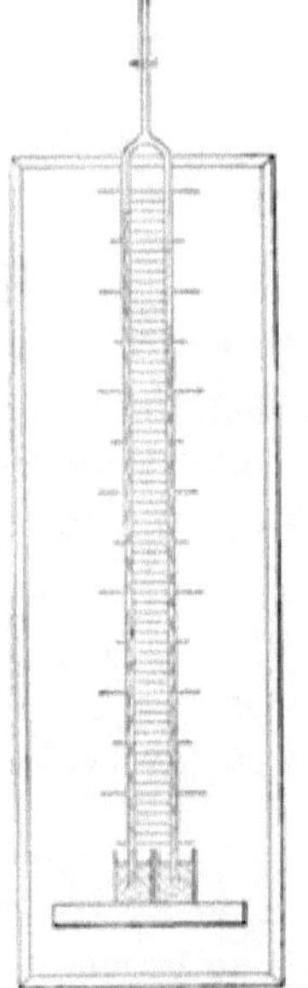

Fig. 37.

The apparatus used in this experiment consists of two vertical tubes open below and connected above to a common tube; the latter tube is provided with stop-cock (see Fig. 37). The two tubes dip into separate vessels, one containing distilled water, and the other the liquid whose density is to be determined. The tubes are fastened to an upright board on which there is a scale.

If the pressure of the air in the common tube is reduced by suction, the liquid will rise in each tube, the heights of the two columns being inversely proportional to the densities of the liquids used.

This may be demonstrated as follows : Let a be the atmospheric pressure, b the pressure of the air in the common tube above the two columns of liquid, both measured in dynes per square centimeter. Let h, h', and δ, δ' be the heights and densities of the two columns of liquid. From Pascal's law we have for any point within the first tube on a level with the surface of the liquid in the open vessel,

$$a = b + h\delta g, \tag{88}$$

and for the corresponding point within the second tube,

$$a = b + h'\delta'g.$$

$$\therefore \ h : h' = \delta' : \delta.$$

Put distilled water into one of the vessels, and the liquid whose density is to be determined into the other. By suction cause the liquids to rise in the tubes until the top of the highest column is near the end of the scale. Adjust the level of the liquid in each vessel until it is at the zero of the scale, and read the heights of the two columns. Then open the stop-cock until the columns have fallen through 6 or 8 cm. Adjust as before, and again read the height of each column. Repeat these readings for several different heights.

Compare in this way the densities of three different liquids with that of distilled water. The tubes should be rinsed with distilled water before and after using each different liquid.

GROUP H: PROPERTIES OF GASES.

(H_1) *Verification of Boyle's law ;* (H_2) *Comparison of the cistern barometer and the siphon barometer;* (H_3) *Coefficient of expansion of air.*

EXPERIMENT H_1. **Verification of Boyle's law.**

The apparatus consists of two glass tubes mounted vertically upon some suitable support and connected at the bottom. One tube is left open at the top, while the other can be closed so as to be air tight. Both are provided with scales to enable the height of the mercury contained in them to be measured. (See Fig. 38.)

I.

To test the law for pressures greater than one atmosphere. — For this purpose one tube should be considerably shorter than the other.

(1) In case the two tubes are not provided with a common scale, determine two points, one on each scale, which are at the same level. This can be done by observing the height to which mercury rises in the two tubes when both are open to the air; or the same thing may be accomplished by means of a spirit level.

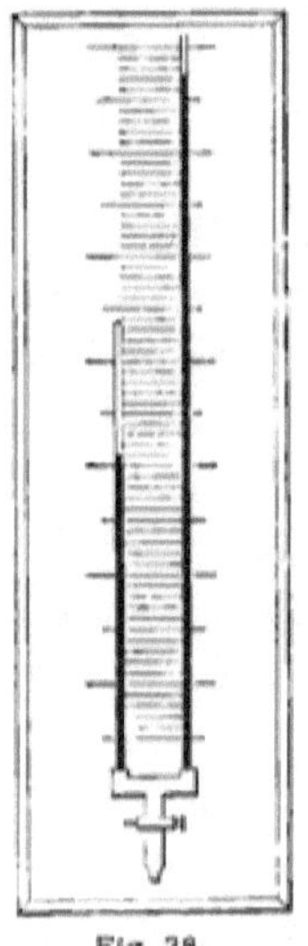

Fig. 38.

(2) The end of the shorter tube being tightly closed, observe the height of the mercury in each tube. Then increase the pressure by pouring more mercury into the longer tube, and again observe the two levels. Continue in this way until the longer tube is filled nearly to the top, taking in all about ten observations. To check these observations the pressure should now be gradually diminished by allowing mercury to escape from the stop-cock at the bottom of the apparatus. Ten more readings should be taken as the pressure falls to its original value.

In each of the observations above, the total pressure to which the air in the short tube is subjected is measured by the difference in level between the two columns of mercury *plus* the pressure of the atmosphere. In tabulating the results each difference in level should therefore be increased by the height of the barometer at the time of the experiment.

If the tube containing the air is of uniform cross-section, the volume of the confined air is proportional to the length of the tube. In this experiment it is sufficiently accurate to assume the tube to be uniform, except at the closed end, where the cross-section is apt to be irregular. The zero point of the scale used with the shorter tube is therefore placed, not at the top of the tube, but a little below the top. If l is the reading on this scale, and V_0 the unknown volume of that portion of the tube above the zero point, then the total volume is $V = V_0 + lA$, in which A is the cross-section. If Boyle's law is true, we should have $PV = K$; or $P(V_0 + lA) = K$. With the exception of P and l, all the quantities in this equation are constant. If a curve is platted with the observed values of l as abscissas and the corresponding values of $1 \div P$ for ordinates, this curve should therefore be a straight line. Determine the equation of this line by the method of least squares, and from this equation compute the values of V_0 and K. Reduce both quantities to C. G. S. units.

The cross-section A may be determined by weighing a small amount of mercury which is allowed to escape from the apparatus, and at the same time observing the alteration in the readings of the two columns. Since the density of mercury is known, these observations are sufficient for the computation of A.

If more accurate results are desired, the short tube must be calibrated by means of mercury,* and the air used must be carefully dried. In all cases great care must be taken to keep the temperature of the air constant.

The student will find it interesting to compute the constant k in the equation $\dfrac{PV}{\theta} = k$, which is true for a perfect gas at all temperatures. If this is done, the results should be put in such a form as to refer to the volume and pressure of *one gram* of air. It will then be possible to compare the value computed for k with those given in various reference books, and a check on the results of the whole experiment is obtained.

---

* See Stewart and Gee, vol. I.

II.

To test the law for pressures less than one atmosphere. — In this case the two tubes should be of the same length. Both tubes are first filled with mercury to within 10–20 cm. of the top. One tube is then tightly closed, and observations are taken as the pressure is reduced by drawing off mercury from the bottom. The pressure should then be gradually increased again until the confined air has returned to its original condition.

In other respects this experiment is exactly the same as the preceding.

EXPERIMENT H_2. *Comparison of a cistern barometer and a siphon barometer.*

The apparatus for this experiment consists of two barometers of the types indicated above, an accurate vertical scale divided to millimeters, and a reading telescope mounted upon a vertical rod. The length of this rod should be at least 80 cm., and the vertical scale should be of the same length. It is essential that the telescope turn freely upon its support with an accurately horizontal motion.

The arrangement of the apparatus which is shown in Fig. 39 is as follows:

The two barometers are mounted side by side upon a substantial block. At points a and b, situated at distances equally distant to the right of barometer B_1 and to the left of barometer B_2, are pins from which the scale S may be suspended. The latter must be adjusted beforehand so that

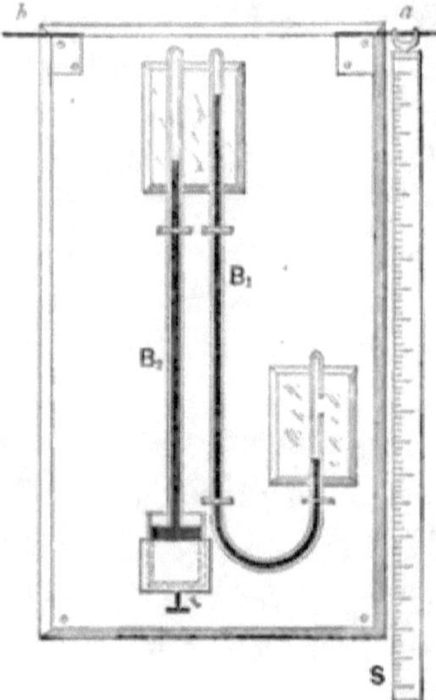

Fig. 39.

when the $\wedge$-shaped opening is placed on either pin the scale will swing freely into a vertical position.

The reading telescope should be set up at as small a distance from the barometers as the length of the draw-tube will permit, and should be in such a position that the meniscus of either mercury column can be seen, and also the scale, in good definition, without change of focus.

These adjustments having been completed, the following observations are to be made:

(1) *Scale hanging at the right.*

(a) The telescope is focused upon the upper meniscus of barometer B_1 (siphon), and the distance from the cap of the meniscus to the fixed cross-hair in the eye-piece is measured by means of a micrometer.*

(b) The telescope is then swung to the right until the vertical scale comes into the field. (In case the scale is not in proper focus, further adjustment must be made by moving it towards or away from the telescope, and not by refocusing the latter.)

(c) The scale divisions nearest the fixed cross-hair are identified and noted, and their distances from the latter are measured by means of the micrometer screw.

(d) These operations are repeated in the case of barometer B_2 (cistern).

(2) *Scale hanging at the left.*

(e) The various operations described as *a*, *b*, *c*, and *d* are carefully repeated.

(f) The telescope is shifted to a position opposite the cistern of barometer B_2, and the level of the mercury in the same is obtained by readings similar to those described under *a*, *b*, and *c*.

---

* In case the reading telescope is not provided with a micrometer eye-piece, the common eye-piece should be furnished with a suitable ruling on glass, which, placed in the focus, makes a very good substitute.

(*g*) The level of the lower meniscus of barometer B_1 is determined as above.

(3) *Scale hanging at the right.*

(*h*) The levels of cistern and lower meniscus are redetermined as above.

(4) *The reading of a thermometer placed midway between the two mercury columns is noted.*

If the conditions indicated in the description of this experiment are fulfilled, that is to say, if the scale hangs vertically both at the right and left, and the telescope moves smoothly in a nearly horizontal plane, the height of mercury column (B_1 and B_2 respectively) will be found nearly the same, whether computed from readings with scale left or scale right. Any discrepancy approaching 0.01 cm. should indicate the advisability of repeating the measurements. The height of the two mercury columns in B_1 and B_2 will, however, differ very appreciably, even when the vacuum is good in both instruments. The difference is due to depression by capillary action, which influences the cistern barometer only. The next step is to determine whether the correction for capillarity will account for the difference of barometric height.

(5) *To calibrate the cistern barometer for capillarity*, note the reading of the meniscus when the screw by means of which the height of the mercury in the cistern * is adjusted, is at almost its lowest position; then add a weighed quantity of pure mercury to the cistern sufficient to produce a rise of about one centimeter in the surface of the contents. The meniscus will rise through a distance precisely corresponding to the change of level in the cistern, and in case the ratio in the cross-sections be not very large indeed, the change of level as compared with that which

---

* The cistern barometer to be used in this experiment should be provided with a cistern which has a flexible leather bottom, upon which a screw impinges as in the Fortin barometer, giving considerable range of level.

would have occurred had there been no loss of mercury from the cistern to supply the increase in the column within the barometric tube, will afford a fair approximation to the diameter of the latter. This determination involves the measurement of the dimensions of the cistern and the computation of its contents per centimeter of vertical height.

In case the difference in the observed height for B_1 and B_2 is not entirely accounted for by means of the correction for capillarity (concerning which see any one of the larger treatises in physics), it is probable that the vacuum in one or both barometers is imperfect. Gross errors of filling may be detected by driving the column of B_2 to the top of the tube, by means of the screw, and watching for a bubble which cannot be made to disappear by pressure, and, in the case of the siphon barometer, reaching the same end by the direct application of pressure to the open end of the tube.

To reduce the readings obtained in this experiment to absolute measure, the scale should be placed upon the dividing engine (Exp. A_3), and compared with some good standard of length, or with the screw itself, if the constant of the instrument is known.

Experiment H_3. The coefficient of expansion of air.

The apparatus used in this experiment is a modification of that of Regnault. It consists of an air thermometer bulb, B (Fig. 40), contained in a jacketed vessel which serves as a bath of constant temperature. This bulb is connected with a mercury manometer by means of a long metallic tube of very small bore.

The coefficient of expansion is to be indirectly determined from the changes of pressure necessary to maintain the air contained within the bulb at a constant volume when subjected to changes of temperature.

Unless the bulb has been previously filled with dry air, it must be so filled by connecting it to an air-pump, and exhausting several times.   After each evacuation, air is allowed to enter the bulb through the set of intervening drying tubes (T, Fig. 40).   The "three-way" stopcock V is arranged to admit of this operation without the necessity of detaching the air-bulb from the manometer.

After having been thus pumped out and refilled at least ten times, the bulb is to be brought into connection with

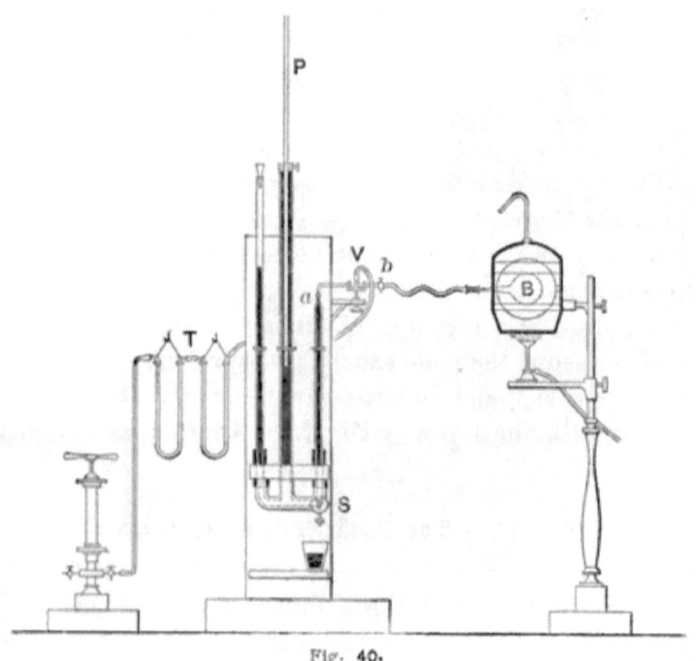

Fig. 40.

the manometer by turning the stopcock V.   There should be no further communication between its contents and the exterior atmosphere.   The two temperatures for which measurements are to be made are that of melting ice and that of boiling water.   To obtain the former, the bulb is entirely surrounded by crushed ice, and is kept thus packed until all upward movement of the mercury column in the closed arm of the manometer ceases.   To prevent an overflow of the mercury into the neck of the bulb, the pressure must be repeatedly lowered by adjustment of the iron plunger P, by small amounts, to compensate for the tendency of the gas to contract. When the temperature of the bulb has become constant, the pressure is raised until the mercury reaches the mark a in the neck of the manometer. The height of both mercury columns is then observed, preferably by the aid of a reading telescope and auxiliary scale, as described in Exp. H_2, and the height of the barometer is determined.

After the completion of these readings, the ice is removed from the constant temperature bath, a proper amount of hot water is supplied, the Bunsen burner is lighted, and the bulb is subjected to the continued action of steam until it reaches the temperature corresponding to that which steam assumes at the pressure under which it is generated within the bath. During the process of heating, the pressure upon the air within the bulb should be readjusted from moment to moment, so that no considerable deviation of the mercury from the mark a takes place. Finally, after equilibrium at the temperature of steam has been reached, a careful readjustment of the mercury column to the mark is made, and this operation is followed by readings of the manometric pressure and of the barometer.

In addition to these data it is necessary to know the contents of the bulb at $0°$ C., and at the temperature of the steam bath; also to apply certain corrections.

For the purposes of practice work, it is well to have a value of the cubic contents of the bulb previously determined with care once for all. In this way, by assuming the accuracy of this value and making use of the same in computation, the tedious process of refilling with dry air before each repetition of the experiment may be avoided.

The *process* of determining the contents may be learned, and the measurement of the coefficient of expansion of the glass may be performed by using a duplicate bulb. This bulb is filled with mercury at $0°$, and the contents is weighed, for which purpose it is divided into as many parts as the capacity of the balance may make necessary. It is then filled at the temperature of steam, and the contents, after cooling, is weighed. The mean coefficient k is expressed as follows:

$$k=\left(\frac{\mathrm{Vol}_t}{\mathrm{Vol}_0}-1\right)\frac{1}{t},\qquad(89)$$

where t is the temperature of the steam bath. The temperature t is to be determined from the pressure of the vapor in

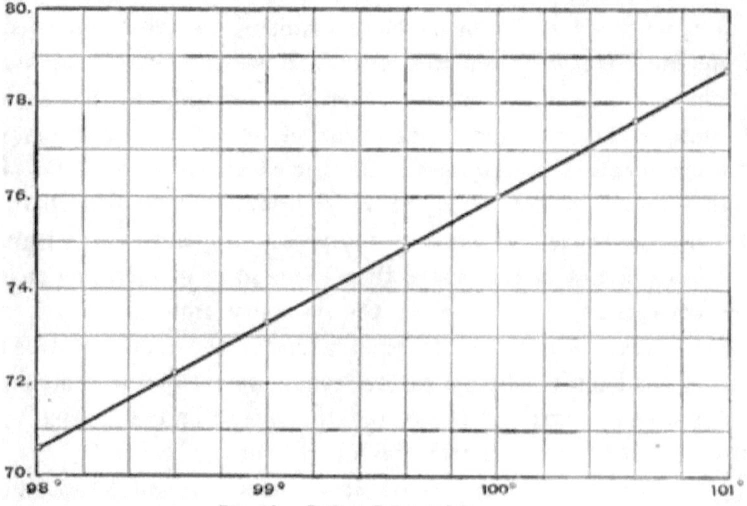

Fig. 41.—Boiling Point and Pressure.

the steam bath, for which purpose the results of Regnault may be used. That portion of his curve which applies to pressures in the neighborhood of one atmosphere is given in Fig. 41.* By means of it the temperature of a steam bath for any ordinary barometric pressure can be obtained without the use of a thermometer.

To compute Vol_0 and Vol_t, the density of mercury must be known at $0°$ and at $t°$. This may be conveniently obtained from the curve of densities, given in Fig. 42.*

* For the data from which the curves are obtained, see Landolt and Börnstein, Tabellen, pp. 41 and 58.

The most important corrections are those arising from the depression of the mercury in the neck of the manometer at a, and from the temperature of the mercury in the manometric and barometric columns. The former is to be ascertained by isolating the bulb from the manometer, by turning V to

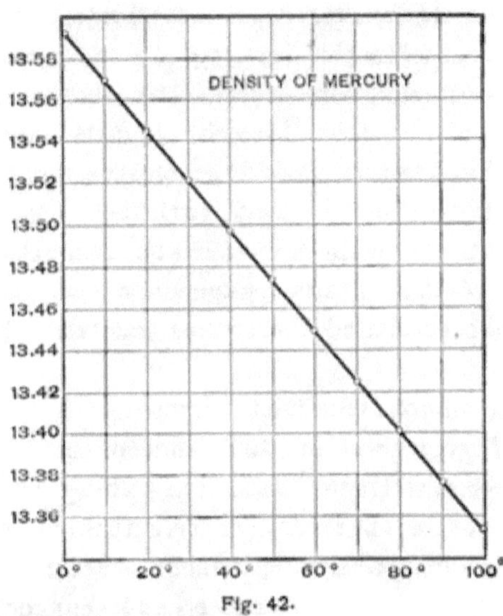

Fig. 42.

the proper position, and bringing the mercury to the mark by means of the plunger. The difference of level at a and in the open tube when the two surfaces are subjected to the same (the barometric) pressure is then noted. This reading is most accurately performed by means of the vertically suspended scale already described, and the reading telescope. The latter correction is that which it is necessary to apply to all barometric and manometric readings on account of the change of density of the mercury with temperature, viz.

$$h_0 = h_t \frac{d_t}{d_0},\qquad(90)$$

where h_0 is the corrected barometric or manometric height,

h, the observed height, and $\dfrac{d_t}{d_0}$ is the ratio of the densities of mercury at the temperature of observation and at $0°$ C.

A less important correction than the foregoing is that due to the fact that a certain volume of the air contained in the apparatus, that, namely, in the tube connecting the bulb with the neck of the manometer does not change temperature. If the bulb is of considerable size (300 cu. cm. or more), and the tube has the contracted bore described above, the volume under consideration will be found to be of little influence. The student should, however, make the measurements and compu-tation necessary to assure himself of the fact. For this purpose a piece of the tubing which is used in the apparatus is provided. The diameter of this is to be gauged and the contents of the connecting tube estimated therefrom, and from the length of the latter.

The neck of the manometer from a to the joint b is frequently of greater volume than the connecting tube. Its contents may be directly determined as follows :

(1) By means of the plunger drive the mercury into the neck of the manometer until it reaches the stopcock V, which must have been previously turned so as to connect the manom-eter neck with the open air.

(2) Turn the stopcock S at the base of the manometer tube so as to isolate the tube leading to the neck.

(3) Turn the stopcock S so as to drain the above tube into a clean beaker, taking care to close S at the moment the level of the mercury reaches the mark a. The mercury which has escaped measures the contents of the neck.

The computation of the coefficient of expansion of the air within the bulb follows readily from these measurements by the application of the laws of Boyle and Gay Lussac. Thus :

A gas possessing a coefficient of expansion a, when heated from $0°$ to $T°$, expands from V_0 to V_T, according to the law

$$V_T = (1 + a\,T)\,V_0. \tag{91}$$

If reduced, when at the higher temperature, to a volume V' by the pressure P_T, we have

$$\frac{V'}{1+\alpha T} = V_0 \frac{P_0}{P_T}, \tag{92}$$

where P_0 is the pressure at which the gas is measured while still at $0°$.

Under the conditions of the present experiment, we have two volumes of gas to consider: that within the bulb, which has a volume V_0 at $0°$ and of $V_0(1+kT)$ at $T°$, and that within the neck, the volume of which is $v_0(1+kt)$. The full expression for the relations between volumes, pressures, and temperatures therefore is

$$\left(V_0 \frac{1+kT}{1+\alpha T} + v_0 \frac{1+kt}{1+\alpha t}\right) P_T = \left(V_0 + v_0 \frac{1+kt}{1+\alpha t}\right) P_0, \tag{93}$$

in which equation k is the cubical coefficient of the expansion of the bulb, and v_0 is the volume of the neck and connecting tube at the temperature $0°$.

In equation 93 we may ignore the influence of temperature upon the volume of the neck, and write for $v_0(1+kt)$ the simpler form v (volume of the neck at temperature of the room t). Equation 93 then becomes

$$V_0\left(\frac{1+kT}{1+\alpha T}\right) + \frac{v}{1+\alpha t} = \left(V_0 + \frac{v}{1+\alpha t}\right) \cdot \frac{P_0}{P_T}, \tag{94}$$

which may be written

$$1+\alpha T = \frac{V_0(1+kT) + v\dfrac{1+\alpha T}{1+\alpha t}}{V_0 + \dfrac{v}{1+\alpha t}} \cdot \frac{P_T}{P_0}. \tag{95}$$

P_T and P_0 are quantities obtained by adding the atmospheric pressure H_1 and H_2, observed respectively at the times of the first and last adjustment of the manometer and the corresponding manometric pressures h_1 and h_2 (which may be positive or negative).

To solve equation 95 we assume the value $\alpha = 0.003665$ for the right-hand member, an approximation to our final actual value which will in no appreciable manner influence the result, since it enters only into the correction of the very small quantity v. The accuracy of the determination of α depends upon our knowledge of the quantities P_n, P_0, T, V_0, and k.*

---

* For a description of Regnault's classical research upon this subject, see Memoires de l'Academie Royale des Sciences, XXI (1847).

CHAPTER III.

GROUP I: CALORIMETRY.

(I) *General statements;* (I₁) *Heat of vaporization;* (I₂) *Heat of fusion;* (I₃) *Specific heat;* (I₄) *Radiating and absorbing power.*

(I). General statements concerning calorimetry.

It may be said in general that calorimetric determinations are subject to a great variety of annoying errors, which can be avoided only by the exercise of especial care and patience on the part of the experimenter. The student is therefore advised to plan his work very carefully before beginning the experiment itself, so that he shall run no risk of omitting essential observations and precautions. It will generally be found that the greatest source of error in calorimeter experiments is the inaccurate determination of temperatures. This may be due to several causes:

(1) The thermometer may indicate the temperature of a *portion* of the liquid ; the rest of the liquid being at a different temperature.

(2) The thermometer may not have had time to acquire the temperature of the surrounding liquid.

(3) The thermometer itself may be inaccurate.

(4) The reading of the thermometer may be at fault.

These sources of error should be guarded against with especial care.

The equations required for the computation of results in calorimetry may all be derived from one general principle.

This principle may be stated as follows: The amount of heat lost by one system of bodies is equal to the amount gained by another system. This, of course, treats potential energy due to change of state as latent heat. The heat lost or gained by a body may be due to two causes:

(1) Change in temperature; the amount in this case is equal to the continued product of the mass, specific heat, and change in temperature of the body.

(2) Change of state; this amount is equal to the product of the mass so changed by a constant quantity of heat necessary to produce such a change in unit mass.

The amount of heat lost by radiation to the air cannot be expressed in either of these ways; but it may be expressed as equal to the product of the time during which radiation takes place, the average difference of temperature between the radiating body and the air, and the radiation constant of the body.

I.

Comparison of thermometers.

When two or more thermometers are used in an experiment, their indications should always be compared, to determine whether their indications agree. Even the best thermometers are apt to differ in "zero point," so that they may give different readings for the same temperature, and yet measure differences in temperature accurately.

To compare thermometers, they should be placed together in a vessel of water (at any convenient temperature), and alternate readings taken for several minutes, the water being kept thoroughly stirred. If they are found to differ, a suitable correction must be made to all subsequent readings.

The numbers, or other distinguishing marks, of the thermometers used should in all cases be recorded.

II.

Determination of the water equivalent of a calorimeter.

When a calorimeter containing water, etc., is heated or cooled, heat is absorbed or given out by the vessel itself in addition to that absorbed or liberated by its contents. The *water equivalent* of a calorimeter is a quantity of water which would absorb the same amount of heat, when warmed through a certain number of degrees, as is absorbed by the calorimeter when heated through the same range of temperature.

To determine the water equivalent, proceed as follows :

(1) Fill the calorimeter nearly three-fourths full of water three or four degrees colder than the air, the weight of the water being known. This water should be kept thoroughly stirred, and its temperature should be observed by means of a thermometer hanging in it.

Add enough hot water, of known temperature, to fill the calorimeter to within one or two centimeters of the top. Stir thoroughly, and record the reading of the thermometer in the mixture at intervals of half a minute, until the temperature becomes practically constant. The hot water should be stirred immediately before it is poured in, and the temperature of both hot and cold water should be observed just the instant before mixing. It is best to choose the temperature of the hot water so that the mixture will come to about the temperature of the air, corrections for radiation being unnecessary if this is done. The mass of the hot water used may be determined by weighing the mixture after the observations are completed. From the data obtained, the water equivalent is to be computed.* The student should make at least three determinations.

---

* The amount of heat that the calorimeter absorbs is very small compared with the amount absorbed by the water which it contains. For this reason slight errors of observation will generally cause a very great error in the computed result. A common source of error is the following: while the hot water is being poured into the cold

If the material from which the calorimeter is made is known, the water equivalent may also be computed, as a check on the above results, from the mass and specific heat.

In the determination of the water equivalent, great care must be used in all temperature readings, or the results of successive determinations will be discordant. This is especially true in the case of small calorimeters. To obtain the best results, a number of separate determinations should be made, and the average of all the results used. No single result should be discarded merely because it differs widely from the rest. A result can be legitimately discarded only when something has occurred during the experiment which tends to throw discredit on some of the observations, or when there is an obvious mistake in one of the readings.

In the most accurate calorimetric experiments it is necessary to determine not only the water equivalent of the calorimeter, but also the water equivalents of the thermometers, stirring-rods, etc. In the experiments which follow, however, this is unnecessary.

In *all* calorimetric experiments, the *temperature of the room* should be recorded, as it will be found necessary in making corrections for radiation.

III.

Determination of the radiation constant of a calorimeter.

The loss of heat from a body which is a few degrees warmer than its surroundings is proportional: (1) to the time during which radiation takes place; (2) to the difference in temperature between the body and the room; (3) to a constant called the *constant of radiation*, depending upon the nature and extent of the radiating surface.

water, it will lose some heat to the air. In the computations this small quantity of heat is necessarily treated as if it were absorbed by the calorimeter, thus giving too large a value to the water equivalent.

Note that this constant depends *only* on the surface, and not upon the nature of the interior of the body. The radiation constant of a calorimeter is, for example, the same when it contains mercury as when it is filled with water. But the rate of cooling will be different in the two cases on account of the difference in the two specific heats. Radiation is essentially a phenomenon which occurs at the surface of a body, and depends wholly upon the nature and temperature of this surface.

The gain of heat by absorption when the body is colder than its surroundings obeys the same laws. The law above stated is known as Newton's law of cooling, and is really only an approximation to the truth. In the case of bodies differing in temperature from their surroundings by not more than $10°$, the approximation is, however, good.

The radiation constant may be defined as the amount of heat which is lost by radiation in one minute when the radiating body is one degree hotter than the air. For a difference in temperature of $\theta°$, the radiation is θ times as great; and for t minutes instead of one minute the loss is t times as great. It will thus be seen that if the radiation constant is known, the loss of heat from a body such as a calorimeter can be readily computed.

In most calorimetric work, corrections must be made for the loss of heat by radiation, or the gain by absorption, during the time of the experiment. The first step in any calorimetric experiment should therefore be the determination of the radiation constant. The method is as follows :

(1) Fill the calorimeter to within 1 or 2 cm. of the top with water considerably warmer than the air (say $10°–20°$ warmer). The mass of the water should be known. Suspend a thermometer in the center of the calorimeter, and observe the temperature at intervals of one minute as the water cools. These observations should be continued for at least an hour, the water being thoroughly stirred before each reading. The temperature

of the room, as indicated by a thermometer hanging near, should also be occasionally recorded.

(2) With the data obtained plat two curves, using times as abscissas in each case, and temperatures of air and water as ordinates. A smooth curve should now be drawn in each case, passing as nearly as possible through all the points platted. Any slight deviations from such smooth curves are probably due to accidental errors in the observations.

From the data given by these new curves, and knowing the mass of water, the statements made above may be verified, and the radiation constant computed.

It should be observed that an approximation must here be made, viz., that the temperature of the surface of the calorimeter is the same as that of the liquid contained in it. If the liquid is kept thoroughly stirred, and if the material from which the calorimeter is made is a good conductor, no great error is, however, introduced.

For example, let the mass of water plus the water equivalent of the calorimeter be 500 grams. Suppose that the temperature fell from 30° to 28° in five minutes, the temperature of the room being 20°. The temperature of the water having changed 2°, the loss of heat is equal to 2 × 500, or 1000 calories. Since this loss took place in five minutes, the loss in one minute was 1000 ÷ 5, or 200 calories. The average difference in temperature between water and air was 9°. The loss for one minute, and for 1° difference in temperature, would therefore be 200 ÷ 9 = 22 + minor calories, which is the radiation constant. Similar computations made with different portions of the data should give nearly the same result. Make eight or ten such computations and use the mean.

In using the constant thus obtained to correct for radiation losses, it usually happens that the temperature of the calorimeter does not remain constant throughout the experiment, so that the rate at which heat is lost by radiation is continually changing. The method to be used in such cases is illustrated by the following example :

Suppose that the temperature of the calorimeter is observed at intervals of one minute and is found to vary as follows: 29°, 26.°5, 24°, 22.°6, 21.°4, 20.°8, 20.°6, 20.°5, the temperature of the air being

22°. The average temperature of the calorimeter during the seven minutes is therefore 23.°18, (found by adding all the readings and dividing by 8). Radiation has therefore taken place for seven minutes at a rate whose average value is that corresponding to a difference in temperature of 1.°18 from the air. If the radiation constant is 20, the loss of heat is 20 × 1.18 × 7 = 165.2 calories.

EXPERIMENT I₁. **Determination of the heat of vaporization of water.**

The apparatus for this experiment may be arranged in a great variety of ways. The essential parts are :

(1) Some vessel in which steam may be generated.

(2) A calorimeter, which may be any metallic vessel of suitable size.

(3) Tubes of metal or glass by which the steam may be conveyed to the calorimeter. The latter should be sheltered

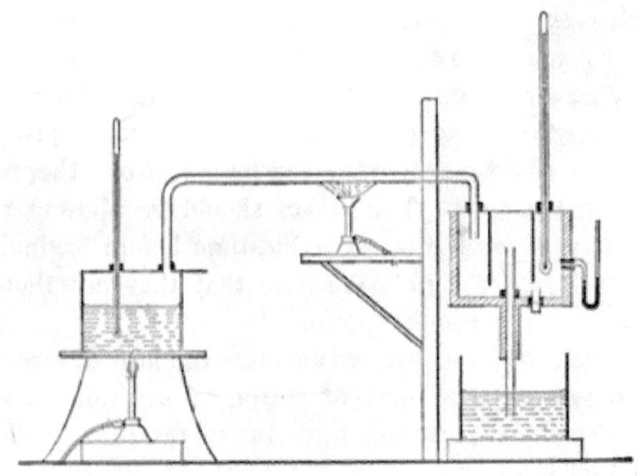

Fig. 43.

from the heat radiated from the boiler, and some device should be supplied to prevent the water which condenses in the tubes from entering the calorimeter. Fig. 43 shows a convenient form of apparatus for this determination.

The water equivalent and radiation constant of the calorimeter used should first be determined as previously described. Observations may then be made as follows to determine the heat of vaporization.

(1) Fill the calorimeter to within 2 or 3 cm. of the top with a known mass of water considerably colder than the air (from 8° to 12° colder).

(2) Pass steam into the calorimeter from a vessel of boiling water by means of the tubes provided for the purpose, keeping the water in the calorimeter thoroughly stirred, and observe its rise in temperature at intervals of one minute, until it has been heated as far above the temperature of the room as it was previously below it.

(3) Determine the mass of steam condensed by weighing the calorimeter and contents at the end of the experiment, the weight of the vessel and of the cold water having been previously determined. These weighings should be made with considerable care, as the mass of the condensed steam may be quite small. To make sure that the steam is dry, it should be slightly superheated by a flame placed under the tube which leads to the calorimeter. The temperature of the steam just before entering the water may be observed by means of a thermometer inserted in the tube. The steam should be allowed to pass through the tubes for a considerable time before beginning the experiment, in order to make sure that they are thoroughly warmed (to avoid condensation).

(4) From the data obtained compute the heat of vaporization of water, or the latent heat of steam. Corrections should be made for the loss or gain of heat due to radiation and absorption, and for the heat capacity of the calorimeter itself.

This correction, due to radiation, may be reduced to a minimum by allowing the flow of steam to continue until the water in the calorimeter reaches a temperature as much above that of the air as it was initially below that temperature. But the correction should always be computed. At least three determinations should be made.

The following tables show the character of the data pertaining to this experiment and the method of arranging them.

COMPARISON OF THERMOMETERS.

No. 12975.	No. 12319.	No. 3.
7.53	7.55	8.3
7.60	7.62	8.3
26.80	26.82	27.4
25.83	25.87	27.2
38.03	38.08	39.
36.89	36.91	37.6

No. 12327 registers 99° in boiling water.

RADIATION CONSTANT.

Time.	Tem. of Vessel.	Tem. of Room.	Radiation Constant.	Time.	Tem. of Vessel.	Tem. of Room.	Radiation Constant.
3-34	30.8	11.2		3-47	28.0	11.1	
35	30.56			48	27.8		
36	30.36			49	27.6		4.15
37	30.12			50	27.4		
38	29.90	11.3		51	27.23		
39	29.70		3.98	52	27.03		
40	29.46			53	26.88	11.0	
41	29.28			54	26.70		3.93
42	29.03			55	26.50		
43	29.83	11.2		56	26.33		
44	28.60		4.22	57	26.15		
45	28.40			58	25.95	10.8	
46	28.20			59	25.80		4.16

Mass of Calorimeter + Water = 492.5 grams.
Mass of Calorimeter = 154.7
$$\overline{337.8}$$
Water Equivalent = 14.8
$$\overline{352.6 \text{ grams.}}$$
Radiation Constant = 4.09 calories.

WATER EQUIVALENT OF CALORIMETER.

	I.	II.	III.
Mass of Calorimeter,	154.7	154.7	154.7
" Cal. + Cold Water,	334.0	344.	340.2
" Cold Water,	179.3	189.3	185.5
" Cal. + Mixture,	478.5	480.5	486.5
" Warm Water,	144.5	136.5	146.3
Tem. of Room, No. 3,	24.0	21.0	21.0
" Cold Water, No. 12975,	9.8	10.2	8.25
" Warm Water, No. 12319,	35.6	36.6	37.4
" Mixture, No. 12975,	20.88	20.85	20.4
Water Equivalent,	12.6	12.6	19.2

Water equivalent = 14.8.

HEAT OF VAPORIZATION OF WATER.

		I.	II.	III.
Mass of Calorimeter,		154.7	154.7	154.7
" Cal. + Cold Water,		438.0	427.7	434.0
" Cold Water,		283.3	273.0	279.3
" Cal. + Mixture,		450.0	440.6	447.2
" Condensed Steam,		12.0	12.9	13.2
Temperature of Room,		21.0	21.0	21.0
" Cold Water,		10.4	8.27	10.82
No. 12319,	TIME.	105°	105°	103°
" " Steam,	$1\frac{1}{2}$ m.	107	105	104°
No. 12327,	3	108		105°
	4	107		
	0	13.4	14.0	12.8
	5	16.2	19.6	13.6
	1.0	18.0	27.2	17.8
" " Mixture,	1.5	20.7	34.4	22.0
	2.0	23.7	35.0	24.7
No. 12319,	2.5	26.5	35.45	28.5
	3.0	31.0		32.9
	3.5	34.4		37.0
	4.0	34.9		37.7
Heat of Vaporization,		545	544	540

Experiment I₂. **Determination of the heat of fusion of ice.**

The radiation constant and the water equivalent of the calorimeter used are first to be determined, as previously described. Observations may then be taken to determine the heat of fusion as follows:

(1) Fill the calorimeter to within 2 or 3 cm. of the top with a known mass of water, $3°$ or $4°$ warmer than the air.

(2) Stir thoroughly and observe the temperature. Then drop in a piece of ice; hold it under water by means of a stirrer arranged for the purpose, and observe the temperature of the water at intervals of half a minute until the ice is melted, and a fairly constant temperature is reached. In case the melting of the ice cools the calorimeter below the temperature of the room, it is well to continue observations of temperature, stirring thoroughly before each reading, until the calorimeter begins to warm again by absorption of heat from the air.

The ice used should be at its melting-point. This is assured by keeping it for some time inside the warm room. It should be carefully dried by means of filter paper just before dropping in the calorimeter.

The mass of ice used may be obtained by weighing the calorimeter and contents after the observations are completed, the weight of the vessel and of the warm water being already known.

From the data obtained compute the heat of fusion.

Corrections are to be made for the loss of heat by radiation, and for the water equivalent of the calorimeter. Make at least three complete determinations.

Experiment I₃. **Determination of the specific heat of a solid.**

(1) Place the metal whose specific heat is to be determined in the calorimeter, and support it in such a way that it does not touch the sides or bottom. Enough water of known weight

should now be placed in the calorimeter to just cover the metal, the temperature of the water being from 8° to 15° above that of the air.

(2) Allow the calorimeter and contents to stand for at least ten minutes in order to make sure that the metal has acquired the temperature of the water. Then add cool water, stir thoroughly, and observe the temperature at half-minute intervals until it reaches a practically constant value. The temperature and amount of the cold water should be such as to bring the final temperatures of the mixture very close to that of the air. A few preliminary trials will show about what the temperature should be. The temperature of hot and cold water, each thoroughly stirred, should be observed immediately before mixing. The weight of the cold water added is to be found by weighing the calorimeter and contents after the other observations are completed.

As the specific heat of any metal is much less than that of water, it will be advisable to take a rather large mass of the metal. For good results, its heat capacity should be comparable with that of the mass of water used. If the metal is not a good conductor of heat, it should be in small pieces.

The method here described is merely one of many which may be used in the determination of specific heat.

The student will find it instructive, if time is available, to check his results by one of the numerous other methods which will be found described in various text-books.

The water equivalent and the radiation constant of the calorimeter used are to be determined as described in the general directions at the beginning of this group.

The weight of the metal being known, its specific heat may now be computed. Corrections are to be made for radiation and for the absorption of heat by the calorimeter itself. At least three determinations should be made.

EXPERIMENT I$_4$. **Radiating and absorbing powers of different surfaces.**

The objects of this experiment are to investigate the radiation and absorption of heat from different surfaces, and to determine the relation between the radiating and absorbing powers of the same surface.

The radiating constant of a surface may be defined as the number of calories that will be radiated from one square centimeter of the surface in one minute, for a difference in temperature of one degree between the surface and its surroundings. In like manner the constant for absorption may be defined as the number of calories that will be absorbed by one square centimeter of the surface under similar conditions.

The radiation constant of a surface may be determined by dividing the heat lost by a vessel in a given time, by the time, the average difference in temperature between the surface and the air, and the area of the vessel. The absorption constant may be computed in a similar manner from the heat gained in a given time.

It is to be observed that radiation and absorption depend upon the temperature of the radiating or absorbing surface, and not upon the temperature of the contents of the vessel. If the walls of the vessel are thin, however, and of some highly conducting material, no great error is introduced by assuming that the contents of the vessel are at the same temperature as the surface.

The method of the experiment is as follows :

(1) Fill the vessel for whose surface the radiation constant is to be determined with water 15° or 20° warmer than the air, and place it upon a poorly conducting support, such that the vessel will be free to radiate its heat in all directions.

(2) Observe the temperature by means of a thermometer hanging in the center of the vessel, at intervals of two minutes, stirring the water thoroughly before each reading. The temperature of the air should also be observed at intervals of about five

minutes, and for good results must remain nearly constant throughout the experiment. Continue these observations for at least half an hour.

A curve should now be platted with times as abscissas and temperatures as ordinates. From this curve, or from the data themselves, make four or five independent computations of the radiation constant. If the constant is computed from the curve, it will be necessary to find the "pitch," $dt \div dT$ ($t =$ temperature; $T =$ time), at different points on the curve, by drawing tangents.

From Newton's law of cooling, the radiation constant R is given by the equation

$$R = \frac{c}{A} \cdot \frac{1}{t - t_a} \cdot \frac{dt}{dT},\tag{96}$$

where c is the heat capacity of the vessel, A its superficial area, and t_a the temperature of the air. The value of c is determined by adding the water equivalent of the vessel to the weight of the water contained in it.

The following method of computing the results will be found instructive as an example of the employment of graphical methods, and may be used instead of the above if desired.

$$\frac{dt}{dT} = \frac{RA}{c} \cdot (t - t_a).\tag{97}$$

$$\therefore \frac{dt}{t - t_a} = \frac{RA}{c} \cdot dT.\tag{98}$$

By integration: $\log (t - t_a) = \frac{RA}{c} T + K,\tag{99}$

where K is the constant of integration.

If, therefore, a curve is platted whose co-ordinates are T and $\log(t - t_a)$ respectively, the result should be a straight line. In the equation of this line, $\frac{RA}{c}$ enters as one of the constants. Note that the logarithm which occurs in the above equation is the

Napierian logarithm. Ordinary logarithms may, however, be used until the final result is reached.

The constant for absorption can be determined in a similar manner by filling the vessel with water 15° or 20° colder than the air, and observing the gradual rise in temperature due to absorption.

These observations should be repeated with three or four vessels which are of the same size and shape, but differ widely in the character of the radiating surface. Polished metal and lampblack surfaces will probably be found to differ most widely in their radiating powers. No difficulty should be experienced in carrying on the observations with four vessels at the same time.

It is to be observed that a slight error is introduced in this experiment by assuming that all the heat is lost by radiation, for part of the loss is really due to convection. For small differences of temperature, however, the loss by convection is small, and may be treated as though it obeyed Newton's law. The radiation constants obtained represent, therefore, the sum of the losses due to the two causes.

(In connection with this experiment, see the general directions for calorimetric work.)

CHAPTER IV.

GROUP P: STATIC ELECTRICITY.

(P) *General statements;* (P₁) *Electrostatic induction;* (P₂) *The principle of the condenser;* (P₃) *The Holtz machine;* (P₄) *Further experiments with the Holtz machine.*

(P). General statements concerning static electricity.

Whenever a body or system of bodies becomes electrified, equal quantities of positive and negative electricity are produced.

Many experimental facts lead to the conclusion that the energy of electrification exists in the insulating medium between the bodies containing these two equal quantities of positive and negative electricity. These experimental facts prove that the insulating medium is in a state of strain. Therefore the energy of electrification is the potential energy of an electrical field, in an insulating medium, bounded by bodies containing what are called "charges of electricity."

If an electrified body or system of bodies be placed within a closed conducting surface, the charge of electricity on this surface is equal, and of opposite sign, to the charge of the body or system of bodies. This law has been deduced directly from experiment. However, it may be shown to be directly deducible from the following theorem.

Let F denote the resultant electrical force at a point on a small element of the surface of a charged body: the integral of the quantity FdA, taken over the entire surface of the charged body, is numerically equal to $4\pi Q$, in which Q is the number of units of electricity in the body.* This is known as Green's theorem.

Another way of stating this fact is as follows : The number of lines of force, or of unit tubes of force, issuing from the surface of a body charged with Q units of electricity, is $4\pi Q$. These lines of force, or tubes of induction, must end on some other body or bodies. On the surfaces of the conductors where these $4\pi Q$ lines of force end, there must be Q units of induced electricity of the opposite sign to the electricity on the first conductor.†

To completely discharge a conductor, and cause to vanish the field surrounding it, it will be necessary for these two equal quantities of electricity of opposite signs to unite.

The conception of free and bound electricity helps to the understanding of this and other phenomena of static electricity. The term "free electricity," or "free charge," is applied to that portion of a charge which will escape to the earth, when the conductor containing it is connected to earth, while a bound charge is that portion

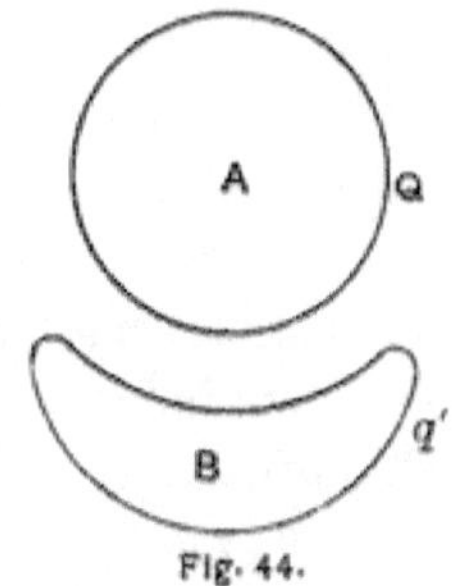

Fig. 44.

which is held by the induction of some other near-by *insulated* charge.

Suppose A (Fig. 44) to be an insulated conductor charged with Q units of positive electricity. Suppose B to be a conductor which has been grounded and afterwards insulated. The charge Q induces on B, q' units and on the walls of the room, q'' units of negative electricity, such that

$$Q = -(q'+q'').$$

---

* Gray, Absolute Measurements in Electricity and Magnetism, vol. I, p. 10.

† This is more general than the second law above given, but it is based on the assumption that an electrical field does not extend indefinitely in a direction in which there are no charged bodies.

That part q' of the electricity induced on B is bound by the charge Q. None of it will escape to the earth, for its potential has been reduced to zero by grounding it. The charge q' on B binds, by induction, a *portion* of the charge on A ; so that if A were grounded, only a portion of the Q units of electricity would escape. That which escapes is free electricity ; the remainder is bound by the negative charge on B.

It is very important to keep clearly in mind the distinction between the *character* and the *potential* of a charge of electricity. In the above example, before A was grounded, B was at zero potential, but it had a negative charge ; after A was grounded, the potential of B became negative, although its charge was unchanged. A, however, was reduced to zero potential, but it still retained a positive charge.

Positive and negative electricity always exist at the positive and negative ends respectively of electrical lines of force ; or, as some may prefer to put it, at the positive and negative boundaries of an electrical field of force. The potential of the body containing the positive charge must always be positive with respect to the body containing a negative charge at the other boundary of the field ; but the potential of either or both of these bodies may be anything with respect to the earth, whose potential is usually taken as zero.

The potential of a conductor is positive, when, upon being grounded, positive electricity is discharged to the earth ; when negative electricity is thus discharged, the potential is negative, and when no discharge occurs, the conductor is at zero potential.

It is a very instructive exercise to map out a field of force with equipotential surfaces and lines of force.* It is not difficult to do this in an approximate manner, if the student keeps clearly in mind the definitions, the fact that lines of force and equipotential surfaces are mutually perpendicular,

---

* In this connection the beautiful maps of the electrostatic field at the end of the first volume of Maxwell's Electricity and Magnetism should be inspected.

and the fact that the surface of every conductor is an equipotential surface.

Let it be required to map a section of the field within a hollow conductor at zero potential, containing two insulated conductors. One of these conductors is positively charged, and the other has only an induced charge.

It will be found easier to draw the lines of force first.

(1) They must always be drawn between conductors of different potentials.

(2) They must issue from a conductor at right angles to its surface.

(3) Lines of force must always issue from a body containing a positive charge, and end on a body containing a negative charge.

If lines of force are drawn fulfilling these conditions, they will be as indicated in Fig 45.* It may be assumed, approximately, that along the shortest distance between the two conductors the potential falls uniformly. Assume that the difference of potential between them is nine. Divide the distance into nine equal parts, and through each point of division draw a line, and continue it so that it is everywhere perpendicular to lines of force. Each of these lines must be a closed curve. And from definition, each of them must lie in an equipotential surface.

By definition, the same amount of work is done in carrying a charge from one point in an equipotential surface to any

---

* The equipotential lines and lines of force in Fig. 45 were computed by C. D. Child.

This computation was made as follows: Known charges were supposed to be concentrated at points. A series of points were then found which had the same potential, according to the formula $V = \Sigma \frac{q}{R}$. All the equipotential surfaces, from 3 to 15 inclusive, were determined in this way. A conductor connected to the ground was then supposed to coincide with the equipotential surface 3. This reduced the potential of every point within by three units. A conductor was then supposed to surround a charge of $+ 40$ units, and coincide with the equipotential surface 12; while another conductor was supposed to surround charges of $+ 10$, $- 5$, and $- 5$ units, and coincide with the equipotential surface 3. These two conductors in no wise changed the potential of any point in the field of force, while it was perfectly allowable to suppose the charges within them to be transferred to their outside surfaces.

point in another equipotential surface. Therefore, the field must be strongest where these surfaces are closest together. Strength of field is sometimes represented by the *number* of lines of force per square centimeter. Therefore, where the

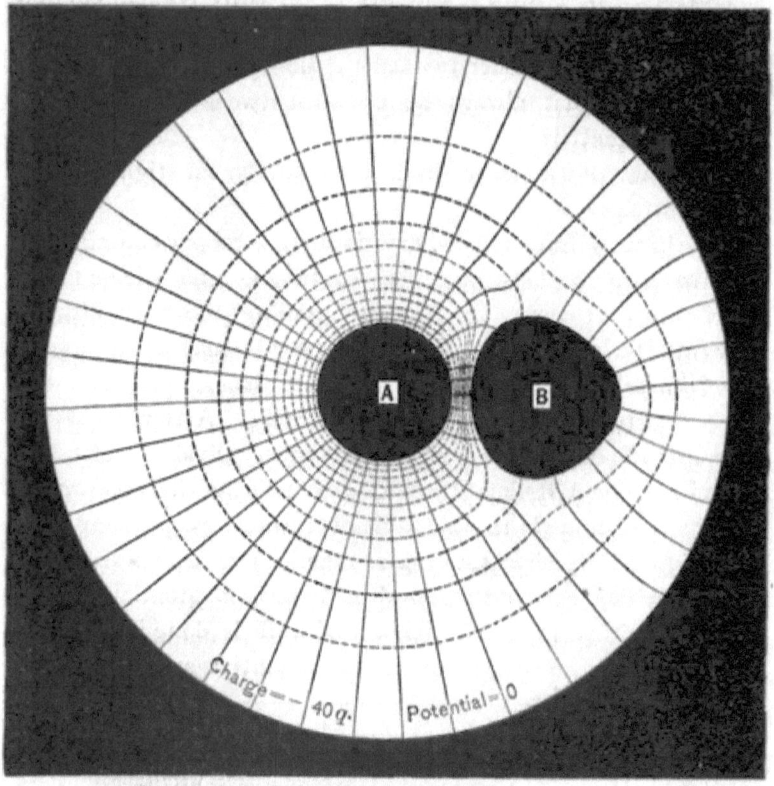

A is a conductor [Potential 12 ; charge 40 q].
B is a conductor [Potential 3   Induced charge — 10 q and + 10 q]
Fig. 45.

equipotential surfaces are closest together, the lines of force should be most numerous.

It should be noticed that one of the conductors has lines of force issuing from it and also ending on it. It follows that there is a positive and a negative charge on this conductor, although the whole of it is at the same potential.

Nearly all experiments on static electricity are more successful in cold weather than in warm. This difference is probably due to a difference in humidity. In moist air, bodies are rapidly discharged, so that it is relatively much more difficult to accumulate charges when the surrounding atmosphere is moist. In cold weather the absolute humidity is usually much less than in warm weather. In an artificially heated room, the absolute humidity remaining the same as the outside air, the relative humidity is very much lessened on account of the higher temperature.

From the definition of a line of force, a positively charged body (an insulated pith-ball, for example) tends to move along the lines of force from positively charged bodies towards negatively charged bodies. If the body were negatively electrified, it would tend to move in the opposite direction. This offers a means of testing the direction of lines of force, and consequently the character of the charge on a charged body.

If an insulated pith-ball be positively electrified (by being brought in contact with a glass rod which has been previously rubbed with silk), and then be suspended in a region supposed to be a field of electrical force, surrounding a charged conductor, one of three things will occur:

(1) The pith-ball will tend to move *from* the body supposed to be charged. This proves that the region is an electrical field with lines of force *issuing from* the body, which is therefore positively charged.

(2) The pith-ball will not tend to move at all. In this case we infer that the electrical field is too weak, or that the charge on the pith-ball is too weak to produce a perceptible effect.

(3) The pith-ball will tend to move *towards* the charged body. This indicates that the region is a field of force with lines of force *entering* the body, which is therefore negatively electrified. We say "indicates," for it only proves that there is *now* a field between the pith-ball and the body, and that *one* of them was originally electrified before they were brought near together.

We know that if the pith-ball were originally neutral, it would move toward a strongly charged body when brought near it. If the conductor were strongly charged, and the pith-ball weakly charged, both with positive electricity, the motion would be the same. Moreover, if the conductor were neutral, a charged pith-ball brought near it would tend to move towards it.

These facts may be readily explained on the theory of induction. What is to be learned from this is that an electrical field of force, and the character of the charge on a body, cannot be certainly determined from the motion of a charged pith-ball *towards* the body. Under these circumstances, the pith-ball should be charged negatively (by being brought in contact with vulcanite previously rubbed with fur), and again experimented upon.

Sometimes it is better to first bring the pith-ball into contact with the body supposed to be charged, and then to test the nature of the charge on the pith-ball by bringing it near electrified glass and vulcanite rods in turn.

The electrification of a body may often be tested more reliably by the use of a proof-plane and a gold-leaf electroscope. In using the electroscope, it must be remembered that it is the *first* motion of the leaves, as the charged proof-plane is brought near it, that is to be noted. If the proof-plane has a considerable charge, whose sign is opposite to that of the leaves, it will cause them to collapse, and afterwards to diverge, as it is brought quite near to the electroscope.

EXPERIMENT Γ_1. **Electrostatic induction.**

Every insulated conductor in the neighborhood of a positively charged body has induced upon its surface equal quantities of positive and negative electricity. The positive electricity is on the side farthest from the charged body, and the negative on the side nearest.

The object of this experiment is to investigate this and other phenomena of electrostatic induction.

For this experiment, a rather large insulated conductor is required. A Leyden jar, in which the small knob is replaced by a sphere 10 or 12 cm. in diameter, and connected with the inner coating, is excellent for this purpose on account of its great capacity. Such a conductor will usually retain its charge for the whole time of the experiment. A second insulated conductor, preferably an elongated cylinder with hemispherical ends, is also required.

Charge the sphere connected to the Leyden jar by means of an electrical machine. Place the second conductor in the electrical field produced by the charged conductor. The two conductors should be not more than 2 or 3 cm. apart.

The nature of the charge on different parts of the second conductor should now be investigated. This may be done, either by means of a pith-ball suspended by a silk fiber, or by means of a proof-plane and gold-leaf electroscope. Some idea may be formed of the direction of the lines of force in the electrical field surrounding the conductors by the direction in which a positively charged pith-ball tends to move.

After testing as above, remove the conductor, still insulated, to a distance from the charged body, and test again. Place the conductor again in proximity to the charged body, ground the conductor, and test with the pith-ball as before. Then move the conductor closer to the charged body, and note any change in its condition. Finally, remove the conductor to a distance from the inducing body (the connection with the ground having been first broken), and test again.

Throughout the experiment care must be taken not to allow any discharge from the charged body to the second conductor.

To secure uniform results it will generally be necessary to repeat these tests several times. This experiment will give satisfactory results only when the air is rather dry. It succeeds best in cold weather, when the room is artificially heated.

Addenda to the report:

(1) Define the following: unit electrical charge; electrical field of force; field of unit intensity; electrical difference of potential; unit difference of potential; electrical potential at a point; equipotential surfaces; electrical line of force; unit line of force, or unit tube of force; electrical capacity; **unit** of capacity.

(2) Give a demonstration of the fact that lines of force and equipotential surfaces are mutually perpendicular.

(3) **State** the general relation which the quantity of induced electricity on the conductor bears to the quantity on the charged body and the distance between them.

(4) Assuming that the charge of the charged body is positive, what is the *potential* of the conductor in each of the five cases investigated? What would be its potential if the charged body were negative?

(5) Draw a vertical section of the two conductors showing equipotential surfaces and lines of force.

(6) Draw two such figures, one when the conductor having the induced charge is insulated, and one when it is grounded.

EXPERIMENT P_2.   **The principle of the condenser.**

When a conductor connected to the earth is brought near a charged body, the potential of the charged body is reduced. If the conductor almost surrounds the charged body, and is very close to it, its potential will be very greatly reduced, although the amount of the charge remains absolutely unchanged.

Another way of viewing this fact is to consider that the conductor lessens the quantity of free electricity on the charged body. **The remainder** of the charge is bound by the electricity induced on the near-by conductor. If, instead of maintaining the charge constant, the potential of the charged body is maintained constant, it will be found that the charge must be rapidly increased as the conductor connected with the earth is brought very near.

A combination of two conductors, very close together, one of which is connected to the earth, is called a condenser. The capacity of such a condenser is enormously greater than the capacity of either of the conductors of which it is composed when measured in the absence of the other.

In order to become familiar with the phenomena of the condenser, two forms are to be experimented with :

I.

The first form is an apparatus consisting of two vertical, parallel metal plates. These plates are both insulated, and are capable of motion along a line joining their centers.

(1) Fasten a pith-ball by means of a conducting thread to one plate, so that the ball rests against the plate.

(2) Connect the second plate to the earth, and charge the first one by means of an electrical machine.

(3) Move the plates to and from each other, and note the effect on the pith-ball.

(4) When the plates are quite near together, insulate the plate that was formerly grounded, and afterwards discharge the other plate by grounding it. Then separate the plates, and note the effect on the pith-ball.

(5) Fasten a pith-ball, as above, to the second plate also. Charge the plates while 1 or 2 cm. apart by connecting them to the opposite terminals of an electrical machine. Insulate the two plates without grounding either of them, and determine the character of the charge on each plate, by bringing a charged body whose condition is known near each pith-ball in turn.

(6) Connect one of the plates to the ground for an instant, and observe the effect on the sign and magnitude of the charges. Do the same with the second plate. Continue grounding alternately the two plates until they are both very nearly discharged.

(7) Charge the plates again, and observe the effect of connecting them by means of a good conductor. Repeat these

observations with a glass plate between the metal conductors, the latter being very close, or in contact with the glass.

II.

The other form of condenser to be experimented with is a Leyden jar.

(1) Place the jar on an insulating support, and charge it by connecting the two coatings to the opposite terminals of an electrical machine.

(2) Disconnect from the electrical machine without grounding either coating, and experiment as with the plate condenser.

(3) Determine the number of alternate groundings of the two coatings necessary to reduce the charge to a definite fraction of its original value. For the purpose of this determination, the assumption may be made that the charge is proportional to the length of spark, when either coating is grounded, the other coating having been previously grounded and then insulated.

(4) When the jar is fully charged, make metallic connection between the two coatings. After a few minutes connect the coatings again, and note the existence of the "residual charge."

(5) Try to charge the jar by connecting only one coating to the electrical machine, the other coating being insulated. Investigate the nature of charges on the two coatings, and afterwards discharge the jar, observing whether the spark is comparable with that obtained when the jar was charged by the method first given.

The above-described experiments should be repeated several times in order to be certain of the results and to become familiar with the phenomena.

Addenda to the report:

(1) Indicate whether in the case of a condenser with a gas or a liquid as dielectric, there would be anything comparable to the residual charge of a Leyden jar.

(2) Indicate why it requires a very large number of alternate groundings of the two coatings of a condenser to perceptibly reduce its charge.

(3) Assume that the alternate groundings of the two coatings are at equal intervals of time, and draw two curves with times as abscissas and potentials of the two coatings as ordinates.

(4) Draw a vertical section of the jar, with coatings quite wide apart and showing lines of force and the vertical sections of equipotential surfaces.

(5) Draw two such figures, one in which the potential of one coating is zero, and one in which the surface of zero potential lies between the coatings.

(6) Determine approximately the electrostatic capacity of the jar from its dimensions.

(7) Assume the difference of potential between the coatings to be 100 electrostatic units, and compute the electrostatic force in the glass between the coatings.

(8) Compute the total charge in the jar under the above conditions.

(9) Compute the energy of the charge.

EXPERIMENT P_3. **The Holtz machine.**

In all influence machines, mechanical energy is directly transformed into the energy of electrification. The object of this experiment is to familiarize the student with the use of such machines and the principles involved in their action. Any type of influence machine may be used. The following is the procedure:

(1) Run the machine a few seconds until it is fully charged. The poles should be a few centimeters apart. Then stop the machine, and determine, by means of a pith-ball, the character of the charge on every part of the machine. Repeat these observations several times, and observe whether the polarity of the machine becomes reversed.

(2) While the machine is charged and at rest, gradually bring the terminals together until a discharge takes place, and observe the effect upon the pith-ball. Determine the character of the charges on different parts of the machine when it is running steadily with the terminals too far apart to allow a discharge.

(3) Observe the difference in the discharge when the Leyden jars are removed, also when they are replaced by larger ones.

(4) Determine the maximum distance between the terminals, at which a discharge will pass when the machine is running steadily, but not very rapidly. Remove the crossbar, and determine the maximum length of spark between the terminals when the machine is running at the same rate as before.

(5) Reverse the direction of rotation, and determine under what conditions the machine will work.

(6) Take the machine into a dark room, and run it steadily (*a*) with the crossbar in position, and the terminals in contact ; (*b*) with the crossbar in position, and the terminals very wide apart ; (*c*) without the crossbar, and with the terminals first in contact, and afterwards widely separated. Observe carefully the brush discharge between the revolving plate and the combs in all these cases.

Addenda to the report :

(1) Indicate the results, by positive and negative signs, upon carefully drawn diagrams of the machine.

(2) Explain how the machine becomes highly charged when one armature is given a small initial charge, and the plate is steadily revolved.

(3) Indicate the function of the crossbar, and the most advantageous position for it.

(4) Indicate the function of the Leyden jars.

EXPERIMENT P_4. **The Holtz machine** (*continued*).

After performing Exp. P_3, the following further experiments with an electrical machine will be found very instructive :

I.

Remove the Leyden jars, and connect to each terminal of the machine one coating of a condenser whose capacity may be varied in a known manner. Connect together the remaining coatings of the two condensers. Condensers formed by coating the whole of one side of a glass plate with tin-foil, while on the other side are several pieces of tin-foil insulated from each other, and of equal area, serve very well for this purpose.

Place the terminals at a fixed distance apart of 2 or 3 cm., and run the machine *uniformly*, counting the number of discharges per minute. Vary the capacity of the condensers connected to the terminals, and repeat these observations.

If the machine works uniformly, it will be found that the number of sparks per minute varies inversely as the capacity of the condensers. This fact may be readily shown to follow from the assumption that the amount of electrical work done when the machine is running uniformly is directly proportional to the time, and independent of the capacity of the condenser used.

On account of the uncertainty of the conditions, it will be necessary to take a large number of observations, and to use their mean in testing the truth of the above statement.

II.

An electrical machine is a generator of electricity, and under conditions that are not variable it has a constant electromotive force, and a constant internal resistance.

If the machine is in good working condition, and is rotated uniformly in an atmosphere of constant humidity, its electromotive force and internal resistance will not be greatly variable, provided that the external resistance is not greater than a few million ohms.

To verify this statement, connect the terminals of the machine to the terminals of a high-resistance sensitive galvanometer. Turn the machine uniformly, and observe the galvanometer readings for current, both direct and reversed. Place in series with the machine and galvanometer a resistance of 100,000 ohms. The change in the galvanometer deflection will probably be imperceptible. This shows that the internal resistance of the machine is enormous, and that the electromotive force is probably very great.

In order to determine these constants, the method of Exp. S_2 may be used. Place in series with the galvanometer and machine a variable resistance of several megohms.* Observe the galvanometer readings for several different resistances producing quite different deflections. For each deflection, the current in amperes may be calculated if the constant of the galvanometer is known.

As in Exp. S_2, we have

$$I = \frac{E}{R + R_0}. \tag{100}$$

If E and R_0 are constant, they may be determined from any pair of observations giving two values of R and two of I. If several different values of R are used, plat a curve with resistances as abscissas, and reciprocals of currents as ordinates. This will be a straight line from whose constants E and R_0 may be determined.

Owing to the difficulty of maintaining a uniform rate of rotation, and other unavoidable causes affecting the current, the values of the current used in computations should be the mean of several observations.

It must be remembered that the potential difference of the terminals of the machine, and consequently the electromotive force, is enormously greater when the terminals are separated by several centimeters, and the resistance between them is thousands of megohms.

---

* Heavy black-lead lines on wood will serve for high resistances. If divided into sections of about a million ohms, these resistances may be measured by means of a Wheatstone bridge.

III.

Replace the Leyden jars by large ones. Separate the terminals to a distance of 8 or 10 cm., and run the machine until the jars are charged. Then slip off the belt, and stop the revolving plate with the finger. Under favorable circumstances, the plate will start to rotate backwards, and continue to do so for quite a number of turns. After a successful trial, it will be found that the jars are very nearly discharged when the plate ceases to rotate.

Addenda to the report:

(1) If the electrostatic capacity of the condenser used is known, as well as the electrostatic difference of potential producing the sparks of known length, calculate the electrical work done in ergs per second, in watts.

(2) Prove upon theoretical grounds that the number of sparks per minute is inversely proportional to the capacity of the condenser used.

(3) Indicate the kind of battery that would produce an effect similar to that of the machine in the second experiment of this section.

(4) Indicate the cause of the backward rotation in the third experiment above.

CHAPTER V.

GROUP Q: MAGNETISM.

(Q) *General statements;* (Q_1) *Lines of force and the study of the magnetic field;* (Q_2) *Determination of the magnetic moment of a bar magnet by the method of oscillations;* (Q_3) *Determination of magnetic moment by the magnetometer;* (Q_4) *Measurement of the intensity of a magnetic field;* (Q_5) *Distribution of free magnetism in a permanent magnet.*

(Q). General statements concerning magnetism.

The phenomena of current electricity and of magnetism are almost, if not quite, inseparably connected. In the medium surrounding a conductor conveying a current of electricity, magnets are acted upon by a force. Such a region is naturally called a magnetic field of force.

Imaginary lines showing at all points the direction in which the force acts are called *lines of force.* Greater intensity of a field of force is usually represented by a greater number of these lines intersecting a given area. If masses of iron are brought into such a magnetic field of force, the intensity of the field is greatly increased, in the neighborhood of those parts of the iron where the lines enter and emerge. The same is also true of some other substances. This fact may be explained by saying that these substances are much better conductors of lines of force than the air or ether, or that their "permeability" for lines of force is greater than the permeability of the air. Such good conductors of magnetic lines of force are called magnetic substances.

Those portions of the magnetic lines which lie within a magnetic substance are called *lines of magnetization.* A magnetic substance containing these lines is said to be magnetized, and is called a magnet. Some magnetic substances, steel for example, may be removed from the magnetic field where they have been magnetized, without losing their magnetic properties. The magnetic field surrounding the magnet moves with the magnet, and seems to have a fixed connection with it, independent of any other magnetic field. Such a body is called a permanent magnet.

In all localities where the experiment has been performed, such a magnet is acted on by a force. It follows that there is a magnetic field surrounding the earth. A magnet suspended in a magnetic field so as to turn freely about its center of gravity always comes to rest with its longer axis in a particular direction. The direction of this axis is always tangent to lines of force, the positive direction of the line being the direction in which the end of the magnet points, which points north in the earth's field. The end of a magnet which points north in the earth's field is called the positive end, the other end being called negative.

If such a suspended magnet be brought into a field about the negative end of another magnet, it will set itself with its positive end pointing towards the negative end of the other magnet. The reverse is true in the field about the positive end of the second magnet. It follows from this that the lines of force of the field due to a magnet diverge from its positive end, and converge towards its negative end. Such a region within a magnet, towards which the lines of force converge, or from which they diverge, is called a pole.

A convenient statement of the fact that a magnet always tends to point in a particular direction in a magnetic field may be based upon the principle just laid down ; viz. :

The positive pole of a magnet always tends to move along magnetic lines of force in the positive direction, and the negative pole in the negative direction. The mutual action of two magnets when brought near together may also be stated in the following form: *Like poles repel each other, and unlike poles attract each other.*

In a real magnet, lines of force diverge from a *region* in the positive half, curve around through space, and converge to a *region* in the negative half, and then pass on through the magnet as lines of magnetization. The idea of a pole, as a *point* towards which lines of force converge, is a highly idealized conception. It is a very useful conception, however, and by most authors is made the basis of the whole system of electromagnetic units. This ideal conception of a magnet pole is not likely to lead to error except in one case; namely, when the intensity of the force at a point in a magnetic field is expressed as a function of the strength of its poles, and the distance between them, as in Exp. Q_3.

An ideal magnet with ideal poles of a given strength and a given distance between them may be conceived, such that the magnetic field would be at four symmetrical points, exactly like the field produced by a real magnet. But the field of the real magnet would be different at all other points from the field of the ideal magnet. For example, the field of a magnet, quite close to its middle point, is such as would be produced by an ideal magnet with poles comparatively close together, while the reverse is true for a point near either end of the magnet. The error introduced into Exp. Q_3 by the assumption made is quite small whenever $L > 3\,l$.

Notwithstanding what has been said about magnet poles, the term "magnetic moment" has a perfectly definite physical meaning. If a magnet be placed in a magnetic field with its axis at right angles to the lines of force, it will be acted upon by a turning force. If the moment of this turning force be represented by G, and the intensity of the field by H, the magnetic moment of the magnet may be defined by the relation

$$MH = G, \qquad (101)$$

in which M is the magnetic moment.

Experiment Q₁. Lines of force and the study of magnetic fields.

Surrounding every magnet and every current of electricity there is a magnetic field. The earth also has a magnetic field surrounding it. The object of this experiment is to investigate the direction in which the force acts in such fields; that is to say, the direction of the lines of force.

For this purpose place a sheet of glass immediately above the magnet whose field is to be investigated, and scatter over it iron filings, allowing them to drop from a height of 8 or 10 inches. If the magnet is sufficiently strong, the filings will arrange themselves in "lines of force." A slight tapping or jarring of the glass will probably make the magnetic curves more perfect. Sheet metal (not iron) or paper may be used instead of glass if desired, but the glass plate has the advantage of allowing the position of the magnet to be clearly seen. Permanent records of the curves may be obtained by allowing the filings to arrange themselves upon a sheet of blue print paper, and exposing the latter to the sun while the filings are still in position.

Among cases which may be studied to advantage in this manner are the following:

(1) The field of a single "horseshoe" magnet.

(2) Two magnets with like poles near each other.

(3) Two magnets with unlike poles near each other.

(4) A bar magnet placed in the neighborhood of a horseshoe magnet.

(5) The field of two horseshoe magnets placed vertically, their four poles forming a square.

Many other more complicated arrangements will suggest themselves. Observe also the effect of pieces of soft iron, placed in different positions in the field, upon the form of the curves obtained. If the piece of soft iron seems to produce little effect, bring it in contact with one pole.

The direction of the magnetic force at any point will be indicated by the direction in which a small compass needle will set itself when placed at that point. By shifting the compass from place to place, the direction of the force can thus be found at any number of points.

To study the field by this method, place one or more magnets in the middle of a large board ruled in squares, which has been previously set with two opposite edges parallel to the magnetic meridian. The board should be so large that at the edges the field due to the magnets is decidedly weaker than the earth's field.

By means of a small compass determine the direction of the lines of force for a large number of points. There should be enough of these observations, so that the direction in which the compass needle would point if placed anywhere on the board may be known within rather narrow limits.

Make a diagram (to scale) of the board and magnets, and at each point where the compass was placed draw a little arrow to show the direction of the force. An arrow should also be drawn somewhere on the board to show the direction of the earth's field. Map the whole field on the board by means of lines representing the lines of force. These lines do not need to pass through the arrows, but should be so drawn as to represent the direction in which the compass needle would point if placed upon corresponding points on the board.

The field so mapped is the resultant field of the magnets and of the horizontal component of the earth's field. Therefore, it must not be expected that all the lines of force will enter a magnet.

In the neighborhood of every magnet or system of magnets there are in general two or more points where the magnetic field due to them exactly neutralizes the earth's field. At these points there will be no directive force acting on the compass needle, and on opposite sides of these points the needle will point in opposite directions. Locate these points on your diagram.

Addenda to the report:

(1) State the law of magnetic force.

(2) Define: unit magnet pole; magnetic field of force; field of unit intensity; magnetic difference of potential; magnetic potential at a point; equipotential surfaces; magnetic lines of force; unit line of force, or unit tube of force.

(3) Show that lines of force and equipotential surfaces are mutually perpendicular.

(4) Indicate the reason why, in this experiment, the filings move away from points directly above the magnet, especially in the neighborhood of the poles.

(5) Draw the horizontal sections of several equipotential surfaces whose potentials differ by equal amounts.

(6) Assume that the potential of any point a centimeter from the north pole is 100, and that the surface of zero potential bisects the distance between the poles, and determine approximately from the map and from the assumptions already made, the magnetic force at several points 10 or 20 cm. distant from the magnet.

EXPERIMENT Q_2. Determination of the magnetic moment of a bar magnet by the method of oscillations.

A magnet suspended by a torsionless fiber with its axis horizontal will come to rest with its magnetic axis in the magnetic meridian. If the magnet is turned so as to make a *small* angle with the magnetic meridian, the moment of the force tending to restore the magnet to its position of equilibrium is directly proportional to the angular displacement. The resulting motion of the magnet, when left free to vibrate, is therefore a simple harmonic motion.

The periodic time is dependent upon the magnetic moment of the magnet, its moment of inertia, and the horizontal intensity of the magnetic field in which it is suspended. The following equation may be derived by equating the kinetic energy of the magnet at its mid-position to the potential energy when at the end of its swing. The method of derivation is the same as that pursued in Exp. E_1.

$$MH = \frac{4\pi^2 K}{T^2}.\tag{102}$$

To perform the experiment:

(1) Place the magnet in a small wire stirrup, and suspend it by a few untwisted silk fibers. It should be suspended in a box with glass ends, to avoid the effect of air currents, and a position should be chosen at a distance from movable masses of iron. If the bar is rather strongly magnetized, the torsion of the silk fiber may be neglected, or, if desired, it may be eliminated by determining the ratio of the moment of torsion to the moment of the magnetic forces.*

(2) Set the magnet to vibrating through an arc of not more than five degrees. Determine the period of oscillation by the method of Exp. A_5, or by counting the number of passages in the same direction during five or six minutes. The period should be determined several times, and as carefully as possible.

(3) Measure the length, diameter, and mass of the bar, and from these data compute its moment of inertia. If the value of the horizontal component of magnetism for the place where the magnet was suspended is known, the value of M may be computed from the above equation.

The method of oscillations may be used, if desired, to determine the value of H in different parts of the laboratory; in which case the period of oscillation must first be determined from observations taken in a locality where H is known.

If this experiment and the following one be performed with the same magnet and at the same place, both H and M may be determined in absolute measure.

---

* Kohlrausch, Physical Measurements, p. 128.

Addenda to the report:

(1) State the effect upon the period of oscillation, if in the above experiment the magnet were not quite horizontal.

(2) State the effect upon the period, if the magnet were bent into the form of a horseshoe, without changing its intensity of magnetization.

(3) Determine the average intensity of magnetization in the magnet experimented with, and indicate in what part of the magnet it is the greatest, and in what part the least.

(4) Compute the ergs of work that would be required to rotate the magnet 180° about a vertical axis in the earth's field from the position of rest.

(5) Assuming the dip 75°, compute the work required to rotate the magnet from a vertical position through 180° about a horizontal axis.

EXPERIMENT Q_3. **Determination of magnetic moment by the magnetometer.**

When two forces act at right angles to each other, their resultant makes an angle with each of the forces such that the tangent is the ratio of the two forces. See Fig. 46, in which a and b are the forces and α and β the angles which their resultant r makes with them respectively.

Obviously, $\tan \alpha = \dfrac{b}{a}$ and $\tan \beta = \dfrac{a}{b}$.

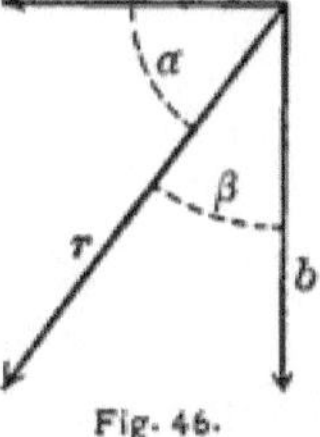

Fig. 46.

This fact may be used to determine the ratio of the intensity of two magnetic fields at any given point.

When a magnet is so placed that the field due to it at a given point is at right angles to the field due to the earth, a short magnetic needle placed at that point will be deflected from the magnetic meridian through an angle whose tangent is equal to the ratio between the intensities of the two components of the field at that point.

The needle must be *short* with respect to the distance to the magnet, for otherwise its ends would extend too far beyond the point at which the field of the magnet has the intensity given below.

The strength of the field at any point due to a magnet is a known function of its magnetic moment, the distance between its poles, and the distance of the point from the magnet.

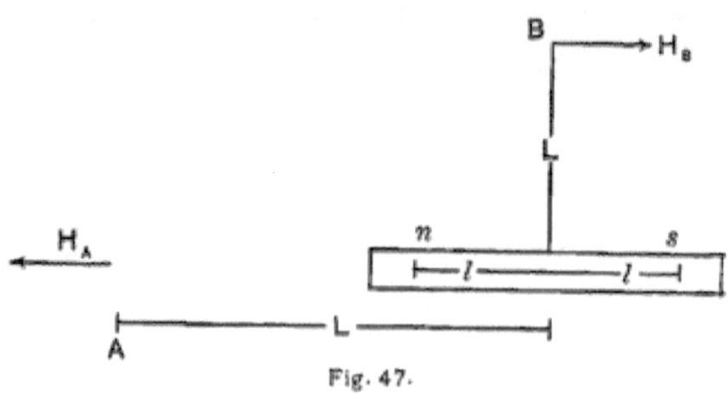

Fig. 47.

For example, the strength of the field at A, due to a magnet whose poles are at n and s (Fig. 47), is

$$H_A = \frac{2\,ML}{(L^2 - l^2)^2} \tag{103}$$

At B, the strength of the field due to the same magnet is

$$H_B = \frac{M}{(L^2 + l^2)^{\frac{3}{2}}}, \tag{104}$$

in which M is the magnetic moment of the magnet, $2\,l$ the distance between its poles, and L the distance of A or B from the center of the magnet.

If the magnet is at right angles to the magnetic meridian, a magnetic needle placed at A will be deflected from the meridian through an angle δ according to the relation

$$\frac{M}{H} = \frac{(L^2 - l^2)^2}{2\,L}\tan \delta, \tag{105}$$

and there will be a corresponding relation for the position B.

These equations may also be derived by an application of the principle of moments to the magnetic forces acting on the suspended needle.

The magnetometer consists, essentially, of a suspended magnetic needle, a bar, 1 m. or more long, upon which to place the magnet with which the experiment is to be performed, and some means of measuring the angle through which the needle is turned.

In preparation for this experiment, adjust the magnetometer bar at right angles to the magnetic meridian. This may be done with sufficient accuracy with the aid of a small compass needle. If greater accuracy is desired, adjust the magnetometer bar by trial so that the same deflection is produced when the magnet is placed on opposite sides of the magnetometer needle, at the same distance from it, and with the same *pole pointing towards it.*

Having completed the adjustment, proceed as follows:

(1) Place the magnet on the bar with its poles pointing east and west, and at a distance of not less than 20 or 30 cm. east of the magnetometer needle.

(2) Observe the magnetometer reading by means of a telescope and scale, and the mirror on the magnetic needle. Then turn the magnet end for end, keeping its distance from the needle the same, and again observe the reading. Half the difference of the two readings is a measure of the deflection of the needle from its position of rest on account of the presence of the magnet.

(3) Reverse the magnet in this way several times so as to get the average of a number of observations.

(4) Finally place the magnet at the same distance to the west of the magnetometer needle and proceed as before. From the average of all the deflections observed, and the distance between the mirror and scale, compute the angle through which the needle is deflected.

As a check the observations should be repeated with the

magnet at such a distance from the needle as to produce a deflection which is considerably greater or less than that first used.

The following table gives typical data and shows the method of presenting them.

MAGNETIC MOMENT BY THE MAGNETOMETER.

North Pole Pointing.	Distance of Center of Mag. from Needle.	Scale Reading.	Deflection in Scale Div.	
		48.37		Distance between poles of magnet, $2l = 22$ cm.
West	54 W.	3.04	45.33	Horizontal intensity $= 0.145$
East	54 W.	94.62	46.25	Average deflection $= 45.91$
East	54 E.	95.63	47.37	Distance from mirror to scale $= 91.1$ scale division
West	54 E.	3.57	44.69	$\tan 2\theta = 0.5037$
		48.26		$2\theta = 26° 44'$
				$\tan \theta = 0.2376$
West	80 W.	35.86	12.40	Magnetic moment $= 2436$
East	80 W.	60.68	12.42	Average deflection $= 12.43$
East	80 E.	60.85	12.59	$\tan 2\theta' = 0.1364$
West	80 E.	35.95	12.31	$2\theta' = 7° 46'$
		48.26		$\tan \theta' = 0.0679$
				Magnetic moment $= 2426$

In the above formula, $2l$ is the distance between the poles of the magnet, and is therefore less than the length of the bar itself. The position of the poles, and therefore the length $2l$, may be approximately determined by the aid of a small compass.

If H is known, M may be computed; or, if the product MH is known, both M and H may be computed in absolute measure. This product may be obtained by the method described in Exp. Q_2.

If the magnetometer admits of it, a similar series of observations should be taken with the magnet placed at points north and south of the magnetometer needle, its poles pointing east and west as before.

Addenda to the report:

(1) Determine the strength of each pole of the magnet experimented with.

(2) Calculate the magnetic force and potential due to the magnet for two or three points in its neighborhood.

(3) Calculate the work required to carry a magnet pole of strength equal to either pole of the magnet, from one pole face to the other pole face, along any path.

(4) Compare the pull on either magnetic pole with the pull of gravity on one gram for a case in which the inclination of the earth's lines of force is $75°$.

EXPERIMENT Q_4. **Measurement of the intensity of a magnetic field.**

The intensity of a magnetic field at different points may be compared with the intensity of the earth's field by either of the methods made use of in Exps. Q_2 and Q_3. In the following experiment, these methods are to be used in measuring the magnetic field at a series of points in the neighborhood of a permanent magnet.

I.

Place the magnet with its axis in the magnetic meridian, its negative pole pointing north. For all points to the east or west of the middle of the magnet, the intensity of the field will be the arithmetical sum of the earth's horizontal intensity and the intensity of the field at that point, due to the magnet. For all points to the north or south of the magnet, the intensity of the field will be the difference of these two quantities.

Determine the period of oscillation of a small magnet of any shape, for a series of points on a line at right angles to it, and bisecting the distance between its poles. Do the same for a series of points north or south of the magnet. For each point, the number of oscillations produced in three or four minutes should be determined.

As the intensity of the field due to the magnet varies most rapidly near it, the points of observation should be closer together the nearer they are to the magnet. A good series of distances is the geometric series $\frac{1}{16}L$, $\frac{1}{8}L$, $\frac{1}{4}L$, $\cdots 2L$, in which L is the length of the magnet.

As in Exp. Q_2, we have

$$H_P \pm H = \frac{4\pi^2 K}{M T_P^2} = \frac{C}{T_P^2},\qquad\qquad (106)$$

in which H_P is the intensity of the field due to the magnet at the point where the time of vibration is T_P, H is the horizontal intensity of the earth's magnetism, and C is a constant depending upon the magnet. C may be eliminated by taking the time of vibration at a distance from the magnet where H_P is zero. H_P can then be computed in terms of H, or if H is known, it may be computed in absolute measure.

Plat a curve with distances from the magnet as abscissas, and corresponding values of H_P as ordinates.

II.

Place a large bar magnet at right angles to the magnetic meridian, as in Exp. Q_3. For points "A" and "B," the ratio of the intensity of the field, due to the magnet and the earth's horizontal intensity, will be equal to the tangent of the angle through which a magnetic needle will be deflected from the magnetic meridian, if placed at that point.

Place a compass with a circle graduated to degrees at a series of points "A," at distances from the magnet as in I above. For each point determine the deflection from the meridian as follows: Read both ends of the needle, then reverse the magnet and read again. The angle through which the needle has been turned is double the angle of deflection from the meridian. In the same manner make a series of observations for points "B." Plat a curve with distances from the magnet as abscissas, and the intensity of the field due to the magnet as ordinates.

Addenda to the report:

(1) From the equations in Exp. Q_3, and several points on one of the above curves, compute values of M. The points taken should not be observed points unless these points happen to fall exactly upon the curve.

(2) Note whether these values of M show a progressive increase or decrease, and if so, indicate cause of the variation.

EXPERIMENT Q_5. **Distribution of "free" magnetism in a permanent magnet.**

For purposes of calculation, the distribution of imaginary magnetic matter in a magnet may be considered in two ways: as a distribution throughout its volume, or over its surface. The volume distribution or intensity of magnetization is greatest midway between the poles. The surface distribution is greatest near the ends, and is vanishingly small midway between the poles. This imaginary magnetic matter is supposed to be so distributed as to produce by its attraction or repulsion the same field of force that the magnet produces. From this we see that the quantity of surface magnetism, or "free" magnetism, as it is called, is everywhere proportional to the number of unit lines of force which enter or emerge from the magnet.

I.

The distribution of magnetism may be determined by measuring the force necessary to detach a small, soft iron armature from the magnet. For measuring this force use a pair of balances or a spiral spring, whose extension can be readily determined.

Determine in this way the force necessary to detach the armature for ten or twenty points along the magnet from one end to the other. The magnet may not be symmetrically magnetized; if not, the forces at symmetrical points will not be equal. Plat a curve with distances from the center of the magnet as abscissas, and the forces necessary to detach the armature as ordinates.

In considering that this curve represents the distribution of magnetism along the magnet, two things should be remembered:

(1) By induction, the distribution of magnetism is slightly changed on account of the presence of the armature. If the armature is quite small with respect to the magnet, this may be neglected.

(2) The force with which the soft iron armature is attracted to the magnet is proportional to the square of the magnetism at that point. This is true, since the force is proportional to the product of the magnetism of the magnet and the magnetism of the armature, in the immediate neighborhood of the point of contact, but the induced magnetism of the armature is itself proportional to the magnetism of the permanent magnet.

II.

The distribution of magnetism may also be determined by the method of oscillations.

Place a bar magnet in a vertical position, and determine the period of oscillation of a small magnet for a series of positions along the magnet, and quite close to it. These points should be north or south of the magnet.

As in experiment Q_4, we have

$$H_p \pm H = \frac{C}{T_p^2},\qquad(107)$$

in which H_p is the intensity for the point P of the field due to the magnet, resolved in a direction perpendicular to its length.

If the point P is quite close to the magnet, H_p will be proportional to the free magnetism at the corresponding point of the magnet. As in (1), plat a curve with distances from the center of the magnet as abscissas, and corresponding values of H_p as ordinates.

CHAPTER VI.

GROUP R: THE ELECTRIC CURRENT.

(R) *General statements;* (R$_1$) *The law of the tangent galvanom-eter;* (R$_2$) *Measurement of current by electrolysis;* (R$_3$) *Measurement of the constant of a sensitive galvanometer;* (R$_4$) *Theory of shunts;* (R$_5$) *Measurement of current by means of the galvanometer.*

(R). General statements concerning the electric current.

The electric current may be defined as the rate at which electrification is transferred, or the amount of electricity which passes through a given plane cutting the circuit at right angles to the lines of flow, in a unit time. When two bodies which differ in potential are connected by means of a conductor, the fleeting phenomena which accompany the electric discharge occur, and we have a transient current; if the difference of potential be maintained constant by the expenditure of work, there will be a permanent current.

If current were always measured by electrolysis, the idea of current would be a derived conception involving *time.* Since, however, when a current flows in a conductor there is a magnetic field surrounding the conductor, the intensity of which at any given point is always directly proportional to the current, it is more convenient to measure the latter by means of the field which it produces. In this way we reach a conception of current which does not directly involve time.

Those instruments which measure currents by comparing the field produced with the earth's magnetic field, or with the earth's field as modified by controlling or regulating magnets, are called galvanometers..

The lines of force surrounding a wire carrying a current may easily be mapped by the aid of iron filings. Figs. 48 and 49 are such maps showing the field around a straight wire. The former was obtained by cutting a sensitive plate and passing the conductor, the field of which was to be mapped,

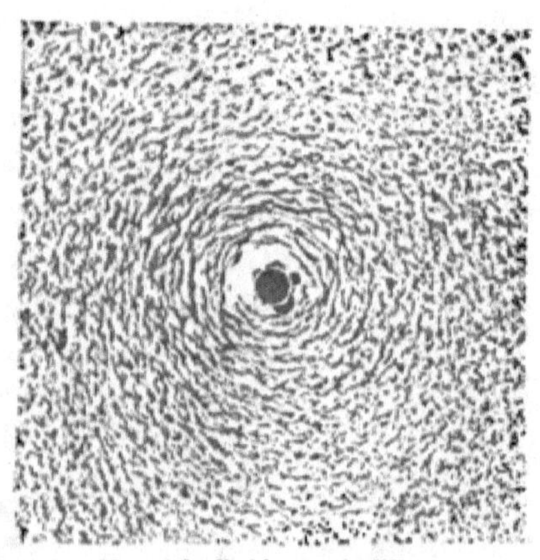

Fig. 48.—Map of the Field around a Wire carrying Current (from a Photograph).

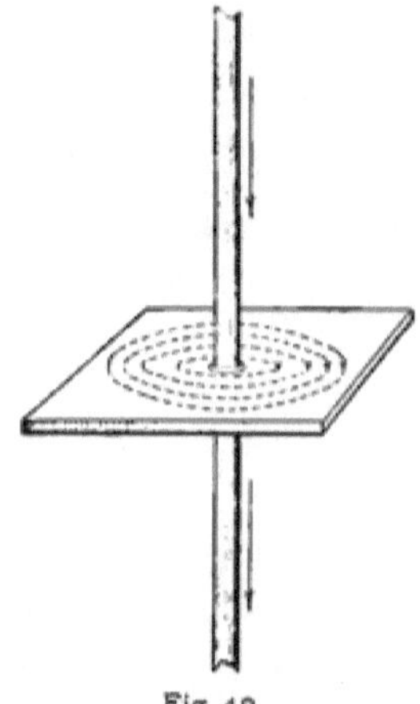

Fig. 49.

through the hole. The plate was then fastened in a position at right angles to the conductor. Current was sent through the latter, and the surface of the film was strewn with iron filings. These operations having been completed by the red light of the developing-room, the plate was then exposed for three seconds to gas-light, after which the photograph was developed, giving the map.

The direction of the lines of force, at any point in the field, produced by a current, is always at right angles to the plane containing the point and the current. The intensity of this field may be deduced from Laplace's law, of which the following equation is a statement :

$$dH_p = \frac{I \sin \theta ds}{r^2} \tag{108}$$

In this expression, dH_P is the intensity of the magnetic field at the point P, due to the short element ds of the current of intensity I; r is the distance from the point P to the element ds, and θ is the angle which the direction of the element ds makes with the line drawn from it to the point P.

The absolute unit of current in the electromagnetic system is *that current, a unit length of which will produce unit magnetic field at unit distance from the current.* It follows that the C. G. S. unit current in the electromagnetic system, flowing around a circle of 1 cm. radius, will produce at the center of the circle a field whose intensity is 2π units.

The Chamber of Delegates of the Electrical Congress at Chicago adopted "*as a [practical] unit of current the international ampere, which is one-tenth of the unit of current of the C. G. S. system of electromagnetic units, and which is represented sufficiently well for practical use by the unvarying current which, when passed through a solution of nitrate of silver, in water, and in accordance with the accompanying specifications,* deposits silver at the rate of 0.001118 grams per second.*"

---

* In this specification, the term "silver voltameter" means the arrangement of apparatus by means of which an electric current is passed through a solution of nitrate of silver in water. The silver voltameter measures the total electrical quantity which has passed during the time of the experiment, and by noting this time, the time-average of the current, or if the current has been kept constant, the current itself can be deduced.

In employing the silver voltameter to measure currents of about 1 ampere, the following arrangements should be adopted:

The cathode on which the silver is to be deposited should take the form of a platinum bowl, not less than 10 cm. in diameter, and from 4 to 5 cm. in depth.

The anode should be a plate of pure silver some 30 sq. cm. in area, and 2 or 3 mm. in thickness.

This is supported horizontally in the liquid near the top of the solution by a platinum wire passed through holes in the plate at opposite corners. To prevent the disintegrated silver which is formed on the anode from falling on to the kathode, the anode should be wrapped round with pure filter paper secured at the back with sealing-wax.

The liquid should consist of a neutral solution of pure silver-nitrate containing about 15 parts by weight of the nitrate to 85 parts of water.

The resistance of the voltameter changes somewhat as the current passes. To

The intensity of the field at the center of the galvanometer coils produced by unit current flowing in the coils is called the *true* constant of the galvanometer, and is generally denoted by G. For many galvanometers, this constant may be computed from Laplace's law, and the dimensions, position, and number of turns of the coils.

If a galvanometer coil is placed with the plane of its windings in the magnetic meridian, the field produced by it

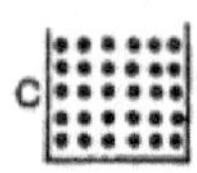

at the center of the coil (or at any point on its axis) will be at right angles to the earth's field. Let CC' (Fig. 50) represent the horizontal section of the galvanometer coil. The intensity of the field at the point O, due to the current I flowing in the coils is, GI. If H represents the horizontal

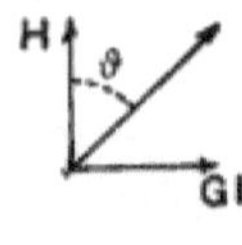

intensity of the field at the point O due to the earth (and regulating magnets), the resultant of these two fields will make an angle δ with the plane of the coils such that

$$I = \frac{H}{G}\tan \delta. \tag{109}$$

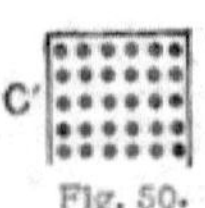

If a *short* magnetic needle be suspended at the point O, it will come to rest with its magnetic axis in the plane of the resultant magnetic field through the point O. That is, it will turn through the

Fig. 50.

angle δ from the position of equilibrium when no current flows. If the magnetic needle is not short, its ends are liable to extend too far beyond the *point* O at which the field due to the current I has the intensity GI. If the current is required in amperes instead of in absolute units of current, the above equation becomes

$$I = 10\,\frac{H}{G}\tan \delta. \tag{110}$$

---

prevent these changes having too great an effect on the current, some resistance besides that of the voltameter should be inserted in the circuit. The total metallic resistance of the circuit should not be less than 10 ohms. — [Extract from Bulletin 30 U. S. Coast and Geodetic Survey, embodying the specifications referred to above.]

The constant quantity $10\dfrac{H}{G}$ is called the "reduction factor," the "working constant," or, for brevity, simply the constant of the galvanometer. If this be represented by I_0, we have

$$I = I_0 \tan \delta. \qquad (111)$$

From (111) it is obvious that the galvanometer constant I_0 is that current which will produce a deflection of 45°.

In this discussion it is assumed that the friction of the needle on the pivot or the torsion of the suspending fiber is negligible. This is generally a safe assumption except in sensitive galvanometers, where a very small needle or an astatic system is used. In such cases, the moment of the force of torsion tending to bring the needle back to its position of equilibrium may be very considerable compared with the moment of the magnetic forces tending to return the needle to the magnetic meridian. Moreover, there may be a twist in the fiber, such that the needle does not return to the magnetic meridian when the current ceases to flow in the galvanometer coils.

In Fig. 50, above, it is obvious that if the galvanometer current is reversed, the direction of the field GI will be reversed. In this case the magnetic needle will be turned through the same angle δ, with its north end pointing on the opposite side of the meridian. This offers a means of setting the galvanometer coils in the plane of the magnetic meridian, if they are not already so adjusted.

For this purpose, we send a current through the galvanometer, and observe the angle through which the needle has turned when it comes to rest. We then reverse the current through the galvanometer, and observe the corresponding angle of deflection on the opposite side of the position of equilibrium. If these angles are not equal, we turn the galvanometer coils in such a direction as to increase the smaller angle of deflection, and repeat until the difference of the two angles is a small fraction of either one of them.   In doing this it must be remembered that if the scale is turned with the galvanometer coils, the needle will come to rest at a new position with respect to the scale ; *i.e.* the galvanometer will have a new " zero point."

In measuring current by means of a galvanometer, angles of deflection should be determined for the current, both direct and reversed.   There are two reasons for this :

(1) If the galvanometer coil makes a small angle with the magnetic meridian, it may be proved* that the mean of the deflections for direct and reversed current will be in error by a small quantity of the second order.

(2) The equilibrium position or zero point of a galvanometer needle is constantly varying, the fluctuations being due to variations in the earth's magnetic field.   Now it is quite as convenient to observe the reading for reversed current as it is to observe the zero reading for every measurement.

In measurements by this method of direct and reversed deflections a commutator, or reversing key, is used.   A simple form consists of a block of wood containing four holes filled with mercury, and a second block containing two U-shaped conductors of heavy copper wire.   The device is shown in Fig. 51.   The wires leading from the battery are to be connected to mercury cups at m_1, m_2, while the galvanometer is connected to the remaining cups.   If the second block (*b*) containing the U-shaped conductors be placed upon the first with the conductors dipping into the mercury cups, the current from the battery will flow in one direction through the

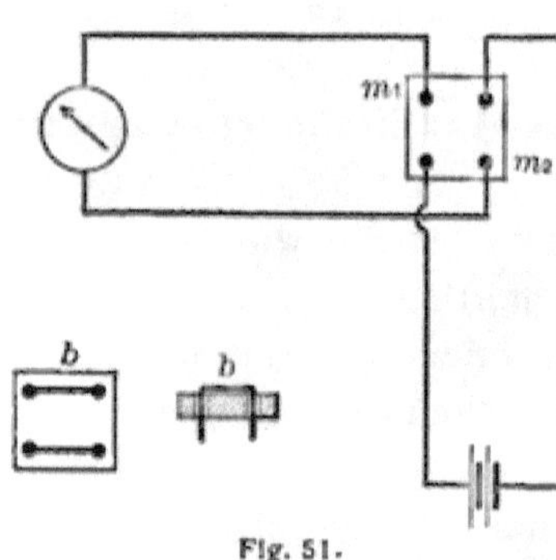

Fig. 51.

---

* See Mascart and Joubert, Leçons sur l'électricité et le magnetism, vol. 2, p. 235; also Nichols, The Galvanometer, Lecture 2.

galvanometer, while the current through the galvanometer will be reversed by lifting the second block, turning it 90° about a vertical axis, and again dropping the conductors into the mercury cups.

The angle of deflection of the galvanometer needle may be determined directly from the reading of a long pointer moving over a circular graduated scale. In this case both ends

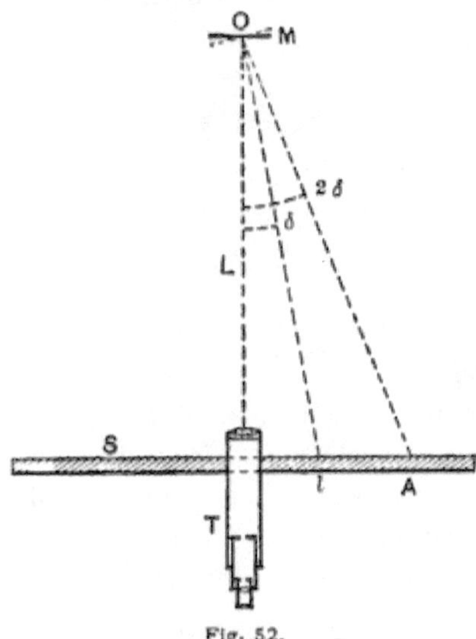

Fig. 52.

of the pointer should be read in order to eliminate eccentricity, as well as to get a more accurate value of the deflection.

In many cases the angle of deflection is determined by means of a small mirror permanently attached to the magnetic needle. With mirror galvanometers either a telescope and scale, or a lamp and scale, may be used. In either case, the angle of deflection is computed in the same way.

Let OM (Fig. 52) be the horizontal section of the mirror attached to the galvanometer needle, S the scale, and T the telescope. The telescope and scale should be adjusted at right angles to each other, and so placed that the portion of the scale immediately below (or above) the telescope is seen reflected from the mirror through the telescope when no current flows through the galvanometer. If the galvanometer needle be now deflected through the angle δ, a new portion of the scale will be seen reflected from the mirror. From the law of reflection, the angle which the ray reflected from the mirror into the telescope makes with the normal must be equal to the angle which the incident ray AO makes with the same normal. It follows that the angle AOT between the reflected and incident rays is equal to 2δ. If l is the deflection along the scale from the zero point, and L the distance of the scale from the mirror, we have

$$\tan 2\,\delta = \frac{l}{L}. \tag{112}$$

From this equation and a table of tangents, δ, and hence $\tan \delta$, may be deduced.

It may be readily shown than when δ is quite small, $\tan \delta$ is very nearly proportional to l. Under this condition it follows that current is very nearly proportional to deflection, and we may use the equation

$$I = I_0 l, \tag{113}$$

in which I_0 is the constant per scale division. The error in using this approximate value for the current is as follows :

When $\dfrac{l}{L} = \dfrac{1}{10}$, the error is about 0.0025.

When $\dfrac{l}{L} = \dfrac{1}{4}$, the error is about 0.0100.

When $\dfrac{l}{L} = \dfrac{1}{2}$, the error is about 0.0600.

From an inspection of Fig. 52 a, it is obvious that a scale might be so curved that deflection of the ray of light, as measured along the scale, would be directly proportional to

$\tan \delta$. This curve would not be one easy to construct, but it can easily be proved that if a scale S' be made upon the arc of a circle whose radius is $\frac{8}{5}$ of the distance from the mirror to the scale immediately under the telescope, the error in assuming that $\tan \delta$ is proportional to the deflection along the scale does not exceed 0.001 for any deflection of the *needle* not exceeding 24°.

When the current is reversed in a galvanometer, it often takes several minutes for the needle to come to rest. Time

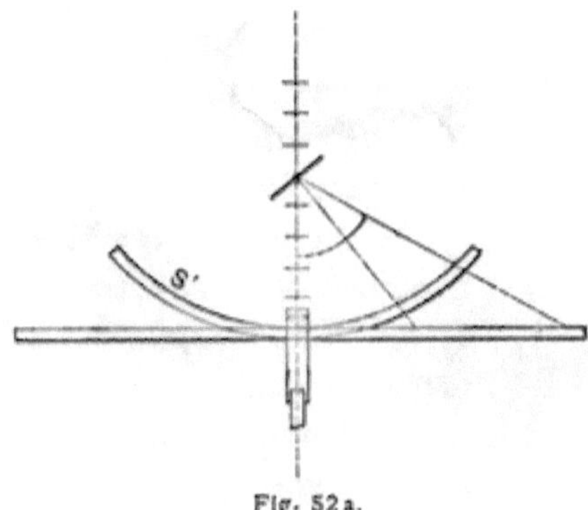

Fig. 52 a.

may be saved by closing the circuit as the galvanometer needle gets about to the end of its free swing in the direction in which the current would deflect it.

There are two principal methods of "damping" the oscillations of galvanometer needles, and making the instrument nearly or quite "dead-beat."

(1) By the attachment of a mica or aluminum vane to the needle. This vane, by friction against the air in an inclosed place, brings the needle to rest much more quickly than would otherwise be the case. The action may be increased by suspending the vane in a vessel of oil.

(2) By suspending the magnetic needle within a cavity in a small mass of copper. As the magnet moves in this cavity, causing the lines of force to sweep through the copper,

currents of electricity are induced. These currents, as stated in Lenz's law, are always in such a direction as to oppose the motion which produced them.

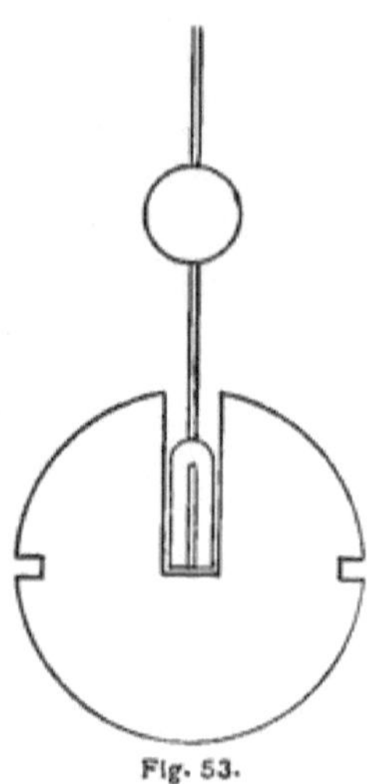

Fig. 53.

The best example of this is found in the type of instrument first designed by Siemens. In this form of galvanometer the magnetic needle is of the horseshoe type, ordinarily called a bell magnet. This magnet is suspended in a hole but little larger than itself in a copper sphere. Fig. 53 shows a vertical section of the copper sphere, with the inclosed magnet; Fig. 54 represents a cross-section of the same magnet.

In the use of sensitive galvanometers, the question will often arise as to what type of galvanometer will be most sensitive for a particular purpose. This question cannot be settled in general terms, on account of the great difference between the different types. The more restricted question as to what number of turns will be most sensitive for a particular purpose may be easily determined.

If the type of galvanometer, the size of the coils, the mass of copper in them, and the closeness of the turns to the needle remain the same, it may readily be proved that that instrument will be most sensitive whose *internal resistance is equal to the external resistance in series with it.*

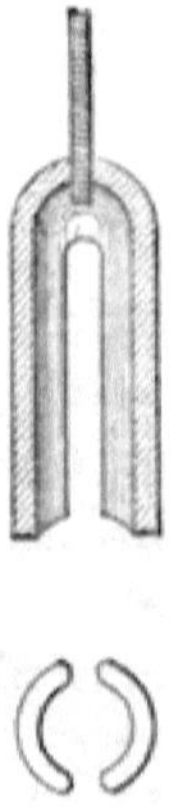

This relation may be demonstrated as follows : Let V be the volume, L the total length, s the cross-section, R_g the resistance, and ρ the specific resistance of the wire to be used in the galvanometer coils. Then we have

Fig. 54.

$$R_g = \rho \frac{L}{s} = \frac{\rho}{V} L^2. \qquad (114)$$

If I_0 is the constant per scale division of the galvanometer, we have $I_0 = \dfrac{C}{L}$, in which C is a constant depending on the type of galvanometer.

If E is the electromotive force, R the external resistance, and δ the galvanometer deflection, we have

$$\frac{E}{R_g + R} = I_0 \delta.$$

$$\therefore \quad \frac{E}{\frac{\rho}{V} L^2 + R} = \frac{C}{L} \delta. \tag{115}$$

If this equation is differentiated with respect to L, we have

$$\frac{d\delta}{dL} = \frac{E\left(R - \frac{\rho}{V} L^2\right)}{C\left(\frac{\rho}{V} L^2 + R\right)^2}.$$

Consequently δ will be a maximum when

$$R = \frac{\rho}{V} L^2 = R_g, \tag{116}$$

a result that coincides with the statement which we desire to verify.

EXPERIMENT R_1. **Law of the tangent galvanometer.**

If a galvanometer coil is placed with the plane of its windings in the magnetic meridian, the magnetic field due to a current circulating in the coils will be (in the axis of the coil) at right angles to the earth's magnetic field. The resultant of these two fields will therefore make an angle with the magnetic meridian whose tangent is the ratio of the intensity of the earth's field to the field due to the current in the galvanometer coils. A *short* magnetic needle suspended anywhere in the axis of the coil will set itself along this resultant direction. If the needle is not a short one, it will, when considerably deflected from the meridian, extend beyond the axis to points where the two components of the field are not at right angles to each other. Therefore the tangent law will no longer hold.

This experiment is intended to give a method of testing experimentally whether a given galvanometer obeys the law of tangents (*i.e.* whether the tangent of the angle of deflection is proportional to the current).

Connect the galvanometer in series with a resistance box and cell, and place a reversing key somewhere in the circuit so that the direction of the current in the galvanometer can be readily reversed. Then observe the reading of the galvanometer, with current both direct and reversed, for ten or twelve different values of the resistance in the box, choosing the resistances so that the deflection of the galvanometer is varied from the smallest that can be accurately observed up to the largest that can be used.

From the data thus obtained, plat a curve, using resistances as abscissas and cotangents of deflections as ordinates. If a reflecting galvanometer is used, it will be necessary to compute the angle of deflection from the linear deflection and the distance between mirror and scale. If the galvanometer obeys the tangent law, the curve obtained by platting as above should be a straight line. Draw a straight line, therefore, that passes as nearly as possible through all the points, and produce this line backward until it intersects the horizontal axis. The distance between the origin and this point of intersection is a measure of the resistance in the circuit outside the resistance box ; *i.e.* if we call this resistance R_0, then R_0 = galvanometer resistance + battery resistance + resistance of connecting wires.

Now, if E is the E. M. F. of the cell, and R the resistance in the box, then

$$I = I_0 \tan \delta = \frac{E}{R_0 + R}. \tag{117}$$

If E is known, and R_0 determined from the curve, as stated above, the constant of the galvanometer can be computed. In

making this computation, take the E. M. F. of a gravity cell as
1 volt.*

In some reflecting galvanometers in which the deflection is
small, the deflection itself is nearly proportional to the current;
i.e. if the deflection on the scale is δ, then $I = I_0 \delta$. To test
whether this is true in the case of the galvanometer used, plat a
curve with box resistances as abscissas, and reciprocals of deflections as ordinates. If $I = I_0 \delta$, the line obtained will be straight.

By some students, the following method of using the data
may be preferred. From the data, determine the value of R_0,
as in Exp. T_5. Compute the value of the current in each case

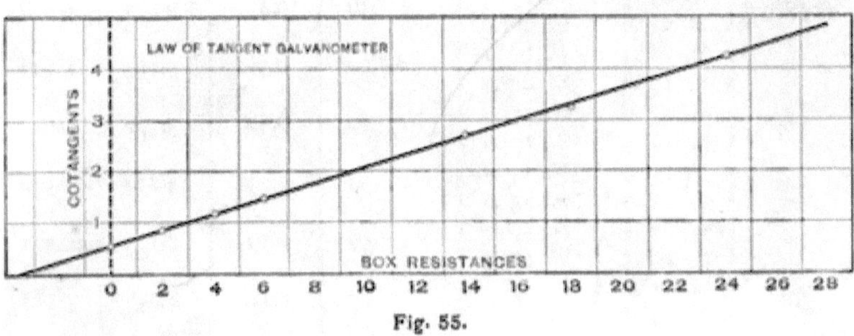

Fig. 55.

from Ohm's law. If the galvanometer obeys the tangent-law,
the ratio of current to tangent of deflection will be a constant.

The following data are typical of the results to be obtained,
and will serve to indicate the method of arranging and tabulating readings. The curve given in Fig. 55 shows the graphical
method of testing the deviation of the instrument from the law
of tangents.

---

* The E. M. F. of the battery used in taking the following data was 4 volts.

Law of Tangent Galvanometer.

Resistance in Box.	Galvanometer Readings.		Mean Deflection.	$\tan \delta$	$\cot \delta$	I_0
	Direct.	Reversed.				
0	N. 62°.5 S. 62°.0	N. 63°.0 S. 63°.5	62°.70	1.937	0.516	0.613
2	N. 50°.6 S. 50°.0	N. 50°.0 S. 50°.2	50°.20	1.200	0.833	0.625
4	N. 41°.5 S. 41°.0	N. 41°.0 S. 41°.2	41°.20	0.875	1.142	0.623
6	N. 34°.8 S. 34°.2	N. 34°.5 S. 35°.1	34°.80	0.695	1.439	0.616
10	N. 25°.5 S. 25°.0	N. 25°.5 S. 26°.0	25°.50	0.477	2.096	0.628
14	N. 20°.4 S. 19°.8	N. 20°.1 S. 20°.6	20°.20	0.368	2.718	0.627
18	N. 17°.0 S. 16°.5	N. 17°.0 S. 17°.6	17°.00	0.306	3.271	0.610
24	N. 13°.4 S. 12°.9	N. 13°.2 S. 13°.8	13°.30	0.236	4.230	0.620
30	N. 10°.9 S. 10°.3	N. 10°.9 S. 11°.4	10°.90	0.193	5.193	0.621
50	N. 7°.0 S. 6°.5	N. 7°.1 S. 7°.6	7°.05	0.124	8.086	0.613

From curve $R_0 = 3.33$ ohms.
"   " $I_0 = 0.620$ amp.

Last column computed assuming value of R_0 obtained from plat.

Experiment R_2. **Measurement of current by electrolysis.**

One of the most accurate methods of measuring current is by means of the amount of copper or silver deposited in a voltameter through which the current flows.

The voltameter deposit represents the integrated value of the current extending over considerable time; that is, it is a measure of the total quantity of the current which has flowed through the voltameter. This instrument, therefore, can only give an *average* value of the current. On account of this and other disadvantages, the voltameter is chiefly used to calibrate or determine the constants of instruments which depend for their indications on the magnetic field produced by the current.

In this experiment the spiral coil voltameter devised by Professor H. J. Ryan is to be used.* Two coils are to be prepared for each cell by wrapping copper wire on cylindrical forms. The size of the coils depends somewhat on the strength of the current used. With a current of from one to three amperes, a coil made of one and a half meters of wire of 1.5 mm. diameter will give satisfactory results.

The coils should be of about the same length, but should differ in diameter by 3 or 4 cm., so that the smaller may be placed inside the other without danger of touching. (See Fig. 56.) At one end of each coil the wire is to be brought out parallel with the axis for several inches for convenience in making connections. These two coils are to be used as the electrodes of a voltameter cell, current passing in through the outer coil and leaving the cell by the inner coil. The amount of copper deposited in a known time is then sufficient to determine the average current flowing. (One coulomb deposits 0.000328

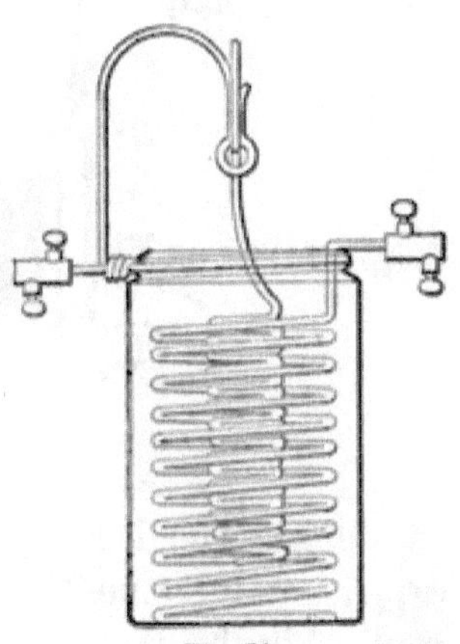

Fig. 56.

gram of copper.) The amount of copper dissolved is always slightly in excess of the amount deposited, and for various reasons is not so reliable a measure of the current.

In preparing the gain coils, great care must be used to have them thoroughly clean. A wire of suitable length for the purpose should be fastened by one end and then cleaned with sandpaper. When thoroughly cleaned, the wire is coiled upon a

* See Ryan, Transactions of the American Institute of Electrical Engineers, vol. 6, p. 322.

suitable form, the latter being first covered with clean filter-paper. After cleaning with the sandpaper, the coil should not be touched by the hand anywhere except at its terminal. If this work has been well done, the coils will be ready for use without any further cleansing. If not, pass the coil through a non-luminous Bunsen flame to remove oil, plunge it in a very dilute solution of sulphuric acid, and then into distilled water. To dry the coil rapidly and without danger of oxidation, it is first rolled on filter or blotting paper until only a thin film of water remains. This is rinsed off by dipping into strong alcohol. After again rolling on filter-paper, what little alcohol is left will quickly evaporate, leaving the coil dry and ready for

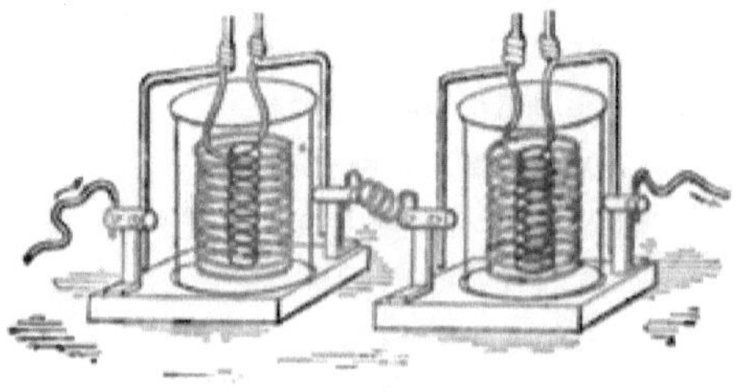

Fig. 57.

weighing. The loss coil should also be cleansed with sand-paper, but it is unnecessary to use the precautions that are required in the case of the gain coil.

The density of the copper sulphate solution should lie between 1.10 and 1.18. A few drops of sulphuric acid will improve the action of the solution. The direction of the current should be determined by a compass needle before the voltameter is placed in the circuit. The connections can then be made in such a way as to make the deposit occur on the inner coil.

In this experiment the voltameter is to be used in determining the constant of a tangent galvanometer. Two voltameter cells (Fig. 57) are used as a check on the weighings, the two cells being connected in series with the galvanometer and with each other. Figure 58 gives a diagram of the connections. A steady current is sent through the circuit for some measured length of time, and the strength of the current is computed from the amount of copper deposited. The deflection of the galvanometer having been also observed, the constant is readily computed.

A reversing key should be used in connection with the galvanometer, the construction of the key being such that the current through the galvanometer can be reversed without breaking the current in the main circuit. Deflections, both direct and reversed, are to be observed at intervals of two or three minutes throughout the experiment.

The gain coils must be weighed with great care, and placed in the solution only a few minutes before the current is started. At the end of the experiment they should be immediately removed, dipped in distilled water, and dried, as described above. The second weighing should be made as soon as possible after the coils are dry.

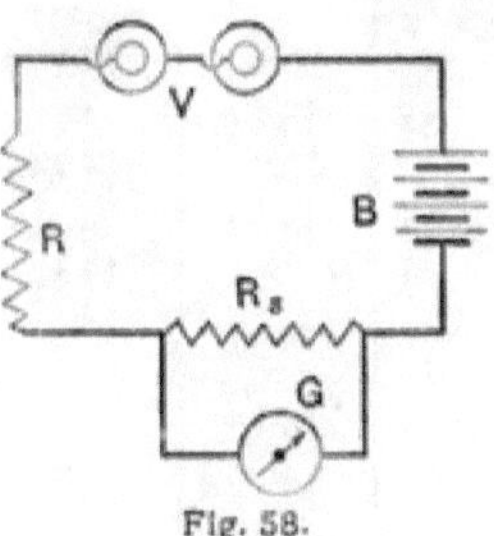

Fig. 58.

The constant of any galvanometer may be measured by this method.

In the case of instruments, the sensitiveness of which is so great that currents of the magnitude adapted to the voltameter cannot be measured directly, a shunt of suitable resistance, R_s (Fig. 58), should be placed across the galvanometer terminals. The ratio of the current in the voltameter to that which flows through the coils of the galvanometer can readily be computed.

The following table gives the results obtained in the calibration of a tangent galvanometer, and shows the method of arranging them :

GALVANOMETER CONSTANT BY COPPER VOLTAMETER.

Time.	Galvanometer Readings.		Other Data and Results
	Current Direct.	Current Reversed.	
hr. min.			Distance of mirror from scale = 50, scale div.
9 49	Circuit	completed.	Average double deflection = 32.27, "
51	—	42.40	$\tan 2\delta = 0.3227$ $2\delta = 17° 53'$
54	74.62	—	$\delta = 8° 56\frac{1}{2}'$ $\tan \delta = 0.1573$
57	—	42.43	
10 1	74.62	—	Two voltameter cells in series :
5	—	42.43	
9	74.68	—	

Two voltameter cells in series :

	Before.	After.	Gain.
Cathode A . . .	27.434	28.686	1.2520
" B . . .	27.5715	28.624	1.2525

Time.	Current Direct.	Current Reversed.
13	—	42.39
17	74.70	—
21	—	42.38
25	74.67	—
29	—	42.32
33	74.70	—
37	—	42.31
41	74.57	—
45	—	42.30
49	74.56	—
49	Circuit	broken.

Duration of run = 3600 sec.

Intensity of current $I = 1.059$ amp.

For tangent galvanometer, $I = I_0 \tan \delta$;

$$\therefore I_0 = 6.73 \text{ amp.}$$

Galvanometer, one turn, needle at center :

Diameter of ring = 77.7 cm.

True constant $G = 0.1617$.

$$I_0 = 10\frac{H}{G}; \quad \therefore H = 0.109.$$

EXPERIMENT R_3. **Measurement of the constant of a sensitive galvanometer.**

It is frequently impracticable to calculate the constant of a sensitive galvanometer from its dimensions and from the value of the horizontal intensity of magnetism at the point where the needle hangs. The constant of such a galvanometer can best be determined by measuring the deflection of the needle which a *known* current produces. The constant can then be determined from one of the equations :

$$I = I_0 \tan \delta,$$
$$I = I_0 \sin \delta,$$
$$I = I_0 \delta, \tag{118}$$

according to the law of the galvanometer.

There are three principal methods of determining the constant of such a galvanometer, depending upon the method of determining the current flowing through the galvanometer coils.

I.

The current may be measured by means of a tangent galvanometer whose constant is already known. For this purpose it will be necessary to put a shunt across the terminals of the sensitive galvanometer, since the latter will usually be very much more sensitive than the instrument whose constant is already known.

The method of procedure is as follows :

(1) Connect the tangent galvanometer in series with a battery of constant E. M. F., a reversing key, and a variable resistance.

(2) Connect the sensitive galvanometer so that it shall be in multiple with a portion of the variable resistance, as in Fig. 59. The variable resistance should be so adjusted that the deflection of the tangent galvanometer is the most suitable (about 45°, if the deflection of the needle is read directly, or nearly as large a deflection as the scale will permit, if the reading is made by means of a mirror).

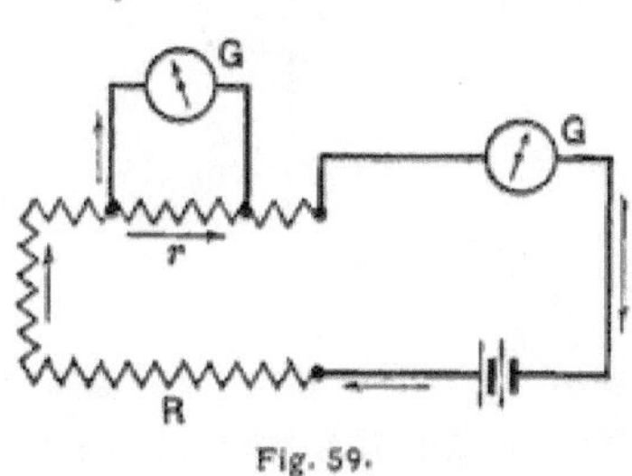

Fig. 59.

(3) Adjust the resistance in multiple with the sensitive galvanometer, until its deflection is nearly across the scale. Observe the readings of both galvanometers for direct and reverse current, and repeat these observations several times to get a good average. As a check, take another series of observations with a different resistance in multiple with the sensitive galvanometer, producing a deflection varying considerably from the first.

From the deflection of the tangent galvanometer, the current flowing in the main circuit is known ; and from the law of divided circuits, the fraction of the current flowing through the sensitive galvanometer can be computed, provided the *ratio* of the galvanometer resistance to the shunt resistance is known.

II.

If the tangent galvanometer be replaced by a voltameter, the current in the main circuit can be measured as in Exp. R_2. The rest of the experiment is the same as above.

It may happen with a very sensitive galvanometer that a current strong enough to produce a suitable deposit in the vol-

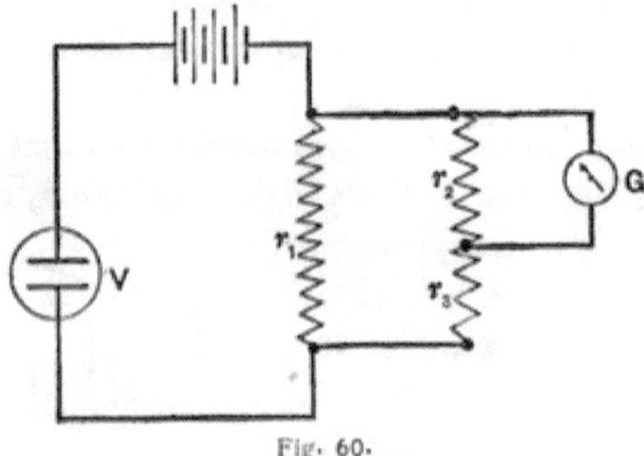

Fig. 60.

tameter will require a shunt of excessively low resistance in multiple with the galvanometer. Under these circumstances, it will be advisable to connect the galvanometer in multiple with a branch which itself is in multiple with a portion of the main circuit, as in Fig. 60.

If the ratio of the resistance in each pair of branches is known, the current flowing in the coils of the galvanometer may be calculated from the current flowing in the main circuit.

It is to be observed that both of the above methods determine the constant independently of the value of *any* resistance. They simply depend upon a knowledge of the *ratio* of resistances.

III.

The current flowing may be determined from Ohm's law, provided the E. M. F. of the battery is known in volts, and the resistance of each portion of the circuit is known in ohms.

For the purpose of this determination, a standard Daniell cell may be very easily constructed as follows: Place an amalgamated zinc rod in a porous cell containing a saturated solution of zinc sulphate. Coil around the porous cell eight or ten turns of rather large copper wire, which has been previously cleaned with sandpaper. Place the porous cell in a larger vessel containing a semi-saturated solution of copper sulphate. The two vessels should be thoroughly cleaned before using.

Such a cell at 15° has an E. M. F. of 1.074 volts. It should be used immediately, although its E. M. F. will change very little for several hours. The internal resistance of such a cell is usually negligible compared with 10,000 ohms. But if it is thought desirable to do so, its resistance may be afterwards determined by the method described in Exp. T_6. The Clark cell affords a more accurate standard, but it is more difficult to construct, and it possesses the disadvantage of a high internal resistance.

The following is the procedure:

(1) Connect the galvanometer in series with a resistance of at least 10,000 ohms, and a Daniell cell, or a Clark cell.

(2) Observe the galvanometer readings, and repeat them several times to get a good average. As a check, repeat these observations with two or three different resistances in series with the cell and galvanometer. The galvanometer deflection may be deduced from the readings, and the current flowing may be calculated from Ohm's law. An application of one of the above equations will then give the galvanometer constant.

It may happen that the galvanometer used is so sensitive

that the deflection is too great to be read even when all the available resistance is in the circuit. In this case the deflection may be diminished as in I above. In this case it will be better to make the observations for the check by varying the resistance in multiple with the galvanometer. This may be done simply by shifting the points at which the galvanometer is connected to the main circuit.

In the above it has been assumed that the law of the galvanometer is known. In nearly all galvanometers, some one of the equations given above hold pretty accurately up to 10° or 20°, which is the maximum deflection that should be used with reflecting galvanometers. If the galvanometer deflection is read directly by means of a pointer moving over a graduated scale, the maximum deflection may be much greater. In this case current may not be at all proportional to the tangent of deflection.

In all such cases the galvanometer should be calibrated. For this purpose proceed as in any of the above experiments, and observe the resistances that correspond to deflections, varying by approximately equal increments from zero to the maximum reading that the scale admits. At least ten or twelve such observations should be taken.

Plat a curve with currents flowing through the galvanometer as abscissas, and galvanometer deflections as ordinates. This curve is called the calibration curve of the instrument.

If the galvanometer is furnished with a regulating magnet, its exact position should be noted at the time of performing the experiment.

Addenda to the report:

(1) Indicate the difficulties which make it impracticable to calculate the constant of a sensitive galvanometer from its dimensions.

(2) Calculate the constant of the instrument considered as a tangent galvanometer. From this constant and the hori-

zontal intensity of the field where the magnet hangs, calculate the *true* constant of the galvanometer.

(3) If the instrument is a reflecting galvanometer, calculate the constant per scale division.

(4) Discuss the influence of the position of a regulating magnet upon the sensitiveness of the galvanometer. Where should the magnet be placed in order to change the zero point by a few scale divisions and yet have the least effect in changing the galvanometer constant?

(5) How could a magnet be placed quite near the galvanometer and yet have an inappreciable effect, either to turn the needle, or to change the galvanometer constant?

Experiment R_4. **Theory of shunts.**

Whenever a current flows in a divided circuit in which there is no E. M. F., the currents in the branches are inversely as the resistances in those branches. This relation may be stated as follows:

$$I_s : I_g = R_g : R_s \qquad (119)$$

The object of this experiment is to verify this relation. The procedure is as follows:

(1) Connect a resistance box in series with a gravity battery of one or more cells.

(2) Connect the terminals of the resistance box through a reversing key to a galvanometer. (See Fig. 61.)

(3) Insert in the main circuit a high resistance (100 or more times as great as R_g). Under these circumstances, the current in the main circuit may be assumed to be constant, no matter how much the resistance in the

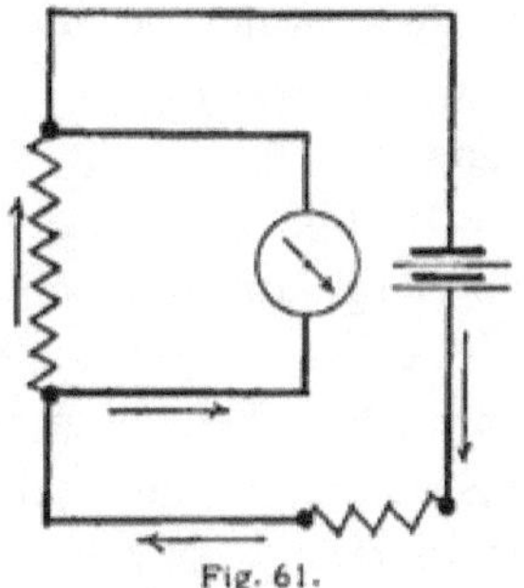
Fig. 61.

resistance box is varied. If I stands for current in the main circuit, the above equation to be verified becomes

$$I_g R_s + I_g R_g = I R_s, \qquad (120)$$

in which the variables are R_s and I_g.

(4) Observe the reading of the galvanometer with current, both direct and reversed, for a number of different resistances in the box, including the reading when the circuit is broken through the box. This last reading obviously represents the constant current in the main circuit. The resistances taken should be such as to make the galvanometer readings vary by approximately equal steps.

If the resistance of the galvanometer (including connecting wires in multiple with the resistance box) be now measured, sufficient data will be obtained to make a number of verifications of the above equation. As current appears in every term

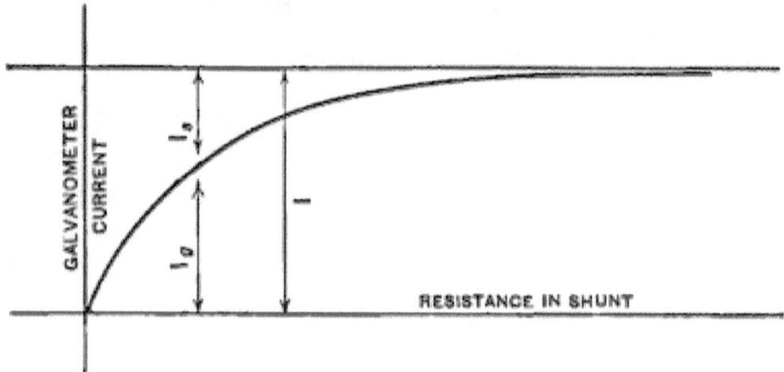

Fig. 62.

in the first degree, any quantity which is proportional to current may be substituted for it ; as, galvanometer deflection, or its tangent.

If the observations be platted with box resistances as abscissas, and tangents of galvanometer deflections as ordinates, the curve obtained will be a hyperbola, with an asymptote parallel to the axis of abscissas. (See Fig. 62.) Knowing the resistance of the galvanometer, the constant current in the main circuit may be calculated from the co-ordinates of *any* point on the curve. If the values thus obtained are equal, the above equation is verified.

If the observations be platted with *reciprocals* of box resistances as abscissas, and cotangents of deflections as ordinates, the resulting curve should be a straight line, the intercept on the axis of abscissas being equal to $-\dfrac{1}{R_g}$.

The following table gives a typical set of data from such readings, and shows the method of arranging them. If these results be platted as indicated above, they will be found to give a curve the form of which is that of Fig. 62.

TABLE.

Resistance in Shunt.	Galvanometer Readings.		Galvanometer Deflection. Proportional to Current.	Other Data and Results.
	Current Direct.	Current Reversed.		
∞	66.00	10.95	55.05	When circuit broken through shunt, $I_g = I = 55.05$
20	64.60	12.25	52.35	
5	61.20	15.64	45.56	From curve $R_g = 1.04$
3	58.50	18.00	40.50	Values of I computed from points on curve.
2	56.08	19.85	36.23	
1	51.40	24.43	26.97	
0.6	48.10	27.95	20.15	$I_g = 8 \qquad I = 54.2$
0.3	44.15	31.80	12.35	$I_g = 16 \qquad I = 55.6$
0.2	42.40	33.60	8.80	$I_g = 30 \qquad I = 55.0$
0.1	40.26	35.55	4.71	$I_g = 40 \qquad I = 54.7$

Addenda to the report:

(1) Calculate the current in the main circuit from several points on the curve which are not observed points.

(2) From the curve platted, find what must be the resistance of a galvanometer shunt so that the current in the galvanometer will be $\frac{1}{2}$, $\frac{1}{4}$, $\frac{1}{10}$ of the total current in main circuit.

EXPERIMENT R_5. Applications of the galvanometer to the measurement of current.

I.

Measurement of the current from a battery with different arrangements of the cells.

For this experiment a tangent galvanometer of small sensitiveness and of very low resistance is required. The galvanometer should have two or three separate coils, giving different degrees of sensitiveness.

(1) Connect a closed-circuit battery * of four or six cells in series with the tangent galvanometer. The circuit should contain also a variable known resistance and a reversing key.

(2) Measure the current for several different resistances, ranging from zero to some resistance that will reduce the current to a quarter or less of its original value.

(3) Make a similar series of observations for three or four different groupings of the cells. For each current to be measured, that galvanometer coil should be used that will give the greatest deflection, provided that the latter is not much greater than 50°.

(4) Measure the resistance of the galvanometer coils and of the connecting wires. Plat curves with resistances outside of the battery as abscissas, and currents in amperes as ordinates. From the curves determine under what conditions each separate grouping of the cells would produce a greater current than any other grouping.

II.

Measurement of current by the Vienna method.

This method is usually employed with currents so large that they cannot be measured directly by ordinary galvanometers or ammeters. The main current is sent through a heavy wire of German silver or similar material, whose resistance changes very little with temperature, and a galvanometer is connected in multiple with this resistance. A constant small proportion of the current will always pass through the galvanometer, and can be measured. From the resistance of the German silver coil, together with that of the galvanometer, the ratio of this measured current to the total current can be computed, and the latter is therefore determined.

---

* Any battery which does not suffer marked polarization will serve for this purpose.

The practice of the method may be illustrated by the measurement of the current from a non-polarizing cell of high electromotive force and low internal resistance. In place of a cell a commercial thermo-battery may be used.

Before beginning the experiment, compute the resistance of the shunt that must be put across the terminals of the galvanometer, in order that the maximum readable galvanometer deflection will be produced when the maximum current to be measured flows in the main circuit. This can be done if the galvanometer constant is known; but it will be necessary to assume approximate values for the electromotive force and internal resistance of the battery.

Having determined the proper resistance of the shunt, proceed as follows:

(1) Connect the cell in series with a variable resistance, and with the shunt which is in multiple with the galvanometer.

(2) Observe the galvanometer readings when several different resistances are used in series with the cell. These resistances should vary from one to ten ohms.

(3) Plat a curve with resistances as abscissas, and reciprocals of currents flowing in the main circuit as ordinates. This curve should be a straight line, and from its constants the electromotive force and internal resistance of the cell may be computed.

III.

To investigate the effect of polarization upon current.

(1) Take a Le Clanché cell, or some other cell that polarizes rapidly, and connect it in series with five or ten ohms' resistance.

(2) Connect a sensitive galvanometer whose constant is known in multiple with a portion of this resistance, such that the galvanometer deflection is quite large.

(3) Observe the galvanometer readings both direct and reversed every three or four minutes for half an hour or longer. Then break the circuit, stir the solution in the cell, and in the

course of ten or fifteen minutes close the circuit, measure the current flowing, and repeat three or four times.

(4) Take another cell as nearly as possible like the first one, and make a similar series of observations, but with a resistance of 50 or 100 ohms in series with it.

(5) Compute the current flowing in the main circuit, and plat a curve for each cell, with times as abscissas and currents as ordinates.

CHAPTER VII.

GROUP S: DIFFERENCE OF POTENTIAL AND ELECTRO-MOTIVE FORCE.

(S) *General statements; (S$_1$) Comparison of two electromotive forces; (S$_2$) Ohm's method for the measurement of the E. M. F. of a battery; (S$_3$) Potential difference at the terminals of a battery as a function of the external resistance; (S$_4$) Fall of potential in a wire-carrying current; (S$_5$) Beetz' method of measuring electromotive forces; (S$_6$) Lines of equal potential in a liquid conductor; (S$_7$) Variation in the E. M. F. of a thermo-element with change of temperature.*

(S). General statements concerning difference of potential and electromotive force.

The indiscriminate use of the terms "electromotive force" and "difference of potential" has given rise to much confusion. The following treatment of the subject, though different from that of many writers, is believed to be entirely consistent with the facts. Moreover, it is hoped that it will make clear to the mind of the student the relation between two ideas which, though intimately related, are nevertheless entirely distinct.

The difference of potential between two points is that difference in condition which tends to produce a transfer of electrification from one point to the other point. The *measure* of this difference of potential is the amount of work that would be done by or against electrical forces in carrying unit quantity of electricity from the one point to the other point.

Any generator of electricity (whether it be a battery, dynamo, or electrical machine) is capable, when energy is supplied to it, of *maintaining* a difference of potential between its terminals, even though they are connected by a conductor. It is to this capability of maintaining a difference of potential, that we apply the name of *electromotive force*. The electromotive force of a generator is measured by the *maximum* difference of potential which it is capable of producing when no current flows. Or, when a current is allowed to flow, it is measured by the difference of potential at the terminals, plus the fall of potential due to the resistance of the generator.

From these definitions it follows :

(1) That there is a difference of potential between any two points of a circuit conveying a current.

(2) That the electromotive force of a circuit is always *located* in the generator. The source of a counter electromotive force may always be looked upon as a negative generator. So far as our present knowledge extends, there is never any electromotive force in a perfectly homogeneous conductor which is not moving relatively to a magnetic field.

The above meaning of the term "electromotive force" is always in mind when it is said that a given conductor is the *seat* * of an electromotive force, as in the case of a wire moving in a magnetic field ; also when it is said that there is no electromotive force in a given branch of a multiple circuit. Counter electromotive force is the true negative of electromotive force *as above defined.*

Ohm's law as originally stated, using modern terms, is : *The current flowing in a (perfectly homogeneous) conductor (not moving relatively to a magnetic field) is directly proportional to the difference of potential between the terminals of the conductor.* If the conductor between two points is in any way varied subject to the above conditions, the current will be *equal* to the difference of potential between the points divided by a quantity known as

---

* See Gray's Absolute Measurements in Electricity and Magnetism, pp. 142–146.

the resistance of the conductor between the points.   From which we have

$$I = \frac{V_a - V_b}{R_{ab}}, \text{ or } I = \frac{dV}{dR}.$$ (121)

The statement that the current flowing in a *circuit* is equal to the total electromotive force in the circuit, divided by the total resistance of the circuit, is a *deduction* from Ohm's law.[*]

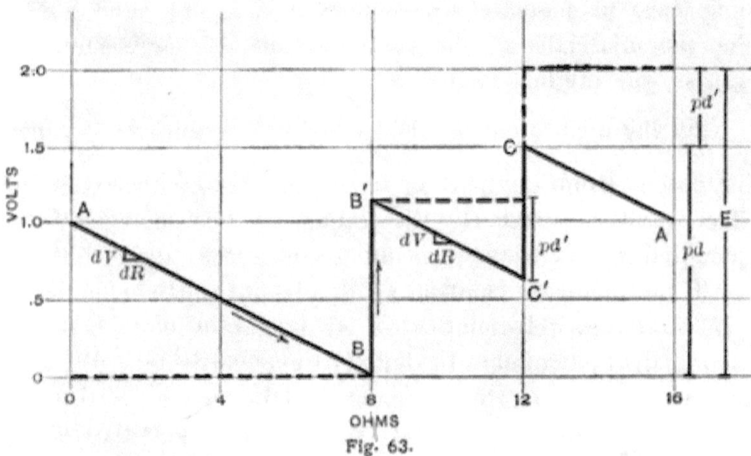

Fig. 63.

The above discussion may be fixed in the mind of the student by the following graphic treatment of two particular cases.

Let *BC*, Fig. 63 a, be the two poles of a cell whose electromotive force is two volts, and internal resistance four ohms. The negative pole of the cell is maintained at zero potential, by being

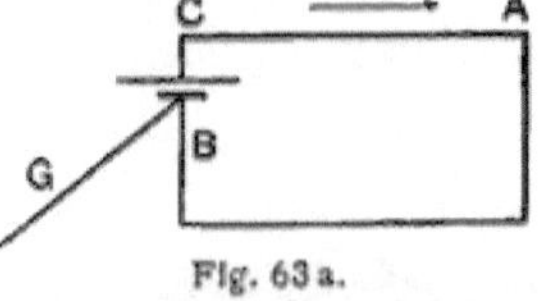

Fig. 63 a.

grounded, and the two poles are connected by a homogeneous conductor of twelve ohms' resistance: *CA* four ohms, and *AB* eight ohms.

If a curve be platted showing the relation between potential and resistance, with resistances counting from *A* in the di-

---

* See Gray's Absolute Measurements in Electricity and Magnetism, pp. 142–146.

rection of the current as abscissas and potentials for ordinates, the result will be as given in Fig. 63. From A to B the potential falls uniformly; between the negative pole and the liquid there is a finite difference of potential represented by BB'; in the liquid, supposed homogeneous, there is a fall of potential, at the same rate as in the outside conductor; between the liquid and the positive pole there is a finite difference of potential represented by $C'C$, and from C to A the potential falls at the same rate as before, reaching, of course, the original value.

By the application of Ohm's law the current, $I=\dfrac{dV}{dR}$, may be derived from any part of the circuit that is homogeneous. The result is obviously the same whether increments of potential and resistance are infinitesimal or of any magnitude.

If the conductor is cut at A, Fig. 63 a, then the potential of AB will immediately fall to zero. As no current flows, there will be no fall of potential in the liquid; the potential of C will therefore immediately rise by the amount of the former fall through the liquid. The broken line represents the potential in the cell and conductor after the circuit is broken. The electromotive force of the cell E is measured by the maximum difference of potential between its terminals when no current flows. This is obviously equal to $pd+pd'$, in which pd is the difference of potential between the terminals before the circuit is broken, and pd' is the fall of potential in the cell due to its resistance. It is obvious from the geometry of the figure that $\dfrac{E}{R}$, in which R is the total resistance of the circuit, gives the same value for the current as $\dfrac{dV}{dR}$ taken in any homogeneous part of the circuit.

Figure 64 represents the potential as a function of the resistance in a circuit, in which the generator is a dynamo. In this case the potential is not a discontinuous function of the resistance. The electromotive force is not located at a point (or at a surface) in the circuit as in the case of a cell, but it exists in all those parts of the armature which cut lines of force. With this exception, the above discussion applies to the present case, word for word. If the circuit is broken as before, the broken line shows the condition of affairs, provided that the *resultant* * magnetic field remains

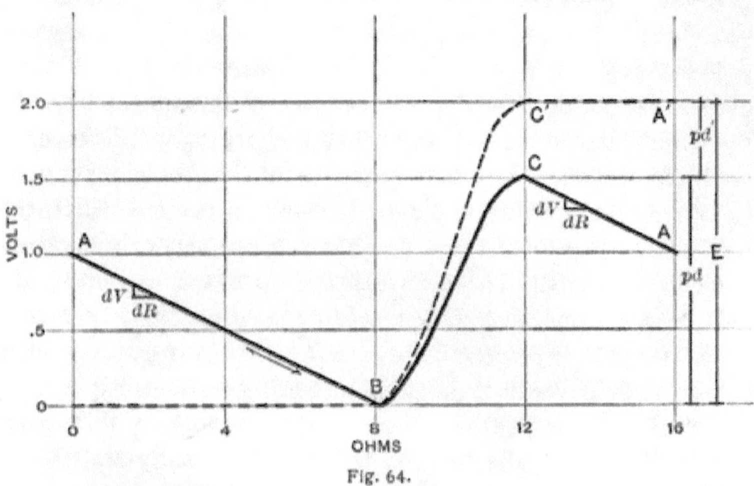

Fig. 64.

unchanged after the circuit is broken. This assumption does not hold true, of course, in the case of the series-wound dynamo.

The above graphic representations of the potentials in a conductor carrying a current, bring prominently forward the fact that in a conductor not containing an electromotive force the current always flows from points of higher potential to points of lower potential; but that in a conductor or in that part of it containing an electromotive force producing a current, the current always flows from points of lower to points of higher potential.

---

* By *resultant* field is meant the field that is the resultant of the field due to the field magnets *and* to the current in the armature coils.

The figure also illustrates the fact that the electromotive force in a circuit is a constant which is independent of the resistance of the generator and of the external circuit, while the difference of potential between two points is not independent of those quantities.

In the case given, the electromotive force is two volts, but the greatest difference of potential between any two points is 1.5 volts. If the cell be replaced by two cells of half the electromotive force and half the internal resistance separated from each other by six ohms' resistance, the electromotive force in the circuit would be two volts, but the greatest difference of potential between any two points would be only 0.75 volt. So we might imagine a circuit in every part of which there was an electromotive force directly proportional to the resistance of that part. The electromotive force and current would still be the same, *but there would be no difference of potential between any two points of the circuit.* In any part of such a circuit, the difference of potential due to its resistance is exactly balanced by the electromotive force generated in that part. This does not invalidate Ohm's law as originally stated, for that law is no longer applicable.

By way of illustration, imagine a perfectly uniform and homogeneous ring moving with respect to a uniformly magnetized cylindrical bar magnet, their axes remaining coincident. This would constitute a circuit containing an electromotive force and carrying a current, but in which there would be no difference of potential.

From definitions it follows that whenever electricity is transferred along a circuit, work is done between the points a and b, according to the relation

$$W = k(V_a - V_b)It.$$

The difference of potential between a and b is one electromagnetic unit, if work is done at the rate of 1 erg per second, when the current flowing is one electromagnetic unit. This choice of unit potential difference makes k unity in the above equation.   The electromagnetic unit of electromotive force is that electromotive force which is capable of producing unit difference of potential.   It may be proved that the electromagnetic unit of electromotive force is produced whenever unit magnetic lines of force are cut at the rate of one per second. The practical unit of difference of potential is called a "volt." It is equal to 10^8 electromagnetic units.

EXPERIMENT S_1.   **Comparison of two electromotive forces.**

I.

From Ohm's law we have, if a tangent galvanometer is used,

$$I = I_0 \tan \delta = \frac{E}{R + R_0}. \tag{122}$$

If the two cells whose E. M. F.'s* are to be compared are allowed to send a current successively through the *same* resistance, the ratio of their E. M. F.'s will be equal to the ratio of the tangents of the angles of deflection.   To perform the experiment we proceed as follows :

(1) Connect one of the cells in series with a sensitive galvanometer and a high resistance (500 or more times as great as the resistance of the cell).

(2) Observe the galvanometer readings (both direct and reversed).

(3) Repeat these observations with the other cell connected in series with the *same* resistance.   A number of independent determinations of the ratio of the two E. M. F.'s may be made by varying the high resistance in the circuit; or by varying the sensitiveness of the galvanometer by means of a controlling magnet.

---

* In this and subsequent directions for the performance of experiments, this well-known abbreviation will be used for electromotive force.

II.

The method above described assumes that the resistance of each cell is negligible compared with the total resistance of the circuit. If this is not the case, the following method is always applicable.

When the two cells are connected so as to assist each other, the two electromotive forces are added; when they are connected so as to oppose each other, the current in the circuit is that due to the difference of the two E. M. F.'s. Since the resistance of the circuit is the same in both cases, the two currents observed are proportional to the sum and difference respectively of the electromotive forces. The two currents being deduced from the galvanometer deflection, the ratio of the two electromotive forces can be computed.

If it is not known which cell has the greater electromotive force, it should be observed whether the deflection is reversed or simply lessened when the terminals of the given cell are reversed.

The cells are first connected in series with a galvanometer, and such a resistance is placed in the circuit as will make the deflection one that can easily be read. We then reverse one of the cells so that the two act against one another, everything else about the circuit remaining the same, and observe the deflection.

A number of independent determinations should be made as described above.

If the E. M. F.'s are very nearly equal, great care should be exercised in reading the galvanometer when the cells are opposed to each other. It is better, in such a case, to use two cells of the kind having the smaller E. M. F. against one of the other kind.

If this method be used with cells either of which polarizes rapidly, it must not be expected that the results of a series of observations will be entirely concordant.

EXPERIMENT S_2.   **Ohm's method for the measurement of the E. M. F. of a battery.**

The object of this experiment is the determination of an E. M. F. in absolute measure, without reference to any standard cell.   From Ohm's law we have

$$I = \frac{E}{R + R_0},\qquad(123)$$

in which R_0 is the constant unknown resistance of the battery, connecting wires, and galvanometer; and R is the known resistance which may be varied at pleasure.

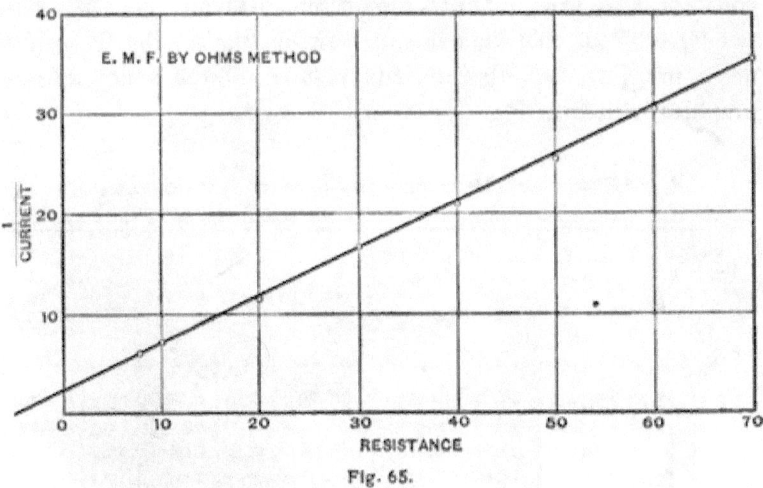

Fig. 65.

The procedure is as follows :

(1) Place in the circuit of the generator a resistance R, whose value in ohms is known, and measure the current in amperes by means of an ammeter or galvanometer whose constant is known.

(2) Vary the known resistance, and measure the current as before.

These two observations will give two equations between which R_0 may be eliminated, and E determined in volts.

The best results will be obtained if the two resistances are so chosen as to make the two values of the current quite different. As a check, it is best to repeat the observations with a number of different resistances. It is to be observed that the method depends upon the assumption that the E. M. F. is unaffected by changes in the current. With some cells this is only approximately true.

When a number of observations have been taken, the results can be readily computed by graphical methods. To accomplish this, a curve should be platted with resistances as abscissas, and reciprocals of currents as ordinates. If the E. M. F. remains constant, the curve obtained should be a straight line, and from the "pitch" of this line, E can be computed. The following table presents typical data, the results of which are shown graphically in Fig. 65:

E. M. F. BY OHM'S METHOD. — TWO GRAVITY CELLS IN SERIES.

Box Resistance.	Galvanometer Readings.		Double Deflection.	tan 2δ	2δ	tan δ	Current	$\dfrac{1}{\text{Current}}$	E. M. F.
	Right.	Left.							
7	95.70	49.04	46.66	0.4666	25° 1'	0.2218	0.1686	5.93	2.14
10	90.66	53.88	36.78	0.3678	20° 11'	0.1780	0.1353	7.39	2.12
20	83.15	61.28	21.87	0.2187	12° 20'	0.1080	0.0821	12.18	2.11
30	79.92	64.47	15.45	0.1545	8° 47'	0.0767	0.0583	17.15	2.08
40	78.19	66.09	12.10	0.1210	6° 54'	0.0603	0.0458	21.84	2.09
50	77.11	67.13	9.98	0.0998	5° 42'	0.0498	0.0384	26.05	2.14
60	76.35	67.85	8.50	0.0850	4° 52'	0.0425	0.0323	30.96	2.12
70	75.90	68.42	7.48	0.0748	4° 17'	0.0374	0.0284	35.22	2.15

Distance of mirror from scale = 50 scale divisions.

Galvanometer constant $I_0 = 0.76$ ampere.

From curve $R_0 = 5.7$ ohms, $E = 2.14$ volts.

Last column computed assuming value of R_0 obtained from curve.

Addenda to the report:

(1) Show that the best results will be obtained when the two currents vary widely in amount.

(2) If the experiment were performed using cells the E. M. F. of which falls off as the current increases, what would be the form of the curve?

EXPERIMENT S_3. The potential difference at the terminals of a battery considered as a function of the external resistance.

The difference of potential between the terminals of a cell has its greatest value when the external resistance is infinite

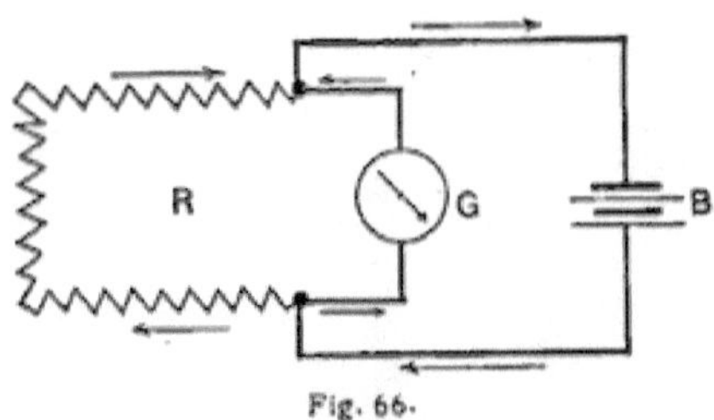

Fig. 66.

(when the circuit is broken), and is then equal to the electro-motive force. As the external resistance is diminished, the E. M. F. remains constant; but the difference of potential between the poles steadily grows less, until the external resist-ance is zero, when the two poles are at the same potential.

The relation between these two quantities may be investi-gated as follows:

(1) Complete the circuit of the battery by a resistance box.

(2) Connect a high resistance galvanometer through a reversing key to the terminals of the resistance box. (See Fig. 66.) The resistance of the galvanometer used should be so great (1000 ohms or more) that the current passing through it is too small to modify appreciably the current in the main circuit. Under these circumstances, the galvanometer merely serves to measure the difference of potential between the terminals of the cell.

Let I_g be the current flowing in the galvanometer, R_g its resistance, and pd the potential difference between its terminals; then we have

$$\frac{pd}{R_g} = I_g = I_0 \tan \delta.$$

The product $R_g I_0$ is a constant for which may be substituted the symbol pd_0. This is the constant of the instrument used as a potential galvanometer,

$$\therefore \; pd = R_g I_0 \tan \delta = pd_0 \tan \delta. \tag{124}$$

When R_g is very great, this will be very nearly the potential difference that would exist if no galvanometer were used. It

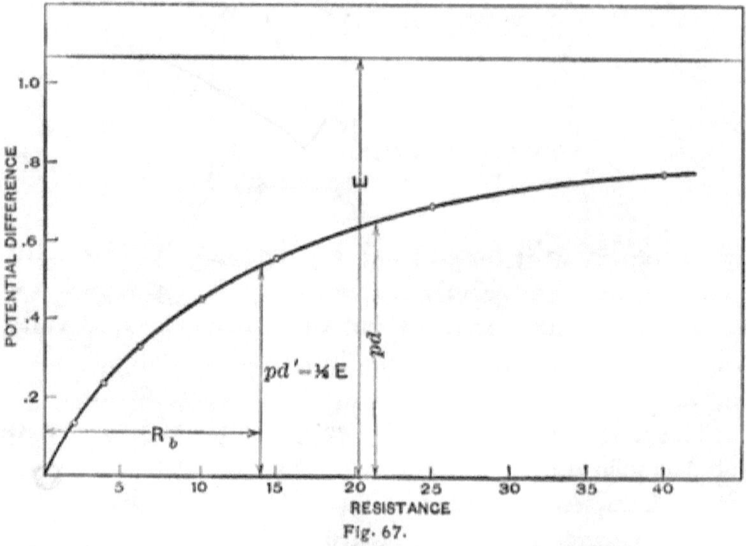

Fig. 67.

may be here noted that the potential difference between the terminals of the galvanometer, the battery, and the resistance box are practically identical, since the connecting wires are supposed to have negligible resistance.

(3) Observe the reading of the galvanometer for a number of different resistances in the box, and also when the circuit through the box is broken. These resistances should be such

that the galvanometer deflections vary by approximately equal steps.

If I is the current in the resistance box, R its resistance, and R_b the resistance of the cell, including the connecting wires to the box, we shall have

$$I = \frac{E}{R_b + R} = \frac{pd}{R},$$

or $$pdR_b + pdR = ER. \tag{125}$$

If the observations taken be platted with box resistances as abscissas, and potential differences as ordinates, the resulting curve should be a hyperbola, with an asymptote parallel to the axis of abscissas.

Results obtained by the method just described are given in the following table. The relation between resistance and potential difference is shown graphically in Fig. 67.

POTENTIAL DIFFERENCE BETWEEN TERMINALS OF GRAVITY CELL.

RESISTANCE IN BOX.	GALVANOMETER READINGS.		GALVANOMETER DEFLECTION PROPORTIONAL TO pd.	POTENTIAL DIFFERENCE IN VOLTS.
	Direct.	Reversed.		
∞	65.26	9.80	55.46	1.065
200	63.40	11.70	51.70	0.991
80	61.06	14.00	47.06	0.904
40	58.06	17.07	40.99	0.787
25	55.30	19.87	35.43	0.680
15	51.90	23.30	28.60	0.549
10	49.25	26.10	23.15	0.444
6	45.95	29.35	16.60	0.319
4	43.90	31.50	12.40	0.227
2	41.20	34.28	6.92	0.133
0.8	39.20	36.20	3.00	0.057

Constant per scale division of galvanometer used as potential instrument $= I_0 R_g = pd_0 = 192 \times 10^{-4}$.

From plat. $R_b = 13.6$ ohms.

If the constant pd_0 is not known, any quantity that is proportional to the potential difference may be substituted for it in platting the curve.

If the observations be platted with *reciprocals* of box resistances as abscissas, and cotangents of galvanometer deflections as ordinates, the curve should be very nearly a straight line, whose intercept on the axis of abscissas is equal to $-\dfrac{1}{R_b}$. R_b may also be obtained from the first curve. It is the abscissa corresponding to the ordinate which is half the maximum ordinate.

Addenda to the report:

(1) From the curve platted, determine the external resistance so that the terminal potential difference shall be $\frac{1}{2}$, $\frac{1}{4}$, $\frac{1}{10}$ of the E. M. F. of the battery.

(2) Compute the resistance of the battery.

EXPERIMENT S_4. Principle of fall of potential in a wire carrying a current.

This experiment is intended to illustrate the fact that the difference in potential between any two points on a simple circuit in which a current is flowing is proportional to the resistance between these points. This proportionality of fall of potential and resistance holds true in the case of any simple circuit, provided that there is no electromotive force between the two points considered. It is a direct consequence of Ohm's law, and may be stated as follows:

$$pd = Ir, \tag{126}$$

in which pd is the difference of potential, r the resistance between any two points of a simple circuit, and I the current flowing.

The most direct method of testing this proportionality would undoubtedly be to measure the difference of potential between selected points of a circuit by means of an electrometer.

In this case the measurement would depend upon electrostatic forces, and the current flowing in the circuit would not be modified. The following method will, however, give results that are quite closely correct if the galvanometer resistance is sufficiently large.

The procedure is as follows :

(1) Connect a resistance box in series with a gravity battery of one or more cells, and take out all the plugs corresponding to the low resistances.

(2) Connect a high resistance galvanometer through a reversing key *s* to side plugs, and by this means put the galvanometer

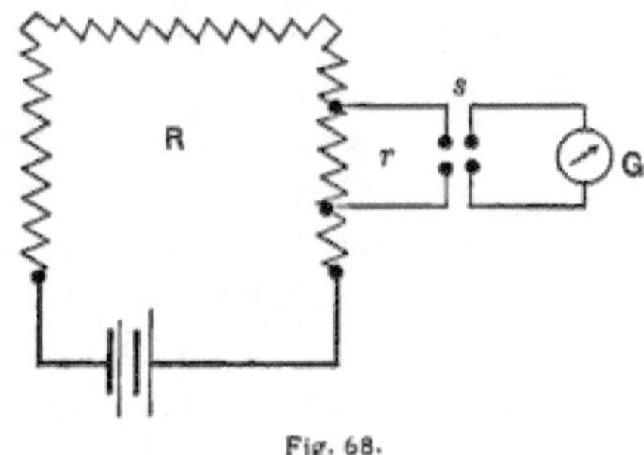

Fig. 68.

in multiple with a portion of the resistance in the box (Fig 68). In order that the galvanometer shall not perceptibly alter the fall of potential in the main circuit, the resistance between the points to which it is connected should not be greater than 0.005 that of the galvanometer. If the galvanometer deflection is not a suitable one, it should be made so by varying the resistance or E. M. F. in the main circuit.

The side plugs should now be shifted from place to place on the box so as to include different resistances between them ; and for each value of the included resistance the deflection of the galvanometer (both direct and reversed) should be observed. Ten or twelve different values of the resistance included between the plugs should be used, ranging from the smallest that will give a readable deflection, to the largest that can be used without throwing the galvanometer reading off the scale.

Since the resistance of the galvanometer remains constant throughout the experiment, the current passing through it is in each case proportional to the difference of potential between the side plugs.

The results may be best used to test the principle of fall of potential by platting a curve in which resistances between side plugs are used as abscissas and the corresponding galvanometer deflection as ordinates. (If the galvanometer is a tangent galvanometer, tangents of deflections must be used; if a sine galvanometer, sine of deflection, etc.). The curve should be very nearly a straight line, very slightly concave towards the axis of abscissas.

This experiment will be even more instructive if a straight wire 60 or 80 cm. long whose resistance is about 0.005 that of the galvanometer, be substituted for the resistance box with side plugs. If this is done, one terminal of the galvanometer should be connected to one end of the wire and the other terminal to a sliding contact, by means of which the length of wire between the galvanometer terminals may be varied at pleasure. If the cross-section of the wire is uniform, it will be found that difference of potential is proportional to the length of wire included between the galvanometer terminals.

The principles involved in the use of a galvanometer as a voltmeter will be brought out quite clearly if a new series of observations is taken in which the resistances between the side plugs range up to $\frac{1}{5}$ or $\frac{1}{4}$ of the resistance of the galvanometer. This may be done by very greatly increasing the resistance of the main circuit. If in this case the observations be platted as before, there will be a very decided curvature toward the axis of abscissas; but if the true *multiple* resistance between the side plugs be used as abscissas, the curve rigorously becomes a straight line.

Addenda to the report:

(1) Indicate the circumstances under which there would be no curvature in a series of observations platted as above.

(2) Why does the curve become straight when platted as described in the last paragraph of the directions?

EXPERIMENT S_6. **Beetz's method of measuring electromotive forces.**

This experiment depends upon finding two points, A and B, (Fig. 69) in the circuit of the battery whose E. M. F. is required,

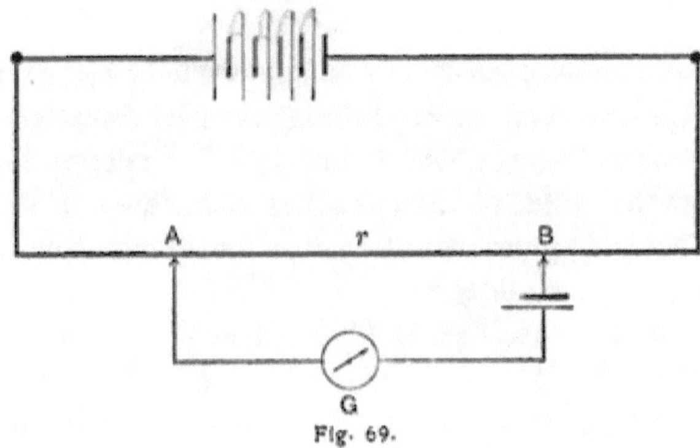

Fig. 69.

such that their potential difference shall equal the E. M. F. of a standard cell. If r is the resistance between these points, R the total resistance of the circuit exclusive of the battery, whose resistance is R_b, pd the fall of the potential between A and B (which is equal to the E. M. F. of the standard cell), the current in the principal circuit will be equal to

$$\frac{E}{R+R_b} = \frac{pd}{r} \qquad (127)$$

If a new value of R is taken, r must also be changed. This will give another equation similar to the above, and between them R_b may be eliminated and the ratio of E to pd computed.

The method may also be employed to determine the battery resistance R_b, but good results cannot be expected unless R is always comparable with R_b.

To perform the experiment :

(1) Connect the unknown E. M. F. in series with a known resistance which may be varied at pleasure. If the current in the main circuit flows from A to B, connect the negative pole of the standard cell to B and the positive pole to a galvanometer. The other terminal of the galvanometer is connected to A.

(2) Vary the position of the point A or B or both, until no current flows through the galvanometer. Under these circumstances the fall of potential from A to B due to the current in the main circuit is equal to the E. M. F. of the standard cell.

The experiment consists in finding a number of values of R and r such that no current flows through the galvanometer. From any two pairs of values both E and R_b may be determined. Or better, plat the values of R as abscissas, and those of r as ordinates. This will give a straight line from whose constants E and R_b may be determined.

The standard may be a Daniell cell in the form of a U-tube in the bottom of which is placed plaster of Paris to prevent the mixing of the two solutions, or a Clark cell. In either case the internal resistance will be very large ; but if the galvanometer is sufficiently sensitive, this fact has no influence on the results.

If the battery whose E. M. F. is to be measured is subject to rapid polarization, the current should be allowed to flow only for an instant before closing the circuit of the galvanometer.

By this method it is obvious that the E. M. F. to be measured must be greater than that of the standard cell. Unless the galvanometer is very sensitive, it should be three or four times as large.

Addendum to the report :

Show that when no current flows in the galvanometer the potential difference between A and B is equal to the E. M. F. of the standard cell.

EXPERIMENT S_6. **To trace the lines of equal potential in a liquid conductor.**

The apparatus for this experiment consists of a shallow vessel provided with a glass bottom and filled with some poorly conducting liquid, such as ordinary water. A telephone is also required, and some means of obtaining an alternating or interrupted current. A small induction coil is suitable for this purpose.

If two electrodes are placed in the liquid and a current passes between them, the current will flow from one electrode to the other by every possible path. The potential varies along each of these paths, having its greatest value at the positive pole and its least value at the negative pole. For each value of the potential between these limits, there is therefore a point on each of these "lines of flow." Since all these points are at the same potential, they lie upon one of the equipotential lines of the liquid. The object of this experiment is to determine the shape of these equipotential lines.

Connect two wires to the terminals of the telephone, and fasten one of them so that its end dips into the liquid. If the end of the second wire is also placed in the liquid, a sound will in general be heard in the telephone, due to the rapid make and break of the current. By shifting the position of the second wire, however, a position can be found such that this sound is no longer heard. When this position is reached, the ends of the two wires must be at the same potential, and are therefore points on the same equipotential line. Keeping the position of the first wire unaltered and varying that of the second, enough points can be found in this way to locate the equipotential line with considerable accuracy. These lines should be traced quite carefully near the edge of the conductor, and in the neighborhood of a line separating a good conductor from a bad conductor. It will be found convenient to place a board ruled with equidistant lines beneath the glass bottom of the vessel, and to record the position of the points by reference to these lines.

A diagram can afterwards be drawn on which the equipotential curves are accurately represented. To avoid annoyance from the noise of the interrupter on the induction coil, it is advisable to place the latter in a separate room.

In the manner described above, the form of the equipotential lines may be investigated when electrodes of different shapes are used, or when the relative position of the electrodes is altered. In each case, at least five or six lines should be located, the intervals between them being so chosen that the field in all parts of the liquid is clearly shown. Diagrams should be drawn to scale, representing the position of the electrodes and the limits of the vessel, as well as the equipotential curves. Since the lines of flow must be at all points perpendicular to the equipotential lines, the former can also be drawn.

Very instructive results may be obtained by placing between the electrodes a piece of metal of high conductivity. Since the resistance of the metal is less than that of the liquid, the field will be distorted, and the modified form of the equipotential lines can be determined by the telephone. A piece of some poorly conducting substance, such as glass or paraffin, will also give instructive results.

It may sometimes be desirable to use a galvanometer instead of a telephone in tracing the equipotential lines. In this case, a continuous instead of an alternating current must be used, and the liquid conductor may be replaced by a sheet of tinfoil. The equipotential lines are determined by finding a series of points, such that if the galvanometer terminals be connected to any two of them, no current will flow through the galvanometer.

On account of the analogy that has been found to exist between lines of flow and magnetic lines of force, the results of this experiment have important bearings on magnetic problems, such as occur in dynamo work.

Addenda to the report:

(1) Indicate the reason why the equipotential lines are always normal to the edge of the conductor.

(2) Indicate the part of the conductor in which the current density is the greatest.

(3) Indicate the part of the conductor in which the fall of potential is most rapid.

EXPERIMENT S_7. **Variation in the E. M. F. of a thermo-element with change in temperature.**

There is always a difference of potential between points on opposite sides of the junction between two different metals. If two metals be joined so as to make a complete circuit, there will be a fall of potential at each junction. Since these two changes of potential are equal and are opposed to each other, no current will be produced. In a word, the whole of one metal will be at one potential, while the whole of the other metal will be at a different potential.

This contact difference of potential depends upon temperature. Therefore, if the two junctions are at different temperatures, these two differences of potential will not, in general, annul each other, and a constant current will flow through the circuit. Such a combination of two metals with the two junctions at different temperatures constitutes a thermo-element. It is the seat of a true E. M. F., as that term has already been defined.

It is the object of this experiment to determine the relation between this E. M. F. and the temperatures of the two junctions.

The procedure is as follows:

(1) Construct a simple form of element by soldering together the ends of two wires made of different metals: for example, German silver and copper, or copper and iron. Then cut one of the wires in the center, so that the free ends will form the terminals of the element.

(2) Connect the terminals of the element through a reversing key to a sensitive galvanometer. It will be advisable to place a resistance box somewhere in the circuit, so that the resistance of circuit may be under control. The resistance of the whole circuit should be great enough so that it will not be appreciably altered by changes in the temperature of the element.

(3) One junction of the element is now to be kept at a constant temperature, while the other is placed in a bath of oil or water whose temperature can be readily varied. The E. M. F. corresponding to any observed difference in temperature between the junctions is then proportional to the galvanometer deflections, or its tangent, as the case may be. It is important that the terminals of the element be kept at the same temperature. This can usually be accomplished by placing them side by side and wrapping them with paper.

The junction whose temperature is to be varied should be inserted in a test-tube for protection against the chemical action of the bath. Its temperature may be measured by a thermometer placed in the same tube, the bulb of the thermometer being on a level with the junction. To prevent air currents it is best to fill the upper part of the tube with cotton waste or asbestos. For rough work, the other junction may be left in the air, provided it is protected from draughts. It is better, however, to place the junction in some constant temperature bath, such as boiling water, melting ice, or water that is nearly at the temperature of the room. In this case the junction should be inserted in a test-tube, as described above.

Observations of temperatures and galvanometer readings should be taken throughout a considerable range, the differences of temperature between the junctions varying from 0° to 100° or greater. Considerable difficulty is often experienced on account of the uncertainty of the exact temperature at the instant the galvanometer is read. To reduce this source of error as much as possible, take several galvanometer readings and several temperature readings, while the temperature is maintained as nearly constant as possible, and use their average in . the computations.

(4) From the galvanometer constant, the resistance of the circuit, and the galvanometer deflections, compute the E. M. F. of the thermo-element for each observed difference of temperature.

(5) Plat a curve with temperature differences as abscissas and E. M. F.'s in microvolts as ordinates.

The E. M. F. of the thermo-element may be determined by a method similar to that used in experiment S_5. For this purpose place in the main circuit a galvanometer to measure the current flowing. Replace the standard cell by the thermo-element, and adjust the points A and B so that no current flows through the sensitive galvanometer in the branch circuit. The fall of potential between A and B can be determined from the resistance between those points and the current flowing. This difference of potential is equal to the E. M. F. in the branch circuit.

CHAPTER VIII.

GROUP T: THE MEASUREMENT OF RESISTANCE.

(T) *General statements; (T$_1$) Measurement of resistance by the Wheatstone bridge; (T$_2$) Measurement of resistance by the method of fall of potential; (T$_3$) Specific resistance; (T$_4$) Determination of the temperature coefficient for resistance of carbon and of various metals; (T$_5$) Measurement of the internal resistance of a battery by Ohm's method; (T$_6$) Resistance of a battery by Mance's method; (T$_7$) Resistance of electrolytes.*

(T). **General statements concerning resistance.**

When two points of a homogeneous conductor are maintained at different potentials, a current will flow in the conductor. The magnitude of this current depends upon the substance and dimensions of the conductor. The *conductivity* of a conductor is that quantity which must be multiplied into the potential difference at its terminals to give the current which flows. The *resistance* of a conductor is the constant ratio between the difference of potential at its terminals and the current which this potential difference produces.

The *absolute unit of resistance* is the resistance of a conductor such that unit electromagnetic difference of potential at its ends will cause unit electromagnetic current to flow. It may be shown experimentally that the resistance of a conductor varies directly as its length, and inversely as its cross-section. On account of the relative ease with which a conductor of some standard substance of given length and section may be constructed, it is more usual to define the practical unit of resistance in these terms. The Chamber of Delegates at the Chicago Electrical Congress adopted, "*As a unit of resistance the international ohm, which is based upon the ohm equal to* 10^9 *units of resistance of the C. G. S. system of electromagnetic units, and is represented sufficiently well by the resistance offered to an unvarying electric current by a column of mercury at the temperature of melting ice,* 14.4521 *grams in mass, of a constant cross-sectional area, and of a length of* 106.3 *centimeters.*"

In current electricity it is necessary to have variable resistances, such that any known value may be inserted in a circuit at pleasure. This demand is met by constructing a series of coils of wire of different resistances and enclosing them in a box, the whole being called a rheostat or resistance box. These coils are constructed of insulated wire, usually of German silver. This metal is used for two reasons: (1) its specific resistance is considerably greater than that of copper or iron, thereby giving the same resistance with less length of wire; (2) the change of resistance with change of temperature is much less than in the case of any pure metal. These coils are non-inductively or doubly wound, so that their self-induction shall be as small as possible. The ends of each coil are connected to separate brass blocks which are electrically connected by removable brass plugs. When all of these plugs are in place, the resistance between the binding-screws of the box is inappreciable. Any desired resistance may be introduced into the circuit by removing the plugs corresponding to the proper resistance coils.

In the use of resistance boxes it should always be remembered that the resistance apparently in circuit is not the true resistance unless each plug in place makes good connection between the adjacent brass blocks. If the plug be simply dropped into place, or if it be not thoroughly clean, the resistance between it and either brass plug, instead of being infinitesimal, may have a large value. Unless care is taken, the unknown resistance thus introduced into the circuit is likely to be a considerable fraction of an ohm. If the resistances used are small, this becomes of great relative importance. To avoid this difficulty, each plug when it is inserted should be twisted in its seat, thus securing good contact. Sometimes it is necessary to clean the plugs and brass blocks with emery paper.

The coils of resistance boxes are generally wound with small wire, hence they should only be used for weak currents.

EXPERIMENT T_1. **Measurement of resistance by the Wheatstone bridge.**

By far the most accurate method of measuring resistance is by means of the Wheatstone's bridge.

Let ABC and $AB'C$ (Fig. 70) be the two parts of a divided circuit containing no E. M. F. If by means of a battery a

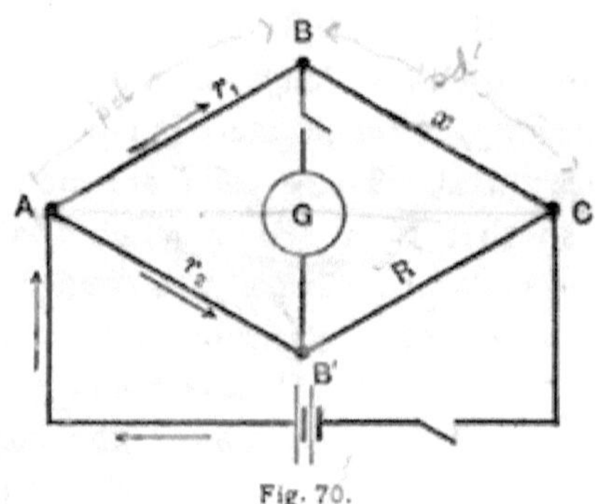

Fig. 70.

current is made to flow from A to C, the potential will fall from A to C along both branches. Let B and B' be points in the two branches having the same potential. Let pd and pd' be the differences of potential between A and B and between B and C respectively. Let the resistances be r_1 and x. As no current can flow through the branch BB', we have from Ohm's law :

$$\frac{pd}{r_1} = \frac{pd'}{x}$$

As B and B' are at the same potential, the difference of potential between A and B must equal that between A and B'. Therefore, in the lower branch we have

$$\frac{pd}{r_2} = \frac{pd'}{R},$$

whence
$$x = \frac{r_1}{r_2} R. \qquad (128)$$

A Wheatstone bridge is an apparatus consisting of three sets of wire coils whose resistances are known. R is a rheostat or variable resistance in which any resistance may be obtained from 0.1 to 10,000 ohms. r_1 and r_2 are called "ratio arms," each consists of a series of resistances, which may be made 1, 10, 100, or 1000 ohms at pleasure.

To measure a resistance with this apparatus, connect the three sets of resistance coils, r_1, r_2, and R, the unknown resistance, a sensitive galvanometer, and a battery, as in the diagram. By removing plugs, make $r_1 : r_2$ any convenient ratio, say 10 : 100. Vary the resistance in the rheostat until no current flows through the galvanometer connected between B and B'. The unknown resistance may then be computed from the known resistances of three of the four branches.

In measuring resistances with the Wheatstone bridge, two contact keys should be used — one in the battery branch and one in the galvanometer branch. In order to eliminate the effect of thermo-currents, a reversing key should be included in the battery branch.

It is essential for accurate results that the battery key should be closed first, and held closed long enough for the current to become steady, before the galvanometer circuit is completed. Otherwise a deflection may be produced on closing the battery circuit even when the bridge is properly balanced. This is due to the fact that the distribution of a current when first started is determined largely by the relative values of the self-induction in different branches of the circuit, and does not depend solely on the resistances, as is the case when the current has become steady. The effect of disregarding this precaution when measuring inductive resistances, such as electromagnets or the field coils of a dynamo, is always to make the resistance appear larger than it really is.

This fact may be illustrated by selecting as one of the resistances to be measured an electromagnet of rather high self-induction. After the resistance in the rheostat has been so adjusted that no current passes through the galvanometer when the keys are closed in the proper order, observe the effect of closing the keys in the reverse order. After the galvanometer needle has come to rest, observe the effect of opening the galvanometer key while the battery key remains closed.

Wheatstone's bridge is often made in the form known as the slide wire bridge. In this pattern r is a rheostat, and the branch $AB'C$ is a straight wire, a meter long, of uniform cross-section. At B' there is a key which makes contact with the bare wire. This key is moved along the wire until a point is found having the same potential as B. Since resistance is proportional to length (assuming the wire to be cylindrical and homogeneous), we have

$$\frac{r_1}{x}=\frac{a}{b},\qquad(129)$$

in which a and b are the lengths of the two segments of $AB'C$.

Addenda to the report:

(1) Explain the effect observed in measuring an inductive resistance if the galvanometer key is closed first.

(2) Prove that the battery and galvanometer may be interchanged without affecting the balance of the bridge.

EXPERIMENT T_2. **Measurement of resistance by the method of fall of potential.**

In any part of a simple circuit not containing an E. M. F., we have, from Ohm's law,

$$pd=IR,\qquad(130).$$

in which pd and R are the difference of potential and resistance between the points, and I is the current flowing. In any other part of the same circuit, we have

$$pd' = IR', \tag{131}$$

the current being the same in all parts of the circuit.

If one of these resistances is known (r, Fig. 71), and the ratio of the two differences of potential is determined, the unknown resistance may be readily calculated. This ratio may most easily be determined by means of a potential galvanometer (see Exp. S_4). In order that the fall of potential to be measured shall not be perceptibly lessened, when the galvanometer is connected to the two points, its resistance should be 1000 or more times as great as the unknown resistance. If the galvanometer resistance is not large, the unknown resistance may still be determined if we know the galvanometer resistance. The relation is proved as follows:

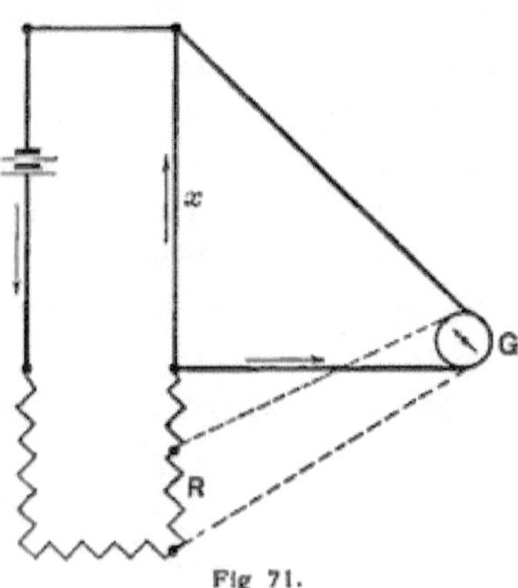

Fig 71.

Let pd and pd' be the potential differences between the terminals of the galvanometer, when connected in multiple with the standard and unknown resistance, respectively; then we have

$$pd : pd' = \frac{RR_g}{R+R_g} : \frac{R'R_g}{R'+R_g}. \tag{132}$$

This assumes that the *total* current in the main circuit remains constant throughout the experiment.

This method of measuring resistance is especially useful in measuring very small resistances. It is commonly used, for example, in determining the specific conductivity of a wire of which only a small sample is available. (See Exp. T_3). It is also a convenient method of measuring resistance in determining the temperature coefficient of a wire (see Exp. T_4), or when the variation of resistance is used to measure temperature changes.

The unknown resistance x (Fig. 71) is connected in series with the standard, a variable resistance, and a battery of constant E. M. F. (The variable resistance may be a *standard* resistance box.) Since the unknown resistance and the standard are in series, the same current is flowing in each.

The fall of potential is measured by connecting the galvanometer, through a reversing key, first in multiple with the unknown resistance, and then in multiple with the standard, and observing the deflection in each case. The ratio of the two deflections is then equal (very closely) to the ratio of the two resistances.

In preparing for this experiment, the galvanometer should first be put in multiple with the unknown resistance, and the resistance or E. M. F. in the main circuit varied, until the deflection is a suitable one. The resistance in the main circuit should not be very small, for under these circumstances the battery is more apt to polarize, and the current to change during the experiment.

To eliminate various errors, it is best to have two reversing keys, one in the battery circuit and the other in the galvanometer circuit. For each position of the key in the main circuit, the direct and reversed reading of the galvanometer should be observed. The reversal of the main current eliminates errors due to the thermo-currents caused by differences in temperature between different portions of the circuit; while the reversal of the galvanometer circuit eliminates any error that might be caused by a direct magnetic action of the current in the unknown resistance upon the galvanometer needle. In order to be sure of good contact, it is best to make the connections at the terminals of the unknown and standard resistances by means of mercury cups.

Several independent determinations should be made. This may be done in either of two ways:

(1) Keeping the standard the same, vary the galvanometer deflection, (*a*) by changing the sensitiveness of the galvanometer, (*b*) by varying the resistance or E. M. F. in the main circuit.

(2) Keeping the current in the main circuit constant, vary the standard, by putting the galvanometer in multiple with different coils of the standard resistance box.

In taking observations, it is well to alternate between the unknown and standard resistances, so as to eliminate the error which might be introduced by a progressive change in the conditions.

Addenda to the report:

(1) Explain by diagram the necessity of having *two* reversing keys.

(2) Compute the error introduced in your case by using a galvanometer whose resistance was not infinite compared with the unknown resistance.

Experiment T_3. **Measurement of specific resistance.**

The specific resistance of a substance is usually defined as the resistance in absolute units of a conductor, 1 cm. long and 1 sq. cm. in cross-section. Specific resistance is sometimes defined in terms of mass instead of volume; *i.e.* it is the resistance of a conductor 1 cm. long whose mass is 1 gram.

If the resistance, length, and cross-section of a wire be measured, it is obvious, since resistance varies directly as length, and inversely as cross-section, that its specific resistance may be readily calculated. The temperature at which the resistance has been determined, should be noted and stated.

I.

If the sample furnished has a resistance of several ohms, the resistance may be measured by the method of the Wheatstone bridge. The measurement should be made with great care, using several different ratios, reversing the ratio arms, reversing the battery current, and taking every precaution to make the determination accurate. The temperature of the bridge coils as well as that of the wire whose resistance is being determined, should be observed. From these data, knowing the temperature coefficients of the wire and the bridge coils, and the temperature at which the bridge is correct, the resistance of the wire at $0°$ can be computed.

II.

If the resistance of the sample to be experimented on is one ohm or less, it should be measured by the fall of potential method. (See Exp. T_2.)

In either case the length and diameter should be measured with the greatest care. The diameter may be directly measured in a number of places by means of a micrometer wire gauge ; or, better, the mean cross-section may be indirectly determined from the mass, length, and density of the specimen. The density should be determined by weighing in water.

Addenda to the report:

(1) Calculate the volume specific resistance.

(2) Compute the specific resistance in terms of mass.

(3) Compute the relative conductivity, assuming that of copper to be 100.

EXPERIMENT T_4. **Determination of the temperature coefficient for resistance of carbon and of various metals.**

The resistance of all conductors varies with the temperature, and the temperature coefficient for resistance is defined by the equation

$$R_t = R_0(1 + at^\circ), \tag{133}$$

in which R_t and R_0 are the resistances at temperatures t° and 0°, respectively, and a is the coefficient. For metals a is positive.

I.

Method of the Wheatstone bridge.

The wire to be tested should be insulated, and coiled in the form of a solenoid sufficiently small to slip into a long test tube, or ordinary glass tube sealed at one end.

Heavy insulated copper wires are to be soldered to the two ends of the coil and brought to the terminals of the Wheatstone's bridge. Make the test wire of such size and length that its resistance will be from two to ten ohms (the higher, the better). Place a thermometer in the tube with the wire, the bulb being at the center of the coil, and fill the upper part of the tube with waste cotton, asbestos, or similar material to prevent the circulation of air. Then immerse the tube in a water bath and measure its resistance at different temperatures, ranging from zero to the boiling-point. Readings of resistance should be taken both for increasing and decreasing temperatures, and the thermometer should be read before and after each measurement, the mean of the two readings being used. Let the changes of temperature take place *very* gradually, and keep the water thoroughly stirred.

For practice determinations of the temperature coefficient of carbon, an incandescent lamp may be used instead of a wire.

From the results obtained, plat a curve on cross-section paper, using temperatures as abscissas, and resistances as ordinates. This curve, in the case of most metals, will be very nearly a straight line. Draw a straight line as nearly as possible through all the points, and determine its equation. From this equation determine the temperature coefficient a and the resistance at 0°.

II.

Fall of potential method.   (See Exp. T_2.)

In this case, a wire of low resistance can be used to advantage. Two wires, not necessarily large, are to be soldered to each end of the test wire, one pair serving to carry the current, and the other pair leading to the galvanometer.

When the coil is at the temperature of the room, adjust the resistance in series with it, so that the galvanometer deflection is about two-thirds the distance across the scale. It is very important that the temperature remain very nearly constant during an observation of the galvanometer reading. The temperature should be taken as nearly as may be at the same instant the galvanometer reading is observed, both direct and reversed. The mean of these two temperature observations is to be used in the computations.

For the determination of the temperature coefficient it is not necessary to have any absolute standard of resistance. Since galvanometer deflections are proportional to resistance, we may substitute for R_t and R_0 the deflections δ_t and δ_0 (equation 133), or their tangents, if a tangent galvanometer is used.

After making the necessary readings, a curve should be platted, with temperatures as abscissas and galvanometer deflections as ordinates. The equation of this line is then to be determined, and from its constants the temperature coefficient and deflection for $0°$ are to be calculated.

Addenda to the report:

(1) Justify the substitution of galvanometer deflection for resistances in the above equation.

(2) Using the coefficient determined, calculate the resistance at absolute zero of wire whose resistance is 100 ohms at $0°$ C.

EXPERIMENT T_6. **Measurement of the internal resistance of a battery by Ohm's method.**

This experiment requires the same observations as Exp. S_2, and the battery resistance may be calculated from the observations taken in that experiment, provided the resistance of the galvanometer and of the connecting wires is known. It is not necessary, however, to know the constant of the galvanometer.

From Ohm's law we have

$$I = \frac{E}{R_b + R_g + R}, \tag{134}$$

in which R is a known resistance, R_b and R_g the battery and galvanometer resistances respectively. The last named includes the resistance of the connecting wires. For I may be substituted $I_0\delta$ (or $I_0\tan\delta$, in case the current is proportional to the tangent of the deflection of the galvanometer needle).

If two different values of R be taken, and the corresponding galvanometer deflections observed, we shall have two equations similar to 134. If one of these equations be divided by the other, both E and I_0 will be eliminated, and R_b will be a function of known quantities.

This experiment furnishes an excellent example of the general principles discussed on page 4. The precautions there suggested should be followed here; that is to say, the difference between the two currents in the observations by means of which E and I_0 are eliminated, and R_b is determined, should not be far from the value of the smaller one. Furthermore, the resistances used should be comparable in magnitude with the battery resistance. In order to meet these conditions it will be necessary to use a non-sensitive galvanometer of low resistance, or to adjust a sensitive galvanometer with a shunt of proper resistance placed across its terminals.

The procedure is as follows :

(1) Connect the battery in series with a resistance box, the galvanometer, and a reversing key.

(2) Observe the galvanometer readings for eight or ten different resistances. These readings should be taken several times for each resistance used, and the mean deflection derived from them should be utilized in the computations.

(3) From each suitable pair of observations compute the resistance of the battery.

It will be found instructive to determine the resistance from the observations graphically, and if a considerable number of observations are taken, that will usually be the least laborious method and sufficiently accurate.

To do this, plat a curve with known resistances as abscissas, and reciprocals of currents, or of galvanometer deflections as ordinates. The intercept on the axis of abscissas will be the resistance of the circuit outside of the resistance box.

The resistance of a cell is sometimes determined by connecting two cells, first in series, and then in multiple, and observing the galvanometer deflections in each case. Between two equations representing these observations, E and I_0 may then be eliminated, and R_c may be determined. This method assumes that the E. M. F.'s and internal resistances of the two cells are identical. To test this assumption, connect the two cells in series, but so that their E. M. F.'s are opposed. If no current flows, their E. M. F.'s are equal. Next connect each cell in turn in series with the galvanometer and the same *low* resistance. If the currents are equal, their internal resistances are equal (provided their E. M. F.'s are equal).

The following modification of the method, which is especially useful when the law of the galvanometer is unknown, may be used to check the results:

(1) Connect the two cells in multiple, and observe the deflection produced when some known resistance is used in the box.

(2) Join the cells in series and adjust the box resistance until the deflection is the same as before.

(3) From the values of the two box resistances and the galvanometer resistance, compute the resistance of a single cell.

The method of this experiment is not applicable to batteries that suffer marked variation from polarization.

EXPERIMENT T_6. **Resistance of a battery by Mance's method.**

It is a rather difficult matter to secure a satisfactory measurement of the internal resistance of a battery. Mance's method is perhaps the most accurate for a battery that is not subject to rapid polarization.

The battery whose resistance is required is made one arm of a Wheatstone bridge, the other three arms being adjustable resistances of known value. The battery usually employed with the bridge is removed and replaced by a wire, the battery key being retained in its old place. In this use of the bridge, a current flows through the galvanometer at all times, and it will be found advantageous to keep the galvanometer key closed.

The measurement now consists in so adjusting the resistances in the bridge that the opening or closing of the battery key has no effect upon the deflection of the galvanometer needle. When this adjustment has been obtained, the resistance of the cell can be computed from the ordinary law of the bridge.

If the deflection of the galvanometer is too great to be read on the scale, a permanent magnet may be used to bring the needle back. This magnet should be kept as far away as is possible, however, in order not to diminish the sensitiveness of the galvanometer. Judgment must be used in the choice of the resistances placed in the various arms, so as to secure the greatest sensitiveness and at the same time as little inconvenience as possible from large and variable deflections. If the resistance of the battery is not very great (thousands of ohms), it will be best to adjust the resistance of the three arms of the bridge, so that the greatest resistance is in series with the battery and galvanometer.

If the battery polarizes, even very slowly, there will be a drift of galvanometer reading. This change of the current through the galvanometer must, of course, be disregarded. Sometimes the observations are still further complicated by the existence of some small self-induction in the bridge coils.

The effect of this is to give the galvanometer needle a slight inductive throw, even though the conjugate condition of the four arms of the bridge has been reached.

Addenda to the report :

(1) Prove that the ordinary law of the bridge holds for Mance's method.

(2) A dynamo is like a battery in the fact that it is the seat of an E. M. F., and has internal resistance. What difficulty would be experienced in measuring, by this method, the internal resistance of a dynamo while running?

Experiment T_7. Resistance of electrolytes.

When a current is passed through an electrolyte, the electrolyte is decomposed, and a counter E. M. F. is always set up. Often there is also an evolution of gas at one or both ends of the electrodes. These effects complicate the experimental determination of electrolytic resistance, but the difficulties which they introduce may be, in great part, avoided by the use of an alternating current of short period.

The Wheatstone's bridge method of measuring resistance may be adapted to the determination of electrolytic resistance as follows :

(1) An alternating current is supplied by replacing the battery by the secondary circuit of an induction coil.

(2) The galvanometer is replaced by some means of detecting alternating currents. A telephone will serve this purpose very well. The method of working is analogous to that described in Exp. T_1. The resistance of the bridge arms is varied until no sound is heard in the telephone, and the unknown resistance is determined by the ordinary law of the bridge. Since the current flowing is a rapidly fluctuating one, it is of the utmost importance that the bridge arms have no self-induction. For this reason, a special form of bridge is generally used.

If the vessel containing the electrolyte is a tube or a prismatic trough with electrodes filling the ends, the specific resistance may be computed as in Exp. T_3. In this way we may determine the specific resistance of different solutions, or of the same solution at different temperatures and densities. The temperature of the solution should always be noted at the time of the experiment.

If the vessel used does not admit of accurate measurement, it should be standardized a follows :

(1) Make a 10 per cent solution of zinc or copper sulphate.

(2) Fill the vessel and determine its resistance.

(3) From this resistance and the specific resistance of the electrolyte taken from tables, compute what must be the length of the electrolyte if its cross-section is one square centimeter.

The apparatus having been thus standardized, the specific resistance of any other solution may be determined.

Before putting a solution into the vessel, care should always be taken to scrupulously clean the vessel, and to rinse it with distilled water. The resistance of a solution is sometimes greatly changed by even slight traces of other substances.

CHAPTER IX.

GROUP U: ELECTRICAL QUANTITY.

(U) *General statements;* (U$_1$) *Constant of a ballistic galvanometer;* (U$_2$) *Logarithmic decrement;* (U$_3$) *Comparison of capacities;* (U$_4$) *Capacity in absolute measure.*

(U). General statements concerning electrical quantity.

The electromagnetic unit of quantity is that quantity of electricity which is transferred by unit current in unit time. The practical unit of quantity, or the coulomb, is the amount transferred by a current of one ampere in one second.

The total quantity of electricity transferred by any current is the product of the current by the time during which it continues.   If the current is variable, this becomes

$$Q = \int I dt$$

taken between the proper limits.

Quantities of electricity are considered when we deal with,
(1) The total amount of an electrolyte decomposed.
(2) The charge and discharge of condensers.
(3) Momentary induced currents.

In cases 2 and 3 the duration of the current is usually very brief, and since the magnetic field produced is equally transient, it is obvious that the quantity of electricity transferred cannot be measured by means of a galvanometer used in the ordinary manner. The quantity of electricity transferred through the coils of a galvanometer by a momentary current can be measured, however, by the " throw " or " swing " of the needle due to the magnetic impulse of the momentary current.

A galvanometer used for measuring such impulses is called a ballistic galvanometer from its analogy to a ballistic pendulum.

Any galvanometer can be used as a ballistic galvanometer, simply by observing "throws" instead of permanent deflections, provided that the motion of the needle be so slow that the end of the swing can be determined accurately. It is also desirable, in the case of galvanometers used ballistically, that the damping should be as small as possible. These two requisites are secured by making the needle heavy, thus securing slow motion and small factor of decrement. In using a ballistic galvanometer, it must be remembered that the magnetic moment of the needle enters the constant of the instrument. Therefore the needle should be a magnet whose moment is not subject to rapid change.

EXPERIMENT U$_1$. **Measurement of the constant of a ballistic galvanometer.**

There are three methods for determining this constant :

(1) By measuring the throw of the galvanometer needle due to the discharge of a condenser.

(2) By measuring the throw of the galvanometer needle produced by the induced current due to the rotation of a coil in a magnetic field.

(3) By computation from the periodic time of the galvanometer needle, and the constant of the instrument used as a tangent galvanometer. The last is the most instructive, and is the one here given.

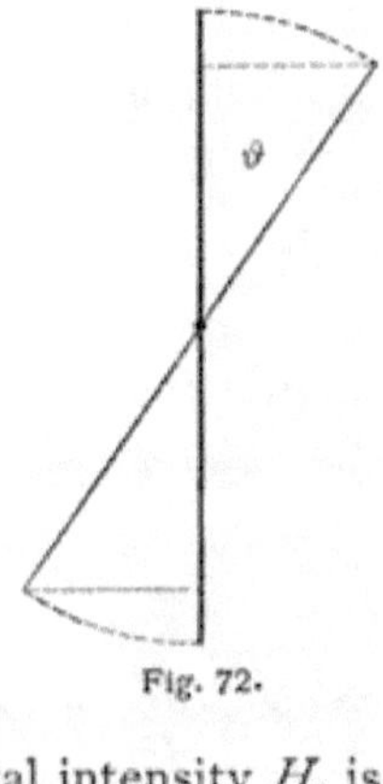

The amount of work done against magnetic forces in turning a magnet through an

Fig. 72.

angle δ (Fig. 72) in a magnetic field of horizontal intensity H, is

$$W = MH\,(1 - \cos \delta) = 2\,MH \sin^2 \tfrac{1}{2}\, \delta. \qquad (135)$$

The kinetic energy of the magnet when it has its greatest angular velocity is

$$E_0 = \tfrac{1}{2} K \omega_0^2. \tag{136}$$

The kinetic energy of the moving magnet at the mid-point is equal to the work necessary to turn the magnet through the angle δ.

$$\therefore \ \tfrac{1}{2} K \omega_0^2 = 2\,MH \sin^2 \tfrac{1}{2}\,\delta. \tag{137}$$

A current of I amperes flowing in the galvanometer coils exerts a force on the galvanometer needle whose moment is $\tfrac{1}{10}MGI$, G being the *true* constant of the galvanometer.   If the moment of this force be integrated over the time during which the current lasts, it must equal the moment of momentum produced.

$$\therefore \ \tfrac{1}{10}MG \int I dt = K\omega_0,$$

whence,
$$\tfrac{1}{10}MGQ = K\omega_0. \tag{138}$$

Force multiplied by time is equal to the momentum produced.   In the same way moment of a force multiplied by time is equal to the moment of momentum produced: but the moment of momentum of a body is also equal to its moment of inertia multiplied by its angular velocity.

If T is the periodic time of the magnetic needle for small oscillations, we have (see equation 102)

$$T = 2\pi \sqrt{\frac{K}{MH}}. \tag{139}$$

If in the equations (137), (138), and (139), K and M be expressed in the form of their ratio, this ratio and ω_0 may be eliminated between the three equations.   This will give

$$Q = 10\frac{T}{\pi}\frac{H}{G}\sin\tfrac{1}{2}\,\delta. \tag{140}$$

Now $10\dfrac{H}{G}$ is the working constant of the galvanometer.

$$\therefore \ Q = \frac{T}{\pi} I_0 \sin\tfrac{1}{2}\,\delta. \tag{141}$$

The constant factor multiplied into the term $\sin \frac{1}{2} \delta$ is the constant of the instrument used as a ballistic galvanometer. Calling this quantity Q_0, we have

$$Q = Q_0 \sin \tfrac{1}{2} \delta. \tag{142}$$

In order to determine Q_0, first determine I_0 as in Exp. R_1, and then the periodic time of the galvanometer needle as in Exp. Q_3. From these values compute Q_0.

If δ is quite small, the quantity of electricity Q is proportional to δ, but δ is proportional to the deflection on the scale. Therefore we have

$$Q = Q_0 \delta, \tag{143}$$

in which δ is the throw in scale divisions, and Q_0 is the constant per scale division. The above demonstration assumes that the whole of the kinetic energy of the needle after the current has ceased to flow is used in overcoming magnetic forces. This is not quite true. The friction of the needle against the air and the current induced in the galvanometer coil by the moving magnetic needle, both require the expenditure of energy, and therefore make δ less than it otherwise would be. The theory of damping leads to the conclusion that $(1 + \frac{1}{2} \lambda) \sin \frac{1}{2} \delta$ should be substituted for $\sin \frac{1}{2} \delta$ in the above equation, in which λ is the logarithmic decrement of the galvanometer needle. (See Exp. U_2.)

EXPERIMENT U_2. Determination of the logarithmic decrement of a ballistic galvanometer needle.

It has already been shown that the quantity of electricity that passes through the coils of the ballistic galvanometer is proportional to the impulse imparted to the needle, which, in its turn, is proportional to the sine of half the angle of throw, or to the angle itself, if the latter be small. This is true, however, only when there is no lost energy due to air friction and induced currents, which damp the oscillation of the needle, and finally bring it to rest.

Since it is by means of the throw that the quantity is to be measured, we must know the correction that is to be applied to the *actual* throw of the needle to give the throw that would have resulted had there been no damping.

When a magnetic needle oscillates under the influence of damping, the ratio of any amplitude to the succeeding one in the opposite direction is very nearly constant, or

$$\frac{\delta_1}{\delta_2} = \frac{\delta_2}{\delta_3} = \frac{\delta_n}{\delta_{n+1}} = r. \tag{144}$$

This constant is the "ratio of damping," and its Napierian logarithm is called the logarithmic decrement, and is generally designated by λ. We have, therefore,

$$\lambda = \log_e \frac{\delta_n}{\delta_{n+1}} \tag{145}$$

The equation of motion of a body oscillating under the action of a force whose moment is proportional to the angular displacement, as has been shown under the head of simple harmonic motion, is

$$K \frac{d^2\phi}{dt^2} + G_0\phi = 0. \tag{146}$$

If the motion is not simply harmonic, but is damped by friction or otherwise, a third term must be introduced. In the case of an oscillating magnet, damping is produced :

(1) By air friction.

(2) By induced currents due to the motion of the magnet near conductors. Both of these retarding forces are very nearly proportional to the angular velocity; consequently the term that must be added to the above equation is $k\frac{d\phi}{dt}$, in which k is a constant. The complete equation of motion of the damped magnetic needle is therefore

$$K \frac{d^2\phi}{dt^2} + k\frac{d\phi}{dt} + MH\phi = 0. \tag{147}$$

If we integrate this equation, we have

$$\phi = \delta_0 \epsilon^{-\frac{kt}{2K}} \sin \frac{2\pi}{T} t, ^* \qquad (148)$$

in which δ_0 is a constant, and T is the period of oscillation of the needle under the influence of damping.

Let time be reckoned from the instant the needle passes the position of equilibrium; and let δ_1, $\delta_2 \cdots \cdots$, be the values of ϕ at the times $= \frac{T}{4}, \frac{3T}{4} \cdots \cdots$. These values of ϕ will be the successive actual amplitudes of the oscillatory motion ; and

$$\delta_1 = \delta_0 \epsilon^{-\frac{kT}{4K}},$$
$$\delta_2 = \delta_0 \epsilon^{-\frac{3kT}{4K}}. \qquad (149)$$

From (149) we have

$$\log_\epsilon \frac{\delta_1}{\delta_2} = \tfrac{1}{4} \frac{kT}{K}, \qquad (150)$$

and by substituting for this quantity λ, as in (145), equation 149 gives

$$\delta_1 = \delta_0 \epsilon^{-\frac{1}{2}\lambda}. \qquad (151)$$

Transposing and expanding the exponential in terms of λ, and neglecting powers of λ higher than the first, we obtain

$$\delta_0 = \delta_1 (1 + \tfrac{1}{2} \lambda). \qquad (152)$$

When there is no damping, *i.e.* when $k = 0$, we have, from (149), $\delta_1 = \delta_0$. Therefore, it follows that δ_0 is the quantity that should be substituted for the first actual throw in using a ballistic galvanometer, and that equation 143 becomes

$$Q = Q_0 (1 + \tfrac{1}{2} \lambda) \delta_1. \qquad (153)$$

The above demonstration is based upon the assumption that both δ and λ are small. If δ is $4°$ and the ratio of damping is 1.05, equation 153 will be in error by about one

---

* See Gray's Absolute Measurements in Electricity and Magnetism, vol. 2, p. 393.

part in a thousand. If δ is $10°$ and the ratio of damping is 1.2, the error will be about one in a hundred.

The object of this experiment is to determine the logarithmic decrement of a galvanometer needle, and to show the relation of the decrement to the resistance in circuit with the galvanometer. It is obvious that the decrement must depend on the resistance, since the damping is, in large part, due to the currents induced in the galvanometer coils by the moving needle, and because these currents are inversely proportional to the resistance of the circuit.

In the performance of the experiment, a galvanometer should be used in which the needle is not strongly damped. From equation 144, we have

$$\frac{\delta_n}{\delta_{n+m}} = r^m, \tag{154}$$

whence
$$\lambda = \frac{1}{m} \log_e \frac{\delta_n}{\delta_{n+m}}. \tag{155}$$

Errors of observation have the least influence when the ratio of δ_n to δ_{n+m} is about 3.

The method of procedure is as follows :

(1) Set the needle to vibrating, and observe the limits of the successive swings to the right and left by means of a telescope and scale.

(2) From these observations determine the successive amplitudes.

The position of equilibrium of the needle will generally be obtained by noting the scale reading when the needle is at rest. Sometimes this position changes during the progress of an experiment. It may then be obtained as follows : Let S_1, S_2, and S_3 be three scale readings corresponding to the extremes of successive throws. We shall then have

$$S_0 = \tfrac{1}{4}[S_1 + S_3 + 2 S_2],$$

in which S_0 is the zero position at the instant when the scale reading is S_2. The deflection required, then, is in scale divisions,

$$\delta_2 = S_2 - S_0.$$

If the angles are not small, these amplitudes should be reduced to circular measure by means of the known distance of the scale from the mirror.

Several values of the ratio of damping should be obtained in the following manner: Suppose the $(n+1)$st amplitude to be about one-third of the first; λ should then be determined from the ratios

$$\frac{\delta_1}{\delta_{n+1}}, \quad \frac{\delta_2}{\delta_{n+2}} \dots.$$

Determine in this way the logarithmic decrement when the galvanometer coils are short-circuited, and are in open circuit, and also for several different resistances, comparable with the galvanometer resistance. Finally, from these determinations plat a curve, with resistances as abscissas and corresponding values of the decrement as ordinates.

This curve will have an asymptote parallel to the axis of abscissas, at a distance from that axis equal to the decrement on open circuit. If the axis of abscissas be made to coincide with this asymptote, the ordinates to the curve will be the decrements due solely to induced currents. These decrements are inversely proportional to the resistance of the circuit. From this relation and from the curve, compute the resistance of the galvanometer.

EXPERIMENT U_3. **Comparison of the capacities of two condensers.**

When the coatings of a condenser are charged to a potential difference, pd, the charge or quantity of electricity stored in the condenser is

$$Q = Cpd, \tag{156}$$

in which C is the capacity of the condenser. It has already been shown in preceding experiments that if the quantity of electricity Q is discharged through a ballistic galvanometer producing the deflection δ, we have

$$Q = Q_0(1 + \tfrac{1}{2}\lambda)\delta. \tag{157}$$

If a condenser of capacity C_1, charged to a potential difference, pd_1, be discharged through the ballistic galvanometer, we have

$$C_1 = \frac{Q_0}{pd_1}(1 + \tfrac{1}{2}\lambda)\delta_1. \tag{158}$$

If another condenser of capacity C_2, charged to a potential difference, pd_2, be discharged through the *same* ballistic galvanometer, we shall have a similar relation. And if the first equation be divided by the second, we shall have

$$\frac{C_1}{C_2} = \frac{pd_2\delta_1}{pd_1\delta_2}. \tag{159}$$

A still simpler relation follows if the condensers have been charged to the same potential difference.

In experimenting with condensers it is generally necessary to use rather large potential differences (from 50 to several hundred volts). Such potential differences may be produced by a water battery of a sufficient number of very small cells. Each cell consists of a short test-tube filled with very slightly acidulated water. The plates are made by soldering together short strips of copper and zinc. Each "couple" is bent into a U-shape, and the copper dipped into one cell, and the zinc into the next cell, as illustrated in Fig. 73.

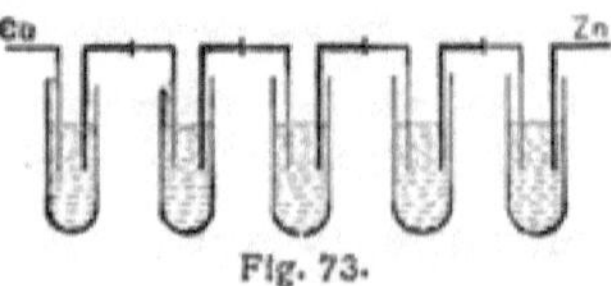

Fig. 73.

In condenser work it is also necessary to use great care in securing good insulation, not solely on account of the use of high potentials, but because the condenser must sometimes remain charged for a few minutes while unconnected with a battery. The procedure in this experiment is as follows:

(1) Connect the condenser in series with the battery and ballistic galvanometer, and place in the circuit a double contact key, as shown in Fig. 74.

(2) Make contact at A, and thus charge the condenser through the galvanometer. The corresponding galvanometer throw should be determined as in Exp. U$_2$.

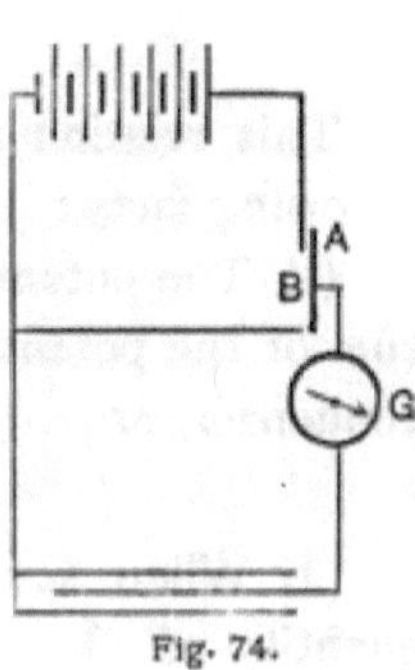

Fig. 74.

(3) Break contact at A, and immediately make contact at B, thus discharging the condenser through the galvanometer. The galvanometer needle will receive an impulse in the opposite direction, which should be very nearly equal to the former throw. These observations should be repeated several times in order to get a good average.

A similar series of observations should now be taken with the condenser replaced by the one with which it is to be compared. If the capacities of the two condensers do not differ greatly, that is, if one is not more than two or three times as great as the other, the same number of cells should be used. If the difference of capacity is very large, the E. M. F.'s of the batteries in the two cases should be adjusted to suit the two condensers, and they should be compared as in Exp. S$_1$.

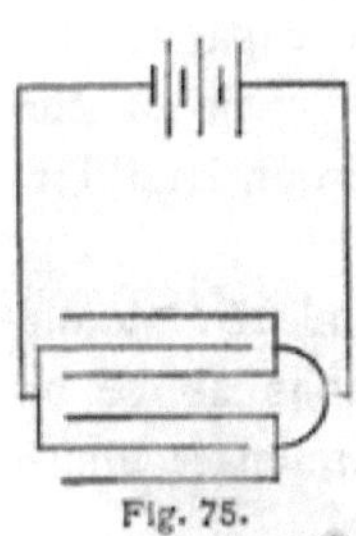
Fig. 75.

When condensers are connected as shown in Fig. 75, they are said to be connected in multiple. If C is the capacity in multiple, we have the relation

$$C_m = C_1 + C_2 + \cdots. \qquad (160)$$

This relation follows directly from the fact that the capacity of a condenser is proportional to the area of either of its coatings.

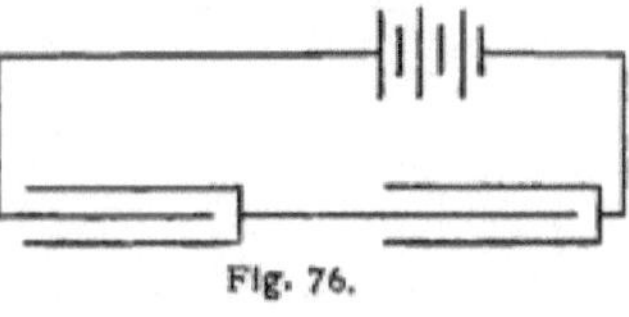
Fig. 76.

When condensers are connected as shown in Fig. 76, they

are said to be connected in series.　If C_s is the capacity of the system in series, we have

$$\frac{1}{C_s} = \frac{1}{C_1} + \frac{1}{C_2} + \cdots. \tag{161}$$

This relation may be readily derived by making use of the following facts :

(1) The potential difference at the terminals is equal to the sum of the potential differences between the coatings of each condenser, or

$$pd_s = pd_1 + pd_2 + \cdots. \tag{162}$$

(2) When several condensers are connected in series, the quantity of electricity on each coating of every condenser is the same, or

$$Q_1 = Q_2 = \cdots. \tag{163}$$

Equation 161 then follows directly from the definition of capacity.　It is also to be remembered that the capacity of a system of condensers connected in series is the ratio of the charge on either extreme coating divided by the potential difference between the extreme coatings.

The relations expressed in equations 160 and 161 should be verified experimentally.　This may be done as above by comparing the series or multiple system with a condenser whose capacity is known.

EXPERIMENT U_4.　**Measurement of the capacity of a condenser in absolute measure.**

If the condenser is charged or discharged through a ballistic galvanometer, we shall have, as in the preceding experiment,

$$C = \frac{Q_0}{pd} (1 + \tfrac{1}{2}\lambda)\delta. \tag{164}$$

If the quantities on the right of this equation are all determined in absolute measure, the capacity will be determined independently of the capacity of any standard condenser.　The constants Q_0, pd, and λ should be determined as described in previous experiments. It should be remembered that the value of λ to be used in this experiment is that obtained when the galvanometer circuit is open.

The procedure is as follows :

(1) The throw of the needle δ is to be determined as in the preceding experiment, by charging and discharging the condenser through the galvanometer.

(2) The values of δ, which always differ in the case of the charge and of the discharge, respectively, should be averaged separately. The former value will correspond to the instantaneous capacity, while the latter corresponds to the capacity of the condenser after a greater or less absorption has taken place.

CHAPTER X

GROUP V: ELECTROMAGNETIC INDUCTION.

(V) *General statements;* (V₁) *Dip and intensity of the earth's magnetic field (method of the earth inductor);* (V₂) *Lines of force of a permanent magnet;* (V₃) *Mutual induction.*

(V). General statements concerning induction.

Faraday discovered that when any portion of a complete circuit is moved through a magnetic field, an electric current circulates in all parts of it.

This fact may be viewed as follows :

Let there be a conductor, shown in cross-section (Fig. 77), which forms part of a complete circuit. Suppose it to be

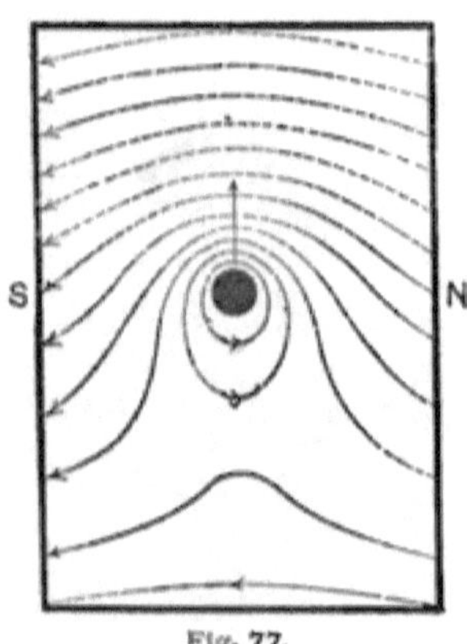

Fig. 77.

moving in the direction of the arrow in a magnetic field originally uniform. The arrangement of the lines of force of this field is indicated by the dotted lines. During the motion of this conductor, the otherwise uniform field will be distorted. The field of force on the side *towards* which the conductor is moving will be stronger than before, and the lines of force will be crowded together, and concave towards the conductor. On the opposite side, the lines of force will be more widely separated, and convex towards the conductor. Immediately around the conductor, and extending to a greater or less distance, according to the intensity of the induced current, the lines of force will be closed curves surrounding it. The positive direction of the lines of force in these closed curves are as indicated in the figure. It follows that if the direction of motion is to the right, and the positive direction of the lines of force vertically upward, the current will be directed towards the observer. Or if the motion is along the x-axis, and the lines of force along the z-axis, the current will be directed along the y-axis, each in the positive direction. (See Fig. 78.)

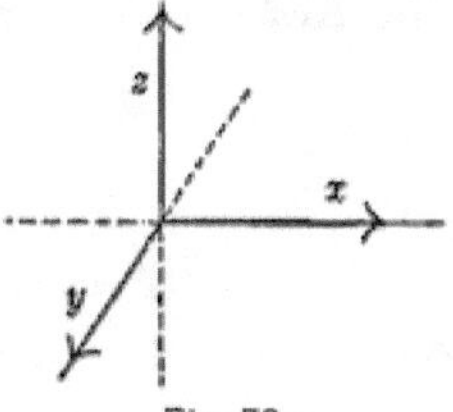

Fig. 78.

Since a current may be produced in this way, it must be that there is an E. M. F. generated in the moving conductor. This E. M. F. exists whether the circuit is closed or not. In the latter case, if the motion is uniform, and in a uniform field, there will simply be a static fall of potential along the conductor in the direction in which current would flow if the circuit were completed.

It has been experimentally demonstrated that the E. M. F. generated in this way is directly proportional:

(1) To the velocity of motion.

(2) To the intensity of the magnetic field.

(3) To the length of the moving conductor; the three directions being mutually perpendicular.

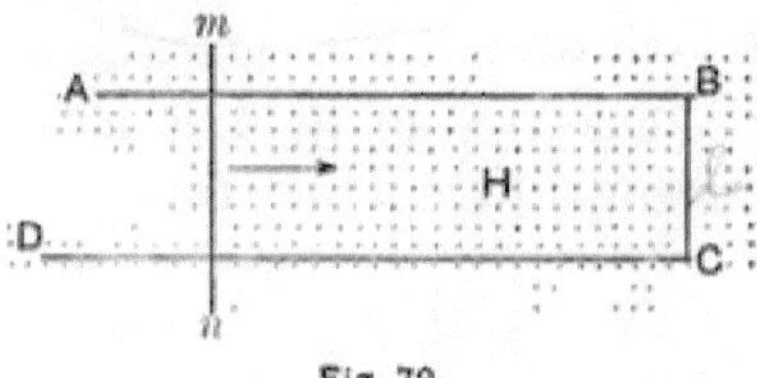

Fig. 79.

Let $ABCD$ (Fig. 79) be a rectangular circuit with one open side, and let it be placed in a magnetic field of intensity H, the lines of force being supposed perpendicular to the plane of the paper. Let *mn* be a conductor resting on the two parallel conductors and completing the circuit. If the length of BC is l, and *mn* moves in the direction of the arrow with a velocity $V = \dfrac{dx}{dt}$, the E. M. F. generated in the circuit will be, in volts,

$$E = \frac{1}{10^8} H \frac{dx}{dt} l. *$$ (165)

When different parts of a circuit cut lines of force at different rates, the total E. M. F. generated in the whole circuit is

$$E = \frac{1}{10^8} H \int \frac{dx}{dt} dl.$$ (165a)

It is obvious that E may be zero both when no lines of force are cut, also when the E. M. F.'s in different parts of the circuit due to cutting lines of force are oppositely directed, and exactly balance each other. For example, let AB, Fig. 80, be a rectangular circuit whose plane is parallel to the lines of force, and capable of rotation about an axis parallel to the lines of force. If this circuit be rotated clock-wise, E. M. F.'s will be generated in the different parts, as indicated by the arrows. These

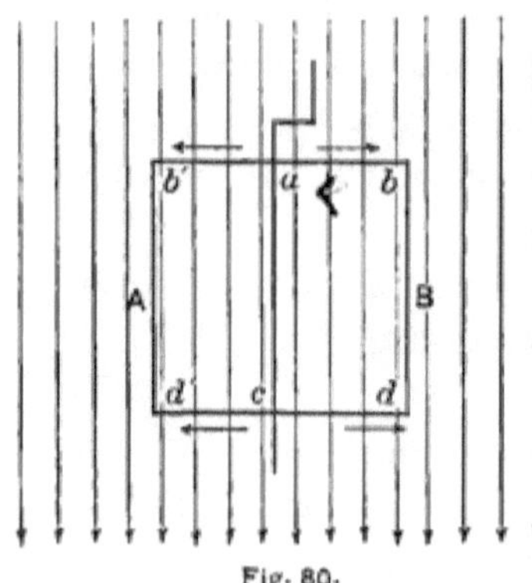

Fig. 80.

obviously annul each other when added around the complete circuit. There is, however, an E. M. F. between a and b producing a fall of potential from a to b, from a to b', from c to d, and from c to d'.

The equation for the E. M. F. generated in a complete circuit may often be simplified in the following manner: Let N be the total number of lines of force that at any instant pass through the circuit. Now if the position of the circuit is changed in the

---

* For the significance of the numerical factor, 10^8, see p. 187.

time dt in such a manner the change in the number of lines of force that pass through the circuit is dN, we have, for the complete circuit,

$$E = \frac{1}{10^8}\frac{dN}{dt} \qquad (165b)$$

If the circuit is composed of n turns, through each of which the N lines pass, we have

$$E = \frac{n}{10^8}\frac{dN}{dt}. \qquad (165c)$$

Furthermore, since $Q = \int I dt$, we have, for the total quantity of electricity produced,

$$Q = \frac{1}{10^8}\frac{N_1}{R}, \qquad (166)$$

in which N_1 is the number of lines of force cut, and R is the resistance of the circuit in ohms.

In making application of the law of induced E. M. F., the following fundamental principles are of service.

(1) The source of the magnetic field is immaterial   It may be due to a permanent magnet, to the earth, or to an electric current.

(2) It is immaterial whether the conductor is moved in a magnetic field, or a magnetic field is moved past the conductor.

(3) Movements of the lines of a magnetic field may be produced in two ways:

(a) By moving bodily a magnet, or a circuit conveying a current.

(b) By causing a current to change, in which case its lines of force will move outwards when the current increases, or move inwards and disappear when the current decreases.

(4) An E. M. F. may be induced in a conductor already conveying a current, and this may either increase or decrease the current flowing.

(5) If the current flowing in a circuit is decreased, the magnetic field due to the current will decrease, the lines of force collapsing on the conductor. This motion of the field will pro-

duce an E. M. F. in the conductor tending to produce a current in the *same* direction as the original current. If the current is increased, the induced E. M. F. changes sign. From this it follows that when current is changed in a circuit, an induced E. M. F. is set up, which opposes that change. This kind of induction is called self-induction.

EXPERIMENT V₁. **Dip and intensity of the earth's magnetic field. (Method of the earth inductor.)**

The earth inductor consists essentially of a coil of wire C, Fig. 81, capable of revolution about an axis A, in its own plane.

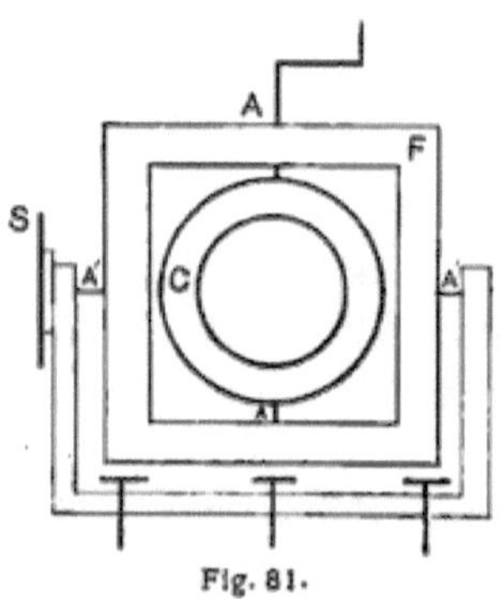

Fig. 81.

Usually this coil is mounted in a frame F, which is itself capable of rotation about an axis A' in its plane, perpendicular to the axis A. To this frame is attached a graduated circle S; by means of this circle the angle which the axis A makes with a horizontal plane can be measured. The instrument is also furnished with stops, which enable the coil to be turned through exactly 180°; and the base is furnished with leveling screws, by means of which the plane containing the two axes of revolution may be made truly horizontal.

I.

To determine the angle of dip.

The angle of dip is defined as the angle which the direction of the lines of force makes with the horizon. If H and V are the horizontal and vertical components of the intensity of the earth's field at any point, we have

$$\tan \beta = \frac{V}{H}. \qquad (167)$$

To determine β, which is the object of this part of the experiment, proceed as follows :

(1) Turn the whole apparatus until the axis, about which the square frame revolves, is perpendicular to the magnetic meridian. This may be done with the aid of a small compass.

(2) Adjust the leveling screws until the square frame containing the two axes of revolution is truly horizontal.

(3) Adjust the stops so that the plane of the movable coil is horizontal in both of the extreme positions.

When thus adjusted, the vertical component of the magnetic field passes through the coil. In other words, V lines of force per square centimeter pass through the coil. If n is the number of turns of the coil, and A is the mean area of the coil, the number of lines of force passing through the coil will be nAV.

(4) If the coil be now turned through 180°, all the lines of force will be cut twice, and we have from equation 166

$$Q_v = \frac{2\,nAV}{10^8\,R},\tag{168}$$

in which R is the resistance of the circuit. If a ballistic galvanometer forms part of the circuit, and if the coil be turned quickly, we shall have

$$Q_v = Q_0(1 + \tfrac{1}{2}\lambda)\,\delta_v = \frac{2\,nAV}{10^8\,R},\tag{169}$$

in which δ_v is the throw of the galvanometer needle. If the angular motion of the needle is not small, $\sin\tfrac{1}{2}\delta$ must be used instead of δ.

(5) If the square frame be now rotated through exactly 90°, as measured by the divided circle, the number of lines of force passing through the coil in its new position will be nAH; and if δ_H is the corresponding galvanometer throw, we have

$$\frac{\delta_v}{\delta_H} = \frac{V}{H}.\tag{170}$$

The constants n, A, R, Q_0, and λ being the same for both positions, are eliminated, and it is not necessary to know their values.

The values δ_v and δ_H used in this computation should each be the mean of ten or twelve determinations.

When the square frame makes an angle with the horizontal equal to the dip, no lines of force thread through the coil in any position; consequently, no current will be produced when it is rotated about its own axis. The position in which no current is produced by the rotation of the coil should be found by trial. The angle through which the frame was turned from the horizontal position furnishes a second determination of the dip.

II.

To determine intensity.

From equation 168 it is obvious that both the vertical and horizontal intensity may be determined in absolute measure, provided Q_0 and λ have previously been determined for the ballistic galvanometer, and n, A, and R are known.

The lines of force make but a small angle with the vertical, and on this account a small error in leveling the coil will produce a relatively great error in the determination of H. This should be remembered in determining the dip as well as in determining the horizontal intensity.

Addenda to the report:

(1) Explain fully the *direction* of the induced current when the coil is rotated about a vertical and a horizontal axis.

(2) Explain from first principles why there is no current when the coil is rotated about an axis parallel to the lines of force.

EXPERIMENT V$_2$. Measurement of the lines of force of a permanent magnet.

The object of this experiment is the determination of the number of lines of force that emerge from the positive half of a permanent magnet.   Before beginning these measurements the constant and the logarithmic decrement of a ballistic galvanometer must have been determined.   (Exps. U_1 and U_2.) These values having been ascertained, the procedure is as follows :

Connect a test coil of a known number of turns in series with the galvanometer.   Place the coil at the center of the magnet, and when the galvanometer needle has come to rest observe the throw of the needle produced by quickly slipping the test coil off the end of the magnet.   This test coil should consist of a considerable number of turns of small copper wire, No. 24–36, according to the resistance of the

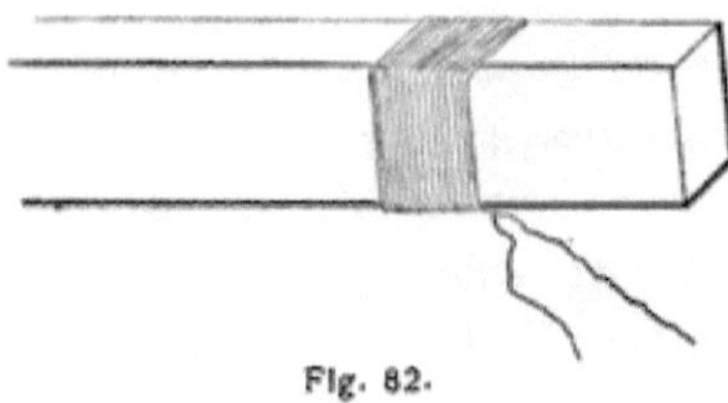

Fig. 82.

galvanometer and the sensitiveness of the latter.   It should be of such a form as to fit easily over the bar magnet to be tested.   (See Fig. 82.)

If N is the number of lines of force that emerge from the magnet, and n the number of turns in the coil, we have from equations 153 and 166

$$Q = \frac{Nn}{10^8 R} = Q_0(1 + \tfrac{1}{2}\lambda)\delta, \qquad (171)$$

in which R is the resistance of the circuit.

The most suitable number of turns for the test coil will depend upon the strength of the magnet, the sensitiveness of the galvanometer, and the resistance of the circuit.   These quantities should be so adjusted that the galvanometer throw is rather large.   Within certain limits this result can be most easily obtained by varying the resistance in circuit with the galvanometer.

If the bar is not symmetrically magnetized, the magnetic center must be found experimentally. To do this, move the test coil along the bar step-wise. When the magnetic center is reached, a slight motion of the coil in either direction may be made without producing a reversal of current in the galvanometer circuit.

By this method the flow of induction from several magnets should be determined, selecting for the purpose both bar magnets and those of the horseshoe type.

Addenda to the report:

(1) From the readings obtained compute the induction per square centimeter through the center of each magnet.

(2) If the magnetic moment is known, compute the distance between the poles, or, more properly, the distance between the "centers of gravity" of the two distributions of magnetism.

EXPERIMENT V_3. **Mutual induction.**

The objects of this experiment are: I, to observe certain of the phenomena of mutual induction; II, to measure the quantity of electricity which circulates in a secondary circuit when the magnetic field in its vicinity produced by a current in a primary circuit is varied.

I.

The primary and secondary circuits consist of two coils of the same size. The primary coil, however, is wound with considerably coarser wire than the secondary coil.

The method is as follows:

(1) Connect the primary coil P (Fig. 83) in circuit with a battery of constant E. M. F., and insert a make and break, key K.

(2) Connect the secondary coil S in series with a ballistic galvanometer and a resistance box. The latter is placed in the circuit to enable the observer to adjust the throws of the galvanometer needle.

(3) Place the primary and secondary coils close together, with their axes coincident.

(4) Observe the galvanometer throws when the current is made and broken in the primary circuit.

(5) The circuit being closed, and current flowing steadily in the primary circuit, observe the galvanometer throws produced by quickly moving the secondary to a distance of a meter; also when the coil is quickly replaced.

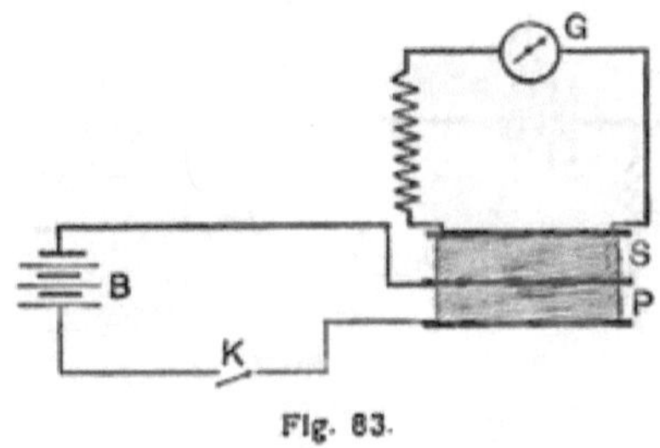

Fig. 83.

(6) Repeat these observations, this time moving the primary instead of the secondary coil.

(7) Observe the galvanometer throw when one of the coils is quickly turned and placed with its opposite face next to the other coil.

(8) Observe the effect upon the galvanometer when a permanent magnet is moved in the vicinity of the secondary coil.

II.

(A) The quantity of electricity which is produced in the secondary circuit is directly proportional to the intensity of the current that is made and broken in the primary circuit. To prove this relationship, use the following method :

(1) Connect a battery, a variable resistance, and a galvanometer in series with the primary coil (Fig. 84).

(2) Connect the secondary coil in series with a ballistic galvanometer, and place the coil, as before, close to the primary with the axes coincident.

(3) Observe the throws of the ballistic galvanometer needle when the primary circuit is made and broken.

(4) Measure also the current flowing in the primary circuit.

Repeat these observations with different currents in the primary circuit.   The resistances of the two circuits should

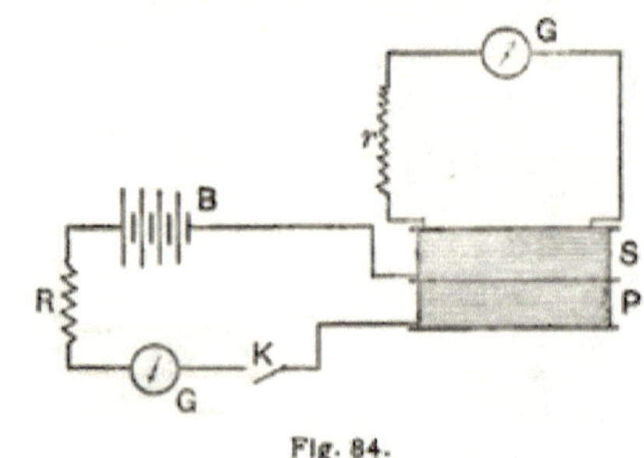

Fig. 84.

be so adjusted that the series of throws on the ballistic galvanometer vary from the smallest that can be accurately determined, to the largest that the scale will allow.   The resistance of the secondary circuit must not be changed during the experiment.

If currents in the primary be platted as abscissas, and throws of the ballistic galvanometer as ordinates, the resulting curve will be found to be a straight line passing through the origin.   This verifies the relation

$$Q_s \propto I_p, \qquad (172)$$

in which I_p is the current in the primary, and Q_s is the quantity of electricity which circulates in the secondary.

The apparatus described above should be further utilized to establish the following relations :

(B) The quantity of electricity which is induced in the secondary circuit is inversely proportional to the resistance of that circuit.

To determine this fact, the same connections as in (A) should be made. Now observe the throws of the ballistic galvanometer when the primary circuit is made and broken, for several different resistances in the secondary circuit. If a curve be platted with resistances in the secondary circuit as abscissas, and the reciprocals of throws as ordinates, it will be found to be a straight line passing through the origin ; thus verifying the relation

$$Q_s \propto \frac{1}{R_s}. \tag{173}$$

If the results of (A) and (B) be combined, we have

$$Q_s = M \frac{I_P}{R_s}, \tag{174}$$

in which the constant M is defined as the coefficient of mutual induction of the two coils. The value of M depends solely on the construction of the two coils and their relative position. If Q, I, and R be measured in coulombs, amperes, and ohms, respectively, M will be expressed in henrys.

(C) If the distance between the primary and secondary coils be varied, the mutual induction will also vary. The relation between these two quantities may be experimentally determined as follows : Make connections as above, place the two coils on a common axis, and observe the throws of the ballistic galvanometer needle corresponding to several different distances between the two coils. From (174) we have

$$M = \frac{Q_s R_s}{I_P}. \tag{175}$$

If the current which flows in the primary while that circuit is closed has a constant value throughout the experiment, the mutual induction will be proportional to the product of resist-

ance in the secondary circuit and the throw of the galvanometer needle, and we may write

$$M \propto \delta R_s. \tag{176}$$

These observations should be repeated with a soft iron core
in the primary coil, and curves platted with distances between
the coils as abscissas, and the above product as ordinates.
If the coefficient of mutual induction is known for any one
position, it can now be computed for any other position by
a simple proportion between the known and unknown coefficients, and the corresponding ordinates to the curve.

CHAPTER XI.

GROUP W: SOUND.

(W_1) *Measurement of pitch by the syren*; (W_2) *Wave length by Koenig's apparatus*; (W_3) *Resonance of columns of air with determination of the velocity of sound*; (W_4) *Velocity of sound in brass*; (W_5) *The sonometer*; (W_6) *Study of the transverse vibration of cords and wires, Moler's method.*

EXPERIMENT W_1. **Measurement of pitch by the syren.**

This experiment consists in the determination, by means of a syren, of the pitch of an organ pipe, first when closed at one end and then when open. Each determination should be made several times. Two observers are needed to make these measurements successfully, one devoting his attention to keeping the syren in unison with the pipe, while the other operates the counter and observes the time. To form an estimate of the degree of accuracy that is attainable, several measurements should be made with a tuning fork of known pitch before beginning observations with the pipe. (See Glazebrook and Shaw, p. 222.)

EXPERIMENT W_2. **Interference and measurement of wave length by Koenig's apparatus.**

In the form of apparatus used a manometric capsule (m_1, m_2) is attached to one end of each of two tubes. The opposite ends of the tubes are brought together at a common opening (Fig. 85), where some sounding body, such as a tuning fork or organ pipe, is to be placed. The two tubes are initially of the same length, but one of them (L_2) is capable of adjustment so that its length can be increased by about 50 cm. From each of the two capsules a tube (g_1, g_2) leads to a small gas jet. The latter will be set in vibration when the membrane of the capsule is disturbed, and can be observed in a revolving mirror. There is also a third jet attached to g_3 which is connected, by tubes of equal length, to both capsules ; so that if a pressure or condensation is sent to it by one of the capsules at the same time

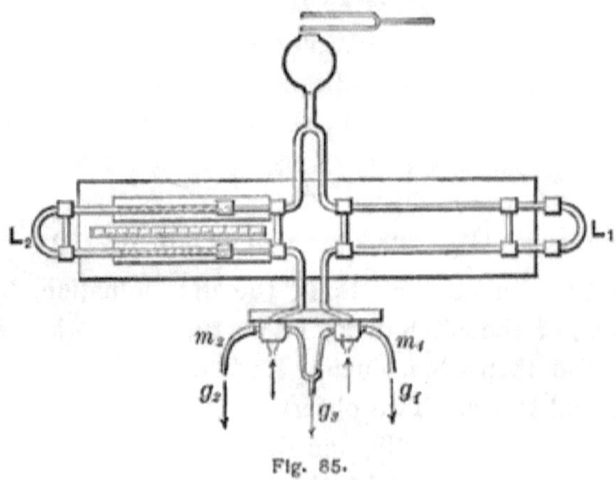

Fig. 85.

that an equal rarefaction is sent by the other, the two acting on the flame at the same instant will not affect it. Each of the single jets will, however, still show the disturbance. In order that a condensation may exist at one capsule at the same time that a rarefaction exists at the other, it is obvious that the two tubes must differ in length by one-half the wave length of the sound that is producing the disturbance, or by some odd multiple of a half wave length. This can be brought about by sliding the movable tube in or out. When the proper adjustment is obtained, the jet that is connected with both capsules should show a minimum disturbance. It will not be found possible to produce complete quiescence in the image of g_3, such as is indicated in Fig. 86. Care must be taken to have the tubes which supply this jet of the same length, and also to have the pressure of gas the same in each. To adjust the pressure, pinch shut one of the tubes, and note the height of flame due to the other; then pinch the second tube and release the first, and adjust the supply of gas until the height of flame is the same in both cases.

Fig. 86.

The wave length being determined as described above, and the pitch of the fork used being known, the velocity of sound can be computed. The result obtained should be compared with the velocity given by the formula

$$v = 332\sqrt{1 + \tfrac{1}{273}t},\qquad(177)$$

where t is the temperature of the room. (See Anthony and Brackett.) If the sounding body used is of unknown pitch, the wave length can be determined as before, the velocity of sound obtained from the above formula, and from these two quantities the pitch can be computed.

EXPERIMENT W_3. **Resonance of columns of air and determination of the velocity of sound.**

The apparatus for this experiment consists of two or more glass tubes containing water, and arranged so that the level of the water can be conveniently altered, several tuning forks of known pitch, a scale for measuring the distance from the top of the water to the open end of the tube, and a thermometer for determining the temperature of the air. A convenient form of apparatus is that shown in Fig. 87.

The experiment is to be performed with each of the tubes as follows: Fasten one of the forks to some firm support so that its prongs are immediately above the end of the tube, and set it into vibration by a blow from a wooden mallet. Then adjust the level of the water until the sound of the fork is reinforced by resonance from the air column contained by the tube. Several positions of the water level will probably be found where this reinforcement takes place; each should be carefully located, and the distance from the top of the water to the open end of the tube should be measured. The distance between two consecutive positions of the water level which produce rein-

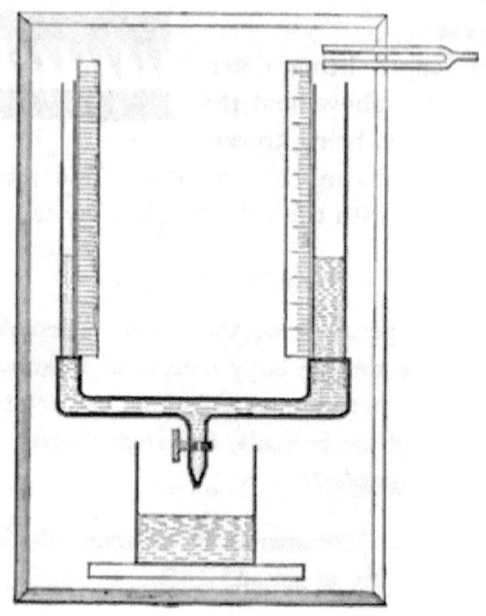

Fig. 87.

forcement is equal to one-half the wave length of the tone given by the fork. Since the pitch of the fork is known, the velocity of sound can therefore be computed. As a check upon the results the velocity of sound may be computed for the temperature of the air at the time of the experiment, upon the assumption that the velocity at $0°$ is 332 m. per second. (See Anthony and Brackett.)

The observations described above should be repeated, in the case of at least one of the tubes, with several forks of different pitch.

To investigate the influence of the diameter of the tube upon its behavior as a resonator, the following method may be followed. Use a number of tubes varying widely in diameter, and determine for each the minimum length of air column that will reinforce a given fork. Care should be used in this work to place the fork always at the same (known) distance above the end of the tube. For a tube of small diameter the length of air column in this case is a quarter wave length; but as the diameter is made greater, the length will be found to vary, this variation being due to the spreading out of the sound waves that travel up the tube as they reach the open end. Try to determine the law of this variation by platting a curve with diameters as abscissas and lengths as ordinates.

The report should contain a full explanation of the resonance phenomena observed.

Experiment W$_4$. **Velocity of sound in brass. Kundt's method.**

A brass rod about a meter long, Fig. 80, is placed in a horizontal position, and firmly supported at its center. To

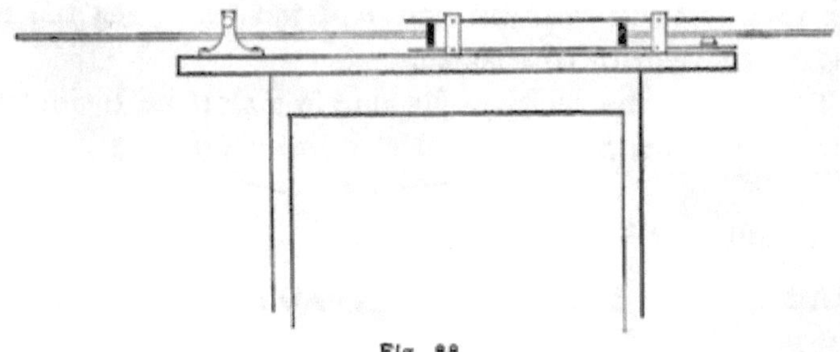

Fig. 88.

one end of the rod is fastened a disk of cardboard or cork, whose diameter is almost equal to that of a glass tube in which it is inserted. The opposite end of this tube is closed by means of an adjustable piston, so that the length of the air

column in the tube can be altered. On setting the rod into
vibration (by rubbing its free end with leather covered with
rosin), the air in the tube will also vibrate, and by placing some
light powder in the tube (such as lycopodium or cork dust),
these vibrations are made evident to the eye. If the length of
the tube is properly adjusted, the dust will be seen to distribute
itself regularly in little heaps, these heaps corresponding to
nodes in the stationary waves set up in the air. Frequently
the dust figures are similar to those shown in Fig. 89.

The experiment consists in so adjusting the length of the air
column as to make this regular distribution of the dust as

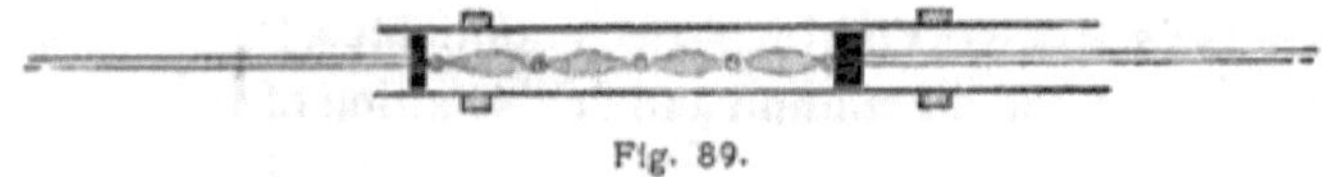

Fig. 89.

marked as possible. The distance between consecutive nodes
is then measured and thus the wave length in air of the sound
emitted by the vibrating rod is determined. Since the rod is
clamped at its center, the wave length in brass of the vibration
produced in it is equal to twice the length of the rod. (See
Anthony and Brackett.) Having the wave lengths of the same
note in air and in brass, the ratio of the two gives the ratio
of the two velocities of sound.

To compute the velocity of sound in air at the temperature
of the experiment, make use of the formula $v = 332 \sqrt{1 + \frac{1}{273} t}$.

EXPERIMENT W_5.   The sonometer.

All the laws of vibrating strings or wires may be expressed
by the formula

$$n = \frac{1}{2\,rl} \sqrt{\frac{T}{\pi d}}, \tag{178}$$

where n is the number of complete oscillations per second, l the
length of the vibrating segment of the string, r its radius, d its

density, and T the tension to which the string is subjected. This formula may also be put in the form

$$n = \frac{1}{2\,l}\sqrt{\frac{T}{m}},$$

where m is the mass of unit length. This form of the equation is often the more convenient. (See Daniell, Glazebrook, and Shaw, or Anthony and Brackett.)

The object of the experiment is to verify this formula experimentally. The apparatus used is a sonometer (Fig. 90), which

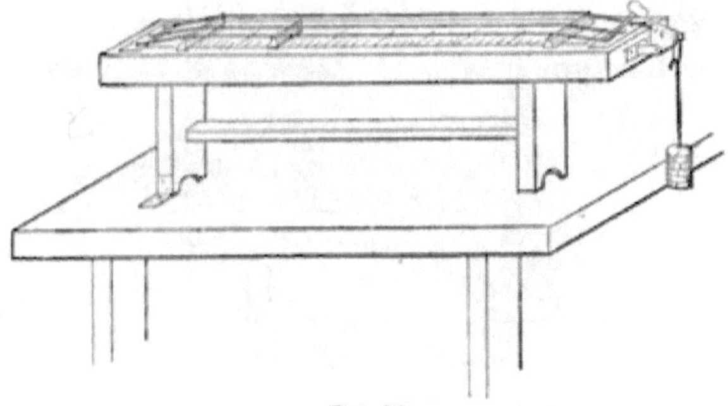

Fig. 90.

consists of a long wooden box, upon which may be stretched two or more wires. One of these wires is stretched by turning a key. The tension of the other one must be known. To secure this, one end of the string is fastened to the box, and the other end to a lever which moves about a knife-edge as an axis. From the other end of this lever weights are suspended. If the two lever arms are made equal, the tension of the string is equal to the weight suspended. The length of the vibrating segment of either of these strings may be varied by changing the position of a movable bridge.

In performing the experiment adjust the length and tension of the string which is to be studied until it vibrates in unison with a tuning fork of known pitch. Having measured the values of r, l, T, etc., compute the pitch of the string from the formula given above, and note how closely the result agrees with the known pitch of the fork. The law should be tested in this way for at least three strings of different diameter and density, and several forks should be used with each string.

On account of the great difference in quality between the note of the string and that of the fork, great care must be used in adjusting the former. If the ear is untrained, a mistake of an octave is not unusual.

EXPERIMENT W_6. **The study of the transverse vibration of cords and wires, by Moler's method.**

The apparatus * for this experiment is a modification of Melde's well-known device. It consists of an instrument de-

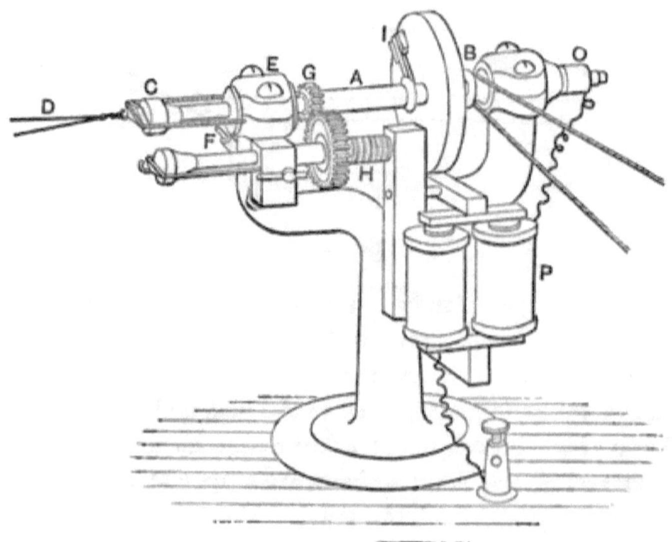

Fig. 91.

signed for the purpose of maintaining in continued circular vibration a cord or wire, the tension of which is adjusted by weights until well-defined loops and nodes are produced.

* For a fuller description, see G. S. Moler's article in the American Journal of Science, Vol. 36, p. 337.

The cord in question is attached at one end to a crank of small throw which is driven at a high speed by means of an electric motor or water wheel. The velocity is maintained constant by the action of an electric brake.

The arrangement of these parts is shown in Fig. 91 In that figure, A is the main shaft, and C the crank pin, upon which a hook is placed carrying the cord or cords D to be put into vibration.

To counteract the tension of these cords, which would otherwise produce too great friction, the crank is attached to the bearing E by a stout cord, the strain upon which is adjustable by means of a tightening pin at F.

In order to drive simultaneously two parallel cords at different speeds, there is a second shaft and crank which can be put into motion at will, by means of the pinion wheels at G and H.

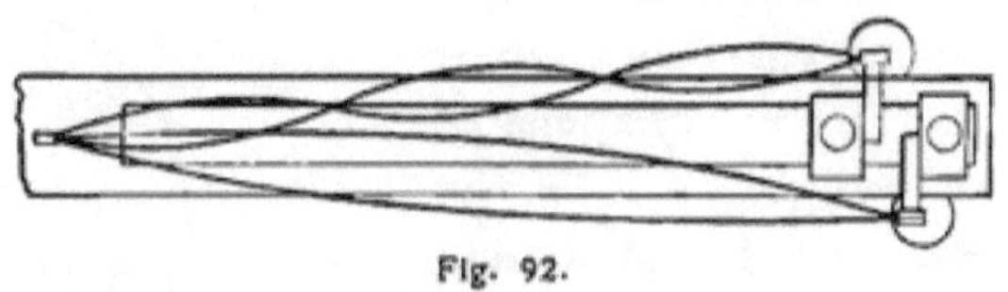

Fig. 92.

The cords, the vibrations of which are to be studied, one end of each of which is fastened to the crank hooks, are carried over pulleys, attached at any desired distance upon the base of the apparatus (see Fig. 92), and are subjected to tension by the application of weights. When these weights are in proper relation to the velocity of the crank, the cord breaks into nodes and falls into a stable condition of vibration which is maintained as long as the conditions upon which it depends continue.

One of the conditions of equilibrium is the speed, and it is for the purpose of regulating this factor that the electric brake is used. This part of the apparatus is shown in Figs. 93 and 94.

In the former figure, J is a lever pivoted at K (see also I, Fig. 91), and this is forced outward with increasing speed until it bends the spring L and makes a contact with M. Thus an electric circuit through the electromagnet P (Fig. 94) is closed and the brake Q is thrown against the periphery of a wheel upon the main shaft. In this way the speed is checked whenever it exceeds a certain desired rate.

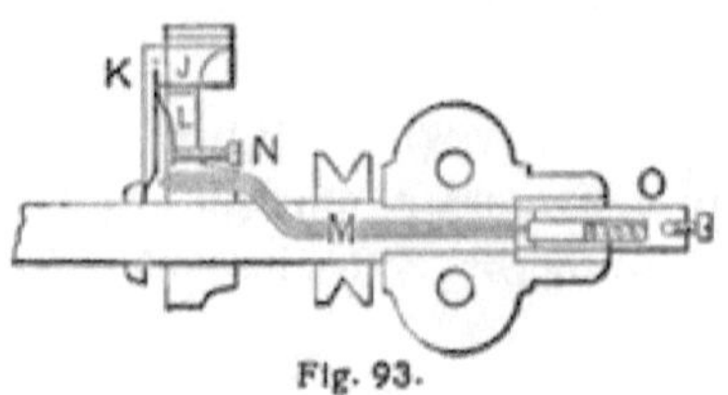
Fig. 93.

It should be noted that in practice this electric regulator has but little to do, since a heavy cord 2 m. in length, or even less, is in itself a very effective regulator of speed as soon as it has once been brought into definite vibration.

It is indeed entirely practicable to perform the experiment without putting the brake into function, provided that two cords be used, one of which is maintained under constant tension and serves as a governor while variations of length and load are made in the case of the other. The governing cord should be of considerable mass.

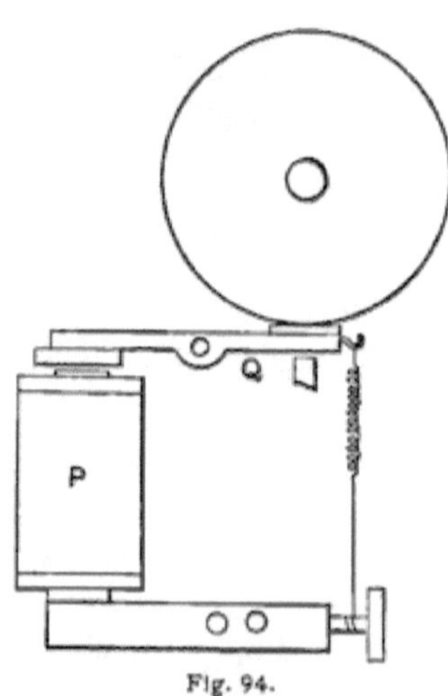
Fig. 94.

The experiment consists in varying the factors upon which the transverse vibration of strings depends, and verifying the relations which exist between them and the rate.

These factors are:

(1) The cross-section (S'), which may be conveniently varied by using several strands of a light cord in common.

(2) The length (L), which is to be changed by shifting pulleys along the base of the instrument.

(3) The tension.

SOUND.

The rate itself may be subject to one change by fastening the cords first to the main shaft and then to the shaft H.

The results are to be arranged as shown in the following table.

TABLE.

Observation.	Cross-Section. S.	Length. L.	Rate of Vibration. N.	Number of Segments. n.	Tension in Grams. P.	Square Root of Tension. $\sqrt{P}$.	Constant $\dfrac{n}{NL}\dfrac{\sqrt{P}}{sd}$.
No. 1		1	2	1	627.	25.04	12.52
" 2		1	2	2	162.	12.70	12.70
" 3	1 strand.	1	2	3	74.	8.60	12.90
" 4		1	2	4	41.	6.40	12.80
" 5		1	2	5	26.	5.10	12.75
No. 6		1	2	1	627.	25.04	12.52
" 7	1 strand.	$\frac{3}{4}$	2	1	266.	16.30	12.22
" 8		$\frac{1}{2}$	2	1	166.	12.90	12.90
No. 9		1	2	1	2500.	50.00	12.50
" 10	4 strands.	1	2	2	625.	20.00	12.50
" 11		1	2	3	280.	16.70	12.52
" 12		1	2	4	158.	12.60	12.60
No. 13		1	1	1	166.	12.90	12.90
" 14	1 strand.	1	1	2	41.	6.40	12.80
" 15		1	1	3	18.	4.20	12.60
" 16		1	1	4	9.5	3.10	12.40

If N be the number of vibrations per unit of time, L the length of the cord, n the number of segments, and V the velocity of transmission of an impulse transmitted to the cord, we have the familiar formula expressing the transverse vibrations of flexible cords :

$$N = \frac{n}{2L} V \qquad (179)$$

If P is the tension of the cord, s its cross-section, and d its density, we have also

$$V = \sqrt{\frac{P}{sd}} \qquad (180)$$

Finally, if λ is the wave length, we may write

$$\lambda = \frac{2L}{n}, \tag{181}$$

$$V = N\lambda, \tag{182}$$

$$\sqrt{\frac{P}{sd}} = N \cdot \frac{2L}{n}. \tag{183}$$

CHAPTER XII.

GROUP X: LENSES AND MIRRORS.

(X₁) Radius of curvature of a lens (by reflection); (X₂) Focal length of a concave mirror; (X₃) Focal length of a convex lens; (X₄) Magnifying power of a telescope; (X₅) Magnifying power of a microscope and focal lengths of same.

EXPERIMENT X_1. **Determination of the radius of curvature of a lens by reflection.**

The apparatus consists of a telescope placed midway between two small gas jets (g, g', Fig. 95), the distance between

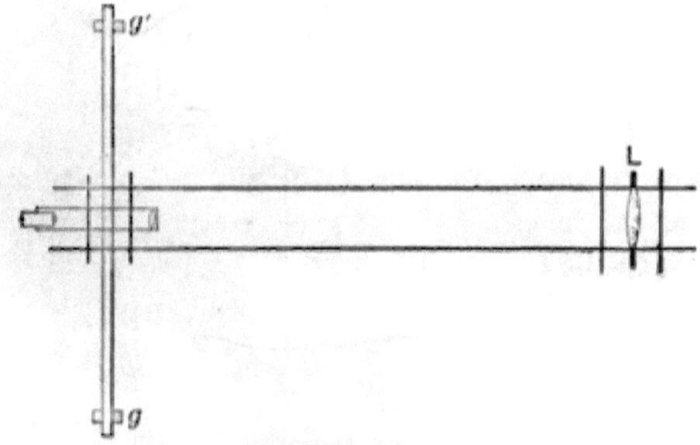

Fig. 95.

the jets being capable of adjustment. The lens (L, Figs. 95 and 96) whose curvature is desired is placed at a distance of from 1 to 2 m., and in such a position that the reflected images of the two flames can be seen in the telescope. The apparent distance between the images is measured by means of a scale (Fig. 97) fastened to the surface of the lens, and from this measurement, together with the distance from the

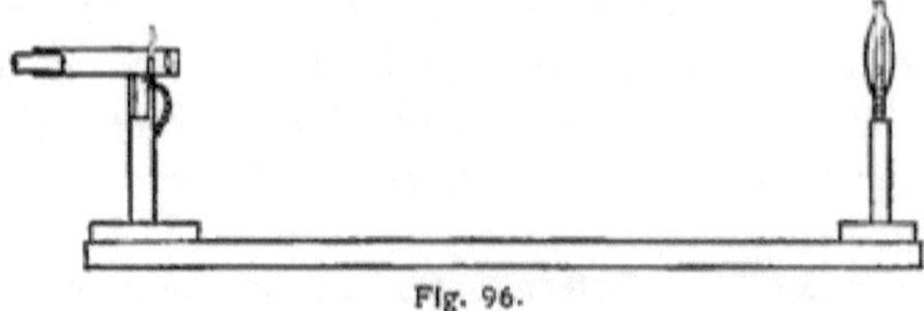

Fig. 96.

lens to the flames, and the actual distance between the flames, the radius of curvature can be computed.

The problem with which this experiment deals consists in finding the radius of curvature $r (= co,$ Fig. 98) in terms of L, the distance between the gas jets (gg'); of D, the dis-

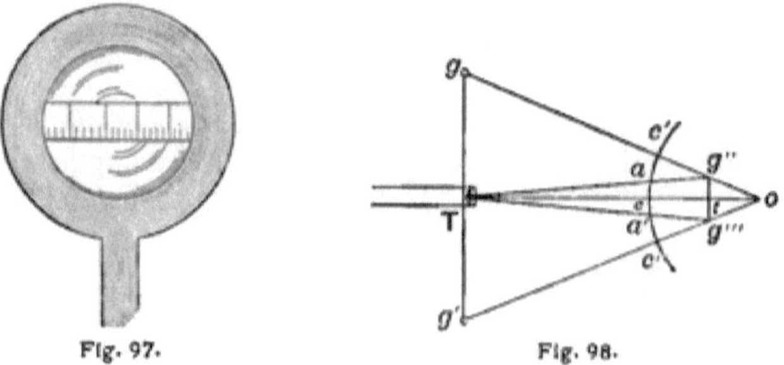

Fig. 97.   Fig. 98.

tance from telescope to lens (cT), and of s, the apparent distance of the images (g'', g''') as measured upon the scale on the face of the lens (aa').

From the relation of conjugate foci we have

$$\frac{1}{gc'} - \frac{1}{g''c'} = -\frac{2}{oc}, \qquad (184)$$

and in case the telescope is at a distance from the lens much greater than L, we may write as an approximation

$$\frac{1}{Tc} = \frac{1}{tc} - \frac{2}{oc}, \qquad (185)$$

or

$$d = \frac{Dr}{2D + r}, \qquad (186)$$

where $d = ct.$

From the geometry of similar triangles we have, also,

$$l = s\frac{(D+d)}{D},\qquad(187)$$

$$l = \frac{L(r-d)}{r+D},\qquad(188)$$

where $l = g''$, g''', which is the distance between the images.

The quantities l and d are to be eliminated, and r is to be expressed as stated above.

Combining equations 187 and 188, we have

$$\frac{s(r+D)}{D} = \frac{L(r-d)}{(D+d)} = \frac{Lr}{2D},\qquad(189)$$

or
$$r = \frac{2sD}{L-2s}.\qquad(190)$$

To obtain accurate results, the conditions of the experiment should be varied by changing the position of the lens, and by altering the distance between the flames. Make five or six determinations for each side of the lens and use the average of each set.

It may happen that two pairs of images are seen by reflection. This is due to the fact that a part of the light from the flames passes through the first surface and suffers reflection at the second. One pair of images will probably be erect and the other inverted, so that no difficulty need be experienced in distinguishing between the two.

Addendum to the report:

Rays from the gas jet g are reflected from the face of the lens, and enter the telescope T. The angles which the incident and reflected rays make with the normal to the surface are equal. From this consideration deduce formula 190, without using the relation of conjugate focal lengths, or the position of the image g''.

EXPERIMENT X₂. **Focal length of a concave mirror.**

The object of this experiment is to verify the formula which shows the relation between the conjugate foci and the principal focus of a concave mirror; viz.

$$\frac{1}{p_1} + \frac{1}{p_2} = \frac{2}{r} = \frac{1}{f} \tag{191}$$

The apparatus required consists simply of the mirror m, a glass scale S, a screen S', and a gas flame.

The mirror should first be mounted (see Fig. 99) in such a way that its principal axis is nearly horizontal. The glass

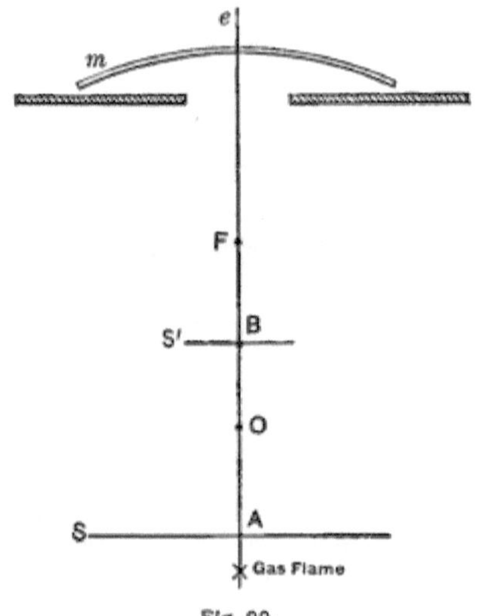

Fig. 99.

scale * may then be placed at some point in this axis, with the gas flame a short distance behind it. It will be found more convenient to work in a room which is partially darkened.

The position of the image of the scale may now be found by trial, a screen S' (preferably of ground glass) being placed

---

* A glass scale is recommended merely because it constitutes an "object" whose image will, in general, be especially sharp.

in such a position that the image thrown upon it is as sharp as possible. This adjustment may be made more accurately if the mirror is partly covered, so that only a comparatively small portion near the center is used. The distances of object and image from the mirror are now to be measured, together with the distance between the lines in the image of the scale. Repeat these measurements for three or four different positions of the scale, the position in each case being such that the image lies between the scale and the lens. The focal length and the radius of curvature are to be computed from each of the observations.

As a check upon the results, the center of curvature may be located by placing a needle, or other pointed object, in such a position that the image of its point shall coincide in position with the point itself. This may be done quite accurately by moving the eye about and noting whether the relative positions of image and object vary.

Addenda to the report:

(1) **From the data** obtained, verify the formula which shows the relation between the size of the image and its distance from the mirror; *i.e.* if the lengths of object and image are respectively l_1 and l_2,

$$l_1 : l_2 = p_1 : p_2.$$

(2) Give a demonstration of the formula above referred to; also the formula for conjugate foci.

(3) Indicate the advantage of using only a small central portion of the surface of the mirror.

EXPERIMENT X₃. **Determination of the focal length of a convex lens.**

The focal length of the lens used is to be determined by each of the four methods described below, a number of observations being made in each case, and the average used.

(1) The lens is made to form an image F, of some object whose distance is so great that light proceeds from it to the lens in rays that are very nearly parallel. The focal length is then equal to the distance between lens and image. The sun is usually the most convenient source of light for use in this method, the rays being rendered horizontal by reflection from a mirror M (Fig. 100). A screen of ground glass or paper

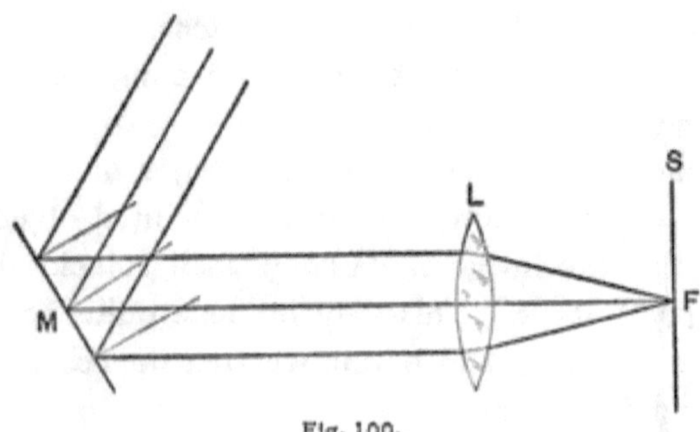

Fig. 100.

is adjusted until the image thrown upon it is as distinct and sharp as can be obtained. The focal length is then equal to the distance from the screen to the center of the lens. This method is not capable of great accuracy, but is more direct than those which follow.

(2) A telescope which has been focused for parallel rays is used to observe some sharply defined object as seen through the lens. The position of the lens having been adjusted until the object is seen to be properly focused in the telescope, the distance between lens and object is equal to the focal length required. In principle this method is practically the same as that first described, and the degree of accuracy that can be attained is about the same in each.

(3) An object is placed at any convenient distance in front of the lens, and a screen is adjusted until the image received upon it is sharply defined. The focal length can then be computed from measurements of the distances of object and

image from the lens. If p_1 and p_2 are these two distances, we have

$$\frac{1}{p_1} + \frac{1}{p_2} = \frac{1}{f}. \tag{192}$$

The luminous object used may be the flame of a candle or gas jet. There are some objections, however, to the use of a flame, on account of the flickering caused by air currents. Better results can usually be obtained by using a fine thread or wire which is stretched across an opening in an opaque screen (Fig. 101). When the aperture is illuminated by means

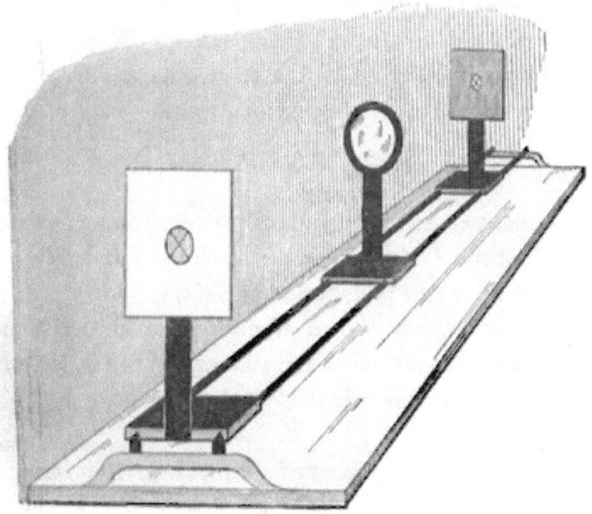

Fig. 101.

of a lamp, the shadow of the wire forms an image which is unaffected by the flickering of the flame, and which can be very sharply focused.

(4) Placing the object at any convenient distance from the lens, adjust the position of the screen until the image is sharply focused. Then, without changing the position of the screen, move the lens until a second position is found, such that a

sharp image is formed. From the distance between object and screen, and the distance through which the lens is moved, the focal length can be computed. If l and a are the two distances,

$$f = \frac{l^2 - a^2}{4\,l}.$$ (193)

This method of determining focal length has the advantage of being uninfluenced by any uncertainty as to the thickness of the lens and the position of the principal points. Since it is merely the distance through which the lens is moved that is required, measurements can be made to any convenient point on the support of the lens, and no correction need be made for the thickness of the glass. For this reason the method will probably give better results than can be obtained by any of the three methods first described.

Addenda to the report:

(1) Sharper images, and therefore more accurate results, will be obtained if the lens is covered, so that only a small region near the center is used.   (Explain.)

(2) From the curvature of each face of the lens and your determination of the focal length, compute the index of refraction of the glass from which it is made.

·EXPERIMENT X$_4$. **Magnifying power of a telescope.**

Focus the telescope upon some large object, such as a scale, which contains sharply defined portions of equal length. The bricks in the wall of a building, or the pickets of a fence, will serve for this purpose. Looking through the telescope with both eyes open, the magnified image of the scale will be seen by one eye, while with the other the scale is observed directly. By a comparison of the two images the magnifying power is determined. For example, if one division of the image seen in the telescope covers ten divisions of the unmagnified image, the magnifying power is ten. To guard against errors due to a difference in the two eyes, it is best to use the left eye in observing the telescopic image as often as the right.

The magnifying power should be determined in this way when the object observed is at several different distances, ranging from a distance that is so great as to be practically infinite, to the least distance for which the telescope can be focused. If any difference is found in the magnifying power, the variation should be shown by a curve in which distances and magnifying powers are used as co-ordinates.

For some one distance of the object observed the distances between the various lenses should be accurately measured when the telescope is focused.

Addenda to the report:

(1) Determine the focal length of each of the lenses, and compute the magnifying power, drawing a diagram to scale to show the position and size of the various images.

(2) Explain the cause of the variation in magnifying power with the distance of the object.

EXPERIMENT X_5. **Magnifying power of a microscope and determination of the focal length of its lenses.**

I.

The "open-eye" method.

This method is similar to that described for the determination of the magnifying power of a telescope.

(1) Focus the microscope upon a finely divided scale and place another scale at the side of the instrument at a distance from the eye equal to the distance of distinct vision (about 25 cm.). By observing the scale with one eye and the image formed in the microscope with the other, the apparent size of the magnified image is determined. The ratio of this to the actual size is the magnifying power.

(2) Measure the distance between the object glass and eye piece and determine the focal length of the latter by one of the methods of Exp. X_8. From a knowledge of the magnifying power it will now be possible to compute the focal length of the object glass.

(3) Construct a diagram to scale to explain the action of the instrument, showing the position and size of each image. (See Gage, Microscopical Methods, p. 65.)

II.

Franklin's method.

The object of this method is to find the focal lengths of microscope lenses from the magnifying power with short and long draw tubes.

The apparatus required is a compound microscope, a micrometer caliper, a stage micrometer, an unsilvered glass microscope slip, and a scale divided to millimeters.

The experiment consists in the following determinations :

(1) The magnifying power (m) of the microscope with short tube.

(2) The magnifying power (m') with long tube.

(3) The change (l) in the length of the microscope tube.

(4) The movement of the objective in refocusing for determination (2). This measurement is to be made by means of the caliper.

The magnifying power, as in the previous method, is the ratio of the apparent size of an object as seen with the microscope to its apparent size as seen with the naked eye at a distance of D centimeters.

Instead of measuring magnifying power by the "open-eye" method, the glass slip is mounted obliquely before the eye piece (Fig. 102), so as to bring an image of the scale (S) into the field.

The theory of the method of computing focal lengths is as follows.

Let p be the equivalent focal length of the eye piece ; p', the focal length of the objective; *a*, the distance from the object to the center of the objective; and *b*, the distance of the image from the center of the objective.

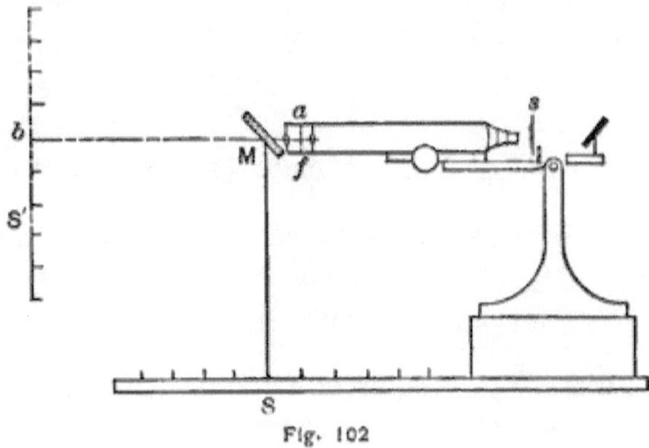

Fig. 102

We have the following equations :

$$m = \left(\frac{D}{p} + 1\right)\frac{b}{a}, \tag{194}$$

$$m' = \left(\frac{D}{p} + 1\right)\frac{b+l}{a-k}, \tag{195}$$

$$\frac{1}{p'} = \frac{1}{a} + \frac{1}{b}, \tag{196}$$

$$\frac{1}{p} = \frac{1}{a-k} + \frac{1}{b+l}, \tag{197}$$

from which these may be obtained.

$$a^2 lm - b^2 km' = 0, \tag{198}$$

$$a^2 - \frac{2\,km'}{m'-m}a - \frac{klmm' - k^2m'^2}{(m'-m)^2} = 0. \tag{199}$$

From equation 199, *a* may be computed, then *b* from (198), then finally *p* and *p'* by combining (194) or (195) with (196) or (197).

The distance D is the distance from the focal plane in the eye piece (which in the case of a negative [Huyghenian] eye piece lies midway between the two lenses, and in the positive eye piece is distant from the eye lens by an amount equal to three-fourths of the distance between the lenses) to the scale (s), Fig. 102.

GROUP Y: THE SPECTROSCOPE AND PHOTOMETER.

(Y_1) *Index of refraction of a prism;* (Y_2) *Flame spectra of the metals;* (Y_3) *Distance between the lines of a grating;* (Y_4) *The Bunsen photometer.*

EXPERIMENT Y_1. **Measurement of the index of refraction of a prism by means of a spectrometer.**

In the spectrometer used (see Fig. 103), the rays of light from the source are made to pass through a narrow vertical slit,

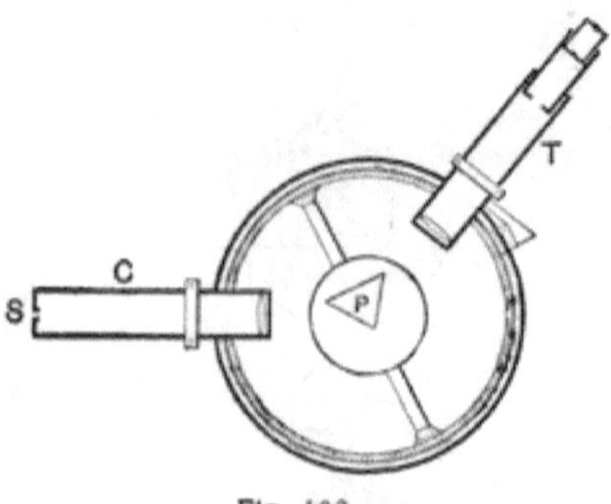

Fig. 103.

and are then rendered parallel by means of a lens. This lens and slit, mounted in a tube to exclude stray light, constitute what is known as the *collimator*. After leaving the collimator, the light is made to pass through a prism, and is finally observed by means of a telescope. Both collimator and telescope are adjusted so as to point towards the center of a horizontal graduated circle, and the telescope is free to rotate about a vertical axis passing through this center. By means of a vernier attached to its support, the angular position of the telescope can be read.

Before beginning observations with the prism, the collimator must be so adjusted that the light leaves it in parallel rays. To accomplish this, take the instrument to an open window and focus the telescope on some object which is so far away that the rays from it are practically parallel. Then turn the telescope so that it points directly at the collimator, and, without changing the focus of the telescope, alter the length of the collimator tube until the image of the slit, as seen in the tele-

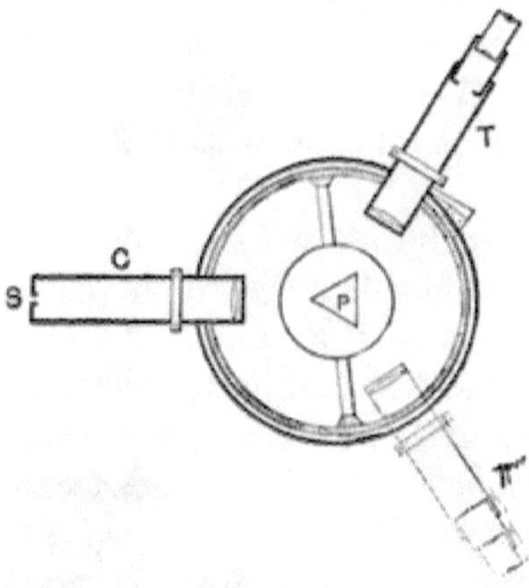

Fig. 104.

scope, is sharply defined. Both telescope and collimator are now properly focused, and should not be altered during the experiment.

In order to obtain the index of reflection, it is necessary to know the angle of the prism, and the angle through which it bends the rays from the collimator when in the position of "minimum deviation."

(1) *To determine the angle of the prism.* — Place the prism near the center of the graduated circle, with its refracting edge turned toward the collimator (Fig. 104). Turn the telescope

until the slit is seen by reflection from one face of the prism, and adjust the position of the telescope until its cross-hair coincides with the image of the slit. Record the position of the telescope as read by the vernier. Then set the cross-hairs in the same way upon the image of the slit, as reflected from the other face of the prism, position T', and again read the vernier. The angle between the two positions of the telescope is then equal to twice the angle of the prism. A number of readings should be taken.

(2) *To determine the angle of minimum deviation.* — Up to this point in the experiment any source of light will serve equally well; but since different colors are bent by refraction in different degrees, it will now be necessary to use some mono-chromatic light. The most convenient light of a single color is that obtained by burning some salt of sodium in the Bunsen flame.*

Place the prism near the center of the horizontal circle, and in such a position that light from the collimator will be refracted through it and pass into the telescope. If, while observing the image of the slit in the telescope, the table which carries the prism is slowly turned, the image will be seen to move across the field, and it may be necessary to shift the position of the telescope in order to keep it in sight. In this way the prism can be set by trial to the position which causes the light to deviate least from its original direction on leaving the collimator; when this position is reached, a slight motion of the table in either direction will cause the image to move toward a position of greater deviation. When this setting is made as accurately as possible, bring the cross-hair into coinci-dence with the image of the slit, and take the reading of the vernier. Several settings should be made in this way, with

---

* If light of a different wave length were used, the index of refraction obtained would, of course, be different. Since this experiment is, however, merely intended to illustrate the use of the spectrometer, it will be found best to use the most con-venient monochromatic light; viz. sodium.

deviations both to the right and left. The index of refraction can be then computed from the formula

$$n = \frac{\sin \frac{1}{2}(\delta + \alpha)}{\sin \frac{1}{2}\alpha}, \tag{200}$$

in which α is the angle of the prism, and δ the angle of minimum deviation.

Indices of refraction are to be obtained in this way for several prisms of different materials.

EXPERIMENT Y_2. **Study of the flame spectra of various metals.**

This experiment should follow that on the determination of indices of refraction (No. Y_1), and can be more conveniently performed if there are two observers. The apparatus required is a spectrometer, or spectroscope, similar to the one used in that experiment.

The substances whose flame spectra are most readily studied are Na, Li, K, Sr, Ba, Ca, Rb, and Cs. A salt of one of these metals, usually either the chloride or the carbonate, is placed in the colorless flame of a Bunsen burner, immediately in front of the slit of the spectrometer. The spectrum of the flame, when colored by the incandescent vapor of the metal, will be seen to consist of several bright lines, whose color and arrangement are characteristic of the metal studied. To map the position of the different lines, the prism should first be adjusted to the position of minimum deviation for sodium light. Then, without altering the adjustment of the prism, set the telescope successively on each of the lines of the spectrum, reading its angular position by means of the vernier. The spectrum can be mapped for comparative purposes from these results. The approximate limits of the visible spectrum, as determined by substituting white light for the metallic spectrum, should be marked on each diagram, and the colors and relative intensities of the lines should be indicated. If it is desired to determine the wave length of each of the lines, a grating may be used instead of a prism ; or, if this is not convenient, the prism may be "calibrated" by reference to the Fraunhofer lines. To accomplish this, the slit should be illuminated by bright daylight, or direct sunlight, and adjusted until the dark lines in the spectrum are clearly seen. The prism is then set to the position of least deviation for the D line, and the angular position of the telescope is observed for several of the more prominent lines. The wave lengths corresponding to these lines being known, a curve can now be constructed, in which angles of deviation are taken as abscissas, and wave lengths as ordinates. By reference to this curve, the wave length corresponding to any observed deviation is readily determined.

The most instructive method of mapping bright line spectra is that employed by Lecoq de Boisbaudran in his work on the

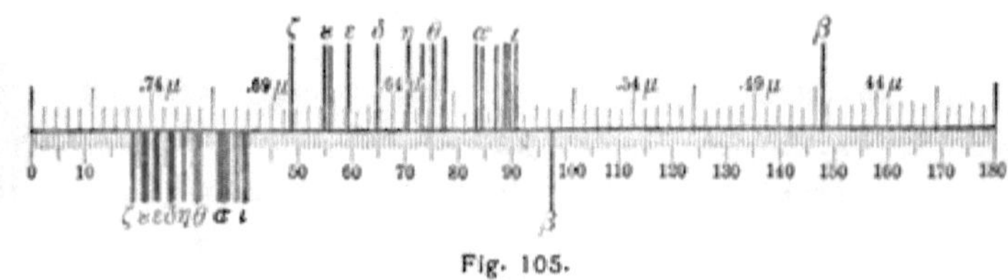

Fig. 105.

spectra of the metals.* An example is given in Fig. 105. As will be seen from the diagram, each spectrum is mapped twice, once above and once below the median line. The former gives the normal, the latter the prismatic spectrum of the substance in question. This method should be employed in reporting upon the results of this experiment.

Considerable difficulty is sometimes met with in working with flame spectra in obtaining sufficient permanence and brilliancy for accurate observation. To obtain the best results the methods of heating must be suited to the salt used. In some cases, a small amount of the salt, when placed on a wire

---

* Spectres Lumineux; Lecoq de Boisbaudran, Paris, 1874.

and heated in the flame, will form a bead which lasts for a considerable time and gives a good spectrum. In other cases the supply of salt will need to be constantly renewed. A piece of asbestos, or wire, which has been moistened by a strong solution of the salt, will sometimes give good results. In general, the results will be more satisfactory when the flame is quite hot. For this reason, the substitution of a blast lamp for the ordinary Bunsen burner is sometimes advisable. The observations can usually be made more rapidly if one observer devotes his attention to keeping the flame in proper condition, while the other observes the spectrum.

EXPERIMENT Y_3. **Determination of the distance between the lines of a grating by the diffraction of sodium light.**

The object of this experiment is to illustrate the principles involved in the formation of spectra by a diffraction grating. It is expected, therefore, that the report should contain a clear explanation of the phenomena observed. (See Kohlrausch, Glazebrook's Physical Optics, p. 183, and other books on light.)

The apparatus consists of a horizontal arm, which may for convenience be provided with a scale, mounted upon a suitable support, and having at its center a narrow vertical slit which may be illuminated by sodium light. To obtain the pure yellow light of sodium it is only necessary to place a wire carrying a bead of some sodium salt in the flame of a Bunsen burner. The grating to be studied is placed in front of the slit with its rulings vertical, and should be mounted on some support so that its distance from the slit can be varied.

On looking through the grating, several images of the slit will be seen on either side, the distance between these images depending upon the distance apart of the lines of the grating. If white light were used instead of the sodium flame, these images would become spectra. By measuring the distance between the grating and the slit (D, Fig. 106), and the displacement of one of the images d, the angle through which the light is bent by diffraction can be determined. From this angle, and the wave length of sodium light, the distance between the lines of the grating is to be computed.

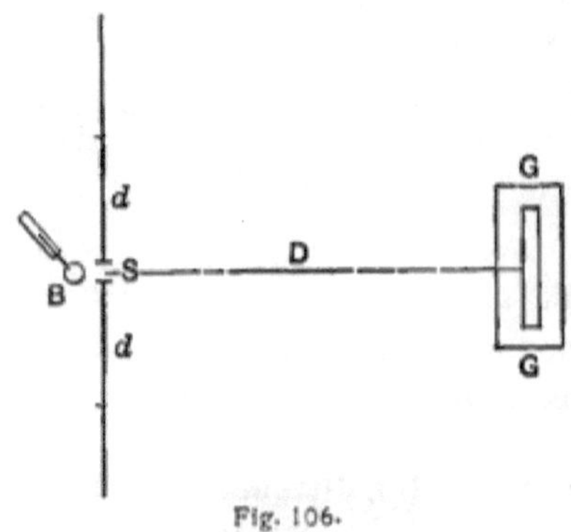

Fig. 106.

In measuring the displacement of the images the following method will be found convenient: Adjust a small rider, which can be clamped to the horizontal arm, until it coincides with the corresponding image on the opposite side of the slit. The distance between the two riders is then equal to twice the displacement of the image. Measurements should be made in this way for four or five different positions of the grating and with different pairs of images. If the measurements are carefully made, the individual results should agree fairly well, and the final average will not be far from the truth. The wave length of sodium light may be taken as 0.000059 cm.

EXPERIMENT Y_4. **Measurement of candle power by the Bunsen photometer.**

In the Bunsen photometer a screen of white paper (D, Fig. 107), a portion of which has been made translucent by the

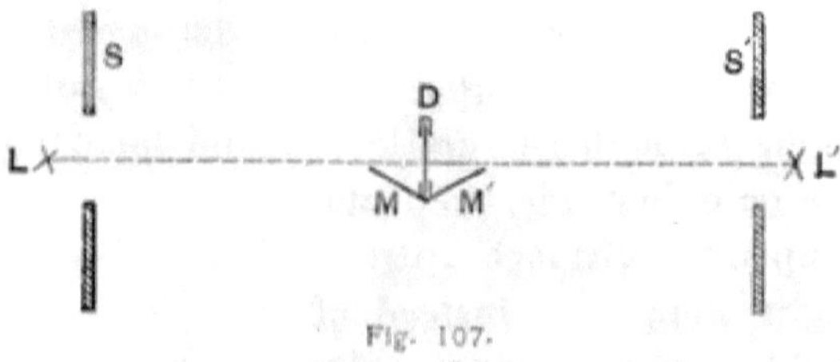

Fig. 107.

application of oil, is placed in a blackened box (technically called the carriage), and mirrors, M, M', are adjusted so that both sides of the paper may be observed at the same time. By means of openings in the carriage, light is admitted from the two sources whose intensities are to be compared. The carriage being placed between the two lights, each face of the screen is illuminated only by light from the source toward which it is turned, while the translucent portion of the paper receives light from both sources. In using the instrument, the carriage is shifted in position until both sides of the screen are seen to be equally illuminated. The distances of the two lights from the screen are then measured, and the relative intensities of the two sources are computed by the law of inverse squares.

Fig. 108.

The translucent spot on the screen merely serves to locate the position of equal illumination with greater accuracy than could otherwise be obtained. If the adjustment is not quite correct, this spot will appear dark on one side and bright on the other (see Fig. 108); but when the proper position has been found, it will almost entirely disappear.

The standard source of light in the apparatus used consists of an Argand burner placed just back of an opaque screen, in which a small oblong slit has been cut. The slit is made so small that it appears entirely covered with light when viewed from the front, and should be so adjusted as to receive only that light which comes from the central portion of the flame. In this way the irregularities due to the flickering of the edges of the flame are avoided. It is to be observed that under the conditions mentioned, the slit itself is the source of light.

Distances should be measured to the plane of the slit, and not to the center of the flame.

To perform the experiment, place the standard and the light to be measured at opposite ends of the photometer bar, and before beginning any actual observations, practice setting the carriage to the position of equal illumination until nearly the same reading is obtained several times in succession. After each reading, the carriage should be shifted two or three feet, in some cases to the right and in others to the left of the proper setting, and then brought back again, without reference to the previous reading, until the two sides of the screen appear to be equally illuminated. The uncertainties of the observation, together with slight variations in the intensities of the two lights, will make it impossible to obtain coincident settings, but after a little practice the successive readings should agree to within three or four per cent. Constant differences are often observed between the settings of different persons. These are due to differences in the eye, and cannot be avoided.

After sufficient practice has been gained in reading, the photometer may be used to measure candle power in some one of the cases which follow. It is to be observed that the scale on the bar is located without regard to the positions of the two lights, so that suitable corrections will have to be made at each end.

(1) By comparison with a standard candle the absolute intensity of the standard light may be determined. At least ten or twelve readings should be taken to get a good result.

(2) The light from a fish-tail burner or an oil lamp may be measured as the flame is seen from different directions. It will probably be found that the flame differs in illuminating power according as the broad surface or the edge is turned toward the photometer. To investigate this variation first set the flame so that its plane is parallel with the photometer bar, and measure its intensity. Then turn it about a vertical axis

and measure the candle power at intervals of 30° until the flame has been turned through a complete revolution. The results should be shown graphically by a curve, in which the angular position of the flame, and the observed intensity of the light, are used as polar co-ordinates. Such a curve is very commonly used to show the distribution of the light from any source, and has the advantage of showing at a glance the intensity of the light in all horizontal directions.

(3) The absorbing power of substances which are nearly transparent may be determined. To accomplish this, measure the intensity of any source as seen direct; then interpose the substance to be investigated, and see how much the light is diminished. From the two measurements the percentage absorption can be computed. Investigate in this way the absorption of sheets of glass of different thickness, and of cells containing various liquids. It must be remembered, however, that some of the light which is apparently absorbed is really lost by reflection. If it is desired to separate the effects of reflection and absorption, more elaborate methods will be necessary.

Numerous other interesting problems will suggest themselves in the solution of which the photometer may be used. For further details concerning photometry, see Vol. II of this Manual; also Palaz, Photometrie Industrielle.

TABLES.

[In these tables the admirable arrangement made use of in Bottomley's *Four-Figure Mathematical Tables* has been followed.]

	0	1	2	3	4	5	6	7	8	9	1	2	3	4	5	6	7	8	9
10	0000	0043	0086	0128	0170	0212	0253	0294	0334	0374	4	8	12	17	21	25	29	33	37
11	0414	0453	0492	0531	0569	0607	0645	0682	0719	0755	4	8	11	15	19	23	26	30	34
12	0792	0828	0864	0899	0934	0969	1004	1038	1072	1106	3	7	10	14	17	21	24	28	31
13	1139	1173	1206	1239	1271	1303	1335	1367	1399	1430	3	6	10	13	16	19	23	26	29
14	1461	1492	1523	1553	1584	1614	1644	1673	1703	1732	3	6	9	12	15	18	21	24	27
15	1761	1790	1818	1847	1875	1903	1931	1959	1987	2014	3	6	8	11	14	17	20	22	25
16	2041	2068	2095	2122	2148	2175	2201	2227	2253	2279	3	5	8	11	13	16	18	21	24
17	2304	2330	2355	2380	2405	2430	2455	2480	2504	2529	2	5	7	10	12	15	17	20	22
18	2553	2577	2601	2625	2648	2672	2695	2718	2742	2765	2	5	7	9	12	14	16	19	21
19	2788	2810	2833	2856	2878	2900	2923	2945	2967	2989	2	4	7	9	11	13	16	18	20
20	3010	3032	3054	3075	3096	3118	3139	3160	3181	3201	2	4	6	8	11	13	15	17	19
21	3222	3243	3263	3284	3304	3324	3345	3365	3385	3404	2	4	6	8	10	12	14	16	18
22	3424	3444	3464	3483	3502	3522	3541	3560	3579	3598	2	4	6	8	10	12	14	15	17
23	3617	3636	3655	3674	3692	3711	3729	3747	3766	3784	2	4	6	7	9	11	13	15	17
24	3802	3820	3838	3856	3874	3892	3909	3927	3945	3962	2	4	5	7	9	11	12	14	16
25	3979	3997	4014	4031	4048	4065	4082	4099	4116	4133	2	3	5	7	9	10	12	14	15
26	4150	4166	4183	4200	4216	4232	4249	4265	4281	4298	2	3	5	7	8	10	11	13	15
27	4314	4330	4346	4362	4378	4393	4409	4425	4440	4456	2	3	5	6	8	9	11	13	14
28	4472	4487	4502	4518	4533	4548	4564	4579	4594	4609	2	3	5	6	8	9	11	12	14
29	4624	4639	4654	4669	4683	4698	4713	4728	4742	4757	1	3	4	6	7	9	10	12	13
30	4771	4786	4800	4814	4829	4843	4857	4871	4886	4900	1	3	4	6	7	9	10	11	13
31	4914	4928	4942	4955	4969	4983	4997	5011	5024	5038	1	3	4	6	7	8	10	11	12
32	5051	5065	5079	5092	5105	5119	5132	5145	5159	5172	1	3	4	5	7	8	9	11	12
33	5185	5198	5211	5224	5237	5250	5263	5276	5289	5302	1	3	4	5	6	8	9	10	12
34	5315	5328	5340	5353	5366	5378	5391	5403	5416	5428	1	3	4	5	6	8	9	10	11
35	5441	5453	5465	5478	5490	5502	5514	5527	5539	5551	1	2	4	5	6	7	9	10	11
36	5563	5575	5587	5599	5611	5623	5635	5647	5658	5670	1	2	4	5	6	7	8	10	11
37	5682	5694	5705	5717	5729	5740	5752	5763	5775	5786	1	2	3	5	6	7	8	9	10
38	5798	5809	5821	5832	5843	5855	5866	5877	5888	5899	1	2	3	5	6	7	8	9	10
39	5911	5922	5933	5944	5955	5966	5977	5988	5999	6010	1	2	3	4	5	7	8	9	10
40	6021	6031	6042	6053	6064	6075	6085	6096	6107	6117	1	2	3	4	5	6	8	9	10
41	6128	6138	6149	6160	6170	6180	6191	6201	6212	6222	1	2	3	4	5	6	7	8	9
42	6232	6243	6253	6263	6274	6284	6294	6304	6314	6325	1	2	3	4	5	6	7	8	9
43	6335	6345	6355	6365	6375	6385	6395	6405	6415	6425	1	2	3	4	5	6	7	8	9
44	6435	6444	6454	6464	6474	6484	6493	6503	6513	6522	1	2	3	4	5	6	7	8	9
45	6532	6542	6551	6561	6571	6580	6590	6599	6609	6618	1	2	3	4	5	6	7	8	9
46	6628	6637	6646	6656	6665	6675	6684	6693	6702	6712	1	2	3	4	5	6	7	7	8
47	6721	6730	6739	6749	6758	6767	6776	6785	6794	6803	1	2	3	4	5	5	6	7	8
48	6812	6821	6830	6839	6848	6857	6866	6875	6884	6893	1	2	3	4	4	5	6	7	8
49	6902	6911	6920	6928	6937	6946	6955	6964	6972	6981	1	2	3	4	4	5	6	7	8
50	6990	6998	7007	7016	7024	7033	7042	7050	7059	7067	1	2	3	3	4	5	6	7	8
51	7076	7084	7093	7101	7110	7118	7126	7135	7143	7152	1	2	3	3	4	5	6	7	8
52	7160	7168	7177	7185	7193	7202	7210	7218	7226	7235	1	2	2	3	4	5	6	7	7
53	7243	7251	7259	7267	7275	7284	7292	7300	7308	7316	1	2	2	3	4	5	6	6	7
54	7324	7332	7340	7348	7356	7364	7372	7380	7388	7396	1	2	2	3	4	5	6	6	7

	0	1	2	3	4	5	6	7	8	9	1	2	3	4	5	6	7	8	9
55	7404	7412	7419	7427	7435	7443	7451	7459	7466	7474	1	2	2	3	4	5	5	6	7
56	7482	7490	7497	7505	7513	7520	7528	7536	7543	7551	1	2	2	3	4	5	5	6	7
57	7559	7566	7574	7582	7589	7597	7604	7612	7619	7627	1	2	2	3	4	5	5	6	7
58	7634	7642	7649	7657	7664	7672	7679	7686	7694	7701	1	1	2	3	4	4	5	6	7
59	7709	7716	7723	7731	7738	7745	7752	7760	7767	7774	1	1	2	3	4	4	5	6	7
60	7782	7789	7796	7803	7810	7818	7825	7832	7839	7846	1	1	2	3	4	4	5	6	6
61	7853	7860	7868	7875	7882	7889	7896	7903	7910	7917	1	1	2	3	4	4	5	6	6
62	7924	7931	7938	7945	7952	7959	7966	7973	7980	7987	1	1	2	3	3	4	5	6	6
63	7993	8000	8007	8014	8021	8028	8035	8041	8048	8055	1	1	2	3	3	4	5	5	6
64	8062	8069	8075	8082	8089	8096	8102	8109	8116	8122	1	1	2	3	3	4	5	5	6
65	8129	8136	8142	8149	8156	8162	8169	8176	8182	8189	1	1	2	3	3	4	5	5	6
66	8195	8202	8209	8215	8222	8228	8235	8241	8248	8254	1	1	2	3	3	4	5	5	6
67	8261	8267	8274	8280	8287	8293	8299	8306	8312	8319	1	1	2	3	3	4	5	5	6
68	8325	8331	8338	8344	8351	8357	8363	8370	8376	8382	1	1	2	3	3	4	4	5	6
69	8388	8395	8401	8407	8414	8420	8426	8432	8439	8445	1	1	2	2	3	4	4	5	6
70	8451	8457	8463	8470	8476	8482	8488	8494	8500	8506	1	1	2	2	3	4	4	5	6
71	8513	8519	8525	8531	8537	8543	8549	8555	8561	8567	1	1	2	2	3	4	4	5	5
72	8573	8579	8585	8591	8597	8603	8609	8615	8621	8627	1	1	2	2	3	4	4	5	5
73	8633	8639	8645	8651	8657	8663	8669	8675	8681	8686	1	1	2	2	3	4	4	5	5
74	8692	8698	8704	8710	8716	8722	8727	8733	8739	8745	1	1	2	2	3	4	4	5	5
75	8751	8756	8762	8768	8774	8779	8785	8791	8797	8802	1	1	2	2	3	3	4	5	5
76	8808	8814	8820	8825	8831	8837	8842	8848	8854	8859	1	1	2	2	3	3	4	5	5
77	8865	8871	8876	8882	8887	8893	8899	8904	8910	8915	1	1	2	2	3	3	4	4	5
78	8921	8927	8932	8938	8943	8949	8954	8960	8965	8971	1	1	2	2	3	3	4	4	5
79	8976	8982	8987	8993	8998	9004	9009	9015	9020	9025	1	1	2	2	3	3	4	4	5
80	9031	9036	9042	9047	9053	9058	9063	9069	9074	9079	1	1	2	2	3	3	4	4	5
81	9085	9090	9096	9101	9106	9112	9117	9122	9128	9133	1	1	2	2	3	3	4	4	5
82	9138	9143	9149	9154	9159	9165	9170	9175	9180	9186	1	1	2	2	3	3	4	4	5
83	9191	9196	9201	9206	9212	9217	9222	9227	9232	9238	1	1	2	2	3	3	4	4	5
84	9243	9248	9253	9258	9263	9269	9274	9279	9284	9289	1	1	2	2	3	3	4	4	5
85	9294	9299	9304	9309	9315	9320	9325	9330	9335	9340	1	1	2	2	3	3	4	4	5
86	9345	9350	9355	9360	9365	9370	9375	9380	9385	9390	1	1	2	2	3	3	4	4	5
87	9395	9400	9405	9410	9415	9420	9425	9430	9435	9440	0	1	1	2	2	3	3	4	4
88	9445	9450	9455	9460	9465	9469	9474	9479	9484	9489	0	1	1	2	2	3	3	4	4
89	9494	9499	9504	9509	9513	9518	9523	9528	9533	9538	0	1	1	2	2	3	3	4	4
90	9542	9547	9552	9557	9562	9566	9571	9576	9581	9586	0	1	1	2	2	3	3	4	4
91	9590	9595	9600	9605	9609	9614	9619	9624	9628	9633	0	1	1	2	2	3	3	4	4
92	9638	9643	9647	9652	9657	9661	9666	9671	9675	9680	0	1	1	2	2	3	3	4	4
93	9685	9689	9694	9699	9703	9708	9713	9717	9722	9727	0	1	1	2	2	3	3	4	4
94	9731	9736	9741	9745	9750	9754	9759	9763	9768	9773	0	1	1	2	2	3	3	4	4
95	9777	9782	9786	9791	9795	9800	9805	9809	9814	9818	0	1	1	2	2	3	3	4	4
96	9823	9827	9832	9836	9841	9845	9850	9854	9859	9863	0	1	1	2	2	3	3	4	4
97	9868	9872	9877	9881	9886	9890	9894	9899	9903	9908	0	1	1	2	2	3	3	4	4
98	9912	9917	9921	9926	9930	9934	9939	9943	9948	9952	0	1	1	2	2	3	3	4	4
99	9956	9961	9965	9969	9974	9978	9983	9987	9991	9996	0	1	1	2	2	3	3	3	4

	0′	6′	12′	18′	24′	30′	36′	42′	48′	54′	1	2	3	4	5
0°	0000	0017	0035	0052	0070	0087	0105	0122	0140	0157	3	6	9	12	15
1	0175	0192	0209	0227	0244	0262	0279	0297	0314	0332	3	6	9	12	15
2	0349	0366	0384	0401	0419	0436	0454	0471	0488	0506	3	6	9	12	15
3	0523	0541	0558	0576	0593	0610	0628	0645	0663	0680	3	6	9	12	15
4	0698	0715	0732	0750	0767	0785	0802	0819	0837	0854	3	6	9	12	15
5	0872	0889	0906	0924	0941	0958	0976	0993	1011	1028	3	6	9	12	14
6	1045	1063	1080	1097	1115	1132	1149	1167	1184	1201	3	6	9	12	14
7	1219	1236	1253	1271	1288	1305	1323	1340	1357	1374	3	6	9	12	14
8	1392	1409	1426	1444	1461	1478	1495	1513	1530	1547	3	6	9	12	14
9	1564	1582	1599	1616	1633	1650	1668	1685	1702	1719	3	6	9	12	14
10	1736	1754	1771	1788	1805	1822	1840	1857	1874	1891	3	6	9	12	14
11	1908	1925	1942	1959	1977	1994	2011	2028	2045	2062	3	6	9	11	14
12	2079	2096	2113	2130	2147	2164	2181	2198	2215	2232	3	6	9	11	14
13	2250	2267	2284	2300	2317	2334	2351	2368	2385	2402	3	6	8	11	14
14	2419	2436	2453	2470	2487	2504	2521	2538	2554	2571	3	6	8	11	14
15	2588	2605	2622	2639	2656	2672	2689	2706	2723	2740	3	6	8	11	14
16	2756	2773	2790	2807	2823	2840	2857	2874	2890	2907	3	6	8	11	14
17	2924	2940	2957	2974	2990	3007	3024	3040	3057	3074	3	6	8	11	14
18	3090	3107	3123	3140	3156	3173	3190	3206	3223	3239	3	6	8	11	14
19	3256	3272	3289	3305	3322	3338	3355	3371	3387	3404	3	5	8	11	14
20	3420	3437	3453	3469	3486	3502	3518	3535	3551	3567	3	5	8	11	14
21	3584	3600	3616	3633	3649	3665	3681	3697	3714	3730	3	5	8	11	14
22	3746	3762	3778	3795	3811	3827	3843	3859	3875	3891	3	5	8	11	14
23	3907	3923	3939	3955	3971	3987	4003	4019	4035	4051	3	5	8	11	14
24	4067	4083	4099	4115	4131	4147	4163	4179	4195	4210	3	5	8	11	13
25	4226	4242	4258	4274	4289	4305	4321	4337	4352	4368	3	5	8	11	13
26	4384	4399	4415	4431	4446	4462	4478	4493	4509	4524	3	5	8	10	13
27	4540	4555	4571	4586	4602	4617	4633	4648	4664	4679	3	5	8	10	13
28	4695	4710	4726	4741	4756	4772	4787	4802	4818	4833	3	5	8	10	13
29	4848	4863	4879	4894	4909	4924	4939	4955	4970	4985	3	5	8	10	13
30	5000	5015	5030	5045	5060	5075	5090	5105	5120	5135	3	5	8	10	13
31	5150	5165	5180	5195	5210	5225	5240	5255	5270	5284	2	5	7	10	12
32	5299	5314	5329	5344	5358	5373	5388	5402	5417	5432	2	5	7	10	12
33	5446	5461	5476	5490	5505	5519	5534	5548	5563	5577	2	5	7	10	12
34	5592	5606	5621	5635	5650	5664	5678	5693	5707	5721	2	5	7	10	12
35	5736	5750	5764	5779	5793	5807	5821	5835	5850	5864	2	5	7	10	12
36	5878	5892	5906	5920	5934	5948	5962	5976	5990	6004	2	5	7	9	12
37	6018	6032	6046	6060	6074	6088	6101	6115	6129	6143	2	5	7	9	12
38	6157	6170	6184	6198	6211	6225	6239	6252	6266	6280	2	5	7	9	11
39	6293	6307	6320	6334	6347	6361	6374	6388	6401	6414	2	4	7	9	11
40	6428	6441	6455	6468	6481	6494	6508	6521	6534	6547	2	4	7	9	11
41	6561	6574	6587	6600	6613	6626	6639	6652	6665	6678	2	4	7	9	11
42	6691	6704	6717	6730	6743	6756	6769	6782	6794	6807	2	4	6	9	11
43	6820	6833	6845	6858	6871	6884	6896	6909	6921	6934	2	4	6	8	11
44	6947	6959	6972	6984	6997	7009	7022	7034	7046	7059	2	4	6	8	10

	0'	6'	12'	18'	24'	30'	36'	42'	48'	54'	1	2	3	4	5
45°	7071	7083	7096	7108	7120	7133	7145	7157	7169	7181	2	4	6	8	10
46	7193	7206	7218	7230	7242	7254	7266	7278	7290	7302	2	4	6	8	10
47	7314	7325	7337	7349	7361	7373	7385	7396	7408	7420	2	4	6	8	10
48	7431	7443	7455	7466	7478	7490	7501	7513	7524	7536	2	4	6	8	10
49	7547	7558	7570	7581	7593	7604	7615	7627	7638	7649	2	4	6	8	9
50	7660	7672	7683	7694	7705	7716	7727	7738	7749	7760	2	4	6	7	9
51	7771	7782	7793	7804	7815	7826	7837	7848	7859	7869	2	4	5	7	9
52	7880	7891	7902	7912	7923	7934	7944	7955	7965	7976	2	4	5	7	9
53	7986	7997	8007	8018	8028	8039	8049	8059	8070	8080	2	3	5	7	9
54	8090	8100	8111	8121	8131	8141	8151	8161	8171	8181	2	3	5	7	8
55	8192	8202	8211	8221	8231	8241	8251	8261	8271	8281	2	3	5	7	8
56	8290	8300	8310	8320	8329	8339	8348	8358	8368	8377	2	3	5	6	8
57	8387	8396	8406	8415	8425	8434	8443	8453	8462	8471	2	3	5	6	8
58	8480	8490	8499	8508	8517	8526	8536	8545	8554	8563	2	3	5	6	8
59	8572	8581	8590	8599	8607	8616	8625	8634	8643	8652	1	3	4	6	7
60	8660	8669	8678	8686	8695	8704	8712	8721	8729	8738	1	3	4	6	7
61	8746	8755	8763	8771	8780	8788	8796	8805	8813	8821	1	3	4	6	7
62	8829	8838	8846	8854	8862	8870	8878	8886	8894	8902	1	3	4	5	7
63	8910	8918	8926	8934	8942	8949	8957	8965	8973	8980	1	3	4	5	6
64	8988	8996	9003	9011	9018	9026	9033	9041	9048	9056	1	3	4	5	6
65	9063	9070	9078	9085	9092	9100	9107	9114	9121	9128	1	2	4	5	6
66	9135	9143	9150	9157	9164	9171	9178	9184	9191	9198	1	2	3	5	6
67	9205	9212	9219	9225	9232	9239	9245	9252	9259	9265	1	2	3	4	6
68	9272	9278	9285	9291	9298	9304	9311	9317	9323	9330	1	2	3	4	5
69	9336	9342	9348	9354	9361	9367	9373	9379	9385	9391	1	2	3	4	5
70	9397	9403	9409	9415	9421	9426	9432	9438	9444	9449	1	2	3	4	5
71	9455	9461	9466	9472	9478	9483	9489	9494	9500	9505	1	2	3	4	5
72	9511	9516	9521	9527	9532	9537	9542	9548	9553	9558	1	2	3	4	4
73	9563	9568	9573	9578	9583	9588	9593	9598	9603	9608	1	2	2	3	4
74	9613	9617	9622	9627	9632	9636	9641	9646	9650	9655	1	2	2	3	4
75	9659	9664	9668	9673	9677	9681	9686	9690	9694	9699	1	1	2	3	4
76	9703	9707	9711	9715	9720	9724	9728	9732	9736	9740	1	1	2	3	3
77	9744	9748	9751	9755	9759	9763	9767	9770	9774	9778	1	1	2	3	3
78	9781	9785	9789	9792	9796	9799	9803	9806	9810	9813	1	1	2	2	3
79	9816	9820	9823	9826	9829	9833	9836	9839	9842	9845	1	1	2	2	3
80	9848	9851	9854	9857	9860	9863	9866	9869	9871	9874	0	1	1	2	2
81	9877	9880	9882	9885	9888	9890	9893	9895	9898	9900	0	1	1	2	2
82	9903	9905	9907	9910	9912	9914	9917	9919	9921	9923	0	1	1	2	2
83	9925	9928	9930	9932	9934	9936	9938	9940	9942	9943	0	1	1	1	2
84	9945	9947	9949	9951	9952	9954	9956	9957	9959	9960	0	1	1	1	1
85	9962	9963	9965	9966	9968	9969	9971	9972	9973	9974	0	0	1	1	1
86	9976	9977	9978	9979	9980	9981	9982	9983	9984	9985	0	0	1	1	1
87	9986	9987	9988	9989	9990	9990	9991	9992	9993	9993	0	0	0	1	1
88	9994	9995	9995	9996	9996	9997	9997	9997	9998	9998	0	0	0	0	0
89	9998	9999	9999	9999	9999	1·000 nearly.	1·000 nearly.	1·000 nearly.	1·000 nearly.	1·000 nearly.	0	0	0	0	0

	0′	6′	12′	18′	24′	30′	36′	42′	48′	54′	1	2	3	4	5
0°	1·000	1·000 nearly.	1·000 nearly.	1·000 nearly.	1·000 nearly.	9999	9999	9999	9999	9999	0	0	0	0	0
1	9998	9998	9998	9997	9997	9997	9996	9996	9995	9995	0	0	0	0	0
2	9994	9993	9993	9992	9991	9990	9990	9989	9988	9987	0	0	0	1	1
3	9986	9985	9984	9983	9982	9981	9980	9979	9978	9977	0	0	1	1	1
4	9976	9974	9973	9972	9971	9969	9968	9966	9965	9963	0	0	1	1	1
5	9962	9960	9959	9957	9956	9954	9952	9951	9949	9947	0	1	1	1	2
6	9945	9943	9942	9940	9938	9936	9934	9932	9930	9928	0	1	1	1	2
7	9925	9923	9921	9919	9917	9914	9912	9910	9907	9905	0	1	1	2	2
8	9903	9900	9898	9895	9893	9890	9888	9885	9882	9880	0	1	1	2	2
9	9877	9874	9871	9869	9866	9863	9860	9857	9854	9851	0	1	1	2	2
10	9848	9845	9842	9839	9836	9833	9829	9826	9823	9820	1	1	2	2	3
11	9816	9813	9810	9806	9803	9799	9796	9792	9789	9785	1	1	2	2	3
12	9781	9778	9774	9770	9767	9763	9759	9755	9751	9748	1	1	2	3	3
13	9744	9740	9736	9732	9728	9724	9720	9715	9711	9707	1	1	2	3	3
14	9703	9699	9694	9690	9686	9681	9677	9673	9668	9664	1	1	2	3	4
15	9659	9655	9650	9646	9641	9636	9632	9627	9622	9617	1	2	2	3	4
16	9613	9608	9603	9598	9593	9588	9583	9578	9573	9568	1	2	2	3	4
17	9563	9558	9553	9548	9542	9537	9532	9527	9521	9516	1	2	3	4	4
18	9511	9505	9500	9494	9489	9483	9478	9472	9466	9461	1	2	3	4	5
19	9455	9449	9444	9438	9432	9426	9421	9415	9409	9403	1	2	3	4	5
20	9397	9391	9385	9379	9373	9367	9361	9354	9348	9342	1	2	3	4	5
21	9336	9330	9323	9317	9311	9304	9298	9291	9285	9278	1	2	3	4	5
22	9272	9265	9259	9252	9245	9239	9232	9225	9219	9212	1	2	3	4	6
23	9205	9198	9191	9184	9178	9171	9164	9157	9150	9143	1	2	3	5	6
24	9135	9128	9121	9114	9107	9100	9092	9085	9078	9070	1	2	4	5	6
25	9063	9056	9048	9041	9033	9026	9018	9011	9003	8996	1	3	4	5	6
26	8988	8980	8973	8965	8957	8949	8942	8934	8926	8918	1	3	4	5	6
27	8910	8902	8894	8886	8878	8870	8862	8854	8846	8838	1	3	4	5	7
28	8829	8821	8813	8805	8796	8788	8780	8771	8763	8755	1	3	4	6	7
29	8746	8738	8729	8721	8712	8704	8695	8686	8678	8669	1	3	4	6	7
30	8660	8652	8643	8634	8625	8616	8607	8599	8590	8581	1	3	4	6	7
31	8572	8563	8554	8545	8536	8526	8517	8508	8499	8490	2	3	5	6	8
32	8480	8471	8462	8453	8443	8434	8425	8415	8406	8396	2	3	5	6	8
33	8387	8377	8368	8358	8348	8339	8329	8320	8310	8300	2	3	5	6	8
34	8290	8281	8271	8261	8251	8241	8231	8221	8211	8202	2	3	5	7	8
35	8192	8181	8171	8161	8151	8141	8131	8121	8111	8100	2	3	5	7	8
36	8090	8080	8070	8059	8049	8039	8028	8018	8007	7997	2	3	5	7	9
37	7986	7976	7965	7955	7944	7934	7923	7912	7902	7891	2	4	5	7	9
38	7880	7869	7859	7848	7837	7826	7815	7804	7793	7782	2	4	5	7	9
39	7771	7760	7749	7738	7727	7716	7705	7694	7683	7672	2	4	6	7	9
40	7660	7649	7638	7627	7615	7604	7593	7581	7570	7559	2	4	6	8	9
41	7547	7536	7524	7513	7501	7490	7478	7466	7455	7443	2	4	6	8	10
42	7431	7420	7408	7396	7385	7373	7361	7349	7337	7325	2	4	6	8	10
43	7314	7302	7290	7278	7266	7254	7242	7230	7218	7206	2	4	6	8	10
44	7193	7181	7169	7157	7145	7133	7120	7108	7096	7083	2	4	6	8	10

N.B. — Numbers in difference-columns to be subtracted, not added.

	0′	6′	12′	18′	24′	30′	36′	42′	48′	54′	1	2	3	4	5
45°	7071	7059	7046	7034	7022	7009	6997	6984	6972	6959	2	4	6	8	10
46	6947	6934	6921	6909	6896	6884	6871	6858	6845	6833	2	4	6	8	11
47	6820	6807	6794	6782	6769	6756	6743	6730	6717	6704	2	4	6	9	11
48	6691	6678	6665	6652	6639	6626	6613	6600	6587	6574	2	4	7	9	11
49	6561	6547	6534	6521	6508	6494	6481	6468	6455	6441	2	4	7	9	11
50	6428	6414	6401	6388	6374	6361	6347	6334	6320	6307	2	4	7	9	11
51	6293	6280	6266	6252	6239	6225	6211	6198	6184	6170	2	5	7	9	11
52	6157	6143	6129	6115	6101	6088	6074	6060	6046	6032	2	5	7	9	12
53	6018	6004	5990	5976	5962	5948	5934	5920	5906	5892	2	5	7	9	12
54	5878	5864	5850	5835	5821	5807	5793	5779	5764	5750	2	5	7	9	12
55	5736	5721	5707	5693	5678	5664	5650	5635	5621	5606	2	5	7	10	12
56	5592	5577	5563	5548	5534	5519	5505	5490	5476	5461	2	5	7	10	12
57	5446	5432	5417	5402	5388	5373	5358	5344	5329	5314	2	5	7	10	12
58	5299	5284	5270	5255	5240	5225	5210	5195	5180	5165	2	5	7	10	12
59	5150	5135	5120	5105	5090	5075	5060	5045	5030	5015	3	5	8	10	13
60	5000	4985	4970	4955	4939	4924	4909	4894	4879	4863	3	5	8	10	13
61	4848	4833	4818	4802	4787	4772	4756	4741	4726	4710	3	5	8	10	13
62	4695	4679	4664	4648	4633	4617	4602	4586	4571	4555	3	5	8	10	13
63	4540	4524	4509	4493	4478	4462	4446	4431	4415	4399	3	5	8	10	13
64	4384	4368	4352	4337	4321	4305	4289	4274	4258	4242	3	5	8	11	13
65	4226	4210	4195	4179	4163	4147	4131	4115	4099	4083	3	5	8	11	13
66	4067	4051	4035	4019	4003	3987	3971	3955	3939	3923	3	5	8	11	14
67	3907	3891	3875	3859	3843	3827	3811	3795	3778	3762	3	5	8	11	14
68	3746	3730	3714	3697	3681	3665	3649	3633	3616	3600	3	5	8	11	14
69	3584	3567	3551	3535	3518	3502	3486	3469	3453	3437	3	5	8	11	14
70	3420	3404	3387	3371	3355	3338	3322	3305	3289	3272	3	5	8	11	14
71	3256	3239	3223	3206	3190	3173	3156	3140	3123	3107	3	6	8	11	14
72	3090	3074	3057	3040	3024	3007	2990	2974	2957	2940	3	6	8	11	14
73	2924	2907	2890	2874	2857	2840	2823	2807	2790	2773	3	6	8	11	14
74	2756	2740	2723	2706	2689	2672	2656	2639	2622	2605	3	6	8	11	14
75	2588	2571	2554	2538	2521	2504	2487	2470	2453	2436	3	6	8	11	14
76	2419	2402	2385	2368	2351	2334	2317	2300	2284	2267	3	6	8	11	14
77	2250	2233	2215	2198	2181	2164	2147	2130	2113	2096	3	6	9	11	14
78	2079	2062	2045	2028	2011	1994	1977	1959	1942	1925	3	6	9	11	14
79	1908	1891	1874	1857	1840	1822	1805	1788	1771	1754	3	6	9	12	14
80	1736	1719	1702	1685	1668	1650	1633	1616	1599	1582	3	6	9	12	14
81	1564	1547	1530	1513	1495	1478	1461	1444	1426	1409	3	6	9	12	14
82	1392	1374	1357	1340	1323	1305	1288	1271	1253	1236	3	6	9	12	14
83	1219	1201	1184	1167	1149	1132	1115	1097	1080	1063	3	6	9	12	14
84	1045	1028	1011	0993	0976	0958	0941	0924	0906	0889	3	6	9	12	14
85	0872	0854	0837	0819	0802	0785	0767	0750	0732	0715	3	6	9	12	15
86	0698	0680	0663	0645	0628	0610	0593	0576	0558	0541	3	6	9	12	15
87	0523	0506	0488	0471	0454	0436	0419	0401	0384	0366	3	6	9	12	15
88	0349	0332	0314	0297	0279	0262	0244	0227	0209	0192	3	6	9	12	15
89	0175	0157	0140	0122	0105	0087	0070	0052	0035	0017	3	6	9	12	15

N.B. — Numbers in difference-columns to be subtracted, not added.

	0′	6′	12′	18′	24′	30′	36′	42′	48′	54′	1	2	3	4	5
0°	·0000	0017	0035	0052	0070	0087	0105	0122	0140	0157	3	6	9	12	14
1	·0175	0192	0209	0227	0244	0262	0279	0297	0314	0332	3	6	9	12	15
2	·0349	0367	0384	0402	0419	0437	0454	0472	0489	0507	3	6	9	12	15
3	·0524	0542	0559	0577	0594	0612	0629	0647	0664	0682	3	6	9	12	15
4	·0699	0717	0734	0752	0769	0787	0805	0822	0840	0857	3	6	9	12	15
5	·0875	0892	0910	0928	0945	0963	0981	0998	1016	1033	3	6	9	12	15
6	·1051	1069	1086	1104	1122	1139	1157	1175	1192	1210	3	6	9	12	15
7	·1228	1246	1263	1281	1299	1317	1334	1352	1370	1388	3	6	9	12	15
8	·1405	1423	1441	1459	1477	1495	1512	1530	1548	1566	3	6	9	12	15
9	·1584	1602	1620	1638	1655	1673	1691	1709	1727	1745	3	6	9	12	15
10	·1763	1781	1799	1817	1835	1853	1871	1890	1908	1926	3	6	9	12	15
11	·1944	1962	1980	1998	2016	2035	2053	2071	2089	2107	3	6	9	12	15
12	·2126	2144	2162	2180	2199	2217	2235	2254	2272	2290	3	6	9	12	15
13	·2309	2327	2345	2364	2382	2401	2419	2438	2456	2475	3	6	9	12	15
14	·2493	2512	2530	2549	2568	2586	2605	2623	2642	2661	3	6	9	12	16
15	·2679	2698	2717	2736	2754	2773	2792	2811	2830	2849	3	6	9	13	16
16	·2867	2886	2905	2924	2943	2962	2981	3000	3019	3038	3	6	9	13	16
17	·3057	3076	3096	3115	3134	3153	3172	3191	3211	3230	3	6	10	13	16
18	·3249	3269	3288	3307	3327	3346	3365	3385	3404	3424	3	6	10	13	16
19	·3443	3463	3482	3502	3522	3541	3561	3581	3600	3620	3	6	10	13	17
20	·3640	3659	3679	3699	3719	3739	3759	3779	3799	3819	3	7	10	13	17
21	·3839	3859	3879	3899	3919	3939	3959	3979	4000	4020	3	7	10	13	17
22	·4040	4061	4081	4101	4122	4142	4163	4183	4204	4224	3	7	10	14	17
23	·4245	4265	4286	4307	4327	4348	4369	4390	4411	4431	3	7	10	14	17
24	·4452	4473	4494	4515	4536	4557	4578	4599	4621	4642	4	7	10	14	18
25	·4663	4684	4706	4727	4748	4770	4791	4813	4834	4856	4	7	11	14	18
26	·4877	4899	4921	4942	4964	4986	5008	5029	5051	5073	4	7	11	15	18
27	·5095	5117	5139	5161	5184	5206	5228	5250	5272	5295	4	7	11	15	18
28	·5317	5340	5362	5384	5407	5430	5452	5475	5498	5520	4	8	11	15	19
29	·5543	5566	5589	5612	5635	5658	5681	5704	5727	5750	4	8	12	15	19
30	·5774	5797	5820	5844	5867	5890	5914	5938	5961	5985	4	8	12	16	20
31	·6009	6032	6056	6080	6104	6128	6152	6176	6200	6224	4	8	12	16	20
32	·6249	6273	6297	6322	6346	6371	6395	6420	6445	6469	4	8	12	16	20
33	·6494	6519	6544	6569	6594	6619	6644	6669	6694	6720	4	8	13	17	21
34	·6745	6771	6796	6822	6847	6873	6899	6924	6950	6976	4	9	13	17	21
35	·7002	7028	7054	7080	7107	7133	7159	7186	7212	7239	4	9	13	18	22
36	·7265	7292	7319	7346	7373	7400	7427	7454	7481	7508	5	9	14	18	23
37	·7536	7563	7590	7618	7646	7673	7701	7729	7757	7785	5	9	14	18	23
38	·7813	7841	7869	7898	7926	7954	7983	8012	8040	8069	5	10	14	19	24
39	·8098	8127	8156	8185	8214	8243	8273	8302	8332	8361	5	10	15	20	24
40	·8391	8421	8451	8481	8511	8541	8571	8601	8632	8662	5	10	15	20	25
41	·8693	8724	8754	8785	8816	8847	8878	8910	8941	8972	5	10	16	21	26
42	·9004	9036	9067	9099	9131	9163	9195	9228	9260	9293	5	11	16	21	27
43	·9325	9358	9391	9424	9457	9490	9523	9556	9590	9623	6	11	17	22	28
44	·9657	9691	9725	9759	9793	9827	9861	9896	9930	9965	6	11	17	23	29

	0′	6′	12′	18′	24′	30′	36′	42′	48′	54′	1	2	3	4	5
45°	1·0000	0035	0070	0105	0141	0176	0212	0247	0283	0319	6	12	18	24	30
46	1·0355	0392	0428	0464	0501	0538	0575	0612	0649	0686	6	12	18	25	31
47	1·0724	0761	0799	0837	0875	0913	0951	0990	1028	1067	6	13	19	25	32
48	1·1106	1145	1184	1224	1263	1303	1343	1383	1423	1463	7	13	20	26	33
49	1·1504	1544	1585	1626	1667	1708	1750	1792	1833	1875	7	14	21	28	34
50	1·1918	1960	2002	2045	2088	2131	2174	2218	2261	2305	7	14	22	29	36
51	1·2349	2393	2437	2482	2527	2572	2617	2662	2708	2753	8	15	23	30	38
52	1·2799	2846	2892	2938	2985	3032	3079	3127	3175	3222	8	16	23	31	39
53	1·3270	3319	3367	3416	3465	3514	3564	3613	3663	3713	8	16	25	33	41
54	1·3764	3814	3865	3916	3968	4019	4071	4124	4176	4229	9	17	26	34	43
55	1·4281	4335	4388	4442	4496	4550	4605	4659	4715	4770	9	18	27	36	45
56	1·4826	4882	4938	4994	5051	5108	5166	5224	5282	5340	10	19	29	38	48
57	1·5399	5458	5517	5577	5637	5697	5757	5818	5880	5941	10	20	30	40	50
58	1·6003	6066	6128	6191	6255	6319	6383	6447	6512	6577	11	21	32	43	53
59	1·6643	6709	6775	6842	6909	6977	7045	7113	7182	7251	11	23	34	45	56
60	1·7321	7391	7461	7532	7603	7675	7747	7820	7893	7966	12	24	36	48	60
61	1·8040	8115	8190	8265	8341	8418	8495	8572	8650	8728	13	26	38	51	64
62	1·8807	8887	8967	9047	9128	9210	9292	9375	9458	9542	14	27	41	55	68
63	1·9626	9711	9797	9883	9970	0057	0145	0233	0323	0413	15	29	44	58	73
64	2·0503	0594	0686	0778	0872	0965	1060	1155	1251	1348	16	31	47	63	78
65	2·1445	1543	1642	1742	1842	1943	2045	2148	2251	2355	17	34	51	68	85
66	2·2460	2566	2673	2781	2889	2998	3109	3220	3332	3445	18	37	55	74	92
67	2·3559	3673	3789	3906	4023	4142	4262	4383	4504	4627	20	40	60	79	99
68	2·4751	4876	5002	5129	5257	5386	5517	5649	5782	5916	22	43	65	87	108
69	2·6051	6187	6325	6464	6605	6746	6889	7034	7179	7326	24	47	71	95	118
70	2·7475	7625	7776	7929	8083	8239	8397	8556	8716	8878	26	52	78	104	130
71	2·9042	9208	9375	9544	9714	9887	0061	0237	0415	0595	29	58	87	115	144
72	3·0777	0961	1146	1334	1524	1716	1910	2106	2305	2506	32	64	96	129	161
73	3·2709	2914	3122	3332	3544	3759	3977	4197	4420	4646	36	72	108	144	180
74	3·4874	5105	5339	5576	5816	6059	6305	6554	6806	7062	41	82	122	162	203
75	3·7321	7583	7848	8118	8391	8667	8947	9232	9520	9812	46	94	139	186	232
76	4·0108	0408	0713	1022	1335	1653	1976	2303	2635	2972	53	107	160	214	267
77	4·3315	3662	4015	4374	4737	5107	5483	5864	6252	6646	62	124	186	248	310
78	4·7046	7453	7867	8288	8716	9152	9594	0045	0504	0970	73	146	219	292	365
79	5·1446	1929	2422	2924	3435	3955	4486	5026	5578	6140	87	175	262	350	437
80	5·6713	7297	7894	8502	9124	9758	0405	1066	1742	2432					
81	6·3138	3859	4596	5350	6122	6912	7920	8548	9395	0264					
82	7·1154	2066	3002	3962	4947	5958	6996	8062	9158	0285					
83	8·1443	2636	3863	5126	6427	7769	9152	0579	2052	3572					
84	9·5144	9·677	9·845	10·02	10·20	10·39	10·58	10·78	10·99	11·20					
85	11·43	11·66	11·91	12·16	12·43	12·71	13·00	13·30	13·62	13·95					
86	14·30	14·67	15·06	15·46	15·89	16·35	16·83	17·34	17·89	18·46					
87	19·08	19·74	20·45	21·20	22·02	22·90	23·86	24·90	26·03	27·27					
88	28·64	30·14	31·82	33·69	35·80	38·19	40·92	44·07	47·74	52·08					
89	57·29	63·66	71·62	81·85	95·49	114·6	143·2	191·0	286·5	573·0					

Difference-columns cease to be useful, owing to the rapidity with which the value of the tangent changes.

	0′	6′	12′	18′	24′	30′	36′	42′	48′	54′	1	2	3	4	5
0°	Inf.	573·0	286·5	191·0	143·2	114·6	95·49	81·85	71·62	63·66					
1	57·29	52·08	47·74	44·07	40·92	38·19	35·80	33·69	31·82	30·14					
2	28·64	27·27	26·03	24·90	23·86	22·90	22·02	21·20	20·45	19·74					
3	19·08	18·46	17·89	17·34	16·83	16·35	15·89	15·46	15·06	14·67					
4	14·30	13·95	13·62	13·30	13·00	12·71	12·43	12·16	11·91	11·66					
5	11·43	11·20	10·99	10·78	10·58	10·39	10·20	10·02	9·845	9·677					
6	9·5144	3572	2052	0579	9152	7769	6427	5126	3863	2636					
7	8·1443	0285	9158	8062	6996	5958	4947	3962	3002	2066					
8	7·1154	0264	9395	8548	7920	6912	6122	5350	4596	3859					
9	6·3138	2432	1742	1066	0405	9758	9124	8502	7894	7297					
10	5·6713	6140	5578	5026	4486	3955	3435	2924	2422	1929					
11	5·1446	0970	0504	0045	9594	9152	8716	8288	7867	7453	74	148	222	296	370
12	4·7046	6646	6252	5864	5483	5107	4737	4374	4015	3662	63	125	188	252	314
13	4·3315	2972	2635	2303	1976	1653	1335	1022	0713	0408	53	107	160	214	267
14	4·0108	9812	9520	9232	8947	8667	8391	8118	7848	7583	46	93	139	186	232
15	3·7321	7062	6806	6554	6305	6059	5816	5576	5339	5105	41	82	122	163	204
16	3·4874	4646	4420	4197	3977	3759	3544	3332	3122	2914	36	72	108	144	180
17	3·2709	2506	2305	2106	1910	1716	1524	1334	1146	0961	32	64	96	129	161
18	3·0777	0595	0415	0237	0061	9887	9714	9544	9375	9208	29	58	87	115	144
19	2·9042	8878	8716	8556	8397	8239	8083	7929	7776	7625	26	52	78	104	130
20	2·7475	7326	7179	7034	6889	6746	6605	6464	6325	6187	24	47	71	95	118
21	2·6051	5916	5782	5649	5517	5386	5257	5129	5002	4876	22	43	65	87	108
22	2·4751	4627	4504	4383	4262	4142	4023	3906	3789	3673	20	40	60	79	99
23	2·3559	3445	3332	3220	3109	2998	2889	2781	2673	2566	18	37	55	74	92
24	2·2460	2355	2251	2148	2045	1943	1842	1742	1642	1543	17	34	51	68	85
25	2·1445	1348	1251	1155	1060	0965	0872	0778	0686	0594	16	31	47	63	78
26	2·0503	0413	0323	0233	0145	0057	9970	9883	9797	9711	15	29	44	58	73
27	1·9626	9542	9458	9375	9292	9210	9128	9047	8967	8887	14	27	41	55	68
28	1·8807	8728	8650	8572	8495	8418	8341	8265	8190	8115	13	26	38	51	64
29	1·8040	7966	7893	7820	7747	7675	7603	7532	7461	7391	12	24	36	48	60
30	1·7321	7251	7182	7113	7045	6977	6909	6842	6775	6709	11	23	34	45	56
31	1·6643	6577	6512	6447	6383	6319	6255	6191	6128	6066	11	21	32	43	53
32	1·6003	5941	5880	5818	5757	5697	5637	5577	5517	5458	10	20	30	40	50
33	1·5399	5340	5282	5224	5166	5108	5051	4994	4938	4882	10	19	29	38	48
34	1·4826	4770	4715	4659	4605	4550	4496	4442	4388	4335	9	18	27	36	45
35	1·4281	4229	4176	4124	4071	4019	3968	3916	3865	3814	9	17	26	34	43
36	1·3764	3713	3663	3613	3564	3514	3465	3416	3367	3319	8	16	25	33	41
37	1·3270	3222	3175	3127	3079	3032	2985	2938	2892	2846	8	16	23	31	39
38	1·2799	2753	2708	2662	2617	2572	2527	2482	2437	2393	8	15	23	30	38
39	1·2349	2305	2261	2218	2174	2131	2088	2045	2002	1960	7	14	22	29	36
40	1·1918	1875	1833	1792	1750	1708	1667	1626	1585	1544	7	14	21	28	34
41	1·1504	1463	1423	1383	1343	1303	1263	1224	1184	1145	7	13	20	26	33
42	1·1106	1067	1028	0990	0951	0913	0875	0837	0799	0761	6	13	19	25	32
43	1·0724	0686	0649	0612	0575	0538	0501	0464	0428	0392	6	12	18	25	31
44	1·0355	0319	0283	0247	0212	0176	0141	0105	0070	0035	6	12	18	24	30

Difference-columns not useful here, owing to the rapidity with which the value of the cotangent changes.

N.B. — Numbers in difference-columns to be subtracted, not added.

	0′	6′	12	18′	24′	30′	36′	42′	48′	54′	1	2	3	4	5
45°	1·0	0·9965	0·9930	0·9896	0·9861	0·9827	0·9793	0·9759	0·9725	0·9691	6	11	17	23	29
46	·9657	9623	9590	9556	9523	9490	9457	9424	9391	9358	6	11	17	22	28
47	·9325	9293	9260	9228	9195	9163	9131	9099	9067	9036	5	11	16	21	27
48	·9004	8972	8941	8910	8878	8847	8816	8785	8754	8724	5	10	16	21	26
49	·8693	8662	8632	8601	8571	8541	8511	8481	8451	8421	5	10	15	20	25
50	·8391	8361	8332	8302	8273	8243	8214	8185	8156	8127	5	10	15	20	24
51	·8098	8069	8040	8012	7983	7954	7926	7898	7869	7841	5	10	14	19	24
52	·7813	7785	7757	7729	7701	7673	7646	7618	7590	7563	5	9	14	18	23
53	·7536	7508	7481	7454	7427	7400	7373	7346	7319	7292	5	9	14	18	23
54	·7265	7239	7212	7186	7159	7133	7107	7080	7054	7028	4	9	13	18	22
55	·7002	6976	6950	6924	6899	6873	6847	6822	6796	6771	4	9	13	17	21
56	·6745	6720	6694	6669	6644	6619	6594	6569	6544	6519	4	8	13	17	21
57	·6494	6469	6445	6420	6395	6371	6346	6322	6297	6273	4	8	12	16	20
58	·6249	6224	6200	6176	6152	6128	6104	6080	6056	6032	4	8	12	16	20
59	·6009	5985	5961	5938	5914	5890	5867	5844	5820	5797	4	8	12	16	20
60	·5774	5750	5727	5704	5681	5658	5635	5612	5589	5566	4	8	12	15	19
61	·5543	5520	5498	5475	5452	5430	5407	5384	5362	5340	4	8	11	15	19
62	·5317	5295	5272	5250	5228	5206	5184	5161	5139	5117	4	7	11	15	18
63	·5095	5073	5051	5029	5008	4986	4964	4942	4921	4899	4	7	11	15	18
64	·4877	4856	4834	4813	4791	4770	4748	4727	4706	4684	4	7	11	14	18
65	·4663	4642	4621	4599	4578	4557	4536	4515	4494	4473	4	7	10	14	18
66	·4452	4431	4411	4390	4369	4348	4327	4307	4286	4265	3	7	10	14	17
67	·4245	4224	4204	4183	4163	4142	4122	4101	4081	4061	3	7	10	14	17
68	·4040	4020	4000	3979	3959	3939	3919	3899	3879	3859	3	7	10	13	17
69	·3839	3819	3799	3779	3759	3739	3719	3699	3679	3659	3	7	10	13	17
70	·3640	3620	3600	3581	3561	3541	3522	3502	3482	3463	3	6	10	13	17
71	·3443	3424	3404	3385	3365	3346	3327	3307	3288	3269	3	6	10	13	16
72	·3249	3230	3211	3191	3172	3153	3134	3115	3096	3076	3	6	10	13	16
73	·3057	3038	3019	3000	2981	2962	2943	2924	2905	2886	3	6	9	13	16
74	·2867	2849	2830	2811	2792	2773	2754	2736	2717	2698	3	6	9	13	16
75	·2679	2661	2642	2623	2605	2586	2568	2549	2530	2512	3	6	9	12	16
76	·2493	2475	2456	2438	2419	2401	2382	2364	2345	2327	3	6	9	12	15
77	·2309	2290	2272	2254	2235	2217	2199	2180	2162	2144	3	6	9	12	15
78	·2126	2107	2089	2071	2053	2035	2016	1998	1980	1962	3	6	9	12	15
79	·1944	1926	1908	1890	1871	1853	1835	1817	1799	1781	3	6	9	12	15
80	·1763	1745	1727	1709	1691	1673	1655	1638	1620	1602	3	6	9	12	15
81	·1584	1566	1548	1530	1512	1495	1477	1459	1441	1423	3	6	9	12	15
82	·1405	1388	1370	1352	1334	1317	1299	1281	1263	1246	3	6	9	12	15
83	·1228	1210	1192	1175	1157	1139	1122	1104	1086	1069	3	6	9	12	15
84	·1051	1033	1016	0998	0981	0963	0945	0928	0910	0892	3	6	9	12	15
85	·0875	0857	0840	0822	0805	0787	0769	0752	0734	0717	3	6	9	12	15
86	·0699	0682	0664	0647	0629	0612	0594	0577	0559	0542	3	6	9	12	15
87	·0524	0507	0489	0472	0454	0437	0419	0402	0384	0367	3	6	9	12	15
88	·0349	0332	0314	0297	0279	0262	0244	0227	0209	0192	3	6	9	12	15
89	·0175	0157	0140	0122	0105	0087	0070	0052	0035	0017	3	6	9	12	14

N.B. — Numbers in difference-columns to be subtracted, not added.

INDEX TO VOLUME I.